Mates!

Also by Stephen Outram

Books:
Eulogy, More Than a Speech
The First Five Years: Port Hedland 1965–1970
Wedding Speeches
Dealers: Buying, Selling & Making Money
Public Speaking: Beyond Fear
Advanced Speaking Concepts
There's No Sex in Golf
Life After

Will Public Speaking Be The Death of You? (OOP)

Blog & Articles:
stephenoutram.com

Mates!

By Stephen Outram

Disclaimer: While this work is presented as fiction, it's based upon a true story, and every effort has been made to accurately describe the included events and detail; though with the vagaries of history and memory there may be inconsistencies and errors. People's names who appear in this book have not been changed and represent real people who lived at the time; street names, places, businesses, etc. also are faithful to the period.

Author: Stephen Outram

Date Published: 1 January 20187

ISBN: 978-0-9943327-5-2

Qest Press
PO Box 1770, Broadbeach, QLD. 4218. Australia

Dedication

To Mates

Ray, Kevin, Karen, Ian, Gary, Eden, and to those others that I may not have seen for a while now, thank you for being my mates.

Thanks to my mate Gary Douglas who, in 2012, asked me a question that was a potent catalyst for this book being possible.

With special thanks to my best mate, Simone Phillips. who has edited this book, inspired and contributed to my life in ways she may never fully know.

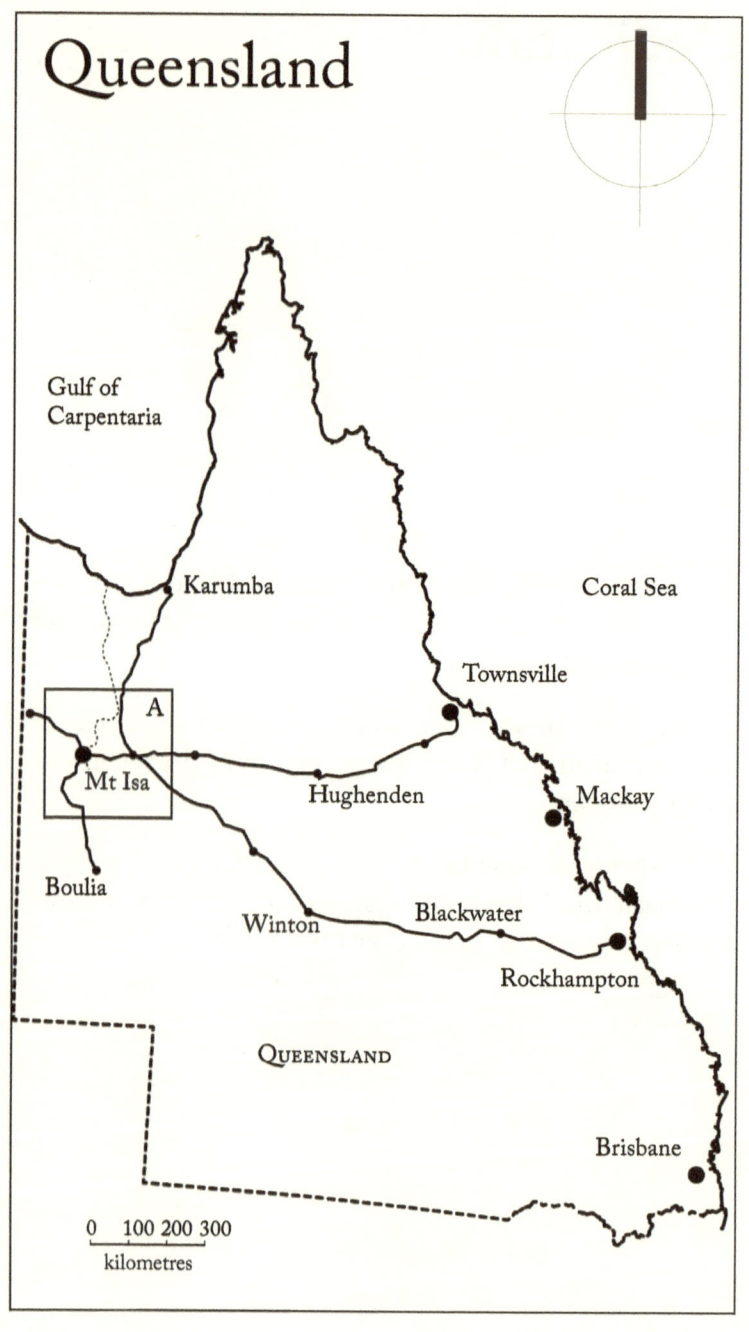

Queensland

Gulf of
Carpentaria

Coral Sea

Karumba

Townsville

A

Mt Isa

Hughenden

Mackay

Boulia

Winton

Blackwater

Rockhampton

QUEENSLAND

Brisbane

0 100 200 300
kilometres

Inset A, Mt. Isa

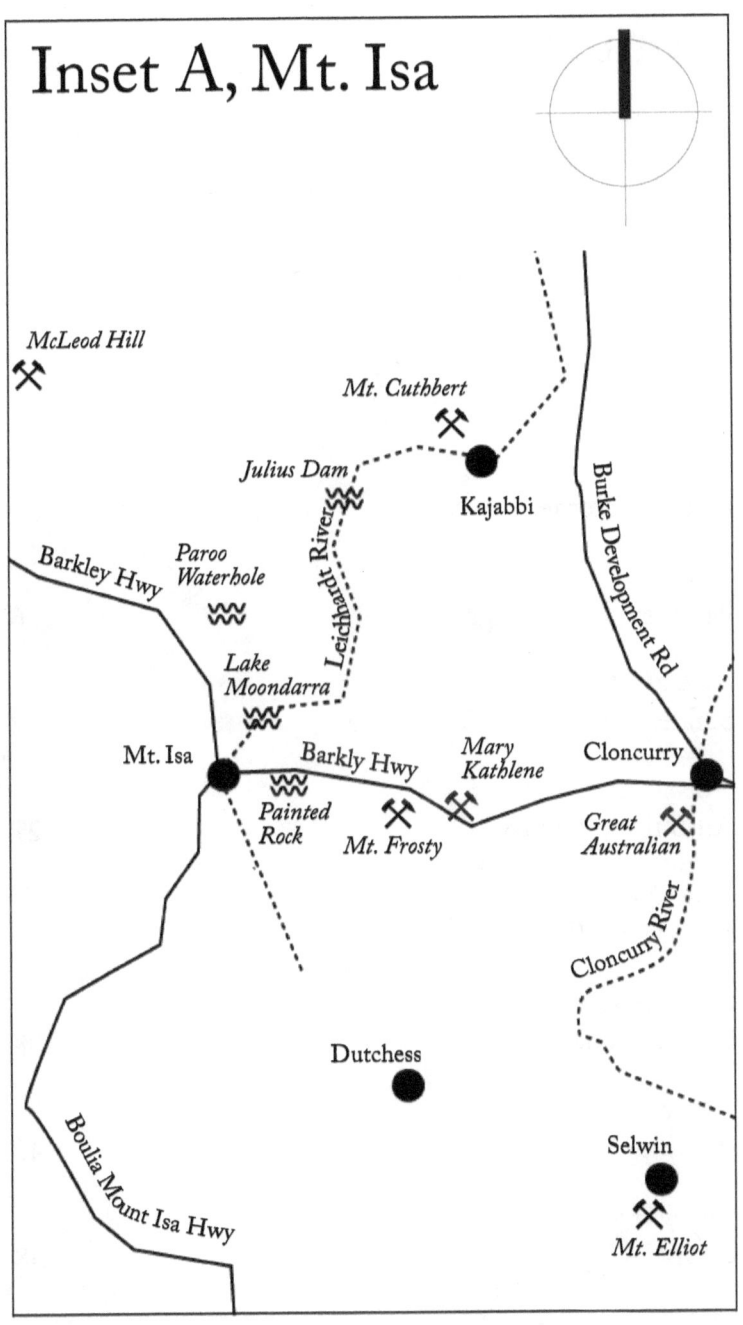

Contents

Bored young men may leave home seeking adventure; but adventure never leaves home seeking bored young men.

Leaving Home

Some choices we make ourselves and others seem to be collaborative; whichever way we choose lives change, families change, people change and can never be the same again.

> "I have learned that if you must leave a place
> that you have lived in and loved and where all
> your yesteryears are buried deep, leave it any way
> except a slow way, leave it the fastest way you
> can. Never turn back and never believe that an
> hour you remember is a better hour because it
> is dead. Passed years seem safe ones, vanquished
> ones, while the future lives in a cloud,
> formidable from a distance."—Beryl Markham

It didn't occur to me that the home I knew, the home that I had contributed to creating, would not be the same without me; that a home evolves and changes over time just like people do; just like sunsets do. When you are in the entity we call Home, it seems to be much the same most of the time; there's a Mum and a Dad, a sister, a dog and from time-to-time a cat, a house, a car, school and living, and me. The basic elements of home are always there, in various guises until someone leaves.

What had been relatively consistent over my 19 years was the four of us: Mum, Dad, my sister Karen and me. Our Golden Labrador Candy joined the family when I was 10; a very welcome and treasured latecomer. We'd had a range of cars that had become part of home and then left, some houses and schools but none had changed our home as much as Candy leaving, passing away in the late 1970s, just as she changed it dynamically with her arrival in 1966. While things that come-and-go can have an effect, it seems that nothing changes a home as much as when someone that you care deeply about, leaves.

Is it different for the one leaving? It seems that the moment they drive off or disappear around the corner they turn into some kind of human hermit crab carrying a new home with them, which might be misidentified as a car or a suitcase except there's more to home than that.

When someone sets-off on an adventure their home can expand to huge proportions becoming a highway, a state or territory, a country or the whole planet and when they settle somewhere, then home shrinks to be a flat or a house in a street. When you're out-of-town visiting someone else's home, then home becomes the town or city where you live but when you're down at the local coffee shop, home is simply the house that you live in. Home is a wonderfully mutable space that can include just about anything or anyone, or a single person.

While it seems that homes can include a great many things or very few things, there is always one thing that is home wherever you live or whatever your home looks like and that's you! So, the idea of leaving home is an odd one.

It's not so much the leaving home that can create feelings of loss and sadness (or is that exhilaration?), but the removing of oneself from everything that is familiar and comforting; all of those things that we use to define and underpin who we are and what we are known as. When a boy leaves home to begin creating his own life he is no longer defined as a boy and becomes known as a man, and though still a son, still a brother, the prime label is now 'Man.' When the man finally returns to the home that he knew as a boy it will have changed almost beyond recognition, except that as soon as he is there, the home that *he* is will be there too and it can seem as if he never left, which is, of course, what's true.

Can someone really leave home or are they the home they think they are leaving? Whatever it is, leaving home is a big choice that creates big changes and at some point in our lives we will all do it for the very first time, and then many times after that.

This story is about the adventure of that very first time; the first time I left home, turned into a hermit crab and then became a man.

Endings, Beginnings

I'd been to the airport many times before: picking up or dropping off friends, flights for my own holidays and sometimes just for a different place to have a quiet drink, watch aeroplanes and be mildly entertained by the general bustle and activity one can find in airports. The terminal building itself was unremarkable; functional and typical of the austere, minimalist design-style of the seventies. Originally sited south of Mount Isa's city centre, the aerodrome was moved north to its current Barkley Highway location in 1950. Following work strengthening and expanding the runway to cater for Boeing's 727 mid-sized aircraft, the terminal was constructed in 1969.

Fronted by a large bitumen carpark, the main building sat low and wide on its site dwarfed by a long run of red-earth hills to the west; the area was sparsely landscaped with a few natives and several cheerful bougainvillea thriving in the arid conditions. A full-width awning jutted out from the building's facade attempting to shade travelers from the biting sun as arrivals made their way into the relatively cool interior and those departing winced, quickly putting on sunglasses as they stepped across the threshold and felt Mount Isa's hot dry air begin to claim the moisture from their skin.

Ray swung his Ford into a parking bay close to the entry, we unloaded my suitcases from its boot and then walked across to the terminal. A pair of aluminum-framed glass sliding doors slid open and beckoned us into a cool, cavernous interior. Passenger check-in was right in front and after all the paperwork was done we walked across to the bar, which looked out over the runway, to the west.

It was September 1979 and the season was hovering on the cusp of spring. I had just turned 23 years old and it seemed unreal that just four years ago, Ray and I had sighted the wizard's wand and driven my Holden HR sedan into the city for the very first time. In an hour I would be leaving Mount Isa for good and even though I hadn't made any special announcement about when I was flying out, there were a bunch of familiar faces in the bar.

"Reprobates!" I called out as we walked in, "You'd use any excuse for a drink."

Several of the accused raised their glasses in confirmation as I looked around the group. Someone moved to one side and through the gap I saw her sitting at a table. My heart twanged a bit; I wasn't expecting to see Sandra Wilson there. Instantly, I wished I wasn't going. She saw me and smiled. I waved back just as a pair of shoulders closed the gap once again. Someone beckoned, offering a pot of cold beer, and gratefully I joined the rowdy throng.

It was an odd feeling chatting with friends in the bar at Mount Isa Airport, knowing that we would not do this again. There would be no more, "Mate, I'll see you at the Irish Club on Tuesday for a game of pool" or "There's a party at Johno's this Saturday. Are you going?" and I knew my departure was going to close the door to any further connection with Sandra. While I knew that leaving The Isa was the right thing for me, my choice came with some challenges. One of them tapped me on the shoulder.

"Are you ignoring me?" Sandra chided and then grinned. God she was cute.

"A bit." I laughed "Leaving is harder than I thought it was going to be." My voice faltered for a moment, "And I won't be seeing much of you anymore."

"Yeh. I know" she said looking up at me, "Maybe you'll come back?"

I hesitated for a moment before replying, "Yeh. Maybe." but we both knew that it was a lie.

"Well," she said, "if I don't see you again I hope you have a great life. I'll miss you. It's going to be strange not seeing you around."

I glanced past her, out to the runway where an aeroplane was landing; smoke bursting off its tortured rubber tyres, "Yeh. I know." I replied softly.

Sandra's lips pulled tight for a moment, wrinkling
her chin. I thought she was going to cry but she held
it together. I gave her a hug, once again feeling the
generous, familiar curves of her body pressed into mine.
I closed my eyes. Inhaled her scent. Soft hair upon my
cheek. Time had almost stopped. Sensation, intense.
The desire to stay, very strong now. I was almost gone. I
breathed in. My mouth opened to whisper. "I can't leave
you. I'll stay." But she broke off. Stepped back. Oh too
soon. Time had stopped. Her hand was still on my arm.
She looked up. Found my eyes. Lingered there. Hoping.
I was frozen. Not a word escaped me. She turned.
Walked away. Rejoined her table. Lips upon a chilled
glass. A red and white striped straw; her favourite. I'd
stopped breathing. I'd watched her go. Lights in her
hair. The movement of her body. Tap of heels. A dance.
The many kisses. The crazy fights. The glorious nights.
All of it had walked away. My heart yearned. My mind
begged her to turn. She didn't look back. My body was
struggling and I inhaled, deeply. Vision cleared. The
truth. It was done. It was truly done. I could go. Space
to move. The airport returned. Noisy. Busy. People. A
glass, cold in my hand. Someone, pressed my shoulder
affectionately. A question. Conversation. Banter.
Laughter … Yes. It was done.

My flight was leaving at four o'clock. I had time for one
quick beer and then came the announcements, calling
for passengers to board. There was a flurry of goodbyes,
"See you at work tomorrow Stephen!" jokes, hand
shaking and back slapping. I shook Ray's hand; he was
staying-on and I was going to miss my old mate not
being a part of this next adventure. I looked around the

bar for Sandra but couldn't see her anywhere and made my way to Departures.

Outside it seemed like I was in a transparent bubble as the voices faded and I waited, isolated by a wire security fence, to have my ticket checked. An air hostess glanced at my boarding pass, nodded and waved me through. Walking out onto the apron towards the waiting aircraft I looked back at the bar's dark tinted windows and waved, having no idea if anyone saw me or waved back. Soon I had climbed up the airstairs, found my seat and was buckled in. I was on the west side of the aeroplane and looked out of its small window towards familiar red-earth hills flanking the runway. I was glad I couldn't see the terminal; I'd probably be looking for Sandra. It wasn't long before the aircraft taxied onto the runway and after a wait, while our pilot talked with the tower, the Boeing's powerful engines roared and I was thrust back into my seat. As its wheels cleared the land my connection with Mount Isa seemed to tear and begin to break apart. I was suddenly lonely, climbing up into the vast space of sky, and cried quietly to myself while watching the long dark scar of Mineside sliding past and then the houses and then the red, red bush.

As sky filled my view the last few threads of connection broke and fell to earth. Mount Isa eased-off her grip and Sandra too, probably on her way home now, let me go. With every kilometre further away I flew I sensed connections, relationships and locations beginning to transform into memories. Some I would keep, some others would keep and some would gradually dissipate and never be known again.

We levelled out and an air hostess took my order for a double Scotch and coke; something to settle me down. The blended whiskey bit into my throat, got to work at warming my stomach and I imagined it seeping into the bloodstream. Soon I felt a familiar buzz and knew it had made its way to my head. I took-in a long deep breath, leaned back in the seat and sipped slowly, feeling my body begin to relax and my brain numb pleasantly. Two hours and twenty seven minutes later we landed in Brisbane and Mum and Dad were there to take me home. They looked older, so was I and we were all different.

Chapter 1

Safari, Wanderlust, Adventure

As Dad shook my hand the sides of his mouth began to turn down in that cheeky smirk I knew so well,

"You'll be back in three months." he said.

Before I could reply Mum playfully pressed her elbow into his ribs and leaned-in for a hug, and then it was my sister Karen's turn. I looked at the three of them standing close together and as the sun tipped-up over the sand dunes at Narrow Neck, I turned and got into my car. I was 18 years old, we had never been apart before and today, I was leaving home.

Dad spoke again, this time softer and deeper in his throat, "Son, if you ever need anything ... "

He left the sentence unfinished and I nodded in reply; he nodded back and we both knew that despite our recent difficulties he would be there for me if I needed it. The Holden HR roared into life and I gunned it a bit, enjoying the sound, grateful for the distraction. Dad winced at the noise and glanced towards the neighbour's windows but said nothing. I slipped the column shift into first, feeling it grumble a little against my palm as the gears meshed together, then released the clutch and drove away, my arm like a lone flag waving out of the open window. For a brief moment orange sunlight flashed in the rearview mirror and I lost sight of them. The car rounded the bend on Pacific Street and took second gear.

It was spring 1976 and I was on my way to pick up Ray Linwood; we'd been friends for a couple of years and were going to the "top end;" to Darwin in Australia's Northern Territory some 3,500 kilometres away.

I left Pacific and wheeled the car onto Cronin Avenue where Gary Hallard and his parents used to live before they had moved to Labrador. I'd met Gary while working at my first architectural job in Southport and we'd become friends. Soon I was on Main Beach's popular Tedder Avenue and then the Gold Coast Highway, cruising over Sundale Bridge towards Southport. Having ignored the warning signs I'd jumped off that bridge many times when I was younger, splashing deep into the Nerang River some six meters below.

Across town in the suburb of Sorrento, Ray lived with his parents and two brothers. I'd met him through Frank Brady who my sister knew; Ray was tall with a slim build, smoked cigarettes and was cool. He was a dedicated Ford man with a 1970 Cortina Mark II. His Dad was a mechanic who had, apparently, done some

"work" on its 1600cc engine. It certainly went well, for a
Ford.

I turned left onto Queen Street and a few minutes
later ran onto Bundall Road; Dad's golf club showed
up on the right and then Gold Coast City Council's
Chambers to the left. It had been nicknamed the
"beehive" and I'd spent many hours there submitting
building plans or talking with inspectors as part of my
job with local architects Burling Brown and Partners.

This trip was different to the others, a surreal mix of
affection for the past and excitement for the future.
I knew every building, road sign, tree ... I'd passed-
by them all many times and who knew when I'd see
them again, if ever. Leaving home, it seemed, was more
than just vacating the apartment and there was much
more to "home" than I had realised. I was not new to
this though, the family had left England in 1964 to
immigrate to Australia, and five years later left the west
coast to drive 4,500 kilometres and settle on the east.
Perhaps life was a series of adventures, moving from
one place to another, or one big adventure assimilating
many moving places. Who knew? I turned right at the
Sorrento shop's traffic lights into Boomerang Crescent
and a few moments later parked outside of Ray's.

The Linwoods had a nice two-storey brick house and
the pathway from the side gate took me past their
swimming pool and on to the front door, which was
ajar. Ray's Mum had a special room upstairs full of
antiques, paintings, fancy furniture and objet d'art. The
boys were not allowed in there but just once she had let
me see inside, which had annoyed the others no-end.
Ray had all of his gear ready. His two brothers, Kevin

and Mark (who was nicknamed Skin because he was so skinny) helped us load the car with a tent, sleeping bags and Ray's stuff. His Dad had already gone to work and they'd said goodbye earlier but Mrs. Linwood came out to see us off. I shook hands all round, Kevin made a joke and everyone laughed, then we got in the HR and drove away. In the rear view mirror I saw that they stayed on the footpath waving until we had disappeared around the road's long leisurely bend—it was called *Boomerang* Crescent for a reason.

Within half an hour we had slipped out onto the highway at Nerang and were heading north towards Brisbane. We had our gear, my car, a few hundred dollars each and this vague idea of going to Darwin and getting a good job there.

Darwin was a big mess! On Christmas Eve 1974 the city had been devastated by Cyclone Tracy, a powerful Category 4 monster that had destroyed 70% of Darwin's buildings and left over 40,000 people homeless; 30,000 of those were evacuated with many never returning. We'd heard stories that the only things left standing were the cold rooms and freezers belonging to butcher shops and hotels. We hoped that there would be a hotel left standing somewhere, serving ice-cold beer as it could get really hot in the top end. We figured there would be a huge rebuild taking place in Darwin and lots of jobs on offer. Exactly how we were going to get there or what we would find when we did, we weren't sure about but, often, that's how great adventures begin.

Ray rummaged around in the glove box, found a music cassette and pushed it into the eight track player that was slung under my blue, sparkle-paint dashboard. It disappeared into the machine and the Beach Boys came to life, pumping out of four dual-cone Pioneer speakers and filling the car with their sound.

> "Let's go surfin' now
> Everybody's learning how
> Come on and safari with me-e ...
> Come-on everybody."

A safari? Maybe. There wasn't much surf where we were going but probably some big salt-water crocodiles. No, this was safari, wanderlust and adventure all rolled into one. We had no solid plans and had simply begun. It was an adventure in the making and even though we didn't know it right now it would be one that Ray and I would never forget, one that would change the course of ours and the lives of people we hadn't even met yet, and one that we would know 50 or more years-on into the future, when we were young men, living in old bodies.

Chapter 2

Ambition, Fantasy

In 1975 the Australian economy was deep in recession. I had lost my job at Burling Brown & Partners as Ron and Darrel downsized their architectural practice due to a turndown in the construction industry. It was disappointing; I'd worked with them during my holidays in their first, small Sundale premises and later at 32 Short Street where they had bought an old two-storey house and converted it into offices. I was studying at Queensland Institute of Technology (QIT) in Brisbane, and joined the firm again during the summer break; Gary Hallard was working there along with Marshall Boyde. Gary had a Toyota Corolla, Marshall drove a Holden Torana and my ride was a Kawasaki 250cc, 3 cylinder motorbike; metallic white with green trim. While the friendships continued, the job had not and the government's economic mismanagement produced high unemployment and difficulty across the country.

Stephe⋂ ꞇ ram

After Burling Brown, I had managed to get part time work at a small Biggera Waters supermarket, stacking shelves, and continued studying at QIT in the evenings and some weekends. After tax, my pay was just $67 a week. Ray, who had started working for Woolworths after he'd left school, had also been put-off and was unemployed.

We got to talking about Darwin and how it would need rebuilding after Cyclone Tracy. Ray didn't have any construction experience but we both knew he could talk himself into just about any job. I knew of one building contractor who had gone to Darwin seeking work but had not heard from him since leaving Burling Brown. It seemed like a good idea to go, for several reasons.

Mum and Dad had recently sold a motel they'd owned—the Marlin Motel in Labrador—and we'd all moved to a two bedroom unit at Narrow Neck, Main Beach. It was nice to live right near the beach, albeit a little crowded, as I was sharing a room with my 16 year old sister Karen. I had discovered alcohol and liked it, had a gloriously noisy hotted-up Holden HR sedan and was running fairly wild with my mates. My parents, who had worked the motel for five years without a holiday, were looking for a quiet, relaxing time in Main Beach, while they figured out what to do with their lives. It wasn't long before Dad and I began to clash, and one day he laid down the law,

"Settle down, fit in or get out!" he told me in no uncertain terms.

Looking back, I don't blame him; I couldn't have been much fun to live with and it really was time to go.

When Ray mentioned a drive to Darwin, I jumped at the idea.

As we chatted excitedly about the trip we quickly defined two simple goals: Ray wanted to earn enough money to buy a Ford GT-HO Phase 3 and I was going to get a Holden Torana GTR XU-1. These were our dream cars and we could see them, smell them, vividly imagine driving them, but we just didn't have them yet. Once we had our new cars then we would drive them home to the Gold Coast, like returning champions, and we would be the envy of all those who had stayed behind! Ah … it was going to be so-o good.

And as Ray and I drove north along the Brisbane Road on our way to Darwin, it wasn't long before the conversation turned to those two cars: which one was faster, what colours they came in, custom paint jobs, how much they cost, top speeds, quarter mile times, who had won the last Bathurst Hardie-Ferodo 1000, our favourite racing drivers—Brock, Moffat, Goss— and so on and so on. It was a conversation that only two young, car-crazy teenage boys could love; and we did! After a while both of us fell silent, lost in our own thoughts; the Beach Boys launched into "409" and the HR sped along the highway towards Brisbane.

Chapter 3

Blackwater Coal

Traffic was slow through Brisbane; eventually we crossed under the Storey Bridge's 36 year old grey-metal arches, swung right into Wickham Street, Fortitude Valley and met bumper to bumper traffic.

There was plenty of time to consider "The Valley's" seedy reputation of gambling, drugs and brothels. I recalled news reports of the Whisky Au Go Go nightclub burning down in 1973 with 15 people dead; an arson attack. And there was the Bellino family who owned night clubs and were rumoured to be Brisbane's mafia with powerful police connections. We passed the Prince Consort Hotel on the left, its verandahs adorned with decorative cast iron balustrades, and then the iconic red-brick McWhirters building that had once housed Myers. The car crawled along in first gear.

A copse of giant Moreton Bay Fig trees rose up majestically on our right as The Valley and it's dark reputation fell behind; the traffic began to pick up speed. We crossed Breakfast Creek where the Brisbane

River meandered in alongside us and motored along Kingsford Smith Drive, through the suburbs of Hamilton, Eagle Farm and onto the Bruce Highway. Brisbane's sprawling outer suburbs quickly gave way and soon enough we were travelling through the Beerburrum State Forests. The Sunshine Coast passed by unseen, 10 kilometres to the east and then the historic town of Gympie squeezed into my rear view mirror.

"Hey Ray!" I said.

"Yeh." he replied.

"Have you noticed how the rear view mirror shows a condensed and receding vision of the past, while the windscreen opens up to the future, relative to the speed one is travelling at? So, when we drive fast the past disappears quicker and the future arrives sooner."

Apparently Ray hadn't noticed and wasn't interested in my new philosophy; glancing out of the window he changed the subject.

"Did I tell you that my Dad reckons there may be work for us out at the Blackwater coal mines? It's just west of Rockhampton."

"Yeh?"

"Yeh."

"We should check it out." I replied.

The Cook Colliery at Blackwater had only been open for a few years with two new mines planned. We were pretty sure that mining paid good wages, so we agreed to go there first and see what was on offer. We had zero mining experience but Ray was confident he could talk us up a job. I knew he could!

Our next major town was Maryborough, where we crossed the Mary River, and later swept through Childers, Gin Gin and Miriam Vale. It was a good run and I opened up the HR and let her stretch her legs on the open highway. Dad had bought the car for me to drive up to Brisbane and attend QIT; it had cost $800 and I paid him back at $10 a week. When I first got the sedan it was a stock 'Special' with Kurrewa Blue body paint and a white roof, it had a three gear column shift and a 161cc, six cylinder red motor and single Stromberg carburetter; it was a little different now.

After about a year the rear engine seal had started to leak oil and Dad and I pulled the motor out in the garage one Saturday afternoon. Dad had been an aircraft engineer and guided me in taking the motor apart and replacing the seal; there was lots to learn and I loved it! We put it all back together and reinstalled it in the car. Happily, everything worked. Yay us! After that the car and I spent a lot of time in the garage as I made various modifications.

I bought a trio of dual-throat Weber carburetters, effectively one carburetter per cylinder, and also installed extractors so that the engine could breathe and exhaust more efficiently; and roar louder! Later I acquired a modified cam shaft, which let more fuel feed into the cylinders. At the same time, I replaced the hydraulic cam lifters with mechanical ones, which provided a more direct link with the tappets and produced a distinct, mechanical clicking sound in the motor. A ported and shaved head showed up, and after I'd cleaned it up with a valve grind and heavier springs the stock head was replaced. One night while I was hanging out in the garage, a neighbour came over and asked if I'd like to buy a set of four, eight inch wide rims with tyres and chrome wheel nuts for $50? Hell yes! On top of that there were all the normal things that a teenager puts in his first car: extra gauges, a stereo, speakers in every panel, fluffy dash cover … and more.

We arrived in Rockhampton about four o'clock in the afternoon, filled the car with petrol, bought a Coca-Cola each and stretched our legs before heading off again. Blackwater was 200 kilometres and just over two hours away. We reached the small town's outskirts around dusk and located the local caravan park. It had a tent site, so we booked-in for the night and then went to the hotel.

Blackwater sat on the Capricorn Highway and was largely known for its coal mines; its population was around 2,500 people and growing. The town was named after Blackwater Creek; apparently someone observed it flowing with black water thought to be from coal deposits. It boasted a couple of hotels and we went to the Capricorn, which we'd spotted when arriving. Ray and I had some beers and then ordered food; the blackboard special was Southern Fried Chicken, coleslaw and chips, simple but good. Later, we got in one game of pool but the public bar was busy and we were both tired, so we drove back to the camp site to pitch our tent.

Ray had a basic two-man tent, which went up easily enough. We pitched it over a ground sheet and threw

our sleeping bags and pillows inside. About 50 metres
from our site a bullmastiff wearing a brindle coat
watched us; it was chained to a very large log. He
barked a few times and tested his chain but seemed
to settle down after a while. We were happy about the
chain and went off to clean our teeth and get ready
for bed. Weary after a long drive and with the alcohol
doing its work, we were soon fast asleep.

During the night I woke briefly; there was some noise
and a bump but I was dopey with sleep and beer, and
must have dozed off again. When morning came and I
opened my eyes I saw that the tent had collapsed and
something heavy was laying against me. I sat up, lifted
the tent up off me and listened … I heard panting.
Oops!

Ray woke up too and we managed to get the front
flap unzipped and crawled out, blinking in the early
morning light. A few things had changed during the
night. For a start the log was now much closer and the
chain was lying over our tent, and there on the other
side where I had been sleeping the large dog stood up,
looked at us and slowly licked its substantial chops. It
was not a pretty sight.

For what seemed a very long moment nobody moved.
There was so much in that moment, it was as if time
had slowed and the seconds became minutes. I was
aware of the sun on my skin, the movement and sounds
of birds, leaves softly rustling and Ray's nervous cough.
Then, someone yelled out from behind us and the
dog's ears pricked towards the sound. Suddenly, like a
big puppy, it jumped up and ran towards the voice; the
chain rattled back over our already distressed tent. A

tall, bearded bloke came over, looked down at the tent and laughed to himself. Shaking his head he offered an apology, unclasped its chain and took the dog away with him, which we were very grateful for. Sometime in the night the dog must have gotten cold and dragged that huge log across the ground so it could snuggle up next to me. It was hard to imagine the brute strength required, but somehow he'd managed it. We were both very glad he was just looking for warmth and not for dinner!

Ray dug around in the boot and produced a small camping stove, a set of army cups and utensils, a tin of powdered milk, small jar of sugar and tea bags.

"What else have you got in there Ray?" I joked. "Is that Dr Who's Tardis?"

We gathered some fallen kindling, lit a small camp fire and soon were drinking hot, sweet tea and chatting about what we would do today. It was decided that after breakfast we would drive out to the mine site office and ask about some work. We relocated the tent to a better spot, away from dogs, logs and chains, and set it up straight again. Once we were showered and dressed I drove us into town where we found a place to have some breakfast.

I realised that we were going to have to do food differently; eating three meals out every day was soon going to gobble up my money. I talked with Ray about getting an esky and making a trip to the supermarket to buy some snacks, tinned food, drinks and other supplies; it would be far cheaper for us than getting food from cafes and roadside stores. I also mentioned we'd be able to keep cans of beer cold too and he liked that idea; we would look into that after our visit to the mine. And with that we finished up, paid our bill and drove out of town heading south along the Blackwater-Rollerston Road.

Coal was discovered in Blackwater in the mid 1800s by Ludwig Leichhardt, but it didn't really start to develop until 1960. About the time my family emigrated to Australia from England, the first mining leases were granted; back then the town had a population of just 25 people. Utah Development Company, a familiar name from my Port Hedland days in Western Australia, built the Blackwater open-cut mine and that's where we were going.

We found the mine site office easily enough and made our enquiries; there was both good news and bad news. The good was that there were positions vacant; the bad was that the unions had taken action to 'close the books' and the mine was unable to take on anyone new. The action had been in place for some time and the people we spoke with did not know when this restriction would be lifted. They suggested we could wait around in Blackwater, but it may be months before they could employ again. Ray and I didn't really understand the union and its activities, but we agreed to be interviewed and spent an hour answering questions, discussing possible jobs and filling in some forms. We figured if things changed with the mine then we could always come back.

After our interviews we drove back into Blackwater and spent the afternoon exploring, buying an esky, ice and some supplies; eventually finding ourselves back at the

Capricorn Hotel. Over a few beers and some dinner we decided to move on; the idea of waiting around was not appealing and Ray was satisfied that he had followed through on his Dad's suggestion. Tomorrow, we would head off and resume our trip to Darwin. And so we had some more beers, several games of pool and then turned in for a good night's sleep, fortunately, without any late night, four legged visitors.

We would always remember Blackwater for its graphic and valuable lesson: you can move just about anything if you really want to!

Chapter 4

First Trouble

We were up early, packed and ready to go. Mackay was about six hours away and Townsville another two. Townsville was where we would leave the coast and turn inland, beginning a 900 kilometer run west to copper city, Mount Isa, where we had a friend.

With the car's sun-visors fully down and the railway running parallel on our right, we drove dead east into the rising sun and back along the Capricorn Highway. Off to the south and rising up out of flat grasslands was the massive Blackdown Tableland, which occupied over 320 square kilometers and spanned the full distance between us and the Dawson Highway, some 120 kilometers to the south. We shot by the tiny towns of Bluff and Dingo, then Duaringa; finally slowing to pass through Gracemere before turning left and joining the Bruce Highway.

To its west Rockhampton was flanked by a series of lagoons and natural wetlands, and guarded in the east by Mount Archer; in the middle, running north-south and winding away to the sea was the Fitzroy River. The city sprawled over both its banks and was joined by two bridges. In 1853 the river was named after a New South Wales Governor, Sir Charles Fitzroy, which makes sense when you realise that Queensland didn't officially exist until 1859; the future state was part of New South Wales.

I followed the Bruce Highway through the city centre and crossed the Fitzroy River Bridge's 360 meter span. Back on land, the road ran alongside Kershaw Gardens for a while and then veered north. Buildings began to thin out and soon we were on open highway, across Belmont Creek and cruising towards the sugar town of Mackay. About 100 kilometers out from Rockhampton we approached Marlborough and then turned west along the Marlborough-Sarina Road; we'd both heard about "Murder Highway."

"Here we go." Ray said quietly.

"Yeh." I replied.

The land north of Rockhampton was a vast area of sparse brigalow scrub that eventually transformed into the lush green sugar cane fields surrounding Sarina. The 250 kilometer section between Marlborough and Sarina was the only way to get to Mackay and was well known, having been widely reported in the news over the years.

In 1967 Joyce and Ron Linfoot, tired after the long drive from Townsville, pulled their caravan over to the side of the road to make camp for the night. Ron was shot in his lower-back and Joyce took a bullet in the shoulder; terrified they huddled in their caravan and lived to tell the tale. A year earlier in the same area, a 25 year old Newcastle man was shot dead while sleeping in his car parked just off the highway, his brother was seriously wounded and their companion's face cut with splintered glass during psychopath Graham Sumner's deadly attack. And just in the previous year in March, Noel Weckert was found shot dead at Connor River, slumped over the steering wheel of his car where he and his wife had pulled over to sleep. The body of Sophie Weckert was discovered five days later at Funnel Creek, some 30 kilometers away. With Marlborough behind us we drove into the "horror stretch" as locals called it, and set off for Mackay but trouble struck before we got there.

The Brigalow Belt is characterised by a hardy wattle tree that grows to 25 metres high; it extends some 450 kilometers north from the township of Taroom to Nebo, near Sarina. Ludwig Leichhardt wrote of Bricklow scrub in his 1844 exploration journal.

> "At the foot of the ridges some fine lagoons were observed, as also several plains, with the soil and the vegetation of the Downs, but bounded on the northward by impenetrable Bricklow scrub."—Ludwig Leichhardt

We drove inland for about 50 kilometers before the road turned northwest at Coppermine Creek; the land was flat, uninteresting, except for a long low range of hills to the east. Bora Creek, Stockyard Creek and Mundi Creek were marked by a rattle of gravel under our wheels, and Clarke Creek produced some vegetation and a signpost to May Downs. A further 20 kilometers on we reached Croydon Station.

In 1965 the Olympic Torch was being relayed by Australian runners to the Melbourne Olympic Games. On the way they were to travel south from Sarina to St Lawrence, but due to heavy rains in the area the route was changed to Sarina - Croydon - Marlborough. This added an additional 36 kilometers to the leg and as the schedule was already set for arrival in Melbourne, the torch bearers were asked to run faster to make up the time.

At Lotus Creek we found a roadhouse and pulled over to get petrol and a hamburger, then continued on to cross the infamous Connor River and later Funnel Creek; we didn't stop to explore and were glad to put them behind us. The road began to curve towards the northeast and I realised we were turning towards the coast. I turned to comment but Ray was snoozing with his head resting against the car's centre pillar.

The Holden had been running well, revelling in the steady high-speed cruise. I'd not noticed the motor gradually becoming noisier; with the wind charging in through wide open windows, music playing and chatting with Ray, it had slipped my attention. It was a mistake. The terrain was getting more interesting as we entered the Great Dividing Range, with Blue Mountain appearing on our left and Sarina Range up ahead. About five kilometers passed the range on a hairpin bend there was a sharp bang from the engine and one of its cylinders dropped out.

I hit the brakes and quickly pulled us over, onto a narrow gravel verge. The motor was making a racket. I turned it off, popped the bonnet and got out. With the motor and music turned off and the noise of driving gone, it seemed eerily quiet. Ray was awake and we looked all over the engine bay, prodded leads, checked links; everything seemed okay. I asked him to start the motor while I listened and all too soon it was obvious where the racket was coming from; tappets.

I had a full tool box in the boot and we removed all of the tappet cover bolts and lifted it off the engine's head. There it was! One of the studs that had held its tappet in place had snapped. We could fix most things but that was not one of them; the broken stud would need to be pulled out and a new one pressed in its place.

My error was that when I had changed the motor's lifters, I had not put lock nuts on the tappet studs. As the tappet rocked, the single nuts worked lose over time and required adjusting. Normally this was easy enough, but with the engine working at high-speed for long periods of time, one of the nuts had completely unscrewed, releasing its tappet and snapping the stud. Actually, we had gotten off lightly as it could have been much worse; lumps of metal flying around in an engine are generally not a good thing!

We assessed the situation and then removed the assembly associated with the broken stud and replaced the cover. It would do no further damage and we could ease the car into Mackay on five cylinders. I cleaned up, packed the toolbox back into the boot and drove off gingerly. The motor sounded weird but ran well enough and after a while we both came off alert and relaxed. Farmland appeared left and right as we eased through Shinfield and then more buildings and people as we drove into Sarina; our journey along Murder Highway was done and we were alive. I turned the car left onto the Bruce Highway and pointed the bonnet towards Mackay. The Malborough-Sarina Road became past in my rearview mirror and the future opened up before us framed with green sugar cane fields on either side.

A road sign informed, "Mackay 23" just before Alligator Creek and the thickening mangrove forests announced our crossing. The tide was out exposing large areas of sandbanks and mud flats; a narrow channel hugged the north bank and wound out of view towards the coast. Farmland lined the Bruce Highway featuring fields of tall, verdant sugarcane stretching out as far as we could see; way off to the west, low and blue, the Great Dividing Range guarded Queensland's central plains. Sandy Creek was next followed by a small gathering of buildings known as Chelona and then Rosella. With the crossing of Bakers Creek, Mackay's outskirts showed up in the windscreen, it was about midday and we headed towards the centre of town. At the Showgrounds the highway broke off sharply to our left, but I turned right into Gordon Street and I pulled the car over to ask for help from some of the locals; a man directed us further along where we found a Holden dealer.

I parked the car and we got out. It was good to feel the ground underfoot again and stretch after the long drive, and to turn off that noisy motor. We went into the dealership and Ray explained our plight to the lady at reception; he worked his magic and she became sympathetic, squeezing the car in for repair that afternoon. Good news! I handed over the keys and we left to get some lunch and explore a little of Mackay.

Mackay was sited on the Pioneer River's south bank and widely known for its surrounding sugar plantations;

the pre-harvest burn off, done at night, could be quite
spectacular. Rising in the Pinnacle Ranges some 60
kilometers southwest of the city, the river formed
a natural harbour where it met the Pacific Ocean.
Docks had been built for cargo ships transporting
sugar products to markets in the south of the country.
In addition, black gold; coal was exported from Hays
Point, which was just south of the main town. Sugar
and coal were not our priority, we were far more
interested in food and found a cafe in the main street.
We took a map of Queensland with us and reviewed the
next main leg of our journey, a 900 kilometre drive from
Townsville to Mount Isa. Later we wandered over to
the river and snoozed on its banks. Around four o'clock,
Ray and I made our way back to the garage to check on
the car.

When we arrived there was a suprise; they were still
working on the car and the head mechanic invited us
into the workshop for a chat. He and several apprentices
gathered around the HR's engine bay to discuss dual-
throat Webers, camshafts, ported heads and all things
hotted-up Holden! Ray, the only Ford man, copped some
good natured ribbing, but responded well and soon
joined in with the juicy conversation; after all, we loved
cars. It was a lot of fun and I watched closely while the
mechanic finished up and reset all the tappets by ear;
listening to the sound they make as he adjusted each
one. The engine's head now featured a shiny new stud
and he told me to keep an eye on it until I fitted a set
of double lock nuts. It was good advice. I paid the bill,
which was very reasonable, and then they rolled up the
workshop door so we could drive out. We shook hands
all round and were asked for a good burn-out on exit.

Happy to oblige, I pumped the accelerator, dropped the clutch and smoked up Gordon Street followed by loud cheers and whistles. It felt good and we were off and rolling again. I found the Showgrounds and turned right onto our old friend the Bruce Highway. Mackay's urban sprawl was temporarily relieved as we crossed over the Pioneer River, and then passed through the outer suburbs of Genella and Farleigh.

Once we were out of Mackay, Ray took over driving and pointed the bonnet north once again, towards Townsville. The motor sounded great; its tappets singing in synchronised unison. After a while the sun began to set and we switched on the headlights; both of us were quiet as our perspective of the world narrowed to the illuminated bitumen in front of us. Our journey slowed dramatically around Bowen, where the highway became engulfed in thick fog and we were creeping along in first gear with just 20 metres visibility. Frogs croaked happily on either side and a choir of crickets sung our passing. Fortunately, traffic was very light and at times it seemed that we were the only humans in a ghostly, clammy and vividly white world. The fog eventually lifted, or thinned out and we drove on.

The Bruce Highway began to climb and we ascended Mount Elliot, skirting east of Bowling Green Bay National Park. The road grade varied and we were up and down in the gears a few times during the steeper sections. When we had reached the top, Townsville's lights came into view; twinkling off in the distance. It certainly lifted our spirits and we chatted excitedly while descending to the plains and farmlands below. Just before Nome we laughed out loud to see a sign that read, "Alligator Creek." Had we somehow looped back in time to Mackay? Thirty minutes later, telltale advertising billboards let us know we were getting close to civilisation.

We were both feeling quite weary as we entered the city's outskirts; it was late and we had no idea about accommodation. Ray pulled the car into a rest area and parked well off to the side, away from a single light pole that was entertaining hosts of flying insects. We slept in the car that night, our sleeping bags rolled out across its blue-vinyl bench seats. I wound all the windows up, leaving a gap for air and then locked the doors. Soon Ray was snoring lightly in the back, but I lay awake for a while, listening. Apart from the insects and the occasional passing vehicle it was fairly quiet and eventually, I fell asleep. It had been a long day and there was another one to come tomorrow.

Chapter 5

Heading West

A family who lives in a large house might look upon someone sleeping in their car as homeless, whereas the person in the vehicle doesn't consider themselves homeless at all, but may judge another who is sleeping under the open sky on a park bench, as such. The homeless person rarely thinks of themselves that way and for some, a life that includes a regular job, mortgage, monthly telephone and electricity bills is a crazy way to live. People in disparate social environments view the world and the way they live very differently–different lives, different viewpoints and different realities.

The surroundings, for example a car or park bench play their part in setting the scene but the sleeper, by making themselves visible; by their actions contribute to being judged and so add substance to the idea of homeless. Together both judge and the judged begin to create the reality of homeless, which others can then agree with, nurturing it to become even more real.

The homeless person, however, may simply be sleeping
in their car until they wake up and move on. Perhaps,
they are creating an adventure of living that the judge
can never know beyond the confines of their conclusion.

Ray had parked next to a thick copse of eucalypts,
which shaded us from the early morning sun; we
woke up just before seven o'clock. I got out of the car
and attempted to stretch away my cramped sleeping
position. My shoulders were wider than the seat and
I'd slept lying on my side most of the night. When
Ray awoke we packed our sleeping bags into the boot,
emptied rubbish out of the car into a nearby bin and
set off again. Abbott Street lead us over the Ross River
where we swung right around the railway goods yard,
made our way over Ross Creek and eventually entered
The Strand adjacent to George Payne's magnificent
1902 Customs House.

In 1971 The Strand had been ravaged when Tropical
Cyclone Althea crossed the coast just north of
Townsville, bringing wind gusts of nearly 200 km/hr.
We had felt the effects of Althea 1,500 kilometres away
on the Gold Coast and watched the news reports with
interest. The effect on Townsville was significant with
three deaths; many houses were damaged or destroyed
including 200 Housing Commission homes. The Prime
Minister Mr. McMahon had visited Townsville and
grandly pledged unlimited financial aid, though in
practice only $150,000 was realised by claimants. In
an effort to better protect the city's historic foreshore,
half of the boulder wall along The Strand was rebuilt to

stand one metre higher than it had before, sacrificing views to the beach. I knew about tropical cyclones having spent my youth in Port Headland, some 3,000 kilometres to the west, and had experienced many of them.

Further along The Strand I spotted some public amenities and parked; we managed a rudimentary wash and felt fresher for it. There wasn't much left in the esky so we had breakfast at a nearby cafe. It was nice to smell salt air and hear seagulls mewing. We were not going to be on the east coast for a while and tried to soak it all up, by osmosis, to take with us. I recalled a similar, perhaps more practical idea from the Gold Coast, where tourists could buy a can of sunshine to take home with them. With our bellies full of coffee, bacon and eggs the next stop was a supermarket, and by nine thirty we had the esky filled with ice, drinks, and snacks and a bag of dry goods stashed in the boot. Townsville's tropical humidity was already impressive and with all windows down we drove to a service station, filled the car up with petrol and checked its motor and tyres; pretty soon we were ready to go again.

The road to Mount Isa was back along the way that we had come into Townsville, so we drove south for a few kilometres and then turned right onto the Flinders Highway. Heading dead south we were soon through Rosenearth and then Brookhill where housing and buildings gave way to the bush. Unseen to our right Ross River Dam sparkled in the morning light, and just after Reid River the rising sun swung-in behind us as the Flinders Highway turned towards the west.

I ran the car through its gears up to 150 km/hr, just for fun, and then settled back down to the speed limit. A glance at the dashboard gauges reassured me that the engine was happy and listening to the exhaust's low steady growl, I settled back more comfortably in my seat.

We had a friend in Mount Isa, Eden Devon, who I'd met via Gary Hallard. Eden had been working for Woolworths on the Gold Coast and was offered a management position in the mining town, which he'd taken, leaving home about a year ago. He was tallish and skinny, had long sideburns, a moustache, smoked mentholated cigarettes and always dressed well. His ride was a 1971 Holden Brougham sedan, sporting a 308cc V8 motor, dark gold metallic paint and the car was absolutely mint. It bought Eden a lot of street cred' that he was the only one of us who had a V8! The Brougham had belonged to his Dad, who had passed it on when he'd been unable to drive anymore. Eden was one of the gang. We'd sniffed each other's engines, drunk beer together, shared a hangover or two and the friendship was sealed.

I slowed a little for the half kilometer wide Burdekin River crossing and 20 minutes later we were driving through the outer suburbs of Charters Towers.

"I'd like to have a look at Charters Towers; the old gold town." I said to Ray.

"Go for it." he replied, lighting up a cigarette.

I slowed and turned off the highway at Milchester and bumped over a level-crossing onto Gill Street. After a few minutes a handsome white building with 1900 set under a large red cross in its gable showed up on the right—it was the Ambulance Building, which later became a Memorial—but it wasn't until we passed Deane Street that I began to connect with the city.

Wherry House with its imposing arched facade and decorative stone balustrades rose up on our left; it had begun life as The Bank of New South Wales in 1889. Then, to the right a show-stopper; built in 1892 the magnificent Post Office building featuring a four storey clock tower commanding the corner of Bow Street. Almost opposite, the massive red brick front of D.S & Co. with its huge arched window ushered us onto Mossman Street revealing views of City Hall and the Stock Exchange with its distinct barrel-vaulted entry.

In Mossman Street, to my eyes, it seemed like we were transported back to the 1870s. I could almost see the street alive with horse drawn carts and hear the sound of raucous laughter coming from the Exchange Hotel; perhaps some gold miners celebrating a glittering find or men in tall hats and waistcoats toasting a big win with some shares.

Ray was getting bored with all the old building stuff and suggested we get back to our trip.

"Hey."

"Yeh?"

"We'd better get going."

"Yeh?"

"Yeh."

I called out, "Come right boys." pulled firmly on the reins and wheeled the HR around and back onto Gill Street, clicking with my tongue. After a while we bumped back over the railway again, turned right and resumed our trip. Hughenden was three hours away and the Flinders Highway stretched out before us like a long black ribbon with red-brown gravel marking its frayed edges. Tall gum trees punctuated the colourful bush on either side and it was very pleasant driving.

Warrigal Creek's dry gravel bed flashed beneath our wheels and then we began a gentle climb up through White Mountains National Park to cross Torrens Creek on the other side followed by a dry, unnamed lake bed. The highway was crisscrossed with dirt tracks leading off into the bush and just before the town of Prairie, we crossed its namesake creek's three kilometer wide floodplain. Ray pulled over and we bought cold soft-drink from the Prairie Hotel and then drove on. A couple of kilometres out of town I spotted a wire enclosure staked to the road's red-gravel verge; the area was littered with thousands of cans and bottles. The idea was to throw your empty drink containers in between the goalposts while the car was in motion; it was obvious that most people were pretty poor shots as rubbish was scattered all over the place. I had a shot and missed, my empty tin bouncing high up off the gravel and joining the others.

As we crossed Skull Creek I commented that for such a dry place there seemed to be plenty of creeks!

"Wait until the wet season." Ray replied knowingly.

While we could see that the highway was tracking a railway line, it wasn't until Hughenden that I realised we had also been running alongside the Flinders River and its massive floodplain. The river's dry sand-bed meandered through the town on its way to the Gulf of Carpentaria in the north, and at over 1,000 kilometres was Queensland longest river.

In Hughenden we stopped briefly to top-up with petrol and check the car. I took over driving and headed off again. Thirteen creek crossings, one train spotting and one and a half hours later we slowed to drive through Richmond and cracked a beer on the other side to celebrate passing the halfway point–490 down and 410 to go. The mighty Flinders River skirted the town less than one kilometre to the northeast, but we turned away in the opposite direction, crossed the railway line and drove on. About five kilometres on, the railway line joined us again and running parallel with the highway. We didn't realise but just 10 kilometers north the great river undulated along beside us. Around Nelia, with consummate concertina locomotion, the Fitzroy flexed strongly and pushed off towards the northwest on its journey through the Gkuthaarn and Kukatj people's land to join the Gulf, some 350 kilometres away.

We too continued, negotiating Alick Creek, Spellary Creek and galloping over Horse Creek; it was five thirty in the afternoon when we crossed Julia Creek where a narrow furrow of dirty water crept sluggishly out from under the bridge, carefully negotiating clumps of long-dead reed stalks, and wormed off to the north. We were in Mitchell Grass country and the surrounding landscape had changed remarkably; it was massively

53

broad, flat and featured very few trees. I drove into town and decided to call it a day.

We pitched our tent at the caravan park and enjoyed a warm, bore-water shower; the water pressure was excellent. A local landmark was the water tower that featured a 30 metre concrete stem, flaring out boldly to imitate a huge, old-fashioned champagne coupe. Local bores provided town water from the Great Artesian Basin, which arrived at the surface heated to a steamy 50 degrees Celsius; the tower allowed water to cool down before it was used. With the road dust and grime washed off and away down the drain, Ray and I walked along Julia Street to find Gannons Hotel on the corner of the Fitzroy Highway. Gannons, rebuilt in 1932 after a devastating fire, had featured in Neville Shute's 1956 movie *A Town Like Alice*. Despite its star quality we opted for the Julia Creek Hotel, a 100 metres or so on down the road.

The hotel looked south to the railway station and beyond that, wide open grasslands. It was a two story, corrugated iron roofed structure with wide verandahs reaching out and claiming the footpath below; characteristic of colonial outback architecture. Upstairs was largely dedicated to accommodation with drinking and eating facilities on the ground floor. We entered where the building's two wings met on the corner of Julia and Goldings Streets via a tall doorway and while not as elegant, it reminded me of the Manley Hostel at Cottesloe Beach, Perth where my family had enjoyed holidays in the late 1960s. Compared to outside, the interior was dark and cool; our eyes adjusted and we found the bar. When they arrived, the first two icy cold pots of beer didn't last long and boy did they taste good!

The barman laughed, "Thirsty boys? Two more?"

"Yes please!" Ray and I said almost in unison.

As we had travelled further and further inland the temperature had risen; it was probably around 35 degrees Celsius outside in the street and a much dryer heat than on the coast. My wallet had also noticed that the price of our three current staples: beer, petrol and food had risen too—no doubt that transporting goods to Central and Western Queensland towns would add to the retail price. Ray struck up conversation with several of the locals who turned out to be a friendly bunch, interested in what we were up to and providing information about the weather and road conditions. We were told that "The Creek" had begun life as a Cobb and Co. exchange station in the late 1800s, and heard their story of the 1974 floods. They described 1,000s of cattle and sheep being swept to the Gulf when four major river systems merged to form a gigantic sea. RAAF helicopters had carried out rescues lifting people off homestead roofs and providing food drops for others; it took nearly two months for the waters to recede. It looked fairly dry outside with little chance of rain, so we ordered some food and relaxed. It was good to stand still for a while and experience an environment for more than just a few seconds. After dinner, a game or two of pool and a couple of hours at the bar we walked back to our camp site and hit the sack.

I woke up during the night and went to the bathroom, then hung around outside for a while. It was amazing to look up into the sky and see millions of stars so clearly and get a sense of the vast space of this country. Back on the Gold Coast, city lights and suburban sprawl obfuscated all but the brightest stars and the growing number of tall buildings in Surfers Paradise had begun to hide the sky from view; new development had a habit of nibbling away at the open space. Back in the relative confines of our tent, I laid out on top of my sleeping bag and listened in the dark for a while; there was the familiar sound of Ray's light snore, a brief rustle or two outside and then nothing until the early morning light woke me.

We took our time in the morning. Mount Isa was less than 300 kilometres away and Eden would not be home from work until after five o'clock in the afternoon; there was no rush and we could play tourist for a few hours along the way. I borrowed a bucket and gave the car a wash; it was nice to see its blue paint again as a layer of red dust, insects and road grime washed away. I emptied the interior of all our rubbish and put it in a nearby rusty, 44 gallon drum. It reminded me of a time in Port Hedland when my Dad was the local rubbish man and everyone's bins were metal drums.

We packed up the tent, drove to the main street and parked; getting out to walk. There were a mixture of buildings and many featured wide shady awnings; testament to the high summer temperatures. The road was wide enough to offer central and kerb parking; we joked that it seemed a bit of a marathon getting from one side to the other, 'Take a compass and cut lunch with you, and send out a search party if I'm not back before tea.'

We nearly made it to the stemware tower at Allison Street, but opted for a distant viewing of the local icon and turned around. After walking back to Julia Street we stopped at an RSL monument, book-ending the central parking.

Ray glanced across at Gannons and nudged me, "Seems a pity not to."

Gannon's was a single story building with two simple gables atop a mass of silver corrugated iron roofing. The roof reached out over the footpath and was supported by hardwood posts that marched around the corner. A corner door beckoned us into the bar and eager to acquaint ourselves with this old movie star, we made our entrance. Unfortunately, we didn't see Virginia McKenna or Peter Finch to say hello to as the bar was deserted; perhaps it was too early and they showed up later in the day for cocktails. We ordered a beer and chatted with the barman for a while, then made our way back out to the car and set off once again. Our next stop was the town of Cloncurry, or "The Curry" as it was known in the area, about 140 kilometres west.

Gannons' barman had told us a joke about a Texas rancher who was visiting Cloncurry from the United States. After many beers in the hotel on Saturday night, the rancher boasted that they ran 100,000 head of cattle on his ranch back in Texas, but hung his head when a local stockman said they had just put 10,000 head in the curry! The barman had laughed enthusiastically, delighted with his joke; I guess they don't get out much in Julia!

Chapter 6

Copper City

About 15 kilometres east of Cloncurry there's an intersection where three roadways meet. It is here that the 750 kilometre long Flinders Highway ends, and is joined by the Landsborough Highway and Grace Street, which takes you into town. It's an unremarkable intersection surrounded by sparse bush-land and featuring a sign directing travellers to turn left to Winton, over 300 kilometres to the southeast. The Landsborough Highway runs over 1000 kilometres through Winton to the town of Barcaldine; from there a driver can turn onto the Capricorn Highway and pass Blackwater on their way to Rockhampton. As the car swept onto Grace Street we didn't realise that we would have saved ourselves around 500 kilometres driving by turning right when leaving Blackwater, instead of left towards Rockhampton and the coast. But that thought never crossed our minds and 15 minutes later, I parked the car on Scar Street near the Post Office Hotel.

Cloncurry's streets were surprisingly generous; the hotel was on the intersection of Scarr and Sheaffe Streets both of which featured two lanes of traffic, each way, centre and kerb parking and wide footpaths. We figured you could put a highrise building on that intersection and still drive cars around it. There were two hotels, the Post Office and Central, an actual Post Office, a retail store and located at its centre was a relatively small stone monument—it was a World War One memorial, originally erected in 1927. We know because we did a "Ludwig Leichhardt" and trekked across the vast intersection (without a cut lunch and a six pack of beer), to have a closer look and read the inscription.

"In Memory Of
the Men of
CLONCURRY and DISTRICT
who gave their lives in the service
SERVICE OF THEIR COUNTRY
during the GREAT WAR
1914 - 1918"

Shading my eyes I looked around the vast intersection. It was hot, dusty and we were both hungry. It seemed like there was an imminent danger of being struck down by sunstroke or carried off by the hordes of black, sticky flies. Fortunately, Ray's survival instincts took over providing us with a third and compelling choice.

"Last one in the door shouts the beers!" he yelled and took-off for the Post Office Hotel; I sprinted right behind him. We jostled for position at the doorway and then squeezed in together, coming to rest laughing and panting in the foyer.

"I'll buy." I said, in between breaths.

The town had taken its name from the Cloncurry
River, which had received its name from the explorer
Robert Burke during the Burke and Wills Expedition
of 1861. "Cloncurry" was the name of his cousin, Lady
Elizabeth Cloncurry of County Galway, Ireland. The
town was officially surveyed in 1876 after pastoralist
Ernest Henry, who was looking for good grazing
land, discovered something completely different—a
significant deposit of copper that become known as
"Great Australia."

Over a cold beer at the Post Office Hotel the barman
told us that the streets were so wide because cattle
and heavy transport drove through town. At one time
Cloncurry had been the administrative centre of the
region though in recent years that role had shifted to
Mount Isa. He warned us that it got pretty hot in The
Curry, with temperature regularly exceeding 40 degrees
Celsius.

"Thank God for ice-cold beer!" I called out and
everyone laughed, raising dew frosted glasses and
nodding heads in agreement.

After a while we ventured back out into the hot
afternoon and resumed our trip to Mount Isa; about
one and a half kilometres out of town we found the
Cloncurry River and crossed its bridge. Looking over
the 200 metre wide stretch of dry sand bed, lined with
gum trees, it was hard to imagine the power of this
river in full flood; and that the road used to be a simple
concrete causeway. Further south, in the early sixties,
a concrete railway bridge was constructed to replace

the old one; damaged by floods. And being stranded in between rivers or creeks during the wet season could be an inordinate test of patience,

> "... as the result of floods, 84 Western passengers at Julia are still stranded in carriages in which they have been living for a fortnight. Fifteen spans of the Cloncurry River bridge have been thrown out of alignment, and parts of the structure have disappeared altogether. The food supplies at Mount Isa are almost exhausted."— The Armidale Express, January 31 1930

The railway line had diverged at Cloncurry, veering southwest, running with Chinaman Creek on its way to Dutchess before turning northwest towards Mount Isa where we would meet up again. Ray and I were heading west again along the Barkley Highway when we saw a road sign, which read "Mary Kathleen."

Mary Kathleen Brown was born in 1914 at Mayfield Station near Windora, in far western Queensland. It seemed that she lived a fairly ordinary life–marriage, worked in a cafe at Longreach, produced four children– and died relatively young of meningitis, 40 years later in Mount Isa where she was buried. Her name, though, was not destined for *ordinary* and it became very well known in Australia and lived-on via a gift from her prospector husband Norm' McConachy, who inexorably bound it to his one great discovery, the Mary Kathleen Uranium Mine.

McConachy had formed a syndicate, which discovered the deposit 56 kilometres east of Mount Isa. The group had insufficient capital to develop a mine and it was offered for sale, to be bought by Australasian Oil Exploration in 1954 for £250,000. Rio Tinto acquired a controlling interest and Mary Kathleen, featuring a town housing 1,200 workers and their families, began production in 1958. The mine produced over 4,000 tonnes of uranium oxide until 1963 when operations were shut down—its major customer, the UK Atomic Energy Authority, had not renewed supply contracts. Just recently though, in 1975, new contracts with Japanese, German and American utility companies had been negotiated, motivating a re-opening and the mine was in production once again.

The project, uranium in particular, was not without controversy and linked with the beginnings of Australia's anti-nuclear movement. In the early 1970s the French were internationally criticized for testing nuclear bombs at Moruroa Atoll in the South Pacific, with Bob Hawk, president of the Australian Council of Trade Unions, speaking out. And there had just been a national one day strike over uranium by the Australian Railways Union, after a Townsville railway-yard supervisor was suspended for refusing to move sulphur bound for the Mary Kathleen mine.

Just before we had begun our trip, in March 1976, and as Mary Kathleen was brought back to life once again, Norman McConachy died of cancer, aged 61 years; he was buried in Mount Isa Sunset Lawn Cemetery next to his wife.

Mildly anaesthetized from our long drive we drove past the sign without a second glance and went on to cross the Leichhardt River's east branch and later, without our normal, "Creek!" yell, George Creek. Maybe we were becoming immune to the charms of this hot, dry bush land and the unending HB black pencil roadway that we drove on.

––––––––––

In the years to follow there would be many times that I drove into Mount Isa along the Barkly Highway. Perhaps due to the combination of terrain and road design or the long distances people tended to drive, the city seemed to appear, as if by magic, and was always a surprise. The Barkly wound through a rocky landscape and up a gentle rise, there was a high-level rugged red-earth outcrop on the left and as we reached a crest in the road *The Isa* was immediately there before us!

It was impossible not to be drawn to the huge red and white barber pole chimney, with its delicate plume of white smoke drifting out across the great red range behind, known geologically as the Western Fold Belt Province and locally as Mineside. Immediately on our left was the Overlander Hotel, a turn to the right would have taken us out to the suburbs of Pioneer and Sunset, but the HR's bonnet was pointed unerringly at the chimney and like an ancient magician's wand it beckoned us in.

We drove straight on and the Barkly Highway became twined with Marion Street to form a wide dual carriageway. Now there were other cars, people, dogs, unfamiliar buildings and I concentrated to keep my speed down to 60 kilometres per hour, which seemed laboriously slow after the open highway. Traffic lights stopped us for a few minutes at East Street and then we drove on past car yards, shops, businesses and some housing. Noticeable was the lack of tall buildings and that the sky dominated my windscreen view. Around 300 metres to the right and perched on a hill, a tall metal-framed tower looked down on us; I'd come to know this later as The Lookout.

The magician's wand moved left-of-screen as Marion Street swung right, but before long came back to centre as we passed by more shops, a large Kmart store, more traffic lights, big wide intersections, petrol stations, a hotel and the ever present tower. A road sign directed us on to Camooweal and Boulia or left to Dutchess; we drove on. A well treed school yard passed by on the right, some sort of civic building off to the left and before I realised it, we were crossing over the sleeping riverbed of the great Leichhardt. On the other side I turned around and put the chimney to my back, returned across the bridge and then turned right into West Street, where we spotted Boyds Hotel and parked.

There seemed to be a lot of Aborigines around; this was unusual for us as we rarely saw an indigenous person on the Gold Coast, where we'd come from. And they were not quiet and inconspicuous, oh no; their high pitched voices, undecipherable language (to us) and presence was right in our faces. After a few close encounters, it became clear that some were quite drunk while others lounged in the shade or bundled themselves into taxis.

One man called out to us, "Hey mate! You got a spare dollar?"

I said, "Sorry mate, we're broke."

The coloured man countered, hopefully, "Got a ciggy then mate?"

64

Unwittingly, Ray made the mistake of handing one over.

"Got a light?" he asked hopefully, squinting at us and putting the cigarette to his lips.

Ray sighed, pulled out his lighter and suddenly, we had a new best friend and it took us over a block to get rid of him.

"Get lost mate! We got nothing else for you."

"Bastards." the man grumbled as he finally turned his back and wandered off; Ray's cigarette smoke trailing out behind him.

Eden had mentioned "Boydies" Hotel in a letter and we knew Woolworths, where he worked, would not be far away. A local shopkeeper pointed us along Rodeo Drive; we turned into Miles Street and found the big retailer at the end. The store was air conditioned and its chilled air felt amazing, at first, then less pleasant as our sweat-dampened clothes began to work against us.

Before I had a chance to ask after Mr. Devon, he had already spotted the two newcomers and called out, "Hey. Fellas!"

With a big smile, even longer sideburns and wearing his customary finery, Eden came over and shook hands enthusiastically. It was good to see him and answer questions about the trip. He sketched us a map to his house and glancing at his wristwatch said that he'd be working for about another hour, and would meet us there later. We pushed our way out through a pair of heavy doors and stepped into a wall of heat on the other side. Phew!

Ray and I were totally over being tourists in outback
Queensland and decided to forgo exploring the town, in
favour of a cold beer and game of pool in Boydies. Our
timing was not the best and as we tried to enter the
public bar, we were barreled off to one side by two burly
men who were fighting. The barkeep had leapt over the
bar and aided by several of his customers, was herding
them outside while skillfully avoiding stray punches.
With the fighter's departure, the bar chatter resumed
and we pulled up a couple of stools and waited patiently
to make our order.

A heavyset bloke at the bar looked us up and down then
winked and said, "You should have been here a couple
of years ago when it was really wild!"

We all laughed and then he turned back to his mate and
said quietly, "I wasn't joking."

The public bar at Boydies was simple, the bar took
up about a third of the room; it was positioned in the
corner and surrounded by bar stools. The external wall
was dotted with frosted glass windows and supported
a ledge that held glasses and ashtrays, and down one
end of the room was the obligatory pool table. The rules
around pool were that you had to beat the current player
to become King of the Table; you stayed on until you
were beaten, which favoured the better or less drunk
players. Gambling on games was common, often for a
pot though sometimes big money changed hands. There
was already a long row of shiny twenty cent coins along
the table's rail, representing the next challenger's turn
and we decided not to add to it. The ceiling was high
and big fans moved the air around. The bar was fairly
busy and we sipped on a pot of cold beer and relaxed

in the lively atmosphere. We noticed that, unlike other country bars we'd been in, there was not one Aboriginal in the place and asked our neighbour about it.

He said that the owner, Marshal Boyd, had banned them all[1] and told us, "A separate place, called The Snake Pit, is all set up for the darkies. If you want a lubra or a fight that's the place to go!"

I nodded and refrained from asking how he'd come by that information.

After a while we left and went back to the car, and made our way over to Eden's place; he was not home yet so I parked outside and we waited. It wasn't long before we heard a horn beep and he pulled up in the driveway. Soon he had the house's front door open and we stepped into its cool interior. Eden opened the refrigerator, pulled out some cans of Castlemain XXXX and handed them around. We sat down at the dining table and chatted; it was good to be in a house, with a mate and the prospect of a proper bed for the night was a welcome one. Eden's house mate arrived and we were introduced to Brian; he worked as a professional photographer and invited us to stay for a few days. They had a spare room and a couch so we were all set.

After some beers, a couple of frozen pizzas (Woolworths', of course) and lots of talking, I was stuffed. We decided to call it in for the night and

---

1   [The following year,] Senator Neville Bonner, an Aborigine, came into Boyds Hotel public bar to challenge local convention and the barmaid refused to serve him, "I am sorry. I can't serve you ... we don't serve coloured people here."— The Age (Melbourne). December 1977

30 minutes later, showered and clean, I lay back and stretched out on the soft cushions. Some light filtered in from the street and apart from a dog barking in the distance and the odd passing car, it was quiet. It seemed like a long time ago that I'd looked into my Dad's eyes and hugged Mum and Karen. I wondered what they were doing and then laughed quietly to myself, probably similar to what I was. I fell asleep.

Chapter 7

Unlikely Meeting

The next morning after the other two had left for work, I had a talk with Ray about money. I was down to my last 50 dollars and Ray admitted he had spent over half of his funds; we didn't have enough to get to Darwin and handle what might show up there.

"So, even if we got work straight away we would not be paid until a week, or perhaps a fortnight later." I suggested.

"Yeh. And we'd better find out how the banks are working up there." Ray added.

"Then there's accommodation; at least we have the tent. We'll be buying food and petrol for the car … "

"And some beers! It's pretty hot up there." Ray infiltrated my logic with the essentials.

I nodded, "Yeh."

"Last night Eden suggested that we get some work in Mount Isa and stay on here for a while. You remember that Brian mentioned there was a big dam building project out of town? He'd heard they were hiring and said we could also try Mount Isa Mines for work too. "

Ray nodded his head in agreement. We talked a bit more and it was clear that Julius Dam was most interesting to both of us; we decided to drive out there straight away and see what they had available.

Our travel instructions from Brian, the previous evening, had been simple, "Drive out of town towards Cloncurry for a couple of kilometres and look for a dirt track on the left; take that and keep going."

Fair enough! I had about half a tank of petrol and being a bit concerned about my dwindling money supply, decided it would be enough for this trip. We stopped and bought a bottle of water from the local store and were soon driving past the Overlander Hotel again, this time it was on the right hand side. Mount Isa quickly disappeared from the rearview mirror as I brought the car up to speed. Brian's estimate of "… a couple of kilometres …" turned out to be a little meagre and as 18 kilometres rolled over on the odometer, I turned left onto an unmarked gravel road. It looked pretty dry out here and I took a swing from the water bottle, wondering if we'd brought enough.

During the 1970s Mount Isa experienced a population boom and by mid-decade numbers had reached 25,000 people. Water consumption had been forecast to exceed the capabilities of the existing supply from Lake Moondarra and Mount Isa Mines commissioned investigations for an additional water source. On the junction of the Leichhardt River and Paroo Creek, 71 kilometres north-east of Mount Isa, a new 107,500 megalitres dam was constructed, creating Lake Julius. In 1976 the project was completed via a partnership with the Queensland government, costing $33 million and featured a multiple-arch and buttress structure with the spillway standing over eighteen metres tall. It was ironic that the jobs Ray and I sought were no longer available as the project had already been completed, however, often the world works in mysterious ways.

The HR's tyres crunched on the loose, graded surface and I noted deep gutters cut into the soil either side, defining a crisp border with the adjacent bush. The road was in good repair and as I picked up speed a great plume of red dust billowed up in the mirrors, and followed us. A very fine dust began to swirl up through the car but we didn't really notice; we were both eyes-front, looking out for a dam. We figured a dam would be quite a large thing and we would see it easily enough.

It was hot. The temperature was around 36 degrees Celsius and a coarse dry breeze punched in through our open windows. Ray and I sipped on the water and gazed out over kilometers and kilometres of open bush, grasses and low level shrubs; it didn't seem a likely site for a dam at all. I slowed down several times as we negotiated the dry creek beds that crossed our path; apart from those the trip was fairly quiet and uneventful. We had been driving for over an hour, with no indication of a dam, when I noticed the fuel gauge needle dipping below a quarter full.

"We might have to head back Ray." I cautioned, "Petrol's getting down. What do you think?"

"Yeah." he said, "I'm not sure how much further this dam is. Let's give it a miss. We can have another go tomorrow, with a full tank."

I changed down into second and slowed the car, then slipped it into first for a perfect three-point turn on the narrow road. The tyres spat gravel as I put my foot down, fish-tailing the rear end a couple of times. We surged out of own dust cloud, straightened up and with the cars bonnet pointing back the way we'd come, picked up speed.

I would have changed into second gear and then third if I could have, but there was a shudder, a clunk and the gears locked; and then I had no gears at all. Depressing the clutch allowed the HR to coast for a short while and begin to slow down. I steered over to the side, bumped through the gutter and stopped, leaving the car straddling it. We got out just as our companion red, dust cloud caught up and began to settle; we both choked a little and I could taste grit in my mouth.

After taking a swig Ray passed me the water bottle and said, "Finish it."

I tipped it up high, washed the dust out of my throat and then threw the empty bottle onto the back seat; it made a hollow sound as it bounced and landed on the floor. Walking around to the back I popped the boot, lifted my toolbox out and took it around to the side of the car. While I was preparing to get under the car Ray put up the bonnet and looked inside the engine bay,

"There's some more water in the window washer reserve," he observed, "and there's always the radiator if we get desperate."

"Yuk!" I grimaced, "Anyone got a cold beer?"

We both laughed, albeit a little nervously. Apart from the dust slowly moving off it was quite still. The sun rose imperceptibly higher in the sky and a trickle of sweat crept from under my hairline and began to negotiate the layer of dust on my forehead; it dripped off my nose as I crawled under the car. The gutter's baked earth bed was hot but the car's shadow took the edge off it. I disconnected the column shift's linkages from the gearbox, and Ray checked the action from above; the gear shift moved freely and it seemed that the issue was with the gearbox itself. We waited for half an hour to let the machinery cool down a bit and then I climbed under again and loosened the oil filler plug, followed by the drain plug and watched dark brown oil begin to drizzle out confirming that there was some oil in the box. After tightening the two plugs back up again I turned my attention to the gear shift levers, rocking them back and forth by hand and then with a spanner but they hardly moved; it became clear that we were stuck with a dead gearbox. What to do now?

Climbing out from under the car I dusted off while Ray leaned in under the bonnet and removed the washer reservoir, then carefully drained its contents into our water bottle.

"Good thing I don't put detergent in there." I joked.

Ray grinned, screwed the bottle's lid on tight and placed our water supply carefully on the front seat. He refitted the plastic reservoir, lit up a smoke and leaned back on the front guard.

We had a few options and didn't really like any of them: we could leave the car and attempt a very long walk back to the Barkley Highway, or wait with the car and hope Eden or Brian would come-a-looking for us when we didn't show up that night. I didn't really want to leave the car as it still had a lot of our gear in it; and after all, it was my car! And Eden may think we had stayed on at the dam construction site, and not come out. Finally, we decided that Ray would take the water bottle and walk back to the highway to get help, while I stayed with the car. We weren't very thrilled with the plan but at least we had a plan. It was just then I noticed something different, far off in the distance.

Wobbling in the shimmering heat and rising up over the bush was a telltale plume of red dust. We watched for a while and it appeared to be getting bigger and hopefully, was moving our way. It had to be a vehicle! I felt both excited and foolish at the same time: excited that there might be some help and foolish that we were stupid enough to break down in the hot bush kilometers from anywhere without water.

There wasn't much to do except wait, so we did. Slowly but surely the dust cloud sailed closer and then a magical thing happened, it began to transform into, not one, but two vehicles and as they got closer we could make out a mustard coloured Land Rover and its companion, a bright yellow Holden One Ton Ute. They pulled up beside us and the passenger window rolled down.

"How you going mate?"

An English accent drifted out from inside the Land Rover.

"Having some trouble?" it asked.

Doors swung open and everyone got out to inspect my disabled HR. We shook hands with Sid (the Pom), Dick and Marty who were coming in from a prospecting trip and going to The Isa. Sid invited us to take a drink from two hessian water bags that were hanging from their front bull-bar; the water was surprisingly cool and tasted incredibly good.

Dick glanced over at the car and then back to us, "So, what are you boys doing out here?"

We told him about trying to get to the Julius Dam project to look for some work.

Dick's right eyebrow went up, "So, why are you driving away from it?" he puzzled in disbelief.

I noted the hint of sarcasm but explained about our petrol getting low so we'd turned around. He raised his eyebrow a little more and then Sid told us that the dam was only a few kilometres away and so we'd nearly made it. Then he dropped the bomb.

"There wouldn't be any jobs there though, it's pretty much finished."

"Really?" I exclaimed. "We were told they were hiring."

"I doubt it." he replied.

And then changing the subject, "You know, it's best to be carrying spare fuel and water out here," he paused for a moment, winked at me and continued, "but I'm not sure too many people would think to bring a spare gearbox!"

It was good and even Dick laughed.

The ice was broken; Ray and Marty lit up a smoke together and we all had a chat, then they offered to tow us back into town. Wow, that was a great relief. They had all the gear and soon the HR was secured to the back of Dick's Land Rover with a sturdy rope. I got the job of steering my car at the back of the convoy and Ray quickly deserted me for a seat in the four wheel drive with Sid and Dick.

We took off with a jerk and within minutes I was eating dust blown up from the Land Rover. The one tonner had gone on up-ahead so its dust cloud drifted off to one side and didn't smoother the following vehicle, but I was locked in about three metres behind my tow and copped it. The water in my bottle tasted terrible, like plastic, but it helped wash the grit out of my throat. About an hour and a half later we turned right onto the bitumen highway and headed home. I drained the water bottle, rinsed my mouth and then spat it out of the open window. We picked up speed and as the cabin cleared of fine dust; I was able to breathe clean air once again.

Our hosts, who I found out later worked for Union Minière, a mining exploration company, took us all the way back to Eden's house; when Ray got out of their vehicle he had a big grin on his face.

"Hey Steve. They want us to work with them." he said excitedly. "We can start on Monday. Two hundred bucks a fortnight!"

Wahoo! Ray had worked his magic and got us both a job. Fantastic. It turned out that their two prospecting hands, Marty and his mate, were finishing up and the exploration company needed some new people; one to go and work with them in the bush on Monday and the other at their yard in town. Ray was to bring his gear ready for a week's camping out near a place called Kajabbi and I would stay in Mount Isa. Sid wrote down Union Miniere's phone number and address for us, and then they drove off to go unload their vehicles.

We were both stoked and went in to clean up. I put some beers in the refrigerator to chill. Eden came home from work bringing steaks, sausages and bread rolls with him. Soon, yellow metal caps were being popped off cold beers, meat was sizzling in the pan and Bob Seger and his Silver Bullet Band were rocking the stereo with *Get Out of Denver*. We told Eden our tale, as he smoked a cigarette and sipped his beer; he just shook his head and laughed.

"You two would have to be some of the arsiest blokes I know! " he exclaimed. "You head out into the bush looking for work, with no clue where you are going, and a job just drives up to you. Unbelievable! You should have saved yourself the trouble and just stayed at home; they probably would have come and knocked right on the front door!"

He went outside, pretending to be Sid and knocked on the door, "Hello. Hello. Is there anyone in here looking for a job? Hello."

It was very, very funny.

Brian came home later and we had to tell the story all over again but we didn't mind. The tale grew to new proportions and of course, Eden had to do his door knocking routine again. It was a great night and when we hit the sack I slept deeply, comforted by the prospect of a job and some money coming in. Things were looking good!

Eden loaned me his car on Saturday morning and I drove out to the auto wreckers; fortunately they had a couple of three speed, full synchromesh gearboxes in stock and I bought one, trading in the old one for a discount. Ray and I spent the afternoon removing the original and fitting its replacement. When the column shift's linkages were finally reconnected we cleaned up and took the car for a test run; it all worked well with gears changing smoothly. We dropped the old box off at the wrecking yard, as agreed, and drove back home.

Now that we had jobs and were staying in Mount Isa, we would need some accommodation. Eden and Brian had been generous but we couldn't stay much longer at their place, sleeping on the couch. I bought a copy of The North West Star and browsed through its classifieds. One advert offered single men's accommodation for 18 dollars per week; I rang the phone number and a woman answered, we arranged to meet up the next day at 11:00 o'clock in the morning.

On Sunday morning I did some domestics: clothes washing, car cleaning and started a letter to the family; then we drove to Simpson Street to meet up with Mrs. Eddleston, the owner. She was in her fifties, thin limbed and greying but there was a sparkle in her eye and she offered a surprisingly firm handshake. The rooms were in a converted house, where residents shared the lounge, kitchen and bathroom. She explained that many of the men who lived here were miners or core drillers and were often out of town or on shift work.

"Don't be too noisy and wake them up; they won't like that." she cautioned.

We were offered a special rate to share one room containing two single beds and a plywood wardrobe. The room was just two metres wide with a bed along each wall; the only floor space was the walkway in between the beds. There was a barred window at one end and the door could be locked.

"You'll be able to reach out and hold hands in the night." Mrs. Eddleston chuckled, joking with us.

The rent was 32 dollars a week with sheets and pillows included; we took it. As we followed our new landlady out Ray nudged me and pointed to a plain, brown, three-seater couch in the lounge; it had no legs but was propped up on beer cans. We nicknamed the place Crazy Cottage and hoped we were going to survive the stay. Outside, Ray paid the first two week's rent in cash and received a set of keys. He said that I could pay the next fortnight after we'd received our wages. That helped me a lot; after buying the gearbox I was getting low on money.

Later in the afternoon, having thanked Eden for
putting us up, we moved into Crazy Cottage. That night
while watching some television in the lounge we met
one of the other residents, but he was not that talkative
and we took our cue to leave him alone. Sid had asked
us to be at the yard at 8:00 o'clock Monday morning
so we turned in early. Sometime in the night the front
door slammed shut, waking me. Someone walked past
our door, the floor boards creaking under his weight.
After a while a toilet flushed, I heard another door close
and then it was quiet. The smell of stale cigarette smoke,
which had crept into our room began to fade away and
I fell back asleep.

Chapter 8

Union Minière

Physiologically, the effect of excitement and anxiety are much the same: heart rate and breathing increase, and adrenalin is released into the bloodstream as the sympathetic nervous system is engaged–fight, flight or freeze. Difficulty can occur when these two get mixed up i.e. when someone thinks they are being anxious when actually, they are excited. Studies have shown that when performers acknowledge the condition and intensify it, they can perform much better than when they try to control and dampen it down. As we drove across town to begin our new job I felt nervous, while Ray was chatty and upbeat.

"What's up Stevie? You're a bit quiet this morning."

Ray always called me "Stevie" when he was being supportive; I told him that I hadn't slept well last night but he saw through my ruse.

"You'll be okay mate." he offered kindly and then lit up a cigarette, blowing smoke out of the open window.

"Just keep the door locked at Crazy Cottage so the crazies don't get in!"

He laughed out loud enjoying his own joke immensely and when Ray laughed that big, wide-open bellow of his, it was infectious and soon I was laughing too.

Union Minière Development and Mining Corporation was a large Belgium company that had an active presence in the Mount Isa area. They had interests in uranium but the commodity was in oversupply and yellow cake's market spot price peaked in 1976, to fall sharply in the early 1980s; Union Minière had changed direction and was exploring for copper. Their yard was out on Ryan Road and consisted of a portable building used as an office, several large metal sheds and a toilet block. As I swung in through the gates we noticed several Land Rovers, the familiar yellow one tonner and spotted Sid walking across the yard dressed in his work-blues and soft hat; he waved and pointed us past the sheds for parking. The whole yard was enclosed by a two metre high steel mesh fence.

"Good morning. I see you got the gearbox fixed." He grinned at us, his black framed glasses glinting in the morning sun.

"Yes." I replied, "I picked one up from the wreckers and we fitted it on Saturday."

"A good skill to have in our line of work." Sid replied. "Come and meet Ray,. He's our Irish mechanic."

Sid took us into a workshop and made the introductions. "Two Rays." he laughed, "Well, that might cause some confusion."

"Only until one of us opens our mouth!" Ray Linwood exclaimed with a big grin.

"True enough; true enough."

The brogue was unmistakable and I nicknamed him Irish Ray. He wiped his hands clean on a rag and then offered us a firm shake.

Irish Ray nodded congenially and then turned his attention back to a two door Land Rover; it was a Series 2B. He'd been repairing its rear drum brakes and had them laid out on the concrete floor in pieces. Sid took us off across the gravel yard to meet Union Minière's chief geologist, and our new boss.

The office building was set up on concrete block piers and we climbed the stairs and entered through a fly screen door. It was a portable type building that I'd often seen on building sites, long and narrow with offices at each end, and a kitchen and storeroom in the middle. We followed Sid to the right, and Ken came out from behind a practical metal framed desk and shook our hands in welcome. He was dressed in green field gear and boots, ready for a trip out to McLeod Hill he told us. His office contained a two-way radio station, book shelves and filing cabinets; there were rock samples and a pointed hammer on his desk, and several photographs of mine sites on the wall; one with a huge brick chimney.

"Mount Elliot mine. Out near Selwyn." he offered when he noticed me looking at the picture. "You'll probably get out there later. It's a great prospect that we're working on."

Ken lifted a mug of coffee up off his desk and took a sip, then chatted with us about the company and what they were doing in Mount Isa. In between sips he spoke about safety in the bush and the yard, and looking after each other, and then handed us back to Sid. I liked him; confident, easy going, intelligent.

Sid showed us around and said I'd be helping Irish Ray in the workshop, and that there was plenty of work to be done around the yard. Sid, Marty and Ray would be working out in the bush near Kajabbi and would return at the end of the week, when Marty was officially finishing up. After that I would be going out on field trips too, as a Prospecting Hand and that would be our main job. I went and found Irish Ray and left the others to organise their trip. The first thing the mechanic did was put on the kettle for a cup of tea and we talked; well, actually, he talked and I listened. In my head I renamed him ole-have-a-chat, but after tea we got to work putting the Land Rovers's brakes back together, then checking the front and servicing the motor.

Around eleven o'clock Sid and his team drove out of the gates taking two vehicles with them; it would take them all afternoon to get to Kajabbi and then set up camp, ready to begin work early in the morning. Irish Ray said that they always took two, in case one got bogged or broke down. They would radio-in each day at five o'clock in the afternoon to let us know all was well or that they required assistance. Dick would be in later in the afternoon to take their call while Ken was away. We finished the 2B, took it for a test run and then called it a day. I got in the HR and drove home to Crazy Cottage; it had been a good first day.

The house seemed to be empty; I showered and drove to Woolworths to shop, parking in Isa Street. My funds were well down and I wondered what I could buy to get me through the two weeks until payday. I chose a large packet of Uncle Toby's Oats, several cans of Heinz Baked Beans and a carton of milk. My plan was 12 days of porridge for breakfast and beans for dinner. I knew I could get a cup of tea at work and hopefully, Eden would buy me a beer. Ray had been lucky as Sid bought all of their food for the trip, saying Ray could fix him up on payday. Sid turned out to be a good friend to both of us.

I went back home, cooked my beans and watched some television. Mount Isa had one station, which was on for a short time in the morning and then again in the evening until about ten o'clock. ITQ8 Mt. Isa first began broadcasting in 1971, in black and white, introducing colour in 1975. The TV set we had in Crazy Cottage was an old black and white Grundig so colour didn't matter much. It was a bit quiet without Ray and I went to bed early with a book; I had a copy of Tolkien's Lord of the Rings, which I loved and was reading for the third time. There was a bit of movement in the house but no one seemed interested in me and eventually, I fell asleep.

———————

Apart from my mundane diet of porridge and beans, the rest of the week was great. I worked on the vehicles with Irish Ray, learned to cut drilled core samples with a diamond saw ready for assay, sat in on the two-way radio conversations with the Kajabi camp and worked

85

cleaning up a big storage shed, which held thousands of catalogued rock samples. It was very different to drawing building plans and I enjoyed the change, being out in the open and doing more physical work. Eden took me out for a couple of beers after work one afternoon, and suddenly it was Friday.

Just before three o'clock in the afternoon two very dirty Land Rovers drove into the yard. Ray was driving one and stuck his arm out of the window with a big thumbs up. He looked good; clear-eyed, suntanned and hair sticking out wildly from beneath his peaked cap.

"How are you mate?" I called out.

"Good." he replied. "Hey, can I borrow your car to go to the shop? I ran out of cigs two days ago!"

I threw him the keys to the HR and he dashed off to get his fix. We all laughed. Sid asked me if I would give a hand to clean the four wheel drives. We emptied both vehicles of all their gear and I gave them a good wash; Irish Ray would check them over on Monday. I stored the gear in a shed and we were done for the week. Even though I hardly knew Marty at all, we shook hands and I wished him all the best; he went over to the offices to pick up his pay. Then Ray was back with a cigarette balanced on his lip and so we went on home.

Ray had picked up a six-pack of stubbies while getting his smokes and we sat out in Crazy Cottage's backyard for a while and talked about what we'd been up to this past week; it was good to hang out with my mate, listen to his stories and share mine. When it was nearly dark Ray said he was going to have a shower and then get a hamburger. I went in the kitchen to put on some beans; when I opened the refrigerator I found a huge cooked bird, the size of a turkey—actually, it was a Brush Turkey. When Ray came out of the shower I showed him. He said that there were lots of them out in the bush, but they were protected[1]. Probably, one of the drillers had shot it, brought it home and cooked the bird.

"Drillers; they're all animals!" said Ray authoritatively. "I met some of them out at Kajabbi!"

"Yeh?" I replied.

"Yeh." said Ray. "They have this big diesel drilling rig hung off the back of a truck. It's stinking hot out there. They stay in the hotel at Kajabbi and drink piss all night, then sweat it out during the day. They make heaps of money but they're all animals!"

While he was gone, one of the other house residents came into the kitchen and told me there was a cooked bird in the refrigerator and I could help myself; there was plenty to go around. I thanked him, sliced off several pieces and dropped them in my beans. Thank God for animal drillers; it was my first animal protein in a week and tasted wonderful and delicious!

On Saturday I went around to see a bloke that I'd met while working at the yard during the week. He owned a really nice Holden HG Kingswood sedan; it had a one

---

1   Australian Brush Turkeys have a featherless red head with either a yellow or blue wattle, and a black body. Adult birds are 60–75 cm long with an 80 cm wingspan, and are protected by law. They are regarded as common by government environment agencies.

186cc six cylinder, red motor and he was interested in
my trio of carburetters. I was going to see if he would
buy the Webers. I was pretty much out of money and
while I hated downgrading the HR to the standard
single, Stromberg carburetter, I needed some cash to
get me through the rest of the week. It was an easy
sale; decent custom car parts were rare in The Isa and
the Webers were a prize. We shook hands on $150 for
the bodies, manifolds, spare air filters, linkages and fuel
lines.

I had stashed the original Stromberg carburetor and its
manifold in the boot, in case I'd have trouble with the
more complex dual-throats, and spent the afternoon in
the HR's engine bay refitting its original fuel system.
When I took the Webers around to pick up my money,
driving the HR was just woeful. That explosive burst
of power I so enjoyed was gone and the car seemed
sluggish, drowsy and dull; even the exhaust note was
different. Looking back, I know that was the moment
I fell out-of-love with my first car and stopped taking
care of it. Still, $150 cash in my pocket felt good and I
went to the shops and got some steak, vegetables and
ice cream; and picked up a carton of 4XXX tinnies on
the way home.

———————

Both Ray and I worked in town the following week; the
boys had brought back trays of diamond drilled rock
core from the Kajabbi area that had to be cut in half
and prepared for inspection. Each length of drill core
was about 50 millimetres diameter by 600 mm long
and came laid-out in aluminium trays. Along side each

piece the animal drillers had written measurements, representing the core's depth down in their drill hole.

Often the core was solid through and sometimes it consisted of broken pieces or crumbly material. We wore ear muffs and protective glasses while using a water-cooled, diamond saw, which screamed as it sliced through the rock, water spray flying everywhere. Occasionally, we discovered thumb-size chunks or veins of gold embedded in the rock, brilliant in the sun after our spinning blade had polished the precious metal. That was always occasion to switch off the noisy saw and call the others over for a look; everyone tried to reach over and touch the prize piece or hold it for a few seconds, while wishing it was theirs. Even though we were exploring for copper, and finding thick veins of that metal was exciting too, the magic of gold was something special and always caused a big stir. It was fun to see everyone's eyes brighten and hear their excited chatter when gold showed its face; it seemed that no one was immune to its charms.

The geologists, Ken and Dick, made visual inspections of every length of cut drill core, noting areas of interesting mineralisation and then selecting portions to be sent off for chemical assay. All assay work was done in Townsville and the rock samples, which were quite heavy had to be labeled, packed and sent by truck to the coast; we placed one half in new aluminium trays and stored the other half in our sheds. It was exciting to receive the assay results back and read off the percentages of copper Cu, gold Ag, lead Pb and various other minerals. Ken always passed the reports around our team so that we were all part of the discovery and realisation of our work.

During the whole process, all information was methodically logged in journals and gradually, a clearer picture began to emerge of what was under the ground that we couldn't see from its surface. I was learning that contemporary exploration involved a thorough process of collecting and recording information, in various ways, to more fully understand what could not be easily seen. From all of this work, hopefully, a significant ore-body would be identified and valued, which Union Minière might develop themselves, keep or sell on. Discoveries became assets and depending on the spot price of a particular commodity over time, contributed or took away from the company's overall value. Like chess masters, Union Minière would wait or act depending on how the market moved, and their skill at the game was crucial to the company's success. And having great discoveries delivered by their various exploration teams around the world was a key pillar in the foundation of this international corporation. So, even though we were a small team covering a very large section of Queensland, Ken was always under pressure to deliver the prize and regularly flew to Brisbane, reporting and presenting to management. As a field hand I wasn't privy to his work, but he must have been good at it as our local operation continued to be funded and supported by its parent.

Our Ryan Road yard was elevated from the city centre, and we had a good view of Mineside and its tall chimney, known locally as The Stack. The iconic structure was over 70 metres tall, decorated with black and red stripes and a black top, and was the most prominent feature of Mount Isa's landscape. Exhausting the lead smelter, The Stack released a white plume of smoke that drifted serenely across clear blue skies. Sometimes the smoke would whip lazily as the winds changed but mostly it drifted east to west, away from us; but not always.

I was working in the yard and looked up to see The Stacks' smoke flying straight over the top of us. "That looks nice." I thought to myself. Over the next 15 minutes I watched, fascinated, as the plume arched down gracefully to gently kiss the ground and lace the air with its acrid, toxic, sulfurous fumes. Suddenly my eyes were stinging like crazy and begun to water, while at the same time the sulphur bit sharply into the back of my throat and choked my lungs. It was horrible! I ran for the shed but the gaseous outpouring was everywhere; there was no escape. Sid and Irish Ray laughed at Ray and I until they nearly fell over. When they had recovered, both shared the sage wisdom of their vast experience.

"You'll get used to it … in a few years." Sid offered with mock sincerity, while Irish Ray guffawed loudly and went back into his workshop.

Over his shoulder he offered the standard Dr. Irish Ray remedy for just about everything that might afflict a person, "A cup of tea will fix you up!" Somewhat desperate and hopeful, we followed him into the shed.

———

While we were working in town, Ray and I began looking for new accommodation. Crazy Cottage had its many charms but two of us living in a two by three metre room was not one of them; Ray and I were mates; we liked each other but not that much!

We found a place overlooking the Leichhardt River, just at the end of Seventeenth Avenue. There were two adjoining flats owned by the Campbell family, who lived in a house next door. Their business was trucks and haulage, and their son Mick had one of the flats; the other had become vacant. We went to have a look and met Mrs. Campbell; she seemed nice enough and led us into a wire fenced front yard with a big, shady grapefruit tree. The flat's front door was up a short flight of concrete steps and we went inside. It had furniture, two bedrooms and combined lounge/kitchen; the bathroom was towards the rear and there was a shared laundry out back. Perfect!

Mrs. Campbell explained the rent was $75 per week and no bond was required; we took it. After we had all shaken hands she told us that the Aboriginal Reserve was right across the river, but not to be concerned because her husband had sorted them out and they didn't cross the river here anymore.

She advised us further, "My husband is a trucky; a big man with a short fuse. Make sure you pay the rent and look after the property and you will never hear from him. You don't want my husband visiting you. Okay boys?"

"Okay!" we said together.

She smiled sweetly and handed over a set of keys; we paid a week's rent in cash and moved-in over the weekend. Wahoo!

Having lived with Mum and Dad my entire life, this was my first flat and I was pretty stoked. The interior was simple, with painted concrete-block walls and linoleum floor coverings; the windows were all glass louvres, there was a stove and a refrigerator, beds and chairs. It was great and we filled a whole shelf in the refrigerator with 4XXX stubbies. After a couple of days we met our neighbour, Mick Campbell; he was in his early twenties, wore navy-blue shorts, a tank top and was well built; he told us that he drove trucks for his Dad. We all sat on the front steps and shared some beers; he seemed like a good bloke.

Mick gave us a few tips, essential for surviving life in Mount Isa.

"Keep the back door shut or at least put the screen door on its latch; the big hill behind us has lot of feral cats and they'll get in your place. Not nice; you don't want that. And don't take any shit from the black fellas."

Mick shared something else too; he was the one who first told us about the Irish Club.

Chapter 9

Out Bush

It was week three at Union Minière and with the departure of Marty, Ray and I were now the official pair of Prospecting Hands. We were scheduled to go and work out near the town of Kajabbi for 10 days and arrived at eight o'clock on Monday morning packed and ready to go; Sid would be going with us and Dick would join our group later in the week. We spent the morning loading the vehicles; we were taking two of the Series III Land Rovers, one of them being Ken's who was staying in-town. These Rovers were fairly new having been delivered earlier in the year, replacing the Series II vehicles. The Toyota Land Cruiser J40 model was becoming popular for off-road work, but Ken had stuck with the proven British workhorse from the local dealership, Western Garage.

Sid and I went shopping at nine o'clock to get supplies from Woolworths; Dick was going to bring out a top-up when he came. We got steak, sausages and bacon, tinned vegetables and fruit, powdered milk, a bag of fresh apples, tea, dried snacks, bread, butter and the like. The meat and other items would be packed in the vehicle's onboard refrigerator and frozen on the drive out. Sid said there was a gas refrigerator out at the Kajabbi campsite where we would be able to keep our food fresh. Ray had Ken's Land Rover loaded when we got back and we all pitched in to get the second four wheel drive ready for the trip.

The long wheel base Land Rovers were very well fitted out for their purpose. Each had roof racks, which held a spare tyre and several green jerrycans; a second tyre was fitted to the bonnet, and on the front a substantial roo bar sporting radio aerials, a duo of spot lights and two hessian water bags. Inside were the two-way radio, 12 volt refrigerator/freezer, shovels, winches, jacks and a plethora of other gear. They had a 2.25 litre six cylinder petrol motor, two separately switched batteries—one dedicated to the engine—and a four-speed manual gearbox. Needless to say they were not particularly fast on-road, but certainly impressive in the bush environment as we were to find out.

We headed out around eleven o'clock and filled our fuel tanks up on the way out of town. The Overlander Hotel slipped by on our right and soon we were on the Barkly Highway; after a while we turned left onto the, now familiar, Julius Dam road and drove into the bush.

It was a hot, clear day and after about an hour and a half, just after crossing Narrowgret Creek, we came to an intersection; Sid, who was driving with me slowed down.

"This is the turnoff to Julius Dam." he said while pointing left. "It's about another 15 kilometres on."

I looked in the direction he indicated and replied, "Funny. If we had made it to Julius three weeks ago then we probably wouldn't be here right now. Drive on Sidney, we have work to do!"

He laughed, put the vehicle into first gear and waved back to Ray as we drove straight ahead.

The surface that we were driving on was a simple graded red gravel track about four metres wide; just enough room for two cars to pass, though we met no one on our way to Kajabbi. The bush either side consisted of grasses, low level shrubs and the occasional Snappy Gum; it was a broad, flat landscape where the sky seemed to dominate the scene. We crossed Narrowgret Creek once again and then the track began to curve gently towards the east; I noticed clumps of taller trees on my left and Sid told me we were running parallel with the Leichhardt River, now downstream from Julius Dam.

It seemed that we had run into our old friend Ludwig Leichhardt again as the river had been named after him by Augustus Charles Gregory, who was the Assistant Surveyor of Western Australia in 1854. During his 1857-58 expedition, Gregory was looking for Leichhardt and his party who had disappeared without trace, he noticed the river was unnamed and in honour of the lost explorer named it Leichhardt River. Gregory reached the Barcoo River and found a tree that had been marked by Leichhardt, but drought conditions ultimately forced him to abandon the search; the fate of Leichhardt remaining unknown.

We joined another track and to the right spotted a large outcropping of pale bleached rock jutting up out of the red soil and crowned with several, spindly young gum trees; to the left I occasionally glimpsed the river through trees lining its banks. The Rovers bumped through Cordelia and Miranda Creeks, and sometime later we drove down into Prospector Creek, roared up its far bank and then turned left onto yet another track. After a few minutes Sid pulled the vehicle up, turned its motor off and the wide, dry, sand bed of the mighty Leichhardt River stretched out before us. Ray pulled up behind and got out to join us; he lit up a cigarette as we all had a quiet moment and took in the scene.

It was strangely humbling to look out across this naked river bed and consider the billions of litres of water that had carved and shaped it over millennia. The track dove down the river's bank and disappeared into a brackish pool of dark water for about 50 metres, before emerging to continue along the sandy bed. The 300 metres that separated us from the far, tree-lined bank was dotted with small copses of juvenile gums that probably, would not survive the next rainy season.

> "Was he trapped by flood when the channels burst, And the north-spawned waters spread?"–
> Bruce Simpson, Leichhardt Land

We were parked on a relatively straight section of the river and Sid told us this was one of the narrowest points to cross.

97

"When the river is in full flood during the big wet, no one can get across." he remarked, "It turns into a raging torrent and isolates Kajabbi."

Ray finished his smoke and we all got back into our vehicles, drove down the bank and across to slip through the tree line on the other side. The track lead us right then wove around Kajabbi's dirt airstrip and a few minutes later we turned into Stanfield Street where Sid introduced us to the only commercial business in town, The Kalkadoon Hotel.

In the early 19th century, Kajabbi serviced several local copper mines and its railway transported cattle from the far northwest, on their way to Cloncurrys' sales yards and the east coast. It had boasted a post office, railway station and the hotel, and a population of about 1000 people. Sid filled us in on a little of Kajabbi's recent history.

"Since the closing of the main copper mines: Dobbyn, Mount Cuthbert and some other smaller ones," he explained, "the town's pretty quiet these days. Maybe 300 - 400 people live around here now. The government will probably close the railway at some point in the future. So, it's mainly the hotel, air strip, the few people who live here and us."

It was about 30 degrees Celsius, and we were parched; Ray and I looked at the hotel, then at Sid and back to the hotel again.

"Oh all right then!" he exclaimed, "A quick one."

The hotel's facade featured a wide shady verandah flanked either end by two gabled turrets; the main roof was hipped and clad with corrugated iron. Its walls were probably hardwood, sheeted only on the inside to expose studs, noggins and other framing timbers. The bar's only two windows were tall with frosted glass, befitting the building's 100 year old status. We walked through the front door into a cooler interior and were greeted by a corrugated iron sheeted bar, lined with stools of all shapes and sizes.

"G'day boys. What'll you have?" asked the barman. Then, "Oh. G'day Sid, I didn't see you behind the young fellas. You out to do some more work down the road?"

Ray and I ordered a beer and Sid had lemonade; they chatted with the barman while I looked around. The ceiling was high, about three metres, fitted with two single-tube fluorescent lights; all of the walls were clad with painted timber boarding. It was a simple, rectangular shaped room dominated by the bar, with a pool table at one end and dartboard the other. Behind the bar were several large glass door refrigerators, an office nook, some shelves with cigarettes, a till and other related paraphernalia. With its grey unfinished concrete floor polished, no doubt, by countless boots, thongs and bare feet, it was rough-and-ready designed to withstand robust use; and looked like it had. It was clearly a place for men, and perhaps some brave women, to drink.

"How did the hotel get its name, Kalkadoon?" I asked the publican.

"Oh my." Sid sighed, "Better get another round in for this story."

"I'm told the building was moved from Mount Cuthbert, "Russel began slowly, gathering his thoughts, "which became a ghost town when the price of copper fell and its smelters were shut down; Mount Elliott Company bought the mine and plant in the mid 1920s. The hotel was rebuilt in Kajabbi and named after the local tribe.

The Kalkadoon's territory went out as far as Boulia, up around Gunpowder and east to McKinley's Gap, and they'd mark the boundaries with an emu foot painted on trees or rocks. They were fierce warriors and protected their territory, and were not very happy with the whites moving in.

The story goes that around the late 1800s a Cloncurry police officer, Beresford, and two of his four black troupers were killed by the very Kalkadoon's they'd been tracking and had captured. The prisoners were corralled in a gorge for the night, but unbeknown to Beresford and his men the clever black-fellas had previously located a stash of weapons in the gorge, and used them to attack the police during the night. A surviving trouper walked 30 kilometres with a barbed spear stuck in his thigh, to raise the alarm.

The whites in the area had a rough time for about a year as the Kalkadoons were in control. Then, a new Sub-Inspector of Cloncurry's Native Police was appointed; he was just 25 years old. Urquhart trained his troupers vigorously and after a short while the Kalkadoon's sent him a message; a challenge, to come and face them. A station owner Alex Kennedy joined forces with Urquhart and took on the black-fellas, giving them a real hard time."

We'd finished our drinks and without missing a beat the publican busied himself refreshing them; then leaned up against the bar and continued.

"Having suffered some losses himself, another station's owner, Hopkins, gathered his men together and joined Urquhart, along with many pastoralists and farmhands from the area forming a large group. The Kalkadoon warriors took note and assembled their warriors; it's said they were 600 strong and some say 900. They lead the whites to a hill about 60 miles north of Cloncurry, where they had stashed a great horde of weapons, and made a stand. Urquhart assembled the horses and dramatically charged his calvary up the hill, but the defenders easily saw them off with spears, boomerangs and rocks; Urquhart himself was knocked unconscious, after being hit in the face with a hard lump of anthill. After several hours he recovered and took command once again, leading an attack on two sides and unsettling the warriors, who broke out of their stronghold to charge down the hill, spears held high. They were mown down by rifle fire, reformed to charge once more but their spears were no match for lead bullets, and soon 200 or more Kalkadoon warriors lay dead upon the slopes.

Not satisfied, Urquhart and his supporters set out and over several days hunted down the remaining warriors, and the fierce resistance of the Kalkadoons was ended. The hill became known as Battle Mountain and was said to have been '... littered with the bleached bones of warriors, gins and piccaninnies.'

As that last sentence drifted away the bar fell silent and then he looked across at me, "So, there you have it young fella."

"Wow." I replied quietly, "Are there any Kalkadoon's around now?"

"Yes." Russel replied. "Though at the time a lot of them got pretty sick after losing so many of their people and land. The last known survivor of Battle Mountain was Tubbie Terrier; he died at Cloncurry in 1930."

We finished our drinks and made our way back out into the heat, got back in the vehicles and drove west along Stanfield Street. I thought about all of the Kalkadoon ghosts; shadows who might still be wandering over their lost territory, unable to touch it, feel the red soil under their feet or claim the land. Their tribe was so totally broken by Urquhart and the whites that it appeared there was little or no nation to be born back into. Looking out over the bush it seemed strangely empty, but was it? I hoped that none of the Kalkadoon spirits came visiting in my tent during the night while we were camping, but I knew they would.

We'd been driving along a dirt track for about eight kilometres when Sid slowed, turned off to the right and followed some tyre tracks to the campsite. He pulled up at the base of a rocky escarpment; there were two tents tucked in amongst shady trees and the blackened remains of an open fire place.

"This is it." said Sid, opening his door. "Welcome to the Kajabbi camp."

I glanced up at the slope, my eyes coming to rest on its white bleached rocks at the top and said, "Tell me this isn't Battle Mountain." but Sid was already out of the Rover.

One of the tents, the largest, contained a refrigerator, table, several metal boxes and low camp beds folded and stacked; the other tent was just for sleeping in. Sid showed us how to start the gas refrigerator; we'd load it with our food later when it was fully cooled. Much of the gear we had brought with us would stay in the vehicles as it was required the next day, for work. Water containers were relocated into the shade and Sid handed over a shovel and asked me to clean out the fire trench and then go gather kindling and fallen timber to make a fire and put on some tea. I worked for about half an hour and assembled a good sized pile. There was a welcome light breeze and the afternoon was beginning to cool down; Sid showed us how to make a fire.

"We dig a trench parallel to the site's prevailing breezes" he explained. "The idea is to lay in some spinifex and kindling and then light it at the end opposite the breeze, so it burns slowly against it. When the fire is burning strongly, add-in the larger pieces of wood. Then when it burns down a bit, lay steel rods across the trench to hold the billy, pots or fry pans. It works well as the trench holds in heat and receives oxygen from each end. Got it?"

"Wow." I said, "That's brilliant."

"Good." Sid replied, handing me a billy, "Now that you know how it all works, get to it so we can all have a cuppa!" and went off to check the refrigerator.

When the water was boiling he came over with a tin containing loose-leaf tea, took a handful and flung it into the steaming billy. As the water's surface frothed up he lifted the container off the flames and placed it off to one side. We waited for about five minutes and watched Sid tapping the metal sides with a spoon, then he poured steaming golden-brown tea into three metal mugs and handed them out. I looked into my mug and there were no tea leaves floating around; it was clear liquid. I looked up at Sid, nodded and he winked back … I got it.

When it was five o'clock in the afternoon Sid's alarm clock jangled; he went and did our radio check-in. I heard him talking with base; the signal was strong out here and Dick's voice was clear though oddly metallic; he would be joining us in a couple of days. There was not much to report and their conversation was fairly short. As the sun slowly dropped lower in the sky, Sid asked if we'd like to wash-up, and have a swim before dark.

"What have you got in mind Sid? joked Ray, "A resort spa and swimming pool? How about some canapes to have with our ice-cold champas?"

"Better than that!" he replied with his customary grin, then picked up his towel and walked out of camp.

Intrigued, we gathered our gear and followed. Sid lead us around the escarpment's base then turned and followed a creek, which disappeared into the rocks. There, hidden away, in amongst a low rock shelter was a natural pool. Towards the rear, where two large slabs met forming a rough v-shape, water trickled down from the higher areas and splashed lightly onto its surface. I looked up and could see blue sky sharply contrasting with the red-brown hill. It was extraordinarily beautiful.

He handed us a bucket each and instructed, "Get some water, soap-up and rinse off out here, and then we don't pollute the pool; you can get in for a soak afterwards."

Ray and I didn't need any urging and soon were starkers, enthusiastically washing off the day's sweat and dust. Once we were all rinsed clean Ray stepped into the pool first.

"Watch out that the yabbies don't bite your arse!" Sid called out.

I smiled to myself as he said "arse" in that British way. Unlike the American "ass" we were beginning to hear more often in Australia these days, what with the US movies, music and TV shows. We all got in and sank down into the water, up to our necks; it was magnificent.

"Resort spa?" said Sid, "I don't think so. I'd rather have this!"

Both Ray and I agreed as the cool water began to take the heat out of our skin and soothe our bodies. It was quiet until, suddenly, Ray jumped up splashing water everywhere.

"I told you." laughed Sid.

I joined in once I realised what had happened; we weren't the only creatures enjoying this water and the local yabbies had found something soft to investigate.

After a while we got out, dried off and walked back
to camp. The sun was setting behind our hill and a
peaceful hush had settled over the bush. It was the
transition from day to night and soon a variety of
nocturnal creatures would come awake and get about
their business. Sid told us that he would cook our
dinner tonight and placed fresh wood on the fire before
rummaging around in the big tent; returning with food,
pots and pans. Unexpectedly, he handed out cans of cool
beer.

"Make it last; I only bought a dozen."

The beer tasted great; I placed a fold-up chair near
the fire and we chatted while the flames turned tree
branches into glowing charcoal. Soon our bush chef
had sausages and onions sizzling, potatoes and carrots
boiling, and slices of bread buttered; he even brought
out a bottle of tomato sauce. The aroma of cooking food
tinged with wood smoke had us both salivating and
when Sid handed out enamel metal plates filled with
steaming food we all tucked-in enthusiastically. After
dinner the billy went on for tea and I washed the dishes
in a bucket. Sipping my tea, looking into the fire's
coals, I realised I was tired; or perhaps just very relaxed.
The temperature had cooled down considerably and I
said good night to the others. In the tent I laid out my
sleeping bag on a camp bed, zipped the fly-screen flap
closed and lay down; within minutes I was fast asleep.
I woke once in the night, just briefly and with no idea
why. I could sense the bush alive all around the tent
and put my hand down to touch the ground. It was
cooler, the heat of the day now released from the land; I

pulled my sleeping bag in more snugly and then settled comfortably in my cot and slept again.

———————

I awoke; it was just light and a flock of galahs were having their early morning conference in a nearby tree. I could hear someone making-up the fire; I got up yawning and went outside to find Sid had put the billy on for tea.

The area we'd be working in was intersected by Six Mile Creek; we'd be in the southern half this week. Sid laid out a map on the Land Rover's bonnet and described the general geology of the mining tenement that Union Minière was exploring[1].

"The Cloncurry Ranges are very unusual," Sid explained. "They're part of an ancient formation known as the Pre-Cambrian belt. What's unusual is that this is one of the few places on Earth that has never been under the sea; no marine fossils have ever been found here. At one time all these hills would have been huge mountains, but they've been eroded over time into the stumps we see now; and all that material probably formed a lot of the surrounding areas, like the Gulf Country."

I looked up at the bare, blunt escarpment sheltering our camp, once a tall pointy mountain.

———————

1   Exploration Mineral Permit, EPM 17527, northwest of Kajabbi.

Sid took a sip of his tea and continued, "Massive erosion exposed many of the deep mineral deposits and gold mining began around here over 100 years ago. Copper was first mined at the end of the 19th Century and over here," his finger waggled over the town of Gregory," there are massive deposits of limestone to the north of the belt that are thought to be the remnants of an ancient barrier reef."

"Wow. Pretty cool Sid." I remarked.

"Yes." He looked over his map fondly, "It's a wonderful old place; has some of the oldest rocks in the world."

Ray had gotten up and we all had some breakfast and got ready. Sid made sure to bury our food scraps well away from the camp so as not to attract ants or rodents. He wanted to get away early so we could work through the cooler morning and then we'd take a break in the middle of the day and continue later, into the afternoon. We drove out of camp around six o'clock and made our way through the bush until we reached the creek and parked the two vehicles under a large gum tree.

The job was to layout a 100 by 100 metre grid across the land; at each intersection a white topped, wooden stake would be hammered into the ground and a reference number marked on it. The grid's two axes ran north-south and east-west, and had already been drafted upon Sid's map; a corresponding origin ensured that both the paper and physical grid were in sync. There were two main purposes for installing the grid: it would be used to facilitate and coordinate a surface and later, a subsurface survey.

Sid retrieved a surveyor's theodolite and tripod from the back of his vehicle and set it up; he would man the instrument while Ray and I walked out, measured distances, placed the stakes and marked them with aluminium tags. There was a stash of stakes ready for us to use, left from previous trips. I'd studied surveying at QIT and understood what Sid was doing, directing us to ensure the stakes were in a perfectly straight line. We worked through the morning and as the sun rose higher in the sky drank, often, from the vehicle's water bags.

The water bags were sewn from a thick-weave hessian fabric that allowed a small amount of water to continually weep out and moisten the material. In the process of evaporation, the water inside the bag was cooled. The small loss of water provided a large, refreshing benefit and I found that as the daytime temperature increased, so did the water's deliciousness; both seemed intimately correlated. By midday, our water was tasting better than beer! I mentioned this to Sid and he shook his head.

"You must be getting delirious in the heat!"

He called us both in and we went back to camp for lunch and a rest.

———————

We worked over several days expanding the grid and then, in the late afternoon of day four, Dick joined us at camp. He brought with him extra food, some tins of Victoria Bitter and several packs of cigarettes for Ray.

109

"Victoria Bitter?" queried Ray; inspecting one of the shiny green tins with feigned suspicion.

"Well, you don't have to drink any of them." countered Dick.

Dick came from Melbourne, Victoria. His real name was Richard but we all called him Dick. Each state had its favourite beer: Queensland produced Castlemain 4XXX, New South Wales had their Tooheys, Western Australia liked Swan Lager and Victoria's beer was Victoria Bitter. Normally, people were very loyal to their state's beer but in the circumstances, Ray and I made an exception to Victoria's own.

Ray opened a tin and took a tentative sip, as if he was taste testing it for poison. "Not too bad, Dick, this V.B. of yours. Not *too* bad."

"Stick around young Raymond." replied Dick magnanimously. "We'll get you educated in appreciating the better things of life. There's hope for everyone, you know, even you."

Everyone laughed, especially Ray with his broad and infectious guffaw. It was a good moment and as humour often does, broke the ice allowing Dick to enter camp and become a member of our group; that afternoon the three became a four.

———————

Dick was lightly built, in his mid to late thirties with thinning, red curly hair and a beard. He was University educated, intelligent and carried a touch of arrogance that people who came from monied families and private schools could sometimes portray. He and Ray developed a kind of love/hate relationship, bantering and teasing each other in a lighthearted way. Though, in the coming year, Dick would show us that his superior airs were a facade; a front that he used to disguise the very kind and caring man he really was. Dick from Melbourne would reveal himself in time.

The next morning we were all up early and gathered around the fire for tea; all except for Dick who had brought a fancy coffee pot and ground beans with him. He said that he had to get roasted beans sent up from Melbourne as there was no good coffee in Mount Isa. He may have been right as his coffee smelled fantastic. Then he placed a couple of slices of bread over the fire, to toast. On the turn Dick produced thin slices of cheese, individually wrapped in plastic, which he carefully unwrapped and placed on the toast to melt. I had not seen these before and asked what they were.

"Gruyere." Dick said, as if that explained everything.

When cheese began to soften and turned glossy, he took them off the heat and ate in between sips of steaming coffee. I made a mental note to see if I could find some Gruyere cheese slices in Woolworths; I so wanted to try them!

Around 5:30 the four of us took two Land Rovers out to the job. While Ray and I continued working with Sid punching stakes into the ground, Dick began working where we had started on Tuesday morning. He walked the grid stopping often to pick up rock samples, dug into the ground with his pointy geologist's hammer or wrote in a thick clothe bound notebook. He was

Stephen tram

using our stakes to locate his observations and at each
intersection noted down the axis' reference markings
from its aluminium tag, then added a description
alongside, of the ground at his feet. When Dick got
back into town he would plot that information on
a map and over time, built up a picture of the land's
surface geology.

When we went back to camp for lunch I asked Dick
to show me what he had written. He seemed surprised
at my interest, then flipped his notebook open on the
bonnet of a nearby Land Rover, to take me through
several of his neatly penned entries. I didn't understand
all of the terms that the geologist used but I got
enough to follow him. He said that while some of the
looser surface material may have been moved around
by flooding, or livestock feeding, he was particularly
interested in outcrops that had become exposed due to
soil erosion. What they were made of and the way the
rock lay; its incline relative to the surface was recorded.
He showed, in his log, that he had found a similar
mineral formation occurring in several different places,
which would be correlated on the map later. This surface
information may indicate an area for future drilling.

Ray's, "Drillers; they are all animals!" jumped into my
head for a moment.

"And that's what you and young Raymond will be
doing next." Dick said; breaking into my thoughts.

"What's that?" I asked.

"The magnetometer." he replied mysteriously; then
closed the notebook and went off to make a sandwich.

"Gruyere cheese, no doubt." I thought to myself.

The magnetometer? It sounded like something that Dr. Smith, of the TV series Lost in Space, would say to Will Robison and the Robot.

"Get the magnetometer dear boy. And you. Robot. Help him. Quickly, there's not a moment to waste!"

I was definitely in!

––––––––––––

Dick stayed with us for three days, working in the Kajabbi heat over the grid we had laid out and filling his notebook with information. When he caught up with us at the grid-face, there was little more to do; Dick said goodbye and drove off, headed for Mount Isa; he'd pullover on the road at five o'clock to participate in our scheduled radio check with Ken. When we got in from work he was gone and the camp was a little emptier without his company. I suggested that he'd run out of his Gruyere cheese and had to get back to town to stock up. I got a couple of smiles, but it was certainly different without our red bearded geologist.

Ray made an announcement, "I'm going to drive into Kajabbi tonight and have a few beers at the Kalkadoon, anyone want to come?"

I thought about it but declined his offer, as did Sid.

"Suit yourselves." said Ray and went off to clean up. Half an hour later he took one of the vehicles and drove off.

"Take a note of the turnoff into camp," Sid called out, "it looks different at night and there's no moon."

Ray waved in acknowledgement and Sid and I settled in to a night around the fire. Later, I took a torch into the bush to clear my bladder before bed. Ray was not back yet. Away from the fire's soft red glow the sky was alight with stars, as it had been for many of the nights that we had been here. It was an extraordinary spectacle, untainted by the harsh glare of city lights. I thought about how far the light that my eyes were receiving had travelled and that it must be very old. It was interesting conjecture that my eyes were responding to starlight that might be thousands of years old, and my brain was interpreting information representing something that probably no longer even existed, but seemed to exist just for me. And so, following through on my theory, bathed in nonexistent starlight I made my way back to camp and bed; awaking briefly when I heard Ray's vehicle return to camp.

———————

Like many things that are thought to be contemporary devices, the magnetometer was first invented in 1833 by a German, Carl Friedrich Gauss. Gauss designed an instrument that was able to detect magnetic anomalies of various types, which could be useful in mineral exploration for probing below Earth's surface. While the technology did not differentiate clearly, for example, between copper and iron, it could identify the difference between iron and sand or clay. When these magnetic differences were plotted upon a map, the results could reveal anomalies below the surface that, combined with other gathered information, painted a picture that was an abstraction to the untrained but fine art to geologists.

When we got to the job on the morning of day eight, Sid did not get his theodolite out from the back of our Land Rover, but another instrument. He showed us how to attach a box, containing the magnetometer, to the top of a four metre long pole and then plug in the base station. One of us would carry the pole, placing it down at each grid intersection, while the other would carry the base station triggering the magnetometer and taking a reading; Sid would then record each reading and it's corresponding stake's reference in a log book.

It seemed simple enough and we set out in Dick's footsteps, walking the grid once again. The magnetic survey was just a bunch of numbers to us and the overall results wouldn't be correlated until much later. So we walked and at every intersection, stopped, then pressed the magic button and gave Sid a number; over and over again. It wasn't all that exciting but we moved along fairly quickly and by day 10 had it completed. It was time to go home, and that was exciting.

Back at camp we did a final radio check and then gathered together our few remaining supplies to cook dinner. It was a bit of a poor man's smorgasbord: a rasher or two of bacon, three and a half sausages, three potatoes, an onion, a tin of peas and some stale bread. Sid wove his culinary magic, once again, and we cleaned it all up with gusto. I put on the billy for tea and after a cuppa and chat around the fire, we all turned in for the night.

The next morning I slept-in until six o'clock. We managed to scrape together Vegemite on toast and a cup of tea for breakfast before cleaning up the camp and getting ready to leave. I buried all of our scraps and waste while Ray raked out the camp and cleared the fire of live coals and ash; Sid was busy in the tents, sweeping them out, packing up the tin boxes with pots, pans and utensils, and turning off our gas refrigerator. When the vehicles were all loaded with what we were taking back to base and there was nothing left to do, we drove out of camp taking the road west to Kajabbi.

Sid had us pull up at the Kalkadoon Hotel, though neither Ray or I conspired for a beer this time. He wanted to let the publican know that we were moving out of the area; the hotel was a hub facilitating local communication, commerce and social activity, and the publican was central to that and well regarded. He came out to the vehicles with Sid and handed over two cold cans of Coca Cola and one of Lemonade; a parting gift from the Kalkadoon.

"See you next trip young fellas." Russel looked at me, "Come and have a beer with Ray next time."

"I will. For sure." I replied.

"Good." he said, nodded and went back inside.

We got back to the Ryan Road yard in the early afternoon and after unloading and cleaning up the vehicles got ready to go home for a four day break. Ken called us into the offices and handed over two pay envelopes.

"I've spoken with Sid and you two have worked very well; I'd like to offer you a full-time job with us here at Union Minière; what do you say?"

"That would be great Ken. Thanks." I replied for both of us, and we all shook hands.

Sid was just outside, " Thanks Sid," I said, " for taking care of us. It's been a good week and we'll see you in a few days."

"So, you're staying." he frowned. "My cooking didn't put you off? I must be slipping!"

"See you later Sir Sid."

We threw our gear in the HR's boot, Ray lit up a cigarette and then I drove us home to the flat; though it was a strange idea after having lived in a tent in the Kajabbi bush for 10 days. It was pretty nice to open the refrigerator and find some ice-cold 4XXX stubbies; we took a couple out to the front steps and sat for a while listening to the city and talking quietly. Ray lit up a cigarette and exhaled a long, satisfying stream of smoke. It was good to be home.

Chapter 10

The Irish Club

On Thursday morning I drove Ray and I into town and we shopped at Woolworths. We loaded our trolley with food, a broom, washing powder, a rubbish bin, fry pan and a whole bunch of other stuff that we figured would be needed for our flat. Eden spotted us cruising through the cereal aisle and came over for a chat.

"So, how was it, out at Kajabbi?" he asked.

"Good mate. Bloody hot! We had to cook on an open fire and sleep in tents! And the bath was this rock pool out in the bush."

"Yeh?" said Eden.

"Yeh." said Ray.

"Wow!" said Eden.

"We had a beer at the Kalkadoon Hotel; that was good."

"Yeh?"

"Yeh."

While we were chatting a girl came over. She was wearing a Woolworths' uniform and Eden introduced us to Claudia Perkins; she was friendly and laughed at our banter.

When she left I asked Eden, casually, "Is she single?"

"I think so," he replied, "she used to have a boyfriend but they split up."

Then his eyes narrowed slightly and he asked pointedly, "Are you interested?"

"Well, she's a girl!" I replied; slightly embarrassed at having been so easily read.

"Stevie's been out bush for a while, Eden" Ray grinned, "he might be a bit toey." The two of them chuckled conspiratorially, as blokes sometimes do. Eden had to get back to work, which let me off the hook.

As he was leaving Eden asked, "Fancy getting a beer at The Tavern tonight; they do great meals there too?"

"Yeh, that would be great." I said.

"Yeh?" said Eden.

"Yeh. What time?"

"Seven o'clock. It's on Isa Street. See you there."

"Okay. See you later boys." and with that Eden turned and strode off towards muesli and health foods.

Later, in fresh fruit, Ray said, "She's nice Steph', you should ask her out."

"Yeh?"

"Yeh."

A short time later, we put our overflowing trolly through the checkout and went home to unpack. I found myself thinking about Claudia, "Yes, she was nice."

We hung around the flat for the day, content to be home. I washed some clothes and finished off my letter to the family, then spent time with the car: a wash, checking the motor and tuning up its single carburetter. Then, at six thirty, we drove off to meet Eden at the Mount Isa Tavern.

The Tavern's bar was like a lounge bar, the floor was nicely carpeted, dining tables with white tablecloths dotted the room and the bar was partially inset along one wall; Eden already had a table and waved us over. Ray offered to get the first round and went up to the bar; he came back bearing three glasses and some bad news.

"I thought we might find Dick here," he said, "because they only serve V.B. on tap."

"Yeh," said Eden, "pity about the beer but the food is great."

I glanced through a menu and it did look good; we'd order a little later. Eden was keen to hear more about our trip to Kajabbi and we told him our stories. I got another round of drinks in and we ordered food: Ray had steak, lamb chops for me and Eden chose fish— 'Barramundi, fresh from the Gulf,' the menu promised.

"Barra!" enthused Eden. "Amazing fish. Blokes drive up north to the town of Karumba in the Gulf of Carpentaria, on fishing trips and bring back heaps of them. It's a great fish."

"What does the name mean?" I asked him.

"I don't know but it's probably aboriginal" Eden replied and then turned to Ray to ask about The Kalkadoon Hotel.

There's an Aboriginal Dreamtime story describing two lovers; their tribe insisted that the girl marry an older man, to look after him. Boodi and Yalima went against the Elders and ran away together, which was breaking the law and punishable by death, so the men of the tribe began hunting them down.

The couple ran far and wide but eventually came to the land's edge where the water began. The hunters found them and they were trapped, and fought for their lives. When the couple ran out of spears and realised they could not survive, they turned their backs and jumped into the water.

Boodi and Yalima swam away as fish; Barramundi and the hunter's spears embedded in their backs can be seen as the spines on the Barramundi's dorsal fin. And so they live, in the shape of the great silver fish, hiding in amongst the logs and reeds of Australia's northern waters.

Our meals arrived, Eden got his shout in and we ate. Eden's fish did look good, the Barra fillet was thick with pearl-white flesh; he flaked off big juicy chunks dripping with a pale cream-and-green-pepper sauce. I

121

decided to definitely come back and have fish another time. True to his word, the food was great. We ended up staying until closing time and got ourselves quite a bit drunk. The boys had a final cigarette out in the carpark; Ray had run out and smoked one of Eden's pulling a few faces at the mentholated taste.

"Jeez Eden, you smoke these?"

We stood around the cars, probably making way too much noise but no one seemed to mind, and then we said good night and headed home. Life in Mount Isa seemed very good, until I woke up the next morning.

"Oh my God! I'm dying." I cried out loud; my eyes weren't even open yet.

My head felt like it was splitting in half and blood was pounding; ping-ponging from one temple to the other, 'Thump, thump, thump.' I staggered off to the bathroom and threw-up in the toilet, which only served to intensify the pain in my head.

"Ouch!"

After washing my face with cold water and noticing a kind of pink syrupy film coating my eyes, I felt my way into the kitchen and managed to locate the kettle and switch it on. I heard a groan and Ray appeared from out of his room; he was not a pretty sight and I told him so.

"You look like shit, Ray!" I winced; it even hurt to talk.

"Who poisoned me?" he asked. "I am never drinking Victoria-bloody-Bitter ever again. Never!" and went off to the bathroom.

We stumbled out of the front door and sat on our front steps, hoping the early morning sun would sooth our heads. The coffee helped to ease my unsettled stomach and hopefully, would begin activating some of my few remaining brain cells. Mick Cambell's front door opened; he took one look and gleefully, started berating us like an Edwardian school master.

"Aha! Been out have we? Got a bit of a head have we? Hmm? Look at you both. You're a mess! You're bringing down the neighborhood you know."

"Who needs mates when we've got you Mick." I responded feebly; my head hurt if I talked too loud.

"We went to The Tavern last night and drank V.B." Ray presented our excuses.

"That will do it." Mick replied unsympathetically. "It's not smart to drink foreign beer; especially from Victoria. It's practically another country, you know."

He sat out with us for a while, had a smoke and coffee, then went off to work; Mick was hauling gravel out near Cloncurry and working over the weekend. Ray went back to bed and I tried to read my book; I could get my eyes to focus on the text but it was hard work so I put the book down and went for a walk along the river.

The Leichhardt ran across the front of our property; there were no fences so I walked through the gums, down a shallow grade bank and into the river bed. There was little surface water but the sand felt cool underfoot in the shade of the trees. It was the dry season and the river looked more like a highway than a waterway; that

Stephen tram

would change in the early part of the new year with the big wet.

Once clear of the treeline I could see several of the Aboriginal Reserve's huts across the other side; the buildings were similar to the Port Hedland community. Nearby, a group of brown-skinned people were sitting under a big shady tree; I waved but got no response and they just watched me. I smiled to myself; there were probably not too many red-eyed, white fellas wandering around in the river.

The main channel ran close to my place and then swept across to the east bank; its flood plain sloping up towards the Reserve's buildings. I wondered if they got flooded during the rainy season—if they did then it was likely that we would as well. I walked north and found I was following a track already worn into the sand, weaving around the young gums and boulders. Up ahead, an Aboriginal man was walking towards me and he nodded as we passed but said nothing; maybe his head was throbbing like mine. After a while I turned and walked back; my head was feeling clearer as I climbed the bank up to the flat. Ray was up and showered, and looked much better for it; I followed his example.

Around lunch time I suggested, "Let's go and join the Irish Club, and have a couple of cold ones, for medicinal purposes only. It's just down the road."

"Yeh. Good idea. I sure could do with some medicine."

We took the car, not feeling strong enough to attempt the 800 metre walk under Mount Isa's midday sun. The Irish Club was at the end of Nineteenth Avenue and commanded a city block; we parked outside and entered via Buckley Avenue. Membership was a couple of dollars and we filled out a form each and handed them over at the bar; the club would post us our member's cards next week and we could use a receipt until then. Ray ordered two pots of 4XXX while I looked around.

The room was simply decorated, quite large, roughly t-shaped with table seating in the main area, four pool tables off to one side and a full sized snooker table in an adjacent nook. There was a good sized crowd and food was being served out from a hatch in one wall; the bar area was busy and all pool tables were in use. We sat on a couple of stools and watched the games; the standard was generally quite high. To get a game the challenger placed a 20 cent coin, in line, on a pool table's rails; when their turn came up they challenged the current King of the Table. It wasn't long before Ray and I had our coins on one of the tables and were soon playing. As the last dregs of V.B left our bodies and was replaced by Queensland's own golden nectar, Castlemaine 4XXX, we felt much better and had a good afternoon playing pool and meeting some of Mount Isa's locals. As the tables got busier during the afternoon, Ray and I partnered-up to play doubles; we did quite well. Often we were invited to, "Play for a pot, mate?" which was friendly enough and occasionally for a dollar. The right to break, considered an advantage, was decided on the toss of a coin, and there was one main local rule—if the black ball was sunk before clearing all of your other balls, then you lost.

We enjoyed a good afternoon and on our way out noticed another room with a large dance floor and stage; we figured this must be where the "Sunday Session" that Mick had mentioned was held, the one that all the chicks went to. We agreed to check that out tomorrow, for sure, and went home for dinner.

I found out about Lake Moondarra from a guy whose job was to harvest the huge floating mats of Salvinia from the lake's surface.

Salvinia's an aquatic plant native to Brazil, but in Australia it was officially categorised as a Weed of National Significance (WoNS). People would buy it for their fish tanks, but unwittingly spread the pest when they cleaned out their tanks and dumped Salvinia in local ponds and waterways.

Gavin drove a flat bottomed, aluminium punt fitted with a big mesh bucket that he used to scoop up the floating plant, which later would be dried and burnt. I laughed as he told me that he really loved his job; out on the water he'd light up a joint or two and just cruise around all day scooping up weed. I nicknamed him Weedman, the guy who had weed inside and weed outside. He seemed pretty relaxed and certainly had a great suntan.

The lake was actually a dam supplying Mt Isa's water. Construction was started in 1956, initially by Utah Construction Company and then finished by Theiss Brothers in 1958; it was the largest water scheme in Australia financed by private enterprise at a cost of £1.7 million. It was a significant enterprise though

Aborigines had business in this area long before the dam.

The Kalkadoons had mined basalt just north of Moondarra producing edge-ground axes. Stone Axe Quarry, covering an area of eight square kilometers, was probably the largest of its type in Australia. We whites tend to think of ourselves as the creators of technology but edge ground axe technology had been the province of Aborigines for 1,000s of years, with Kalkadoon axes traded as far as Lake Eyre in South Australia. In fact, Aboriginal people had established extensive trading routes that stretched from Mount Isa to Kopperamanna, and markets that operated at Boulia, Upper Georgina, Leichardt Selwyn Ranges and Cloncurry where a wide variety of goods and products were exchanged.

The Kalkadoons quarried using a variety of techniques, including flaking, fire to split larger boulders, they also employed poles, creating mechanical advantage to lever stones out of the subsurface; and hammerstones were used to create cracks in rocks and then wedges inserted into these fractures to split them in two or more pieces. Anvils, hammerstones, flaking, knapping and retouching tools were made and used to form the base axe heads; and finally, siltstone or quartzite grindstones with water applied produced the desired and prized bevel edge. It took about 24 hours work to shape the product and a similar time to grind its edge. The basalt went through five stages of manufacture and was moved to different departments for each stage; it was an organised and coordinated process involving groups of workers and craftsmen, producing a range of sized axe products and then getting them to market. Edge ground technology and the commerce it supported had been alive and well in Australia for 35,000 years.

Several people now had mentioned Mount Isa's premier water-recreation destination, Lake Moondarra; Ray and I drove out for a look on Sunday. We headed north out of town along the Barkly Highway and turned right just before the airport, crossing the river on a shallow concrete causeway into Leichhardt River Road—a sign read, "Subject to Flooding" and I could see it wouldn't take much water to make that come true. About 10 kilometres and a couple of small creek crossings later, a large expanse of water showed up on our left; a further four kilometres along and Moondarra[1] revealed herself more fully.

We parked at Transport Bay and walked across a remarkably green stretch of lawn, onto a course sand beach and met the water's edge. It was really nice, a great expanse of water framed by red-earth hills covered with low level scrubs and bushes. It seemed such a shocking contrast to see a huge body of water and then the adjacent bush reflecting a low rainfall, semi-desert environment. But, it didn't seem to be worrying the many pelicans bobbing around on Moondarra's sparkling surface, or the people swimming and picnicking along its green shores. We dropped our towels on the grass and ran into the water; it felt amazing.

---

1   Moondarra is a word from the Kalkadoon people and means, 'place of rain also thunder.'

After a swim we bought a couple of cans of Coca-Cola at the pavilion and drove around to view the dam wall and spillway; a concrete walkway led out across the top so we parked and went to check it out. I stopped halfway across and leaned on the handrail; on one side was a sparkling, lively, abundance of water and I could feel the cool breeze it generated ruffling my hair, and on the other side, the dam wall fell like a massive guillotine to cut through the mighty Leichhardt, leaving its sand bed running wide and dry off to the east as far as I could see. I knew that if the wall was not there, then much of the captured water would be some 300 kilometres away in the Gulf of Carpentaria right now, but it was hard to ignore the stark comparison that was so clearly defined by this vast 250 metre wide concrete and rubble blade.

"Wish I had my rifle," Ray said, taking an imaginary line of sight along his extended arm. "I'd get a good, clear shot at a 'roo from up here."

"You don't have a rifle."

"Not yet." he laughed.

He took a door key out of his pocket and scratched 'Ray' into the now empty Coca-Cola can and then reached out and dropped it over the side; we watched the bright red container bounce all the way down the dam wall to join many more littering its base.

"I might find that one up at Karumba when I go there fishing one day." he laughed and lit up a cigarette, cupping his hand to shield the flame.

129

I looked at my watch and it was time to go; we had to clean up and get ready for the Sunday Session.

"Hey Ray." I said.

"Yeh?"

"Beer, pool and girls all in one place; let's go!"

"Yeh. Let's go!" he echoed and strode off towards then car; I was right behind him.

———

We got to the Irish Club just after four o'clock and went into the Blarney Bar for a game of pool; several tables were free and I racked up the balls while Ray got us a beer. We played a few games and after a while the bar began to fill up. Several blokes challenged for the table but Ray held them off and won a couple of beers. I heard a band start up in the next room and had a final game; handing the table over to the latest challenger.

There was a lineup to get into the dance, but it moved along quickly and soon we stepped through a pair of wooden doors and were inside. The bar was on the other side of the room and I followed Ray across where we bought two pots[2] of beer. A four piece band was playing but there were only a couple of people dancing; most were at the bar or sitting at tables located around its

———

2   The "pot" is local slang in Queensland for a ten ounce or 285ml glass. It is said that Queenslanders prefer a smaller glass because the hot temperatures can warm up the beer. You can drink a pot quickly and enjoy chilled beer all the way down.

perimeter. Someone tapped me on the shoulder; it was Claudia.

"Hello." she said.

"Hi Claudia." Ray and I said together and we all laughed.

"We've got a table over there." she pointed vaguely across the room; "Want to come and join us?"

"Sure thing." I replied and we followed her across the dance floor. Claudia wasn't wearing her conservative Woolworth uniform this time; she had on a shirt, short shorts and a pair of canvas sneakers.

Ray leaned in over my shoulder and whispered, "Nice legs Stevie."

She found us a couple of seats, introduced us to some of her friends and we chatted, drank some beers and had a good time. I soon realised that, for now, we were minor celebrities; the new boys in town. Many of the people at our table had attended local schools and grown up together in Mount Isa; at its heart the city was a country town where families knew their neighbours by name and enjoyed a variety of social interaction. For our new friends, Ray and I were from the glamorous Gold Coast and that gave us a certain status. It was novel for me because on the Gold Coast I had not experienced being invited so openly, into new groups. Often, people did not know their neighbours well, if at all, and many had come from somewhere else to work the tourist season and stay for a few months before moving on. Once again I was reminded of Port Hedland where people were more inclined to connect and form relationships, and there was a strong sense of community. I was enjoying the attention and glancing over, so was Ray as he chatted to a pretty brunette.

As it got closer to the eight o'clock closing-time, the dance floor became really popular. People had been drinking for a few hours now and their inhibitions had fallen away, including mine. I asked Claudia for a dance and Ray got one of the other girls up; it ended up that most of our table came with us and we all danced around together; the wooden dance floor took up about half the room so there was plenty of space. Just before closing time there was a rush for the bar while the band played their last songs, then, the room's main lights flickered on and reluctantly, blinking in the unfamiliar brightness, we all made our way outdoors.

A large crowd of people stood outside talking, laughing and some smoking; it seemed that no one really wanted to go home. We told our new found friends that we'd be working out bush during the week but would meet them again when we were back in town. Gradually everyone dispersed and the Sunday Session was over for another week.

When I got home I noticed the small back and white television we had in the corner of our lounge room; had I really watched almost zero TV since leaving the Gold Coast? Curious, I turned the large plastic dial, switched it on and was presented with a grey-scale test pattern and some white noise; ITQ-8 Mount Isa was done for the night. I turned the set off and got ready for bed.

Later in my room, lying in bed and looking up towards the ceiling I played the evening across my mind's screen

132

and smiled in the dark; I'd had a really good night and danced with a nice girl.

I hadn't had much experience with women. My first and only sex was with Helen on the HR's back seat; parked in the Grand Hotel's carpark at Labrador about two months ago. She was chubby, easy and had big boobs; I'd tagged her with the nickname "Helen's Melons." We were both drunk and I'd fallen asleep; it had taken her an hour to wake me up so I could drive her home; not a great start. Even so it had been fun and I wanted some more of that; a lot more! Claudia was pretty and fun too, and I was really looking forward to seeing her again.

"Things are moving along very nicely." I said quietly to myself as I drifted off to sleep, but Ray was about to stick his big oar in and stir it all up.

Chapter 11

Settling In

The following week saw us working out at Kajabbi again, expanding the grid and taking magnetic readings. Ten days later, we returned to town on Wednesday afternoon for our four days off. Driving home I noticed the HR had begun to develop a knock in the engine; hardly noticeable at first but becoming more insistent— hotting up a motor that had already driven over 100,000 kilometres and then driving it like a boy racer had taken its toll—I needed to find another vehicle, repair or recondition the existing motor. Changing the car seemed a much more interesting proposition to me.

On Friday I went and visited the auto wreckers. From previous visits I knew that they often had cars for sale; fully working, drivable cars that they had fixed up and registered. There were several offerings and I took a fancy to a cream, 1968 Mini Mark II, two door sedan. I took it out for a test drive, they agreed to take my Holden as a trade in and so I bought it and drove home. It was a blast! The Mini certainly lived up to its reputation and, 'sat on the road like a brick,' with hardly any body roll during cornering, and its 848cc, four cylinder engine powered the small body well. When I got home, Ray and I took the car out for a run and slid around several corners while managing to keep all four wheels on the road, and its handbrake slides were terrific. Woohoo! Henceforth it became known as The Brick; not the most flattering of names but apt.

Back on the Gold Coast we would have taken a newly acquired car through the Southport Esses. The Esses were a two kilometre long section of road that ran along Southport High School's west boundary, officially named Brooke Avenue. Beginning at the Smith Street intersection, there were four sweeping curves on a downhill run finishing around Deakin Avenue; perfect to test handling, braking, gear box and general performance. The Esses were deceptive, with steep cambers and deep gutters to handle rainwater runoff; I recall a mate who'd bent his car's suspension when he slid into one of those gutters. Ouch! But we hadn't found any esses in Mount Isa yet and made do with wide, open intersections and loose gravel edges. The Brick boasted a four-on-the-floor manual gearshift, bucket seats and a big round speedometer. Nice! I pulled into a petrol station on the way home, filled it up for just a few dollars and we got back in time to get ready for Friday night out.

The Irish Club had a lounge; officially it was Kennelly's Piano Lounge, named after one of the club's founders, but everyone knew it as the Piano Bar. I dressed up in a collared shirt, jeans and shoes and we went along to find it was very nice with carpet, low comfy seating and

135

timber panelling. Ray stepped up his game and ordered a rum and coke, while I tried an imported bottled beer. We chatted and around eight o'clock a well dressed man began playing the piano. It was very pleasant and as the evening rolled on he introduced a few of those old favourites that everyone who has had a few drinks think they can sing. It began innocently enough with *When Irish Eyes are Smiling*, followed by *My Old Man's a Dustman* and later, *It's a Long Way to Tipperary*. Ray and I, being young people, raised our eyebrows a little at these old songs, but before the night was done found ourselves up at the piano with Victor singing it out with the best of them! After that, Friday night at the Piano Bar with our new friend Victor became a regular thing; with voices well lubricated and our ears immune to any semblance of key, pitch or tone, we sung our way through many an evening.

Victor was slim, wore thick black-framed glasses, had big fuzzy hair, always dressed well and was as gay as they come, and a very kind man. It came as a surprise to learn that this rugged mining town had a thriving gay community, and was responsible for much of the theatre and entertainment in the area. Through Victor, I found out about the Mount Isa Theatrical Society (MITS) and also discovered that the gays held some of the best parties in town. And while I was not gay, they didn't seem to mind at all; it was through their events and friendship that I met many un-gay girls, policemen, councillors, teachers and a variety of local people.

Victor had the largest penis I had ever seen. One night at the Piano Bar I was in the men's toilet standing at the urinal when Victor came rushing in during a break, in between sets. I glanced over to make a comment about the evening just as he pulled what seemed to be a very large snake out of his trousers; he used two hands to aim the thing and then rolled his eyes in relief as his bladder began to empty.

"Ah that's good." he said, "I don't get too many breaks on a Friday night."

When the torrent finally subsided he shook his snake, put it away and then dashed off to get a drink before playing again. The title of the 1966 movie, *A Funny Thing Happened to Me on the Way to the Forum*, popped into my head. I reframed it,

"A funny thing happened to me in the men's toilet at the Irish Club. "

"Really?"

"Yes."

"What happened dear?

"Well, funny you should ask. There I was, innocently minding my own business, when … "

"When what?"

"Give me a minute to get the story out dear."

"Oh. Sorry."

"As I was saying, before I was so rudely interrupted."

"I said I was sorry."

"Accepted."

"Thank you."

"Shall I continue?"

"Please do dear, it's fascinating."

"Well, as I said, there I was innocently minding my own business ... "

I laughed quietly with my reflection in the mirror and then returned to join the happily intoxicated throng gathered around Victor's piano.

Saturday was "DD," Domestics Day. Ray and I handled our domestics; we could have gone food shopping or done our laundry on Thursday or Friday but, somehow, Saturday seemed the right day for these tasks. I met up with Mick in the backyard while I was doing my laundry.

"I never do laundry," he said.

I was surprised, "Really? What do you do with your clothes?"

"Well, mostly I wear navy-blue shorts and tank tops driving trucks, so when I've worn the clothes a few times I just go and buy another set. It saves on laundry powder!" he laughed at his own joke.

"Wow." I replied in amazement, "What do you do with the used clothes?"

He took me into his place and showed me the second bedroom; there in the corner was a one metre high pile of navy-blue clothes.

"I guess I'll get around to them one day; not!"

Mick said he was working on Sunday and invited me to take a run with him in the truck; it seemed like a fun idea and I accepted. Not quite having the income to follow his clothing example, I left to finish off my laundry. When all of the clothes were clean and hung out to dry I took The Brick over to Eden's place, to show him the new car, and then we went over to the Irish Club for beers and some pool; Ray found us there later and we all had a good afternoon.

On Sunday morning Mick knocked on the door and handed me a motorbike helmet; he had a Honda CB750 and drove us out to a large yard where the trucks were kept. He lifted the cab on a white Nissan UD and took me through all his safety checks; I was interested in the big diesel motor where he checked oil levels, radiator, steering and then went around all the tyres. When he was all done, Mick backed the UD up to a pig trailer, coupled it up and we set off. The rig was not loaded yet, so the ride was fairly firm and I was grateful for my sprung seat. Our first stop was not far, just a few hundred metres away at a fuel station; with the tanks full of diesel Mick drove us out to a quarry where the tipper and pig were loaded. The UD sat a lot surer on the road now with its suspension compressed and tyres grasping the bitumen strongly. He worked its gearbox skillfully to get us up to speed.

We did several runs through the morning out to a Main Roads project and then, on the way back to Mount Isa, trouble struck.

"Whoa; the steering is getting bloody heavy!" Mick complained and pulled the rig over onto a gravel verge.

We found that one of the high-pressure power steering hoses had ruptured and every time he turned the wheel, hot oil squirted out; and the oil reservoir was getting low. He elected to drive on but before long the truck required both of us to turn its steering wheel. When we finally got back into the yard we were dripping with sweat. There was not much more that could be done until the hose was repaired. Mick called in the job, we called it a day and biked home to down a couple of very welcome cold stubbies on the front steps.

Later, after we had showered and put on some clean clothes, Mick, Ray and I went to the Irish Club for dinner. Steak, chips and salad went down well and then we wandered into the dance. Mick went off to talk with some mates he'd spotted and I noticed our table of regular boys and girls; we went over to say hello. Soon they had made some room, found us a couple of chairs and we joined them for the night. Ray had met a girl called Margaret, shortened to Margie; she was small, neat, had long brunette hair and was very pretty, and they seemed to be getting on well. I talked with Claudia, got introduced to Margie's best friend Debbie whose Dad worked as a shift boss with Mount Isa Mines and met various other people. I found out that Margie's full name was Margaret Thatcher, same as the United Kingdom's Conservative Party leader, and had some fun with that association.

"Tell me Ms. Thatcher," I said in my best British accent, "just how conservative are you?"

We drank, danced, made a lot of noise and mess at our table, and had a great time but all too soon the lights flickered on and the Sunday Session was over for another week. Everyone moved outside, there was a brief stir in the crowd as two drunken lads pushed each other around and had a scuffle but it soon settled, and then we said good night and went home.

I had only been in Mount Isa for six weeks but it seemed much longer. Ray and I were making friends and finding our way around; we had jobs, a flat, were learning about living in the bush and gaining new skills, and we had met some nice girls ... life was good here and the dream had begun to fade a little. We still talked about XU1s and HTOs but there was so much more going on in our lives now that cars and Darwin didn't get quite as much attention as before. We were flat-out, creating our lives in Mount Isa and it was good; very good. It seemed too that Ray and Margie had really connected as she had asked him around for dinner, to meet the folks. Apparently, with girl friends comes responsibility and new requirements, and just before the symbolic dinner event Ray came home with a surprise; a big orange one.

Chapter 12

McLeod Hill

Ray and I were working in town for the first two days of the week and then Sid was taking us out to McLeod Hill for three days, returning on Saturday morning. McLeod Hill was the name of a mine out near Gunpowder Creek, to the north of Mount Isa, and Union Minière had done significant work in the area and established a working camp. We were to check the campsite over and make sure all was in good order and bring back some gear that was required in town. Ken had also requested new magnetometer work over a small area. The three of us went shopping for supplies on Tuesday afternoon and then prepared the vehicles ready for an early start.

We drove out of the yard just after eight o'clock the next morning and followed Ryan Road to its end, joining the Barkly Highway at Landskey. Then drove northwest for about 90 kilometers before turning right onto a wide graded track called McNamara Road; Sid said we had another 50 kilometres to go from here.

Within a few minutes we had left the bitumen behind and were once again in the bush. Ray was driving the second vehicle and dropped back a good 50 metres to clear our dust cloud.

McLeod Hill was one of a group of mines, including Lady Annie, Mount Kelly, Lady Agnes, The Drifter and others located to the west of Gunpowder Creek. These were all copper mines though some uranium was known to be in the area. The first signs of copper were found here in the early 1900s with Lady Annie having been the most significant discovery, producing some 600 tons of copper to date. All of the mines had been worked intermittently until a copper smelter was established at Mount Isa in 1953, the existing lead smelter was converted using secondhand equipment from Mount Cuthbert and as a result production from the area rose sharply until 1957, when there was a drop in base metal prices. The McLeod Hill lode was reported to have been first discovered in 1942; the mine had an existing shaft sunk to a depth of 33 metres, though no work had been done there for 20 years.

Union Minière had acquired the rights to explore and their team had identified a good sized resource with a grade of 3.5% copper. There was an on-site camp made up of demountable buildings and at one time housed 20 or so people, but now it was under care and maintenance until the company decided what to do next. I wondered whether they would hold it until the price of copper increased and then develop the ore body themselves, or sell it on.

The drive out to camp was subject to numerous creek crossings and there were stretches where the road had been boggy, suffered attempted crossings and had become deeply rutted. Now, in the dry season, the ruts had hardened and required careful negotiation. We had bought a Land Rover and Yellow Terror with us; the one-tonner was not loaded and being light at its rear end, could bounce violently if the vehicle hit pot holes or ruts at speed.

"We can't get out here during the wet;" Sid explained, "these roads get washed out by the creeks. You can see where people have tried and just dug up the surface. Even with a good four wheel drive the area is generally off-limits December through March, and even then it can take a while until repairs and hopefully regrading is done."

We crossed over Johnson Creek and later traversed the Buckley River, which was dry, shallow and not obviously different from the surrounding bush, and there were many little dirt tracks shooting off to the left and right along the way; some ending after just a few metres and others disappearing in amongst the shrubs.

"Small mines and prospects are dotted all over this area." Sid commented. " Most of the copper lodes are small deposits of minerals such as: malachite, chrysocolla, cuprite, azurite, tenorite and some chalcocite; the host-rocks are mainly dolomites and shales with the copper occurring as fine veins or cavity fillings."

I was impressed with his breadth of knowledge and told him so.

Sid smiled and replied, "When you've been doing this for a while you will pick up the lingo Steve; Ken and Dick will tell you a lot about geology if you ask them."

I saw two man-made ponds located alongside the road; they were fed by bore holes drilled down into groundwater reservoirs. The green ponds were soon lost in the dust billowing up from our tyres and though our journey through the low flat landscape was largely unremarkable, there were a few exceptions. At one point all of the immediate vegetation disappeared and we entered into a four kilometre wide bowl of what seemed to be desert, but as I looked closer I could see regularly spaced undulations in its bare red surface, similar to the pattern that waves make. I asked Sid about it.

"Yes." he said, "It's an unnamed dry lake bed. During the wet season it fills and expands out to about five square kilometers in size; not very deep though."

Shortly after Dust Bowl Lake, which I had unofficially named, the road swung towards the west and then continued almost dead north for about five kilometres, where it petered out and turned into a narrow bush track. Sid slowed down and we crunched and bounced through Saga Creek's wide, broken-shale flood plain, eventually turning east onto another track and making our way to the McLeod Hill campsite.

The camp was set-in amongst a small copse of trees and centred around a covered recreational area with benches, chairs, barbecue and the remnants of a dart board. To the south were several buildings—sleeping quarters—and beyond those a roofed shelter containing the site's diesel powered generator. East of centre was an ablutions block with toilets, showers and basins, and a canteen building adjacent. To the north were several offices and stores, and beyond the camp's perimeter I could see a large metal shed with a substantial chain and lock securing its double doors.

Most of the buildings were the white demountable types that I'd seen on many building sites, used as lunch rooms or offices. The camp's centre featured a large timber framed pergola covered with shade cloth and metal sheeting providing relief from the sun. When the camp was eventually broken down and removed, the bush would easily reclaim the space and within a few seasons all traces of the men and women who worked here would be gone; except for the buried rubbish pits that curious fossickers often look for in old settlements.

Sid produced a large ring of keys and opened up a room each for us to sleep in. They featured air conditioning, full sized beds, a wardrobe and mirror; compared to our utilitarian tents at Kajabbi, it was five star!

Luxury! Luxury!" I called out loudly, mimicking Monty Python's famous Yorkshiremen[1] skit, "You know, when I was working in Kajabbi we had to live in tent, deep in bush, surrounded by wild animals!"

"Aye." agreed Ray

"Aye." I replied.

---

1   The "Four Yorkshiremen" sketch was a popular episode of the television comedy show *Monty Python's Flying Circus* that came out in 1967, where four men discuss how deprived their childhoods were, each trying to outdo the other.

"And take paper and spade, and go out into bush to crap; surrounded by wild animals. And during day, we would work under glaring sun putting stakes in the hard, hard ground and later, go back and take readings; magnetic readings, over and over and over again. "

"Aye." said Ray, "And we had to cook our breakfast and dinner over open fire."

"Fire?" said Sid, incredulously, "You were lucky to have fire. In my day fire had not been invented and we had to eat everything raw."

"Aye." said Ray.

"Aye." I replied. "And the hotel, with its cold, cold, beer was miles and miles away. And our pay was so low; a mere pittance that we couldn't afford to buy beer anyway. Except for Victoria Bitter, which was so horrible that they had to give it away for free! "

"Aye." said Ray soberly, "Horrible!"

And then, in perfect unison as if we had rehearsed it, "And you try and tell the young people of today, that, and they won't believe you!"

I was laughing so much that my stomach hurt and Ray had to sit down; Sid was roaring with laughter too. After a while we all got our breath back and could speak again.

"I suppose we should do some work." Sid suggested.

"Aye." said Ray.

"Aye." said I.

"Aye." echoed Sid.

And so, we went off to unload Land Rover, and then hammer stakes into hard, hard ground under glaring sun for mere pittance.

We worked until about four o'clock and then returned to camp, enjoying a cool shower; and no more taking a roll of paper and shovel into the bush to find a private spot. Sid elected to cook on an open fire saying he didn't want to mess up the kitchen for our small group—he really loved being out in the bush camping and the buildings seemed to take some of that away from him—I was good with that as I really enjoyed our chats and tea around the fire with the great star-studded, southern sky glittering high above us.

He took Ray and I for a tour of the camp, explaining all the buildings and their uses, the offices contained two-way radio gear though we'd use the vehicle's equipment to check in at five o'clock. We checked the generator's diesel engine for oil, fuel and water and then fired it up and threw the main power switches; even though it was still day light I could see some of the external lights turn on. Sid opened the big metal shed and swung back its doors to reveal rack after rack of core samples, stacked up nearly to the roof frames.

"Wow!" I said.

"This is the physical proof that we have a good copper deposit here at McLeod Hill." he said proudly, " There's a lot of work sitting there in those racks. We used to have a fair sized team out here." then, somewhat nostalgically, he noted, "It was a good time."

I didn't know a lot about Sid's background, but I did
know that he was from the United Kingdom and had
served in the armed forces; I speculated that he was
Special Services though, mysteriously, he would not
talk about that. He was highly skilled at living, and
perhaps surviving, off the land and it often seemed that
Sid was more at home in the bush than in town. He
was shortish at about 165 centimetres, a little rounded
but very strong with that dependable, hardiness typical
of some English people. Sid lived with his partner, in
town, who had a daughter named Susanna. I didn't
know it then but Susanna was queued to be introduced
later, via another close friend, Mick Campbell.

I unloaded our food from the Land Rover and placed
it into one of the canteen's refrigerators. Ray had
gone off to dig a trench and then collect kindling and
wood; soon he had a fire burning and we all gathered
around and shared a beer while Sid cooked. As the sun
disappeared I enjoyed that special hush that pervades
the bush at dusk; it's when the day hands over to the
night and everything changes.

It was very nice, that night, to sleep in a bed in my
own room with the air conditioner humming quietly in
the background, and off in the distance our generator
reached out with its steady sub-bass rhythm. I got
up during the night, turned off the AC and opened a
window; as the machine's hum dropped away I began
to hear the squeaks, croaks and rustles of the nocturnal
bush. I stood for a while listening, and then returned
to bed not stirring until the sun came silently knocking
and I heard Sid tapping the billy.

We worked through the morning and returned to camp
for lunch; I was curious about McLeod Hill mine and
took a sandwich with me over to the old workings.
It was not hard to find as the area was awash with
discarded rubble that had been pulled out of the earth
and strewn across the landscape. I was standing on a
massive ancient fault that was formed as the planet's
surface had cooled billions of years ago; it was several
hundred metres higher than the adjacent plains and
part of a system of fold belts beginning at Lawn Hill
near the Gregory River, and running in a southeasterly
direction between Mount Isa and Cloncurry, then
continuing on to the ghost town of Selwyn. The geology
supporting most of the mining in the Mount Isa area
was largely contained in three distinct and parallel
provinces:

1. The Western Fold Belt Province, upon which I was
   standing and includes Mount Isa;

2. sandwiched in the middle is the Kalkadoon-Ewen
   Province containing Kajabbi,

3. and then the Eastern Fold Belt Province with the
   town of Cloncurry.

These three massive provinces cover an area in
northwest Queensland of some 50,000 square
kilometres and are known collectively as Mount Isa
Orogen, within this are over 1,800 known deposits.

The focus of McLeod Hill mine was a single one metre
square shaft, diving vertically over 30 metres down into
blackness. There was evidence of a metal ladder having
been fixed to one side, its rusty pins still protruding
out from the shaft walls. I could imagine a tall metal

structure; a hoist frame used to operate a large metal bucket, straddling the hole though long gone now. Copper bearing ore would have been sent off to Mount Isa's smelter, whereas general rubble had been dumped locally. The lighter coloured siltstone shale had cast its stain upon fold's weather darkened surface rocks as it tumbled down inclined slabs to lodge in crevasses and fissures. There were few trees in the area; much of the topsoil had been eroded away exposing broad sections of wind polished rock falling away to the east and the south. A few saplings had taken up residence in pockets of trapped earth, but it was unlikely this area would ever support a covering of local flora. It was barren and the rocks radiated heat absorbed from the sun; I retreated and returned to camp, perhaps underground might be a bit more hospitable but I had my doubts. I returned in time for a long, cool drink and then we went back to work.

Later, in the afternoon, Sid announced that we were all going out for dinner.

"Dinner, Sid?" I queried, "Have you got a nice little Italian restaurant tucked away out here too; you know, with Mama and Papa cooking out the back and the kids up front, serving customers? Mmm, I really fancy some lasagne and garlic bread tonight!"

Sid laughed and explained that he knew some of the geology team working out near Lady Anne and Lady Loretta mines; they had invited us to have a meal in their canteen and so we were going to drive over.

"You mean proper food Sid; cooked in a kitchen?" Ray joked.

"Oy!" replied Sid. "Your next meal at McLeod Hill might be a lot burnt young Raymond."

"What? Like it normally is?"

Sid's eyebrows lowered, his eyes squinted and with jaw clenched he gave Ray his best killer stare!

So sorry. Solly Chef Sid. Very solly." Ray bowed low, managing to combine a Chinese and Indian accent all in the one sentence.

Sid's jaw relaxed enough to allow the sides of his mouth to raise slightly, "All right then, just for you Ray, dinner will be only partially burned as normal."

With the timely mention of dinner we headed back to camp to clean up and put on our *going out clothes*, which were much the same as our working clothes, except a bit cleaner. We all piled into the Land Rover's front seat and took a 40 minute drive through the bush, colored in late afternoon hues and draped in long shadows, and spent a very pleasant couple of hours with Sid's friends. They even shouted us some beers and there was a bonus, ice cream for dessert and no washing up. Woohoo! About nine o'clock we said goodbye to our hosts and Sid successfully navigated us through the darkened bush, back to McLeod Hill. A variety of flying insects were enjoying the camp's outside lights as we pulled in just before ten o'clock. We all headed off to bed because, well, it was quite late for us country folk.

The next morning we finished off Ken's magnetic survey work and returned to camp, then spent the afternoon loading the one tonner with trays of core samples, empty 44 gallon drums and other gear. Somehow, Sid

had managed to hide three tins of Castlemain 4XXX
from us and so we enjoyed a cold beer before dinner.
Ray was chef for the night and I took care of cleaning
up afterwards. Sid found a chess board and offered me
a game; Ray got bored watching our slow paced and
largely silent game and went off to read. We played for
about an hour and Sid proved to be too good; I got
impatient, he took my Queen and then manoeuvered a
winning checkmate. It was a pleasant evening and we
all turned in about nine o'clock.

The next morning, Saturday, we cleaned camp,
shutdown the diesel generator, locked all doors and
made our way back to Mount Isa. Yellow Terror
handled the roads much better now, with a load
onboard, and we arrived back at Union Minière's yard
around midday. Sid said we could unload the vehicles
on Monday, as we were in town the following week.

It was a pay week and Ken had left our wages in the
office; I loved getting those brown paper envelopes full
of cash and tried to leave them unopened for as long as
possible. Ray and I headed home in The Brick, cleaned
up and then spent the afternoon playing pool at the
Irish Club. We were getting really good at the game and
held a table for several hours until our liquid winnings
began to take their toll, simultaneously affecting
coordination and judgement. It was good, though, to
see a long row of shiny twenty cent coins along the rail
as hopeful challengers queued for a chance to knock off
the Kings. Even when our crowns finally slipped off, we
got a few pats on the back and nods acknowledging a
good performance. Yeh! I gave Ray a lift home and then
he borrowed the car to visit ex-prospecting hand Marty,

for a barbecue. I was happy to stay home, watched some television and enjoyed the flat. I opened a stubby, inserted a cassette into the stereo, dug around in the freezer and found sausages, mixed vegetables and ice cream; and cooked up a storm as the Ted Mulry Gang rocked the room with "Jump In My Car."

Later, in bed, my consciousness raised itself a few notches to acknowledge Ray returning home, then I fell deeply and fully into the arms of slow-wave sleep and its blissful neuron silence.

———

Ray and I worked in town the following week but we were scheduled to do a day trip out to McLeod Hill on Saturday; just Ray and I would be going and I asked Claudia if she'd like to come with us. Ray also asked Margie but she was working that morning and couldn't make it. Claudia said, "Yes." and gave me her address and telephone number so I could pick her up. Cool! She lived at 100 East Street with her parents and I went visiting during the week, after work, so they could check me out and make sure I was not some sort of fiendish weirdo. I had ripped my shorts and was grubby from work so didn't make the best impression, but I must have been approved as she was ready on Saturday morning when Ray and I showed up in the mighty Brick.

Their house was setback to the rear of the block and had an attached one bedroom flat that they rented out; Claudia's room was right around at the rear of the house with its own external door. Her Dad, Kurt, had a workshop in the large front yard and there was a good

154

sized vegetable garden built up off the ground. Similar to my family they had immigrated to Australia, though from Eastern Europe; he worked for Mount Isa Mines. Claudia was waiting for us in the front yard, playing with their chestnut-brown bulldog. I bundled her in the back seat of the Mini and we drove off to the Ryan Road yard.

Ray had the yard keys and opened its front gates; we were taking Yellow Terror and it was all ready to go. Sid had given us a map and our mission was to bring some of the 44 gallon drums of diesel and other gear back into town. We had an esky containing lunch and drinks, and set off around nine o'clock. We expected to be back around midafternoon and I was to phone Ken or Dick when we returned to the yard, otherwise one of them would be in at five o'clock to do a radio check and find out where we were.

Claudia had lived in Mount Isa most of her life, but had never been out to a mine, so it was an interesting trip for her. We arrived at the camp around midday and had some lunch; she said she was tired after going out on Friday night and I opened up one of the rooms for her. I was hoping it was an invitation for a bit of fun, but it turned out that she was actually tired and fell asleep easily in the air conditioning. I closed the door and left her to snooze, while Ray and I got busy with our work.

"No luck Stevie?" Ray teased. "No pussy for you today?"

He put his arm around my shoulder and gave a pretend cuddle as we walked over to the fuel store.

"There, there." he grinned and was having such a good time stirring the pot.

"Well, at least she came out today!" I retorted, aiming broadly at Margie's absence.

He missed the jab, "Yes she did Stevie, for a sleep." and laughed.

And with that we got to work, rolling heavy diesel drums up ramps and onto the vehicle's tray, then standing and tying them down securely.

Claudia emerged after about an hour's rest and came to see what we were up to. We finished loading the one tonner while she explored camp, had a look at the mine and its surrounds. When we were done the camp was shut down and everyone piled into the vehicle's front seat to drive back to the yard. Apart from a stop along the Barkly Highway to change a tyre that had blown out we made good time and I reported in to Ken from the yard offices. All done for the day we locked the office door, closed the yard and took Claudia back to her place; she was staying home for the night but I would see her again at the Sunday Session. Ray and I headed home and even though he ribbed me once again I was grateful that he had been there. I was not as confident as he seemed to be with girls and his unwitting chaperone had helped, but I certainly wasn't going to tell him that!

I realised that I was really keen on Claudia but I didn't quite know what to do next. Was she simply being friendly; a friend, or did she want more than that? Was she interested because I was from somewhere else; a novelty item, or was there "a spark" as my Dad would say? Why was my stomach full of butterflies? It was all very intriguing. I'd kissed some girls in high school, had car sex several times with Helen's Mellons but not had a girlfriend before; someone to be with and to care about. I was hoping that Claudia would be my first but I was becoming aware that a relationship was something that both people had to choose and up to now, she hadn't chosen me.

Chapter 13

Lives Changing

The Valiant Charger was introduced by Chrysler Australia in 1971, along with an advertising campaign based on the popular slogan, "Hey Charger." In fact, in the early seventies my somewhat conservative Dad had surprised and delighted the whole family when he brought one home, in fuchsia pink! The two-door, VH coupe was powered by a 215cc six cylinder motor and sold new for under $3,000. When Dad took my sister and I out for a run and put his foot down, I was seriously impressed with the way it pressed me back into the seat and hit 80 kilometres per hour so quickly.

I was also impressed when Ray cruised into our driveway with the 1973 model, a gleaming, orange VJ Charger.

"Raymond! Mate! What have you got there?" I called out enthusiastically as I went to check out his gorgeous new ride. Mick was home too, heard the noise and strolled down to the fence.

"Bloody hell Linwood! A Chrysler? Didn't they have one that was a bit brighter? I'll just go back and get my sunnies so I can actually see what it is."

I couldn't resist and stuck my fingers in the air forming the obligatory, palm out, V shape and said, "Hey. Charger."

Ray played it cool. The tip of his cigarette glowed red, he casually blew a puff of smoke out of the window and replied, "Hey boys."

Then, like a suppressed volcano letting go he roared with laughter, white teeth everywhere, "Whatcha reckon boys?"

Ray swung the car's wide door open, pulled the bonnet release and got out, and like bears to honey we all gathered around the engine bay as he eased up the bonnet; I looked for the prop but he shook his head.

"It's sprung at the hinges Steve; no prop needed."

For the next 20 minutes we inspected every part, sat in every seat; he started the motor and revved it up for us. It was great! I was hoping for a ride; maybe even a drive but Ray was somewhat protective of his new toy.

The next day we cruised to work in Ray's Charger and he got a big reception; there were loud whistles as he pulled up in the yard and everyone came over for a look, and of course there was the usual bonnet raising and engine revving ceremony.

Sid noted the dust that had settled, "Hmm. You'd better get this over to the hose tap Ray and give it a wash;

can't have all this dust on your orange duco. No, no; that won't do at all."

"We won't get any work out of him now," Dick chimed in, "he'll be too busy checking his hair in the reflection."

"I think it will be okay Dick, "responded Irish Ray, "he needs his job to pay for it and fill the hungry beastie with petrol."

Ken sighed, "Well, it's been fun gentlemen but some of us have work to do." and strolled off back to the office.

And with that Ray parked the car and we got on with our day's work.

The next day we drove both our cars to the yard as I was heading out to Kajabbi with Ken and Sid. Ken wanted to review our site and also to get out of the office and into the field. I rode with him and we talked about mining, geology, rocks and dirt. Ken described how the paper work, reports, bookwork and his regular visits to the capital kept him away from the bush; he'd become more of an administrator than a geologist and took every opportunity to strap on his pointy hammer and get back to what he really loved; rocks and dirt.

Ray came and joined us a couple of days later and Ken returned to town. We completed the Kajabbi work and were all going to convoy northwest across the bush to Gunpowder, and then McLeod Hill. There were no established roads and the trip would be navigated with a compass, basing off local landmarks and waterways; the Land Rovers would demonstrate why they had become so popular, world wide, since their early 1948 beginnings. The trip was around 80 kilometres but would take us four or five hours as we'd be in four wheel drive, low gear, a lot of the time; Sid had arranged for us to visit a small working copper mine along the way, where we would stay for dinner and camp in the vehicles overnight. The miners were still on the job when we arrived and I accepted an invitation to go down the shaft in a large bucket and inspect their workings; it would be my first time underground.

The mine shaft was about 60 centimetres in diameter and mostly filled with a rugged metal bucket. Straddling the hole was a simple, three legged headframe with a pulley hanging at its apex. Steel cable ran from the bucket, up around the pulley and down to a diesel motor that wound it around a drum. The bucket only carried one person at a time and I was in first. The diesel came to life with a great puff of black smoke, the bucket bounced as gears were engaged and with a shudder and a creak descended, its metal shoulder squealing as it rubbed past a vertical ladder that I'd not noticed from the surface. The shaft's rock wall was only about 20 centimetres from my face until it eventually widened out some eight metres down where the bucket lurched just short of the ground and came to rest. I looked up and saw a small disk of bright light and blue sky; after that it took a while for my eyes to adjust to the dim underground lighting. I clambered out and yelled up to the operator that I was clear; a few seconds later the bucket jerked up and then began its slow assent back up to the surface. I was in the earth.

My mind flashed to Thorin Oakenshield and his company of dwarfs described in Tolkien's book *The Hobbit*; I could almost hear them singing as they worked deep down in the mines under their mountain home.

> "The dwarves of yore made mighty spells,
> While hammers fell like ringing bells
> In places deep, where dark things sleep,
> In hollow halls beneath the fells."— J. R. R.
> Tolkien, Misty Mountain

As the bucket disappeared its shadow extinguished much of the natural light; faint voices reached my ears and I realised the drillers were working farther out in the mine, their sounds muffled by the massive rock separating us. I was standing on a leveled rock bench, at its far edge a pair of ladder rails poked up above the floor leading down to an access drive and adjacent, there was a narrow loading ramp. While I was aware of the miners and someone descending in the bucket, there was an unusual and imposing quiet; all the noises of the surface world were absent and it reminded me of the atmosphere that was created in great cathedrals, but more intense. I waited for the others.

Ray was next, then Sid stepped out of the bucket and led us around to where the drillers were working. Their operation was much cruder than I'd expected; a single pneumatic hand-drill lay on the rubble at the miner's feet as they plugged the holes they'd drilled with paper-wrapped sticks of gelignite, tamping them down with a wooden rod; lines of Cordex[1] hung out of the rock face like thick spaghetti, waiting to be connected to a firing

---

1   'Cordex' is a trade name for a detonation cord product, which has slipped into use as a generic term for this type of material.

line. The two men wore tough cargo pants and boots, their singlets were stained with sweat and dirt and faces greasy with rock dust. There wasn't room for all of us at the face and Sid went forward to talk with the men; as I watched they pulled a light close to the rock and pointed at the veining and the word "chalcopyrite" drifted back and later "gold." I left the others and walked further on along the main access drive into an older part of the mine and noticed a shovel that looked like it had been leaning there for a long time, its metal blade was in several centimetres of water and looked like it was edged with copper; old railway lines too were tinged with green. A single strand of lights that was threaded along the ceiling, terminated and I decided not to explore the inky blackness in front of me and returned to the others.

"It's a small operation but they're pulling a good grade of copper, and some gold;" said Sid, "both metals are often found together. Sometimes the gold yield will pay the cost of mining and so the copper is pure profit."

"Is it just those two working the mine Sid?" I asked.

"No." he replied, "They've got two shifts running; the men work and live at the mine site for seven days and then get a couple of days off back in town. No drinking on site so the Kalkadoon does quite well."

"I'll bet!" laughed Ray.

"Come on. Let's get topside and clean up; it will be dinner time soon. They've nearly finished charging the face."

As my head emerged into the late afternoon light, eyes blinking, I took in a long, deep breath of relatively cool air. My shirt was soaked with sweat, brought on by the mine's high humidity and musty atmosphere. I poured a drink of water from a canteen hanging on the headframe and sipped while waiting for the others. We all hung around the shaft until the miners were brought up; when everyone was accounted for they connected a couple of wires to a blasting box and without ceremony pressed the red button. The earth thumped beneath our feet and the sharp crackle of explosives was followed by a pressure wave of air and dust that vented up out of the shaft.

"Always a good sign." one of the miners noted, grinning widely at us. "Let's get cleaned up boys, nearly time for a feed!"

And with that we all headed off to line up for a turn in the camp's two showers. These were crudely formed of corrugated iron sheets wrapped around a timber frame and nailed in place. The water was hot, feeding down from a tank that had sat in the sun all day, but it did the job. Refreshed and with a change of clothes we made our way into the mess and sat down to chat with the men and share their food. The cook served up lamb chops with beans, peas and mashed potatoes; there were tall stacks of white buttered bread on the tables to soak up the gravy, a huge steaming tea pot and rice pudding for dessert.

"Maybe we should get one of these places at our camp site Sid," Ray suggested, "and give up on the old trench fire and billy."

Sid slowly shook his head from side-to-side and looked up to the ceiling, his right hand raised palm up, "Dream on young Raymond, dream on." came the expected reply.

There were a few chuckles around the table; it seemed that Sid's love of open camping was well known. When everybody was full and we were all talked out, the three of us said good night to our hosts and walked over to where the vehicles were parked; we emptied out the Land Rovers, threw our sleeping bags in the back and soon enough were fast asleep.

The sky was clear of clouds and it was cool when we woke but cook had his big pot full of steaming tea and we helped ourselves to cereal and toast. The miners and crew were also getting their breakfast and preparing for another day underground. We had finished eating and were saying goodbye when the cook called out.

"Oy! Wait up boys."

He came out of his alcove kitchen and handed over several paper bags packed with sandwiches that he'd made for our lunch. Wow; that was nice. A little embarrassed at our enthusiastic thanks, he quickly shook hands and returned to the kitchen.

We drove off into the early morning and resumed our northwest trek; Sid guided the two vehicles over the Western Fold Belt, navigating rocky canyons, creek beds, narrow bush tracks and flatlands until we reached the Gunpowder area and turned southwest towards McLeod Hill. It was such a blast, four wheel driving across extraordinary country with Sid using a map and compass to keep us on track. The Land Rovers never missed a beat and I learned a whole new set of driving skills that morning. Exhilarated, we drove into the familiar McLeod Hill camp and set about unpacking our gear before enjoying cook's gift of sandwiches, which had kept cool and fresh in the onboard refrigerator. That afternoon we loaded the vehicles with gear to be returned to town and then set off for Mount Isa; Sid pulled us over at five o'clock for a quick radio check-in and 50 minutes later we pulled into the Ryan Road yard.

———————

On the weekend a strange thing happened; it was a first for me and perhaps for Ray too. It affected our friendship and was a catalyst for change in both our lives.

We'd been out socialising with our group of friends at the Irish Club; for some reason or other Ray and I had taken separate cars. In fact, I had bought another car: the Mini's brakes had ceased working and I'd been making do with its handbrake, I'd jury-rigged the car's defunct start button with two wires coming up through the floor, and one crazy night Ray and I had driven to the pub with one flat tyre and managed to roll it off its rim on the way home; we had continued on regardless of the hail of sparks and smoke spitting out from the front end. So, The Brick had gone off with a mate who wanted to turn it into a bush basher; sold for $80 cash. Irish Ray at work drove a company car; a HT Holden station wagon that they were replacing. Ken sold it to me for its trade-in value of $200 and let me pay it off over several pay periods. Everything worked, the body was straight and clean, its tyres were near new and the motor was a 179cc six cylinder. Good to go!

Towards the end of the evening I'd been talking with some new people and lost track of Ray and our other friends; I drove home alone and Ray did not show up for another hour or so.

"Where have you been?" I asked with a wink and a grin.

"I gave Margie and Claudia a lift home." Ray replied scratching his head. Then, "Phew. I'm bushed. Going to bed. Night."

"Night mate." I said.

And with that he went into his room. I was finishing up the kitchen before I went to bed, when he came out again.

"Hey. You know mate. I'm really sorry." Ray began.

I was quite bemused having no idea what he was talking about, but then it all tumbled out.

"I took Claudia home tonight after I'd dropped off Margie, and I know you really like her but we had sex in the back of my car. When I came home and saw you I felt really bad. We'd all been drinking and it just happened. I wanted to do it with her again but she said, 'No. The next one's for Steve.' So she's yours mate, but you need to grab her. I wanted you to know. We're mates and it seemed the right thing to tell you about it. So, sorry but … ."

His voice trailed off and then Ray glanced up at me, like he was expecting something, a reaction, then he

167

shrugged his shoulders, said good night again and went back into his room.

I finished cleaning up the kitchen and took the rubbish bin out; and stood out in the driveway for a while thinking about what Ray had said. I wasn't upset, sad or angry but it seemed that he was expecting it. Should I be upset with him? Was that how this worked?. I mean, my best mate had just shagged the woman I was really interested in, and even though I wasn't going out with her he should have known better; right? Mates don't shag your woman; do they? Perhaps this was a bigger deal than I realised; perhaps I should be upset and maybe I should let him know about it.

So, I decided I'd better make myself angry and teach him a lesson; let him know I was not happy about this and make sure he didn't do it again. I stormed into the flat slamming the front door and drop-kicked the empty rubbish bin across the room while swearing to myself, "Fucking Ray! What a mongrel act! The bastard!" The plastic bin bounced off the far wall and fell to the floor; the flat was dead quiet and in my head I heard, "Do more." I went outside and kicked-in the fly-screen door, making a big noise, then went back inside where I picked up my sleeping bag and went out again kicking the door open on the way. When I got to the station wagon I folded down the station wagon's back seat and climbed in; I certainly wasn't going to sleep in the same place as that rotten louse Ray! I stretched out, laughed to myself at all of the drama and was asleep in minutes.

The next morning my back hurt and my head was fuzzy, "Ouch!"

The early morning sun was streaming in through the HT's windows and my body was suffering the effects of an uncomfortable, unforgiving mattress. I opened a door, climbed out and stretched in the driveway; a stray dog that had come up from the river was sniffing around the rubbish bins. I picked up a rock, vaguely threw it in his direction, then gathered my sleeping bag and walked up to the flat. The screen door's lower plywood panel was broken and the fly-wire had torn at the top; our front door was still open and I went in and filled up the kettle with water for coffee; Ray wasn't up yet.

He must have woken with the sound of boiling water and came out of his room, "G'day mate." I said, "Like a coffee?"

Ray coughed a couple of times and then replied, "Yeh. That would be great. Thanks." and went off to use the bathroom.

I heard the toilet flush and then he came into the kitchen again, "Whoa! That was a weird night. I was worried about you and jammed a chair up against my bedroom door. I thought you might be coming in to get me!"

I stirred in two teaspoons of sugar and then handed him a mug of steaming coffee, "Really? Ha-ha! Yeh. It was a pretty weird night." and that was the last either of us ever said about it.

We went outside, sat on the steps and took in some sunshine; it was very nice to sit there in the quiet of the morning, listening to the birds chatter, not saying much; Ray lit up a cigarette and tobacco smoke drifted

169

serenely across the yard. It had been a weird night but I'd come away with questions and a new awareness.

Firstly, up until now, I'd not experienced someone else sleeping with the girl I thought was mine, and I'd not had a reaction to it. In fact, I'd made one up but Ray had expected a reaction. Somewhere in his life, had he some experience of this, perhaps observing other people, and he already knew what it was like?

Secondly, did our past experiences not only influence the way we acted, but also what we expected others to do in similar circumstances? And the experience didn't have to be personal as I'd tapped into Ray's expectation, which he'd borrowed from someone else in his past. Was all emotion a learned behavior? Did the image of the past, receding in my rearview mirror actually come with me into the future?

And the third thing really intrigued me. I now knew that I could consciously create anger and affect someone else with it, without actually being angry.

The choices we had made that night catalysed significant change in our lives, resulting in two key events: Margaret, who somehow found out about Ray's steamy night of passion on the back seat of his Charger made her move to claim him, before someone else did; and I officially asked Claudia out and within a few months we were living together in our own flat!

Chapter 14

Long Time Gone

From the cusp to its wide, wide base the sky was enormous. I had not seen a sky so immense before that my vision could not encompass it and everywhere I looked, there it was. Though I could not see them, the old mine workings of Mount Elliot were strong in my awareness, sitting in darkness behind. It too called out for attention, the ghosts of past years bound to shattered stone and decaying timbers. But my eyes were fixed on two stars, Shaula and Lasath. Together they formed the needle point of Scorpio's sting, brushing dangerously close to the horizon and though over 500 light years away, they were unmistakable and brilliantly clear.

Covering vast distances in incidental seconds my eyes left the animal's lethal aculeus and traced east across a great curved tail, up into its abdomen where a star named simply as the fifth letter of the Greek alphabet indicated spiny but powerful legs branching out left and right. Along the upward journey to Antares, a further three pairs revealed themselves; pointed tips piercing, penetrating, securing.

Antares, the bright heart star flushed with pink, beat insistently upon the light receptors of my eyes, drawing attention to two colossal claws crowned with armored pincers that curved out and up, coming to rest near Dschubba, the delta star. The mighty arachnid needed no venom or sting that night, I was already paralyzed.

Sid, too, had been watching quietly and even Ray was silent; content to smoke and sip his tea.

Sid spoke softly, "Few white people would have seen this view Steve; at its peak in 1918 there were between 1,000 to 1,500 who worked here and lived nearby in Selwyn while the mine was active, and they have all passed on now."

"It is an amazing view Sidney," I replied, it's quiet now but I can imagine this was a busy place at one time."

Similar to other Queensland towns, rivers and landmarks, Selwyn Ranges and the township of Selwyn were named after someone who had never seen them and lived 1000s of kilometres away. Alfred Selwyn was Victoria's Government Geologist, and the explorer William Hodgkinson immortalised his name in 1876.

Some 20 years later James Elliott was prospecting and discovered a conical hill about 90 kilometres south of Cloncurry that yielded copper, and he took out a mining lease; lacking the funds to develop a mine he sold it on. A shaft was sunk to 16 metres in 1901 and the mine was bought by an enterprising Scot, John Moffat, who floated a new company on Melbourne's

Stock Exchange in 1906. Mount Elliot commanded the attention of British investors who took over the venture and floated Mount Elliott Limited in London.

World prices for copper had been rising steadily on speculation of war, reaching £100 per ton and with new rail links planned for the area, three large companies began to dominate mining and smelting activities in the Cloncurry copper fields: Mount Elliott Limited, Hampden-Cloncurry Copper Mines Limited and Mount Cuthbert No Liability.

A small smelter was erected in 1906 and by August 1910 the general manager William Corbould had built and fired Mount Elliot's new smelters, producing £130,000 of copper by the year's end. Up until 1910 no other mine had made a profit and within a few months the town of Selwyn was under construction, its population swelling to 1,000 inhabitants.

Selwyn boasted four hotels; there was an aerated water manufacturer, three stores, four fruiterers, a butcher, baker, saddler, garage, police, hospital, banks, post office and railway station.

> "On Saturdays and pay nights the streets were monopolised by miners off shift. They fraternised in the "pubs" or in the pool rooms while the women and children fluttered around the shops and stores, glad to be away for a few fleeting hours from the dim light of the kerosene lamps and the overbearing atmosphere of galvanised iron cottages with their myriads of tantalising insects."–P. Fynes-Clinton, The Cloncurry Copperfield

As early as 1912 Mount Elliot was close to exhausting its high-grade ore and acquired additional mines to bolster reserves. Industrial action throughout 1913 rocked the company and management took action to lock out its employees for breach of contract, aggravating the unions. But in 1914 World War I broke out in Europe disrupting world markets, and an agreement was struck where workers would receive half pay until the company could sell its copper. By 1914, with its principal mine all but done, further acquisitions were made to feed the hungry smelters, and shareholders.

War was good for the Cloncurry copper fields, creating strong demand for base metals and the copper price soared to £153 per ton in 1916, though further action by the unions caused a shutdown of Mount Elliott's smelters in 1917. The following year bolstered profits as the smelters treated a record 77,400 tons of ore realising nearly £1.4 million, but in December, as wartime demands decreased the price of copper slumped. Despite a brief 1920 rally in the copper price, Mount Elliott Mine was done and its smelters were finally closed. Selwyn began to empty fast as most workers collected their possessions and left for Townsville. From 1918 - 1920 the town's population had peaked at 1,500 residents, falling sharply to less than 200 by 1921.

Mining towns, it seems, were fickle things that were created to serve one source; one master. Once the source was gone then the town had little reason to exist, becoming a story; history in someone's report or book, or the lost memory of those who once lived there and now were dead.

" The glow that lighted the horizon for miles around with a splendour more spectacular and more realistic than a dozen pyrotechnic displays went out forever."– P. Fynes-Clinton

I looked up at Scorpio again and wondered about the millions of stars that had died; energy exhausted but their light still travelling far out across space long after they had extinguished. What about Selwyn and the mine; was the powerful red glow from its copper smelters still travelling out across space to, one day, be seen by another being on the other side of the Universe?

Mount Isa Mines seemed inexhaustible, probably as Mount Elliott had to its workers, but was it? What would happen when Mineside was no more and its mighty smelters were shut down? And similar to the tall brick chimney standing behind me in the dark, would The Stack; the magician's wand be just another decaying landmark, void of magic?

I must have spoken aloud.

"I don't think Mount Isa will be closing down anytime soon Steve, they've got huge reserves you know." Sid commented.

And with his words, the ghosts of Mount Elliott began to recede; their message, perhaps, delivered for now.

"Yeh. I guess you're right. It's pretty big." I replied." Though one day Sid."

"One day Steve but not today."

I nodded and suddenly was quite tired, "See you tomorrow guys. 'Nite."

It had been an interesting time working with Union Minière this last year and witnessing the litter of abandoned mines first-hand, and to walk amongst their ruins. It had made me realise the folly of expecting something to last forever and the value of being nimble; flexible and able to change. The idea working 40 years for one company and then getting a gold watch was an old one, and the world was different. I would need to be the creator-source of my own life and not expect someone or something else do that for me. I knew that my time with Union Minière was nearly done and something new, a different future beckoned and I was becoming more and more aware of it.

———————

Three alien features dominated the spinifex and eucalyptus landscape: to the left were various mine works surmounting a conical hill that James Elliott might find unrecognisable now, on the right and forward lay a massive black slag heap behind which a tall, red-brick chimney stood; visible from all around. Unseen below the surface, were the empty shafts and drives that once held Mount Elliott's mineral wealth; the main shaft was open to around 200 metres though below that its depth was uncertain, as it had filled with water.

The slag heap lay dark and heavy on the earth like the weathered mass of a rapidly cooled lava stream. Its bevelled edge rose 10 or more metres above the surrounding bush with ragged fissures rippling across the blade, all splayed out from a relatively level but well-pocked oval plateau that with some imagination could have formed the base of a football stadium.

Slag was the by-product of smelting, where crushed ore went through a process of being roasted at high temperature and then smelted to remove impurities. In smelting, these impurities formed a slag which floated on the surface and could be removed to be dumped. It's been estimated that for every ton of copper, about two tons of slag were produced; potentially, Mount Elliott's slag heap weighed over 50,000 tons.

The original 1906 copper smelter was no more, marked only by a red-brick chimney standing tall about 150 metres southwest from the slag. In between the two was a shallow depression; evidence of the first mining activity in 1901; a small open-cut operation. Almost directly south of the slag, about 120 metres away was a conical hill, its base featured remains of the large smelter though the chimney had been struck by lightening and collapsed. Four mighty brick arches, housing the furnace, were positioned low and a crumbling construction of walls, buttresses and platforms stepped up the hill to its summit and the main shaft; its headframe and winding gear long gone. It had been 56 years since mining ceased at Mount Elliott Mine and not one tree or bush had set its roots in that inhospitable slag, preferring instead the dry red earth around its base.

We were working to the southwest of the old mine, adding to a survey that had already been started. Union Minière discovered an anomaly in 1972 based on their magnetometer survey and it was known as the southwest anomaly (SWAN). It took us a couple of days to complete our work during which time Dick joined us. When our work was done we all drove back in convoy; Sid wanted to go via Cloncurry to pick up some gear, and we stopped along the way for a swim.

The Great Australian mine was discovered in 1867 and although being classed as "a mountain of copper" by the geologist Robert Logan Jack, and beginning production in 1885, it had been a largely failed enterprise closing two years later having won only 400 tons of copper. There must have been some more recent open-cut work done but when we arrived it seemed to be a deserted hole in the ground; its weathered benches leading down to a clear turquoise pool, undisturbed and tranquil. Dick drove his Land Rover right down to the lowest dry bench and parked, stripped off all his clothes and dove in naked.

"Jeez Dick," I called out when I got down there, "I forgot to bring my sunglasses; the reflection off your lilly-white Melbourne backside is blinding!"

Dick raised one hand from the water with two dripping fingers making the shape of a "V" and then turned and swam on.

"It's probably a good thing I don't speak sign language Dick." but my jibe fell on deaf ears as the red-headed white whale had already submerged.

I heard a noise, turned, but it was too late; Ray gave me a shove and I tumbled in fully clothed, my hat floating off a few metres with the splash. But Ray was not to escape as Sid was right behind him and soon we were all in, splashing around and enjoying the cool refreshing water. It was quite deep in places but I dove down, managed to touch the bottom and felt the fine light-grey mud that had settled there; a cloud of sediment puffed out as I kicked off for the surface. High up, from a bird's-eye view we must have looked like tiny insects swimming around in a gigantic lake and it was terrific! But evolution was at work and a passing Wedge-tailed Eagle might have witnessed four strange looking white amphibians moving onto the land to dry off in the sun. The eagle would have observed their pale fleshy skins mutate into khaki and cotton before they stood upright, captured metal wagons and drove off as homo sapiens, towards home.

Isn't nature wonderful?

Chapter 15

Kindness in the Rough

"Hello there!" she exclaimed, and gave me a big hug and a kiss. "How was Kajabbi?"

It was good to be home and she looked great; barefoot, brown suntanned legs and wearing a loose shirt tied in a knot at her belly. My hand slid down to rest on the curve of her buttock, pushing out tantalisingly from beneath a pair of high-cut denim shorts.

"It was good," I smiled, kissing her again, "and quite an adventure."

"Yeh?"

"Yeh."

Claudia and I had moved into a flat together; her parents weren't all that happy about it but she had come anyway. It was a simple one bedroom, one bathroom place with combined kitchen, dining and lounge; all of the windows were panels of glass louvres set in galvanised metal frames and there was a back door in the kitchen that opened out onto a concrete pad where the customary Hills Hoist clothes line stood, and a front door on the other side where the lounge was; the roof extended out about 600 millimetres and sheltered a small patio. All the walls were timber framed, lined with cement sheeting and painted pale blue, the floor was covered with marbled linoleum and we loved it; it was ours!

The flat was on Pelican Road and Claudia could walk to the local bakery where she and her Mum worked, as she had done from her parent's house. It was a curious collection of coincidences that Mick Campbell had started going out with a girl named Susanna, who turned out to be Sid's partner's daughter, and they had moved into a flat together a few houses down the road from us! Susanna was the one who, having discovered Mick's pile of work clothes in the second bedroom of his Seventeenth Avenue flat, had washed them all and collected nearly $300 in change and notes from the pockets of his shorts; she was pretty happy about that!

"Sid and I drove over the railway bridge at Kajabbi, in the Land Rover, while the river was in flood!" I said, laying the groundwork for my story, while getting two beers from the refrigerator.

"What? Really?" Claudia looked at me blankly, her brown eyes doing that slightly and very cute unfocussed thing they did, which became progressively more conspicuous with each drink she consumed.

"Yeh. When we got to Kajabbi the Leichhardt was flooding; Sid was driving and put the Rover into four wheel drive and we went in. I could feel the vehicle lifting up off the sand; bouncing along as we went and the water was nearly up to the windows. And then he stopped mid-stream, quickly put it into reverse, backed around and drove across backwards; he said that reverse gear had a lower range than first and we got across the river arse-about."

"Wow!" she said.

"Yeh. Wow. My heart was pumping."

I took a long pull on my beer and continued.

"We went and did our work, breaking down the campsite to bring everything into town, and then drove back to Kajabbi, but the river had risen and we couldn't cross. So Sid and I went to The Kalkadoon to wait a bit and see if the water level would come down, but by mid afternoon it was even higher. Russel, the publican, said we'd have to cross over using the railway bridge and that some miners in a Toyota ute had gone over earlier."

"Over the railway bridge? They are not that wide."

"I know!" I replied, "And it's just the timber sleepers to drive on."

"Whoa."

"So Sid was at the wheel and got us on the line in four wheel drive low, and we drove along the sleepers towards the river. At the bridge, we opened both our doors wide and I hung out one side and he the other to make sure the front wheels stayed on the track; the river was flowing fast, 20 metres deep and just half a metre below us. The problem was that the Land Rover's axles were slightly smaller than the width of the rail tracks and its wheels kept climbing up onto the rails, so Sid was constantly steering off and on the rails and trying to keep it straight. There we were, lurching along from sleeper to sleeper, the engine revving, each with one hand on the steering wheel, leaning out and yelling at each other when a wheel got close to the edge. It was wild!"

I had put my beer down by now as I needed both hands free to enact hanging out the door and steering with one hand, while bouncing up off the chair that I was sitting on.

"Finally, we made it over to the other side but then, because the tyres had gotten so hot they wouldn't grip to steer off the steel tracks, so we had to keep on driving down the railway line bouncing along on those sleepers in four wheel low and hoping there were no trains coming along; because we couldn't get off the damn track!"

"Jeez!" Claudia exclaimed, fully caught up in my story. "What did you guys do?"

"Well, we drove along the line for about two kilometres and came to a set of points, which gave the wheels enough purchase to drive off the line and onto the dirt. Inside the cab, our stuff was all over the place and we had to repack the whole vehicle; then we found our way through the bush and onto the road to come home. It was pretty wild."

She shook her head, I shook my head and we both sipped our beer in silence for a moment.

"I'm glad you made it back okay." she said.

"Me too!"

Claudia looked up at me, her mouth forming a cheeky half grin, "So, get into the shower and let me check that everything is still working, after all that bouncing around."

I laughed and downed my beer, "Yeh. Let's do that."

Claudia was my very first girlfriend and our reasons for getting a flat together were simple, we both wanted more freedom and access to each other, which had proved difficult while she lived with her parents. The relationship seemed to pull out the best and worst of us; everything was intense and being in love was all consuming. Ray and Margie were a couple now and I only saw him at work; these new relationships had almost completely supplanted our Aussie mateship. I thought about how quickly the girls had claimed our attention, time, wallets and even our cars, and how willingly we allowed it. Was it love or sex that intoxicated us so or varying combinations of both?

There was no logic to be found and the sex was fun but with me working away for weeks at a time, Claudia was often home alone. When I was in town it was great but she hated it when I left for another trip away, and we had begun to squabble and fight. Mick and Susanna had come over one day for a coffee and unwittingly came to the rescue; they suggested we all take a weekend trip away to Boulia, for the annual rodeo.

One of Mick's best mates, Greg Summers, was a school teacher in Boulia and we could hang out with them; Claudia and I would sleep in the back of the station wagon and we were all invited to a hāngi party on the

184

Saturday night. It all sounded great, we really liked the idea and Claudia grabbed onto to it enthusiastically; she was very excited about the upcoming trip.

Ray and I were scheduled for a trip out to McLeod Hill; the wet season was easing back and access roads would be open again. We were taking Ken's Land Rover and Yellow Terror and were to bring more gear back into town; the McLeod Hill camp was slowly being broken down and its gear being used on other projects or stored at the yard.

"Take it easy you two; there will be a lot of water lying around and getting bogged is really easy this time of year." Sid cautioned us.

"We'll be fine Sir Sid," I replied, "you have taught us well."

"That may be true," Sid said, "but did you learn anything?"

"Sid!" Ray exclaimed in mock horror, "How can you doubt us? You, our very own bush Dad."

"Go on. Get our of here. And be careful!" He waved us off and we drove out of the yard and turned right onto Ryan Road.

"Remember to check in at five o'clock if you're running late!" Sid called out as we drove off.

I waved out of the window and saw him nod, his glasses catching the sun.

The big wet had been exactly that "Big" and "Wet." I had not been in such a deluge of rain since living in

Port Hedland when the tropical cyclones came visiting.
Mount Isa was transformed into a wetland and I'd
watched the Leichhardt River rage in full flood with
huge trees, animal bodies and various debris smashing
through under the all weather Grace Street bridge
that became the only way to cross over to Mineside.
People told me of the 1974 floods, one of the worst on
record, and that the Gulf Country and huge areas of
Queensland had become vast inland seas. Some 500
people were evacuated from Normanton and Karumba,
while 250 passengers were stranded on the Mount Isa-
to-Townsville rail line and had to be air-lifted out.

> "We were seven weeks without a replacement
> of food, and fruit and vegetables were a thing of
> the past. We had heavy wet seasons but nothing
> what marooned us for months and months
> ..."— Shirley Eckford, Julia Creek

Lake Moondarra was closed, not that many people
could have gotten to it; the Caravan Park on Leichhardt
River Road and its residents became totally isolated as
the causeway disappeared under tonnes of churning
red-brown water. I recalled news reports of Brisbane
in 1974, with water running through the city centre
and nearly 7,000 homes flooded. Mick Campbell
described that he was in Brisbane at the time, in college
with Greg Summers, and had taken a discarded water
damaged television, used a hose to wash the mud out of
it, dried it with a borrowed hair-dryer and got the damn
thing working. Everyone seemed to have one story or
another to tell about the '74 Queensland floods.

Just 500 metres south of the now submerged Isa Street
crossing was Mount Isa Bowls Club, which was located

on a large sand island in the middle of the river; access was by a graded track across the river bed. Often during the wet season the club became isolated when the river rose. The idea was to get the timing right, become entrapped and so have to spend hours and often days at the bar, being unable to report to work due to an Act of God, apparently a legitimate reason to take a sicky. As I listened to the mighty Leichhardt roar past and saw the bowls club's rain smeared lights dancing out in mid stream, I knew I was going to do that one day.

Ray and I had turned off the Barkly Highway and were on the now familiar McNamara Road; almost immediately we could see muddy brown water lying in its gutters and adjacent bush, and splashed through shallow puddles. Someone had been through before us and I could see the gouged out ruts where their tyres had sunk down into the tracks's softer spots; as we progressed the surface material became more unstable, and we drove through large areas of lying water guided only by tufts of bush grass that delineated the edge.

I was in the lead, driving Yellow Terror, when I noticed a nice, well-churned muddy patch up ahead; I slowed and Ray came up behind me. I waited until he was really close and then I floored the accelerator, the engine roared and both rear wheels spun delivering a ragged plume of sticky mud across the Rover's bonnet and windscreen until the Holden's tail began to spin out and I was fish-tailing along the track and picking up speed. I watched the whole thing in my mirrors and laughed out loud when I saw Ray's arm punch up out of the window; his rigid fingers set in a "V" shape signaled a very clear, 'Outram; you bastard!' and it was on!

Stephen Bram

Sid's parting words, "Take it easy you two ... " flew
right out of our heads as we began racing each other
along the muddy track like a couple of deranged rally
drivers. It was such a laugh; the Holden had greater
speed and power but the Rover was sure and steady
over the broken surface. I managed to hold the lead for
a while but the Rover roared past as I was negotiating
a creek crossing and its wake reared up and poured in
through my open window; I could see Ray's clenched
fist up out of his window and the flash of his white
teeth as he glanced back enjoying his dirty work. I
wasn't able to get past the Rover again and followed
Ray as we slid around a corner and turned onto a side
track. I was in close pursuit as we headed for camp but a
couple of kilometres along, Ray lost it.

He must have braked suddenly, trying to avoid dropping
the vehicle's front wheels into a deep mud hole—time
seemed to dilate and it was like watching a slow motion
movie—the Rover's rear end began moving around to
the right and catching up with the front; I saw the two
back tyres bump up in the air and gracefully the whole
vehicle rolled over onto its right side and slid along the
track like a fallen ice skater. I pulled up and turned off
the motor; it was dead quiet and for a couple of seconds
I peered out of my mud splattered windscreen at the
unbelievable view. Then, movement; I saw Ray's hand
grab at an upturned seat, a mop of wild hair appeared in
frame and I flung open my door and sprinted down the
track.

Ray was trying to climb up to the passenger door, which
was now looking up to the sky; I jumped up on to the
vehicle and looked in.

188

"Ray! Mate! Are you all right?" I called out.

The top of his head poked out of the door window, "Can you get the door open?"

I climbed up on top of the Rover and pulled the door handle but it wouldn't release; the door was jammed in its frame.

"You'll have to come out through the window mate." I said.

We were able to open the window fully and he pushed up of the seat and got his shoulders through; I saw his head was bleeding but said nothing about it.

"Come on, you're nearly there."

He eased up and out of the window and rested on the body for a few moments while I looked him over. Ray was pale beneath his tan, he'd banged his head on the door when the Rover hit the track and taken a lot of the force with his shoulder and right side.

"You look like shit mate."

"Thanks buddy." he grinned.

We worked together and got him down off the distressed vehicle and onto the track. Ray sat down on a grass turf and asked if I could find him a cigarette; I climbed back into the Rover, turned off the ignition and located his smokes and matches; I lit one up for him and he took it gratefully pulling smoke deep into his lungs.

Ray glanced over at his Rover, "Jeez Stevie, Ken's not going to be too happy with us."

"Probably not. How are you feeling mate? Can you walk?" I asked.

"Yeh; a bit shaky but I'll be okay."

I inspected his head wound; the cut was bleeding and he winced when I found the egg growing under his hair; Ray's shoulder and right knee were sensitive too.

"You're a bit battered mate. Stay here and finish your smoke. I'll see if I can get the one-tonner past your vehicle; we can go on to McLeod Hill. Okay?"

Ray nodded. "Yeh."

I started up the Holden and began easing it alongside the upturned Rover, two wheels on the track and the other two in water; before I could get past the rear end slid to the right and sunk, its wheels spinning uselessly in mud.

"Damn!"

I got out and found some fallen tree branches, jamming them in under the tyres to provide something to grip on but it did no good; Yellow Terror's wheels spun, slipped off and the car listed further over and settled axel deep in mud. I found it hard to believe that getting our only remaining good vehicle bogged had been so ridiculously easy.

I was exasperated with myself. "Fuck!" I got out and went to talk with Ray.

"We'll have to walk on to camp and call in on the radio at five o'clock. I'll get the battery out of the Holden and we'll take it with us; there may not be a charged one at McLeod."

"Yeh." replied Ray. "Good idea."

It took us an hour and a half to walk to camp, and that car battery got heavier and heavier with every metre I covered. With all the lying water in the area it was humid and we were sweating heavily when, finally, we turned a corner and saw the white buildings; it lifted our spirits to walk into the McLeod Hill camp.

"Woohoo!"

"Yeh." Even Ray, who had been quiet during the walk punched the air, albeit gently.

I put the battery down and stretched my aching shoulders and back.

"I'll go and start the generator. Here's the keys; go and open up. We've got a couple of hours to wait until five."

I handed Ray a set of keys and then walked around to the big diesel. I checked its engine oil and fuel, and then started it without issue. The motor soon settled into a strong steady rhythm and I watched as the pergola's telltale lights flickered on. It felt good to be cocooned in the energy and song of the diesel and have a moment or two to think; I imagined that Ray was chewing over the fact that he'd rolled the boss' Land Rover and I had not been particularly smart bogging our only remaining good vehicle. And we'd blocked the track so no one was going to be able to reach us at camp, which meant another hour and a half walk back, with the Holden's battery. We'd know more after the radio check in and might have to spend the night here; there was probably no food but at least we had a bed. And I wasn't sure how Ray was going, especially with that big bump to his head and his body was probably going to stiffen up with bumps and bruises after being tossed around in the cabin during the roll. I left the generator and went to find him, it would be a good idea to get our story straight when we had to explain what had happened.

"How are you doing mate?" I asked.

Ray was sitting on the steps of the canteen slowly smoking a cigarette.

"My head's sore, and my shoulder; it's worse than a hangover without the fun of drinking."

We laughed quietly and then talked about what had happened.

"We'd better get our story straight; they are going to want to know how it happened." I said.

"Yeh." Ray replied, looking thoughtful and gazing out to the track where we'd walked in.

I knew he was revisiting the accident in his head and I kept quiet.

"I'll say I had a big cough, you know, from the smokes, hit a soft patch and lost it in the mud. It's pretty wet out here."

"Okay." I joined in, "and I bogged the Holden trying to get us through to camp; I didn't realise it was so soft at the track's edge."

"Yeh; that'll do." Ray replied, reaching up and gently feeling the side of his head.

"Let me take a look at that." I said and bent over to inspect his wound. "Come into the canteen and I'll wash it out; there's a first aid kit in there."

I found some cotton wool and saline to clean with and then applied an antiseptic salve to the broken skin. There was a nice big egg just above his ear but we didn't have any ice to put on it, so I placed a soft pad there and wrapped gauze bandage around his head to hold it in place.

"There you go; that will hold it for a while."

"Thanks mate."

I looked around in the cupboards, found tea bags and sugar, and put the kettle on; soon we were sipping hot sweet tea and chatting quietly. Afterwards, Ray opted to go lie down for a while and went off to a cabin. I opened up the radio room, hooked up our car battery and tested the equipment; there wasn't much to do now except wait and I leafed through an old magazine that I'd found in a drawer.

Five o'clock eventually came around and I switched on the camp's two-way radio. We both laughed when we heard Dick's voice crackle out of the speaker, he sounded thin and strangely metallic but it was Dick. Reception was poor and I soon realised that he couldn't hear us. The protocol was to use a system of beeps, one beep was "Yes, " two meant "No."

Dick asked, "Can you hear me? Over."

I beeped once.

"Are you okay. Over."

Two beeps.

"Do you need help? Over."

One beep.

"Do you need someone to come to you? Over."

One beep.

"Is anyone hurt? Over."

One beep.

"Give me one beep for Ray or two beeps for Stephen. Over"

One beep.

"Are you at McLeod Hill camp? Over."

One beep.

"Okay. Understood. I'll come tonight. I can leave in about half hour. Will be with you approximately 20:30 hours. Confirm that you got that, with one beep. Over."

I pressed the button once.

"Good. Understood. Over and out." and he was gone.

I switched the radio off and leaned back in my chair, then looked up at Ray. "We're going to have to walk back, he's not going to get past the two vehicles."

"Yeh." Ray looked at his watch, "Six?"

"Yeh. If we lockup and get away by six o'clock we can meet him on the track."

"Okay."

Ray looked weary, dark circles were forming under his eyes. I went and made him a mug of tea with five heaped teaspoons of sugar in it. He pulled a face after the first sip.

"I'll have a cup of sugar and go easy on the tea please."

The advert for Nestles Quik jumped into my head and I replied, "Drink it Freddy. Drink it."

We both laughed. I left Ray to finish his tea and began closing up the camp, turning the generator off last at six o'clock. It was still light but we took a torch; I hoisted Yellow Terror's battery up on my shoulder and we began the walk back to our vehicles and hopefully to meet Dick. We didn't talk much, occasionally slapped off annoying mosquitos and walked on into the fading light as the bush changed around us; around eight thirty I saw the shapes of the stranded Holden and Rover appear in the torch's light. There wasn't much to do except put the battery back in and wait; Ray lit up a cigarette and I switched the car's parking lights on as Dick would not be expecting to meet us out here.

About nine fifteen I heard an engine and 10 minutes later a pair of lights blazed down the track. The Rover pulled up, Dick swung the door open and got out as we walked over.

"We seems to have done this once before boys. Remember when I first met you; a broken down Holden?" he quipped.

Then, noticing Ray's bandaged head, his normal haughty attitude seemed to disappear; I watched Dick's mask slip and I saw something he'd not shown me before.

Dick placed his hand gently on Ray's shoulder and asked, "How are you Raymond?"

"Not bad. But a bit sore. I got thrown around in the cab and banged my head when she went over."

Dick glanced across at the overturned Land Rover, then back to Ray and stepped in close to carefully check the bandage; he nodded and then turned to me,

"And you Stephen, how are you doing?"

"I'm okay Dick. Tired. We walked to McLeod Hill to do the radio call; took a battery and then came back to meet you here. Hey, thanks for coming out."

He nodded again and then walked back to his vehicle, reaching in over the driver's seat; when he turned back to face us he had three cans of ice cold Victoria Bitter in his hands.

Ray simply said, "Thanks Dick."

There was a lot said in that thanks. It was a moment, the three of us standing on that muddy bush track in a pool of yellow light cast by the Rover's lights; Dick looked at Ray, then me and raised his beer, "Cheers."

"Cheers!"

Condensation from the shiny green can dripped down onto my shirt as I tipped it to my lips and took a long satisfying pull; God it tasted good.

We sipped our beers while Dick casually chatted and asked questions, then he went to work coordinating our rescue. First up we wound out a steel tow cable and hooked one end to Dick's Rover's bull bar and the other onto the rear chassis of the Holden. The bogged vehicle resisted for a moment or two but was no match for the four wheel drive; with a juicy squelch the bog let go and the one-tonner was dragged back onto firm ground. I jumped in, started the engine and parked it further down the track, out of the way. When I returned, Dick nosed his Rover closer to the overturned vehicle and I connected the cable to its chassis. When it was done he backed up slowly, took position centre track and when the cable was taut accelerated backwards; the fallen Rover slid for about half a metre and then suddenly its tyres gripped, the cabin came up off the track and the vehicle slammed onto its four wheels upright.

The driver's side of Ken's Land Rover was a mess; scratched, dented and covered in mud but remarkably the driver's door opened cleanly. I opened the bonnet and checked oil, battery, spark plug leads, brake fluid and had a good look around; it all seemed in good order, and even the lights came on.

"See if it will start." Dick called out.

Ray got in and the motor turned over but wouldn't start; he pumped the accelerator a few time and tried again but it made no difference. Dick got us all to push the vehicle and straighten it up on the track, then eased his Rover in until both bull bars were touching.

"Put it in reverse, Ray and drop the clutch when we get going." he instructed and then began pushing the vehicle backwards.

Dick's headlights flashed and Ray let the clutch out, the tyres bit into gravel and the engine began to turn; after about 10 metres and a cough or two it fired up. He revved the motor a few times and then let it settle down to a steady idle. Dick had parked and we walked over; there were great big grins on all of our faces.

"Bloody vehicle; it's running after all that!" Ray was amazed.

"Yes. That's one of the many reasons we use Land Rovers." Dick said smugly and then yelled out, "Practically indestructible!" We all burst out laughing, our voices bouncing around in the dark but somehow friendlier bush.

"Let's get you home gentlemen."

"Yes." I replied, "That sounds good."

"Yeh." said Ray.

I glanced at my watch in the headlights; it was just after eleven o'clock.

Dick led us home; we put Ray in the middle of our convoy so we could keep an eye on him, and I brought up the tail. We threaded our way along the wet muddy tracks at a much more sedate pace than Ray and I had driven this morning, the Rover's lights cutting through the dark up ahead and spraying out to the sides. At one point, when there was a decent radio signal, Dick called in to base and let Sidney know that we were all okay on our way in and he could go home to bed. I hadn't realised that Sid, our magnificent Sid, had been waiting at the yard all this time in case he was required.

We resumed driving and I thought about Dick, and how people tend to hide some of their greatest capacities until there's an emergency and then they come bubbling up to the surface. Dick had dropped everything, including his normal arrogance, to be something he was not accustomed to being, someone who cared a great deal. Someone who did not care would have sent another person out the next day, would not have thought to bring wonderful cold beers with them and would have never been able to stand on that muddy track with us and calmly observe and assess everything while we drank! Mount Isa was a rough and tumble place and kindness, particularly a man's, might be seen as weakness. Dick's seeming arrogance; his haughtiness, provided the best protection that he could muster to survive in a boisterous frontier environment. But tonight I knew him and would never be fooled again, even though come tomorrow morning his lip would curl up that certain way, his voice would take on that annoying tone and the mask would be fully in place once again.

It was well after midnight when we pulled into the Ryan Road yard and parked our three vehicles side-by-

side. Dick sent us home while he tidied up. Gratefully
we got into our cars and drove off to find a nice warm
shower and get some sleep. Later, as I laid in bed, a few
thoughts about what tomorrow would bring, including
the explanations that Ken would require, floated across
my mind but I pushed them away. I would handle that
tomorrow. Right now a long deep sleep was required.
Claudia stirred and I felt her warm, naked thigh press
against mine as I drifted gratefully into oblivion.

Chapter 16

Mates, Rodeos, Girlfriends

Monday morning was eventful to say the least. When we arrived for work Ken, Dick, Sid and Irish Ray were all gathered around the damaged Land Rover. We parked and Sid waved us over.

Ken seemed calm but I sensed the undercurrents; he looked at us intently and asked, "How's the head Ray?"

"Still a bit sore but it's healing okay." Ray replied, lightly touching his hair.

"Good" said Ken. "So, would you like to tell us all what happened?"

It wasn't really a request and Ray began describing the accident, which didn't take very long.

"I'm really sorry to have damaged your truck Ken," he finished up, "it was muddy and wet, and I just didn't see the pothole until it was too late!"

"You must have been going at some speed to tip a Land Rover over Ray; how fast?" Sid probed.

"Well, not that fast Sid, but it was a fairly straight stretch and the track seemed okay." Ray replied and I sensed he was feeling a lot of pressure.

"Anything that you want to add Stephen?" My heart jumped a bit as Ken's voice suddenly rattled my tympanic membrane.

"Pretty much as Ray said, Ken. I was driving behind so I really only saw the tail go up and over."

Ken nodded. We were all quiet for a while, thoughtful, looking at the Rover; Ken's voice broke into everyone's reverie, "Well, I'm glad that everyone is okay. Ray and Stephen, I'll need you in the office to help fill out some insurance forms and make a statement; come and see me this afternoon. Okay?"

We nodded.

"Sid, we'll need to get a quote for the repairs; will you arrange that with Western Garage please?"

"Yes, I'll take care of it." Sid replied.

"Good. Thanks. Okay everyone, let's get to work."

Ken and Dick strode off towards the office and Irish Ray went to his workshop; when we were alone Sid pulled Ray and I to one side.

"Okay. So you're through the official bit and you've survived that. Now, tell me what happened."

Ray and I looked at each other, then back at Sid and gave him the piece he was after.

"We were probably going a bit fast, for the conditions, Sid." I began.

"And there was water across the track so I didn't see the mud hole until the wheels dropped into it." Ray added.

"I knew it!" Sid replied, gesturing at the Rover. "It takes a fair bit to tip one of these over you know."

"Yeh."

Sid looked from Ray to me and then back to Ray, "Well boys; lesson learned?" he asked pointedly.

We knew what answer was required. "Yeh." we both said together, "Lesson learned."

"Good" Sid seemed satisfied. "No more to be said then. Ray, follow me down to Western in the one-tonner and we'll drop Ken's vehicle in for a quote."

And with that we went off to take care of our various tasks. Ray and Sid returned later and all seemed to be going well until Ray dropped a bomb on me later that afternoon.

We worked through the rest of the morning and broke for lunch as normal. Later, around three o'clock Ken called us into his office; Dick was already there and Sid followed us in. Ken had a claim form on his desk and we answered his questions while he wrote down the details.

"Ray," Ken looked up, "may I have your license please?

Ray pulled a rectangle of paper out of his wallet and handed it over to Ken, "At least I've got a licence; not like Steve." he said.

There was dead silence as everyone's eyes turned upon me, my stomach dropped and I was, literally, shocked at what Ray had just revealed. In effect, all of the heat and all of the attention instantly came off Ray and was directed at me. It was intense.

Ken spoke first; incredulous he asked, "Stephen, you have no license?"

"What!" gasped Dick. "You've been driving our vehicles all this time without a license? Unbelievable!"

Sid, whose chin was cradled in his hand, looked down to the floor and slowly shook his head.

"Stephen," Ken explained, "if you had been driving my truck and had the accident instead of Ray we would have no insurance claim; not for your personal damage or the vehicle's repairs. It puts the company, and me, in a very bad position. What if you had been driving, had an accident and been seriously disabled? You'd have no claim for compensation. The company couldn't help you. You've been foolish concealing this."

They all looked at me, awaiting a response.

My mind was everywhere, frantically searching for something to work with here; some words or anything that would get this pressure off me.

"Well, there's no reason for me not to get a license." I began nervously, "I'm not banned or anything. It's just that when we left the Gold Coast I hadn't gotten around to renewing it and meant to get it handled when we settled down."

"Are you settled down now?" Dick threw back at me.

"Yes." I replied. "Look, I could go and book for my license first thing tomorrow."

Ken looked down at his wrist watch then up at me again, "I'd suggest you finish up for the day Steve and go down to the police station and book in straight away. And in the meantime, no more driving company vehicles please. We'll schedule you to work in town until you can show me a current driver's license. Fair enough?"

"Yes. Fair enough. Thanks Ken." I turned and got out of that office as quickly as I could.

"Stephen." It was Sid's voice, and I turned to find him standing at the top of the steps. "I'll drive you to the police station if you like." His mouth turned up a little at the corners, "You don't have a driver's license; right?"

I grinned and some of the tension went out of my body, "Yeh. Right. Thanks Sid."

We didn't talk much in the car as Sid drove us into town and it turned out he knew the desk officer, which made the whole process of booking in for a test much easier. It took about 20 minutes to fill in the forms and pay a fee and I was all set for the following week. We got back into the Rover and Sid took me home.

I was amazed at how quickly I'd become the bad guy in this event. I mean, Ray was the one who crashed the boss's car, not me. Why did I feel like I was the guilty one? And because Ray had hurt himself he was even getting sympathy; they'd probably let him have a few days off to recover. Recover? Yeh, at the Irish Club no doubt! I found myself getting angry but as we pulled up in front of the flat, Sid's voice cut through my thoughts.

"This may seem a bit rough right now Steve, but it will work itself out. If you'd been a poor worker or someone else, Ken would have sacked you on the spot. He didn't and that's worth something in my book."

I didn't quite get everything he said right then but I was reassured. I still had my job and would get a license next week. I was fine. Sid turned down my invitation to a beer saying that he was going back to the yard to finish up.

"Thanks Sid."

He nodded and then drove off. I went inside, grabbed a beer and then sat out on our small patio sipping the chilled, refreshing liquid and looked down the two red-earth tracks designating our driveway. Across Pelican Street and beyond the houses I saw the taller trees were catching some late afternoon sun, their tops waving gently in the light breeze. I was aware that my relationship with Ray had changed today; his choice to dob me in and mine to be dobbed in had created something different. I say 'mine to be dobbed in' because if I'd had my license then the lack of one could not have been used as a weapon against me; so I'd set myself up for the fall and Ray had simply used it to his advantage.

Ray's tactic was clever; he'd managed to divert all of the attention away from him and onto me. It was brilliant!

But there was a consequence to his action because now I knew that he was willing to sacrifice me so he could survive, and being 'mates' with Ray was not actually what I thought it was. In fact my being mates with Ray, was very different to Ray being mates with me. Perhaps being mates was different for every person and we all had our own version of it. I thought of Claudia and I; perhaps relationships too, were different for every person.

So, what was I left with here? Clearly I had a big blind spot; I believed that what I'd decided mateship was, would be the same for everyone. Well that was pretty stupid! I needed to get smarter because if I continued with this stupidity then every mate would use it against me. Today had shown me that in graphic detail.

At the corner of our building a clump of banana trees waved their broad, verdant leaves playfully at me and I raised my stubby in salute, "Cheers!" My relationship with Ray had changed and the honeymoon was over; it was going to be very interesting to see what it would become. Ray may have won the round but the game was still in play!

———————

We were going to take my station wagon to Boulia and Mick and Susanna would come with us. The windscreen had a creeping fracture and I decided to replace it with one I'd bought from the wreckers. The HR windscreen was a little unusual with its square top corners, and the wreckers only had one in stock. I got to work on it Friday afternoon so it would be done ready for an early start on Saturday morning. Normally a windscreen can

be pushed out from within the car but with the crack
I simply broke it up with a hammer, not willing to risk
cutting my legs if it shattered when I thumped it. After
I'd put all the glass pieces in the bin I cleaned up the
rubber seal and then inserted a long piece of wet, soapy
string all the way around, in a groove where the glass
edge would sit. With the replacement screen in position
I pressed one of its edges down into the rubber and
slowly pulled on the string, which lifted the top rubber
flange up and over the glass. I worked my way around
until the windscreen was fitted fully into its groove.

Claudia came out with a vodka and orange in hand,
excited to see my good work. She chatted away happily
about the trip while I went around the perimeter
tapping it with a rubber mallet to make sure the glass
was snug in the seal. I was nearly done, about three
quarters the way around, when my next tap instantly
turned that shiny expanse of clear glass into thousands
of tiny translucent pieces.

I'd completely shattered the windscreen, all my good
work undone in a second, feelings of self satisfaction
gone, the wreckers had no more, "Damn it!"

Claudia screamed and cried out at me, "Why did you do
that? We can't go to Boulia without a front window!"

She was distraught; irrational. I was angry with myself
and lashed out at her, "Oh go to hell Claudia! Do you
think I did that on purpose so we couldn't go? Don't be
such an idiot."

I stood looking at the useless screen while Claudia ran
inside crying; she had not done this with me before
and I had no idea what to do, so I followed the tears.

Claudia had run into our bedroom and locked the
door—I didn't even know it had a lock—I stood at the
door and could hear her sobbing.

"Claudia, what are you doing; it's only a windscreen.
Come out." I called.

"Go away." was all I got.

So I got a beer from the refrigerator and walked on
down the road to Mick's. We talked and figured that if I
cleared the glass away then we could still drive to Boulia
in the morning; it might be a bit blowy but certainly
doable. It seemed like a great plan and I stayed and had
a couple more beers with the trucker. When I finally got
home the front door was wide open and Claudia was
gone. The next morning I picked up Mick and Susanna
just before nine o'clock in the morning and the three of
us drove off to find a rodeo.

———————

Drivers travelling south will come into Boulia along the
Boulia Mount Isa Highway, having passed the Donohue
Highway intersection on their right and later the local
cemetery on the left. From the Police Station located
at the town's edge they can travel 300 metres and then
turn sharp left; if they elected to drive on a further 1000
metres they will have crossed Boulia Street to discover
the town now in their rearview mirror, over 200 metres
behind them. Ahead they face a 360 kilometre and
five hour drive to Winton, following Winton Road.
The town plan marshalled 11 streets laid out in a grid
creating some 19 urban blocks that contained most of
the buildings and public spaces. A person could stand in

the middle of just about any of the street intersections and see out to natural bush, beyond the town limits. Boulia was certainly not large in size or population but it had a long history and a unique location.

Boulia, effectively an island within the Burke River, was flanked to the west by Georgina, to the east by Hamilton and further out the mighty Diamantina; this confluence of rivers comprised a series of ancient flood plains contained within a region known as Channel Country—150,000 square kilometres featuring numerous intertwined rivulets that, upon occasion, can flood all the way down into Lake Eyre, waiting patiently nearly 700 kilometres to the southwest. Boulia was known as the Capital of Channel Country, a title that could only be fully appreciated from high up in the air.

> " "After crossing the Hamilton River, 5 miles wide with 45 channels, I was out on the high downs ... "—Henry Lamond, Walkabout, 1912

One hundred years ago Boulia was a waterhole known to the local tribe, the Pitta Pitta, but in 1976 around 200 residents lived in town and the numbers swelled to several thousand during the annual rodeo weekend; when my HT cruised past the police station it added three more tourists to the tally.

The drive without a windscreen had been okay. We discovered that having the door windows down produced a wind tunnel effect, but with all the windows fully closed it seemed to create a pressure bubble in the cabin. So, with sunglasses shielding our eyes from flying insects and apart from the sandblasting effect we received from passing oncoming vehicles, a game was started where both passengers would duck below dashboard level leaving the driver to, literally, face the onslaught. We made the trip in relatively good time with most of our skin intact!

We drove along Herbert Street and on out of town to have a quick look at the Burke River. I joked that Leichhardt had been good enough to leave this one to the Burke & Wills team; the other two didn't get it but I knew Ray would have. It was midday, we turned around and drove back to go and find Greg and the other teachers.

"Just drive directly to The Australian Steveo," Mick directed, "he'll be there."

And so he was, yahooing with locals and visitors in the public bar of the Australian Hotel. Soon we all had a cold beer in hand and were being introduced to names and faces that would never be remembered. I smiled to myself and silently thanked the person who had invented the name "Mate;" perfect for situations like this where one was introduced to another, shook hands warmly, looked them in the eye and then instantly forgot their name. "G'day mate. How are you?" would get you by just about anywhere in this country.

The public bar was spacious and simple; a place for drinking. I looked around the room and noticed an older Aboriginal man sitting on a stool at the bar. In all of the loud chatter, bursts of raucous laughter and general hubbub he appeared calm and sat quietly with an untasted pot sitting in front of him, dew glistening on the glass. Like many in town for the rodeo he wore boots, jeans and a check-patterned collared shirt, but seemed out-of-place and I watched him for a while. At one point he glanced my way, held my eye for a few seconds and then nodded, a half smile on his lips. I raised my glass in his direction and nodded in return. Susanna suddenly grabbed my arm drawing me back into the group's conversation. When I looked back the old man was gone though his beer remained, untouched at the bar. A barmaid reached out, picked up the full glass and took it away. It was one of those odd moments when you know there's more to know but you're not quite sure what it is.

We all spent a pleasant afternoon in the pub and then made our way to the house that Greg shared with several of Boulia's other teachers. He was from Brisbane, a "Brizzo," and had recently completed a Bachelor of Education degree. New teachers were encouraged to work for one to two years in Queensland's smaller regional schools before being offered a position closer to home. Boulia State School, established in 1891 on Templeton Street, had some 20 students.

It was late in the afternoon when we left the Australian and a low winter sun was pushing long shadows out across Boulia's wide streets and open spaces.

"Pretty busy in town for the rodeo," Greg noted. "Normally you'd be lucky to see a stray dog on Saturday afternoon!"

"What do you do in Boulia for the other 50 weekends, when it's not rodeo?" I asked.

"Go to the big smoke; Mount Isa!" was the reply and we all laughed.

When we arrived at Greg's house there was a wonderful smell; the tantalising aroma of slow-cooked meat pervaded the air and I was suddenly very hungry. I caught Susanna's eye as we were both sniffing the air; the others soon caught on and like a pack of bloodhounds we followed our host out to the backyard.

"We put the meat down about midday so it should be ready by now." Greg offered, perhaps sensing if he didn't feed the pack then he may well become dinner himself.

"Let's eat!" called out Mick, "I could eat the crutch out of a dead leper."

"Awe, gross; Campbell." chided the teacher, "Can't take you anywhere!"

Greg, Mick and I went off to dig out the hāngi; it didn't take long to retrieve a steaming wire basket; the smell of cooked meat and warm earth was intense.

"Whoa. That smells great." said Mick as he brushed away loose earth and stones.

Greg had put on some gloves and opened up the wire cage, pulling out a Hessian wrapped object; we untied several strings and then peeled back layers of wrapping to reveal a shoulder of lamb covered with whole potatoes and onions. Steam and vapour richly laden with flavourants wafted up into our faces, filling noses and mouths. I had no idea what the others were doing

213

as my eyes closed tightly and I inhaled deeply a big smile shaping my mouth.

The full pack had gathered in close behind us, drawn-in by the enticing aroma; I'm sure I could hear a low insistent growling but told myself it was their stomachs talking.

"Let's eat!"

We all responded to Mick's call to action and took the meat over to a table where it was cut, pulled, torn and dismembered into a big roasting tray, from which we all helped ourselves. With our plates laden with slices of buttered bread, salad, potatoes and succulent fall-off-the-bone lamb the group became quiet, their collective attention centred on devouring the feast. It was great!

After an afternoon in the pub, lots of talking and a "Mighty feed!" as Greg described it, I felt sleepy and said good night. Susanna and Mick had a room in the house and I would sleep in the station wagon. Out at the car I folded down its rear bench seat and lowered the tailgate before laying out my sleeping gear. I sat on the tailgate for a while looking out at the huge, wide sky and thought of Sid, Ray and I sitting near the campfire at Mount Elliot, which was only 120 kilometres away to the northeast. In fact, if I followed the Burke River and survived the trek then I could get pretty close to Selwyn. Though it would be easier to simply drive along the Boulia Selwyn Road. I thought about Claudia too, but sleep's pull was strong and I allowed my body to lay back and sink into blissful abandon. It got cold during the night and I woke briefly to crawl into my sleeping bag; despite the influx of visitors Boulia was quiet and I was back asleep in a few minutes.

Several distinct piles of weathered red-brown bricks and other rubble strewn about were all that remained of the Boulia Native Mounted Police barracks. Sub-Inspector Ernest Eglinton, who oversaw reprisals and numerous shoot-outs against the Kalkadoon people, was based here for six years, from 1878.

Greg had brought us out here for a swim at a waterhole but the surrounding landscape—flat, hard, stoney and devoid of vegetation—gave us cause to doubt his purpose and sanity. We swung right, off the Boulia Selwyn Road's graded surface and onto an unmarked track, then drove on for about a kilometre. I had noticed a ragged, distorted treeline shimmering eerily off in the distance, which gradually stabilised as we got closer.

Mick looked around, "Summers! What are we doing here? Having a dust bath?"

"Settle your brains down Campbell." Greg counselled, We're nearly there."

And so we'd arrived, had a look over the building's remains and then trekked down to the waterhole for our promised swim.

The area looked incredibly ancient. The waterhole was carved out to about six metres below the surrounding bush level and presented a shallow offering of tepid brown water. Rock outcropping, worn and weathered to crumbling, were painted in soft ochres and browns and stood like tired battlements in between runs of steep earthen banks; testament to the force of water that would sweep through the channel during flood.

"They say it never runs dry." the teacher informed us.

"Well I doubt they'll be holding the school's swimming carnival here anytime soon." said Mick, who had walked in and was standing with water barely reaching up to his shins.

Susanna ran in shrieking and tried to push the trucky over. He caught her easily in one arm, maintained hold of his can of beer with his other and sat them both down gently in the water. "Will you tun the taps on please Mr. Summers, we are ready to bathe. Thank you."

Greg glanced at me and we stepped-in together, kicking and splashing them unmercifully. Everyone was yelling and striking the water, and it wasn't long before we were all soaking wet. After a while, somewhat refreshed, we lounged in the water and chatted. I drifted out of the conversation and thought about the policemen stationed out here nearly 100 years ago; did they swim or sit in the shade of a gum tree enjoying a quiet smoke? Surely there were not too many police stations in the area with an attached swimming pool?

In claiming the waterhole, which became known to some as Barracks Waterhole, and building a camp nearby the police denied access to local tribes creating difficulty for them particularly in times of drought. It seemed that Aboriginals had not fared well at the hands of the officers, in the isolation of this place.

Though, long before the whites, I could well imagine the many brown-skinned people gathered at this oasis, splashing and playing in its waters as we did now; the smoke from their cooking fires rising up alongside the chatter of their conversations as they enjoyed the land's surprising bounty.

I got up and left the others bathing and talking, to explore along the banks. Though they were largely bare earth, a thin strip of green vegetation grew just above water-level and some tufts of hardy bush grass peered down from higher up. I followed a small channel up and out to end up in amongst a copse of gums and stood quietly in the shade they offered. I could hear my friend's muted voices, was aware of some movement in the trees and yet there was something else. It was not so much a sound but I had a sense of ... boundless space that somehow, I was part of. I immediately thought of the old black man at The Australian yesterday, sitting calmly; centred in amongst the public bar's bedlam. Was this what some Aboriginals referred to as connection with the land; so vast that it could not be possessed or owned and was actually the other way around—it owned me?

But now there was a new noise, one that was hard to ignore; Mick's bellowed, "Outram!" got my attention and I heard Susanna laugh out loud.

Greg called out too, "It's time for the rodeo. Come on."

"Coming." I called out.

I stood a few seconds longer and quietly said, "Hello." and then walked back to where they were waiting near Greg's car. We all got in and then drove back into town,

217

passing the Rodeo Grounds & Racecourse on the left. We would return there as soon as we'd all cleaned up and dressed—boots, jeans and a checkered collared shirt.

Easter weekend was big for Boulia. While Friday featured a full campdrafting program and Saturday the timed events and later horse racing, Sunday was all about the rodeo. We got there about eleven o'clock and caught the tail end of the morning's activity; steer and bull riding. It wasn't long before we had a cold beer in hand and had found a good spot up in the grandstand. Greg had brought some "tinnie" coolers and handed them around so our beers stayed chilled.

Looking around the crowd I could see plenty of cowboys but also children, mothers, grandmothers and grandfathers; there were even some babies in prams or being held by their parents. And despite all of the noise and adrenalin fueled activity in the arena, people were also standing around in groups talking, laughing and socialising. The Shire of Boulia, known as cattle country, covered 62,000 kilometres with around 450 people living in that huge landscape; rodeo weekend was where the graziers and their families could get together and do something unusual, be neighbourly. Many remote Australian towns and places held annual rodeo or race events that acted as a powerful catalyst to bring people together; they were events where knowledge was shared, news disseminated, the weather discussed interminably, new friendships created and existing ones strengthened, there was space for young men to fight and old men to sit quietly in the shade and snooze, and for young children to play in the dust … it was rodeo.

I got talking to a bloke next to me in the stand; he'd been in the shire all of his life and worked on a station, "You know, it's like a big family and it's a real advantage of living in a small community; we wouldn't want to live anywhere else."

It was announced over the loud speakers that there would be a break for lunch and my neighbour was going off to find his mob and eat. We shook hands and he said in parting, "If you're after a job out here we're always looking for good blokes; you'd be welcome."

"Thanks." I replied. "I've got work in Mount Isa at the moment, but thanks for mentioning it."

"No worries mate." He nodded, tipped his hat, turned and walked away.

I watched as the possibility for a completely different life moved away from me and soon was lost in a throng of hungry people making their way to the shed for lunch. "Wow." I thought to myself. "Some choices are only around for a few seconds." but then I realised that in that ten seconds I'd actually made my choice.

Susanna's hand was tugging at my shoulder. "Come on Steveo, let's get some food."

"Oh yeh!" I responded enthusiastically and turned to follow my mob.

The rodeo arena was located within the race track's infield and we followed the crowd over its finish line and on to the grandstand, which in true outback style was sheeted with corrugated iron; a mighty big tin shed. We refreshed our beers at the bar, ordered some steak

219

burgers and claimed some standing room for ourselves in the crowded area.

I heard Mick say, "It's cozy in here."

The general chat and banter subsided as food arrived and we turned our attention to a slice of nicely charred steak garnished with onions and tomato; decorated with a trying-to-be-cheerful lettuce leaf and all assembled within two slices of white buttered bread. Oh and let's not forget to mention the all important dollop of tomato sauce, designed to leak out with each enthusiastic bite and covertly migrate all over the uninitiated person's shirt-front and shoes.

"The other one you have to watch out for is a bacon and egg sandwich, where the egg yellow is still runny; one bite and it explodes out all over your face!" Greg spoke up over the general din.

"Not a good look when you're out and doing your best to impress the girlfriend's parents!" I shouted.

"Good one Outram." Mick chimed in. "Not a good look at all."

He took a sip of beer and looked at me pointedly, glancing down at my shirt, "Pity about all of that tomato sauce down your front."

"What! No way." but I couldn't not-look to see if it was true. The whole group roared with laughter, including me. Some of our shoulder-to-shoulder neighbours glanced in at the outburst and then joined with the fun.

To the northeast of the grandstand was a camping area with power and an amenities block, but some people had chosen to base themselves in amongst the Burke River's shady treeline, which swung-in to almost touch the racetrack at its most easterly curved edge. Boulia had limited accommodation, one motel and one caravan park, so camping was very much a part of the rodeo experience, and it added to the important social aspect of the Easter weekend event. Those who had brought their horses stabled them in the rodeo grounds and so could take care of their animals; for many, the horses were an integral part of life on the land and considered family or friends.

We noticed that people were beginning to wander back towards the arena and a little later the public address system notified us that events were due to begin again. We picked up a beer each and went to join in an entertaining afternoon of bull riding, barrel races, clowns, horses, cowboys, bronco riding and all things rodeo.

Around about four o'clock Susanna, Mick and I decided to head back to Mount Isa. The rodeo was winding down, awards had been presented to winners and many of the contestants, some bruised and battered, would return to their stations ready to start work early in the morning. We said our good byes and went off to find the station wagon, but Boulia wasn't ready to let us go without a fight. We had some difficulty locating the car due to a clever local disguise that rendered all of the vehicles in the same colour, a thick covering of red Boulia dust! And as there was no windscreen, the dust had managed to recolor much of the interior as well.

"Who needs doors?" I said pretentiously and crawled into the car though the windscreen space; the other two

221

followed my example sending red dust billowing up as they landed on the front seat. Coughing and spluttering we got out again, using the doors this time, and set to work with tee-shirts and towels beating the dust off seats, dashboard and each other. I'm not sure it made a huge difference but we had a good time larking around.

Always thinking of the essentials, Mick had managed to pick up a six-pack of beers and stashed them safely in the esky; we made our way out onto the Boulia-Selwyn Road and 15 minutes later turned right towards Mount Isa. A couple of funny things happened on the way home.

We had been driving for about an hour when a passing truck flicked a rock up off the road verge and launched the deadly 'gibber' right at us. Mick and I both saw it rise up over the bonnet and despite a day at the rodeo, too much sun and having consumed a large number of beers we both managed to lean out of its way and create an opening for the spinning bluestone missile to pass between us. It maintained it's altitude, travelled the full length of the car's interior and smashed dramatically through the rear tailgate window, causing broken glass to explode out of the back. Hundreds of small granular shapes scattered and bounced across the road to be left far behind as our attention turned to a 100 kilometre per hour wind, now howling around our ears and blasting on through the vehicle's cabin. Any thing that was lightweight and loose was instantly sucked up into the vortex; even Susanna's shriek was whipped away and she battled to control long brown hair that

222

was lashing her eyes and head. Mick, who was driving, finally applied the brakes and pulled the car over, allowing the torrent to subside.

"Fuck, that was a close one." he commented.

You saw it too, didn't you? I asked"

"Yeh," he replied. "I didn't want to get hit with the damn thing." He glanced towards the rear of the HT, "Pity about the back window. Maybe I should have headed that gibber out of the way." He tapped his forehead, "Pretty thick you know."

"Nope!" Susanna retorted decisively, "I like your head just the way it is."

"I don't know Susanna," I replied cheekily. "It could have been a big improvement."

The trucky leaned over and thumped me in the shoulder.

"Ouch!" I feigned. "You are so-o sensitive these days Mick."

We walked around to the tailgate and inspected the damage, knocking the remaining pieces of glass out onto the ground.

"Not much we can do with this." I said, "Let's keep going."

And so we all got back into the car and drove off to spend the next two hours shouting at each other over the din, having our hair arranged and rearranged, and receiving an abrasive peppering of fine road dust each time a vehicle passed us. Susanna climbed into the back and sheltered behind the front bench seat but being a man and a mate, I braved it out with Mick in the front. The sun was just about fully set when I looked out through the side glass and with dusk falling rapidly, saw something very unusual.

> " The open plains of the Channel Country are the legendary best site for encountering Min Min lights … . In the Channel Country, sightings are distributed all year round but peak noticeably in midwinter …"— John D Pettigrew, The Min Min light and the Fata Morgana.

A bright orb was tracking us, about 100 metres out and running parallel to the road. I watched it for a while, not quite sure what I was seeing. Susanna had fallen asleep on the back seat and without taking my eyes off the object I reached over and tapped Mick's leg.

"Mick?"

"Yeh?" he glanced my way.

"Can you see that?" I asked.

"See what?"

And I pointed towards the moving light source.

Mick, who was watching the road, glanced to his left several times until his eyes focussed on the distant object.

"Keep an eye on it Steveo." he instructed and took his foot off the accelerator pedal, allowing the car to slow down; I watched the strange light slow down with us. When the car was doing about 20 kilometers per hour Mick put his foot to the floor and we sped off as fast as the HR could go; the light easily matched us then moved ahead until we could both see it through the windscreen opening. It was eerie.

Mick slowed again and pulled over onto the verge; we got out. Susanna woke up and joined us as we looked out at the bright orb of light hovering about two metres off the ground and some 50 metres away.

"Min Min." she said. "Sid has told me about them."

"Yeh. Min Min." Mick confirmed quietly and reached out to hold her hand.

"What?" I asked, "What's a Min Min?."

"Ghost lights. They're legend around here." Mick began, "Lots of people have seen them."

Susanna took over, "There was this hotel out along Winton Road, the Min Min Hotel; it burned down over 80 years ago. Anyway, the local shearers and station hands used to go there to drink on pay day and got ripped off big-time with cheap booze and drugs. Some were killed for their pay packets and then buried in a graveyard, out back. The tale goes that just after the fire, a stockman was riding nearby at about ten in the evening when he saw a glow appear right in the cemetery. As he watched, it got brighter and brighter and grew to the size of a watermelon, and then it came straight at him! He panicked and took-off on his horse but the light followed him all the way to Boulia; terror stricken the man fled into the police station and told

225

his story. They didn't believe him at the time, but over the years thousands of people have reported seeing the ghost lights, but no one has ever explained what they are."

She fell silent for a moment and then added, "You can still go and see the cemetery; there's an old grave there."

We all looked nervously at the light still hovering in mid air before us and then it slowly faded away, as if with the telling of its story it was satisfied. Suddenly it was dark; the bush beyond the car's lights a black void. Our eyes, still registering a white spot wherever we looked, gradually adjusted and I began to see more clearly. It was a weird sensation to be standing out in the dark bush, on the side of a dark road, having just been visited by a ghost light. We all got back in the car and drove off towards Mount Isa, occasionally, perhaps a bit too often, looking back over our shoulders to make sure that nothing was coming in through the rear window opening.

We cruised into Pelican Street around eight o'clock and I dropped Mick and Susanna off at their place, and then went home. I was a bit apprehensive; not sure if Claudia would be there and if she was … . I pulled into the driveway and our flat was in darkness; I realised how much I was hoping that she would be there. I unlocked the front door, turned on the lights and took in my gear. The place seemed empty and dull and suddenly, I missed her terribly. It was like a soft, cotton wool bomb went off in my stomach and slowly spread; it's fibres entangling every part of my body. I nearly cried when it reached my head, at the thought she may never return and we were done.

226

I knew I had to do something about it and got back into the HT and drove around to East Street; her parent's house. I cruised slowly by, not sure what to do and remarkably she was in their front yard with their dog and saw me. I pulled into the kerb and she came over.

"Hi."

"Hi."

"How was Boulia?"

"Good, but it would have been better if you were there."

"Really?"

"Yes. I missed you heaps."

"I missed you too."

At her words the cotton wool began to dissolve and recede. "I'm glad."

What happened to your hair?"

"It was a bit windy without the windscreen. Can we go for a drive and talk?"

"Dad won't like it; he doesn't want me to see you again."

"Just for a talk."

Her brow furrowed. "Hang on, I'll get my bag."

And with that she went into the house. I heard Claudia calling out something to her parents as she ran back out and got in the car. They came out of their house, watched her get into my car and then got into their own sedan as I pulled away. In my rearview mirror I saw their headlights dip slightly as they crossed the gutter and turned our way; the chase was on.

It wasn't that difficult to lose them; I got off East Street and ducked through several smaller roads making my way onto Marian Street. I knew that Ray was taking Margie out to a Chinese restaurant on Simpson Street and was able to hide the HT in their carpark. Claudia and I walked into the restaurant unannounced and quickly sat down with the unsuspecting couple; fortunately for us their table had four seats.

"What are you guys doing here? Ray asked.

"Claudia's parents are after us," I explained, "can we sit here with you for a while."

"What happened to your hair?" Margie asked with a giggle.

"Yeh." Ray joined her, "What's up with your hair Steveo?"

"The windscreen broke on the HR," I explained, "so it was a bit windy driving home from Boulia.

They were all looking up at my hair and laughing, "I'll say. Looks more like a whirly whirly gotcha!"

A waiter came over to inquire if we were eating, drinking or just visiting and I explained it was a short visit. He left us to chat.

Ray wasn't entirely happy that I had high-jacked his intimate date with Margie, but was willing to entertain a short visit.

"So, how was Boulia?" he asked.

I described the trip's highlights while the couple finished off their chicken chow mein, honey prawns and fried rice; it smelt really good. We talked for about a half hour and then Claudia and I left. I was hoping that her parents had given up and gone home and parked up at the Lookout; a high spot which offered 360 degree views of the city. We took a deep breath, looked at each other and then kissed; there wasn't much talking for a while. My hands were everywhere and so were hers; everything else forgotten in the moment.

After a very steamy while Claudia pulled back, "I'd better get home; Mum and Dad will be worried."

"Yeh. I guess so. Are you coming back to the flat?" I asked.

"I'd like that." she smiled at me. "Let me talk with my parents about it."

And so I drove her home and then went on to Pelican Street. When I got inside I went into the bathroom to shower and get ready for bed. I looked in the mirror and finally got why everyone was asking about my hair; it was standing straight up and out like a kind of brown string halo. With my face burned from the sun, eyes red from alcohol and dust, and this new radical hair-do crafted during several hours in a wind tunnel, I looked a total mess.

"Definitely time for a shower." I said to the reflection in the mirror, which nodded back at me in agreement.

Later that week I was invited to Claudia's parents place for dinner. I was nervous but went. We talked about Claudia staying at our flat while I was in town, and then at her parents house when I was working out bush. They said they had a flat next to their place, which was coming due for new tenants soon and asked if we would move in there so they could be close to their only daughter. I agreed it was a great idea and much of the early tension slipped away. We all ate, drank and became quite merry. And at least no one asked me about my hair!

Chapter 17

Initiation

With the summer heat and a massive wet season behind us, temperatures were now very pleasant hovering in the high twenties. The big wet had caused concerns about the new Lake Julius project; with half a metre of rain dumped on the region in just one week there were fears that it could burst its banks. The builders must have done a good job though, as it was still there having survived the onslaught.

I'd given notice at Union Minière and then applied for work at Mount Isa Mines; Ray had stayed on with the prospecting team and it was an interesting change for the two of us, as I drove out of the Ryan Road yard for the final time. Despite the car license incident, Ken and Sid had been happy with my work and offered my job back if the mine didn't work out. I was pleased that they had said that as I too had enjoyed my time with them and it seemed to complete things that mutually, we were both more than satisfied.

Stephe**ꝺ ꞇɩ ram

Despite a good education, I didn't have any mining qualifications or experience but it turned out that my time working in the bush held me in good stead. They were interested in a commitment to staying in the area and apparently 12 months or so already qualified me. After medical, psychological and a variety of other evaluations, Mount Isa Mines offered me a job working in their labour pool starting at $150 per week. Given the psychometric mental gymnastics they had put me through to assess non-verbal skills, and other reasoning tests, I thought I'd at least get a rocket scientist position but no. I joked with the employment officer about it who said there were plenty of opportunities for training and advancement, but laboring is where I would start. Actually I was excited with my prospects, signed on the dotted line and was scheduled to begin induction training the next day.

The training was largely about safety. Mount Isa Mines had an excellent safety record and was regarded as one of the safest mines in the world. Their induction was thorough and often graphic, with one particular segment I would never forget. We listened to an explanation of the use of safety glasses and I cringed through a video showing a ragged shard of metal being pulled from someone's eyeball. The commentary emphasised that no anesthetic or pain-killers could be used during the surgery. At one point the camera zoomed in to show the sclera's surface distorting and bulging out as tweezers pulled on the alien, literally, tearing it out of the eye's delicate white flesh. It was gross, my stomach turned and the memory became indelibly and deeply embedded.

Following induction I was given an ID tag and hard hat, a discount voucher for work clothes and steel capped boots, and instructions on where to go to begin work on Monday morning. Woohoo!

Claudia and I met up with Ray and Margie at the Irish Club for a celebratory drink on Saturday and we talked about taking the girls and friends out to Mount Frosty for a swim the next day. We'd not been before and were keen to check it out. Mount Frosty had been an open-cut mining operation; resulting in several holes in the ground that had begun filling with water and one in particular had become popular as a waterhole. A Sunday swim sounded like a great idea and despite my change of job I still had a strong interest in local mining and the amazing red-earth landscape that we lived in.

Rosebud, Kurrajong, Lady Marie, Wee McGregor and Prince of Wales were just some of the many abandoned mines located south of Mary Kathleen and down towards the town of Ballara. Some had been smaller operations and others supported communities of miners and their families. They were dotted along the Fountain Range Fault, a remarkable formation that appeared up near Kajabbi and trended in a southwest direction down past Dutchess. The range's southerly area featured Fountain Springs, which was the water supply for Ballara from 1913 through to 1927 and one of the only permanent water sources in the area. Ballara Quartzite, named in 1961 after the abandoned railway siding, was a geological formation that extended some 50 kilometres north from its namesake, up past Mary Kathleen Mine, and west towards Mount Frosty. However Mount Frosty Mine was particular to the

233

closely associated Corella Formation, and was actually an old limestone quarry comprising one major and three minor open-cut operations. The limestone had featured a distribution of chalcopyrite and between 1966 and 1977, 156 tonnes of copper metal was known to have been mined, at a respectable grade of 7.2% CU. As with many mines in the area, bush-land rehabilitation had not been a part of the plan and so the large holes-in-the-ground had simply been abandoned to gradually evolve into water-holes or lakes and perhaps, inadvertently, provide a valuable resource for local wildlife and recreation for visiting humans.

With our eskys packed with ice, beers, sausages and steaks, a bag full of groceries and a portable BBQ plate in the boot, we all piled into two cars and drove along the Barkly Highway towards Cloncurry. Ray had Margie and another couple in his Charger and Claudia and I brought Debbie with us in the HR. There were no signposts, but at the 50 kilometre mark we found a dirt road and turned right into Mount Frosty Road, bumped over a cattle grid crossing and headed south into the bush.

The track had not been graded for a long time and was rough but driveable, with care. About two kilometres in we met a dry creek bed and the track dipped down through a deep rut. Everyone except the drivers got out of the cars and very carefully nursed both vehicles across; the Charger was lower to the ground and scraped its sub-frame a little, but came through in good shape. Another half a kilometre along, the road split, but we swung to the right and shortly after that Margie directed us down a track and we parked.

"This is it!" she said

I looked around at the bush and didn't see anything that looked even vaguely like a waterhole.

She read my face, laughed at me and pointed, "It's over here." We all followed Margie through the trees and down a shallow limestone cutting.

It's an extraordinary thing to walk through the hot, dry, dusty bush and then turn a corner to be presented with a vast, shimmering expanse of water. Almost instantly my eyes began to relax their squint, held against the strong sunlight; I felt mildly anesthetised and at the same time was aware of my body's urge to run like a crazy thing and dive deep into the cool green.

"Wow! I exclaimed, "This is amazing."

We had all gathered at the top of a rubble incline to gaze down upon one of Mount Frosty's open-cuts; over the last 10 years it had captured and held rainwater to form a waterhole; copper and other minerals had leached out of the limestone to tint the water turquoise-green, which stood in sharp contrast to the red surrounding bush and bright walls. It measured about 100 metres in diameter; across at the far side a thick limestone column rose up out of the water branching left and right to form two great rough-hewn arches, supporting a mass of overhead stone that was delicately capped with a thin ribbon of exposed red topsoil. From the top down to the water's surface I estimated a 30 metre fall and Claudia, who had been before, pointed out several lower ledges that people jumped from; I knew that I wanted to try that out.

Even though I was tantalised with the water view,
this was clearly an abandoned mine site and we were
standing in amongst bare rock and discarded rubble;
it would take decades before the bush would be able
to reclaim and soften the harsh landscape. We decided
that before taking a swim we'd get our gear from the
cars and set up camp at this higher level, as we had to
scramble down a rubble incline to reach the water and
there was little space down there to put anything once
we arrived.

Motivated by the thought of a refreshing swim it didn't
take us long to unload the cars and find a suitable spot
for our gear. We took our towels and a tin of cold beer
and trekked down into the old pit towards the water.
We were walking on what would have been the main
haulage road leading on to a series of pit benches that
stepped down to the mine's lowest level, the pit floor.
As the water level had risen over the years the benches
were all covered and no one seemed to know how deep
it was. At the water's edge Ray and I had a friendly
tussle, seeing who could get into the water first. He
managed to push me back and I slipped on the gravel
giving Ray the opportunity to leap out; he twisted
mid-air and curled up, made a crude entry and then
disappeared in amongst a great splash. I waited for him
to resurface, planning to bomb him, but then had a
better idea. Amidst a flurry of bubble's his mop of hair
broke through the water; with a great shake Ray sent
water flying everywhere and then opened his eyes.

"Ray! Mate! What's happening to you?" I sounded an
alert, my voice urgent, eyes wide looking intently into
his face.

"What?" he replied, "What's up?"

I pointed dramatically, moving back half a step, "Your skin mate."

"My skin?" he queried; looking slightly confused?

"Yes. Your face."

By now the girls had come on over and lent support to my case.

"Your skin looks really different Ray," Margie frowned followed by Claudia's, "Yeh; what happened to your skin Ray?"

Ray looked from me to Margie to Claudia and then back to me, and rubbed his face. The girls were quiet, expectant and looked to me, waiting for a lead.

"Ray. Mate!" I called out, "You're all green! You're turning into The Hulk!"

For several seconds he looked blankly at me as his brain tried to process the improbability, and then a big, white Ray grin filled his face and his laugh echoed off the surrounding rock walls.

"Nice try Outram!" He lunged forward, grabbed my leg and hauled me into the water. As I fell forward I heard, "Now you can be green too!" and we both went under with a big splash.

I wasn't in very deep, but hung for a while under the surface, just floating; fully immersed in the cool green liquid. My body slowly rose; I flicked hair and water out of my eyes and gazed up at a big blue circle of sky,

framed by the pit's limestone bowl. It was glorious.
The girls, Debbie and the other friends soon joined us
and our voices bounced happily around the old mine
workings. A little later some other groups of local
people arrived to swim and several of us ventured up
onto the lower ledges and flung ourselves out into
space to take the 10 metre flight back down, deep into
the cool green oasis of Mount Frosty. I'm sure that the
miners of old, who toiled out here in the dust and heat
digging the pit, never dreamed that the land they had
cut open and then discarded would be transformed into
such a beautiful thing. It seemed that the energy of
country was potent here, giving new life to heal an open
wound; and in so doing, provided a gift to those who
had once wounded it.

Later, with the waterhole succumbing to the day's
afternoon shadows, and we humans reenergised and
refreshed, we drove back to Mount Isa. Claudia and I
were going to meet friends at the Irish Club's Sunday
Session, while Ray and Margie had been invited to roast
dinner at her parent's house.

"Getting pretty serious Ray; roast dinner with the
parents. Hmm. Watch out; it will be two-point-four
kids and a three bedroom mortgage soon."

I had ribbed him but was also glad he was enjoying this pretty, long haired brunette. They were good together; there was a shared closeness and particularly with Ray, a gentleness I had not seen before. He gave me the forks, his right hand raised with two rigid fingers forming a defiant V, and a grin as they drove off with a roar; the orange Charger's rear tyres spitting out dust and gravel as it disappeared off down the road.

―――――――

At eight o'clock Monday morning, all kitted out in my clean new work clothes, I reported to the main Mineside security gate where I joined several other new recruits. It was change of shift and the gate was busy with men finishing up their eight hour night shift and the day shift workers migrating in. The security guards ushered us off to one side to wait for our Shift Boss; they were busy checking worker's ID tags and occasionally opening a crib box looking for possible stolen gear. I watched the parade, noted that most had carried crib box and realised that there was probably no local sandwich shop and I'd have to bring in my own food. It seemed that lunch was going to be a meagre affair today.

About eight-thirty, Steve, the Labor Pool Shift Boss showed up. He introduced himself, gathered us all together and we followed him around Mineside as he dropped men off at various locations; along the way we visited a store and I was given a pair of black gum boots and leather gloves. Finally, we arrived at the ground floor of No. 2 Crushers where he introduced me to a small gang of men working under one of the massive conveyor belt motors. It was noisy and dusty; the plant was in full operation with all of its four crushers working, ore rattled down onto the belt above us and was hauled across to the concentrators, over 100 metres to the southeast.

I met Merv, the front loader driver, Harry and several others, was handed a long-handled shovel and pitched in to shift ore that had fallen from the belt, into Merv's waiting bucket. The conveyor belts were sprayed with water to keep the dust down and this washed onto our ore pile turning it into mud and increasing its weight considerably. It wasn't long before my nice blue overalls were splashed with mud and I was very glad for my ungainly but very waterproof gumboots! We worked for about half an hour until Steve had gone off to check on another team when Harry announced that it was time for a smoke; I noticed that he kept his shovel handy and I did the same.

"You don't want to overdo it on your first day Steve." he called out over the din.

Harry winked at me and pulled a packet of Drum tobacco and papers out of his pocket, and proceeded to deftly makeup a thin "rollie," which was ceremoniously lit, his hands automatically cupping the flame against a light breeze generated by the conveyor's movement.

He reached out and offered me his makings, one eyebrow raised slightly in question, "Thanks Harry," I said, "but I don't smoke."

"Suit yourself." he replied and tucked the packet safely back into his overalls.

After about 15 minutes we spotted Steve walking
our way and in one remarkably elegant action, Harry
smoothly put the smoke between his lips and swung his
shovel deep into the mud; I followed suit while Steve
nodded and kept on going. When the Shift Boss was
out of sight Harry's shovel went down again and he
finished his cigarette, finally flicking a spent butt into
the loader's bucket and disposing of any evidence.

No. 2 Crushers was a multistory, steel-framed building
partially clad in grey metal sheeting—it was actually
khaki in colour, though disguised under a thick layer
of grey rock dust. The ground floor area where we were
working was mostly open above us. I looked up into
the building's cavernous interior, all the way to the
roof, and through the dust haze saw an overhead crane
spanning full-width and featuring a small operator's
cabin hanging underneath at one end; it must have been
40 to 50 metres above me. My gaze fell down through
the great open hall to take in four huge cone crushers
occupying their own floor and on a level just below
them, four electric motors each the size of a small car.
Everything was supersized and we people seemed like
tiny ants in comparison. Apart from the sunlight it
wasn't hard to imagine being deep in Tolkien's Mines
of Moria, looking up in awe at the dwarven kingdom's
great hall with its unbelievably tall stone pillars and
arched ceilings, just before drums were heard beating
out their warning from the deep ...

Suddenly it became relatively quiet as the crusher's ore
feed was turned off, and even more so as conveyor belts
began to run empty. Gradually, as dust settled out of
the atmosphere, our eyesight seemed to improve and

241

the building's structure sharpened. Steve had joined us again and indicated that we were all going somewhere; several of the gang jostled for a position in the lift, but I followed Steve up a set of steel stairs to the crusher floor.

Breaking rock was no easy thing. A method known as "fire setting" can be traced back to China's Tang dynasty and was later used by the Romans. It involved heating the rock face with fire and then letting it cool or throwing water upon it, which caused cracking. Other early miners forced wedges into natural cracks and fissures and later, a technique of hand drilling where a steel rod was hammered into a face to create a hole capable of holding gunpowder; the rod was turned by hand after each hit. Before explosives, the breaking of rock was done by hand using hammers, chisels rock wedges and pole picks; it was laborious and took a lot of time. With the coming of the Industrial Revolution, steam engines and other machinery, the work of rock breaking was transformed and men were able to put down their hammers as powerful crushers began handling the coarse material.

The crushers were impressive and even though they were spinning in idle, there was no missing their size, mass and power; they were designed and built to do just one thing, break rock. I walked around one of them and touched steel nuts that were bigger than my hand could span; this was machinery at a scale I'd not seen before. I noticed that my heart rate was up a bit and it felt good; I was excited. The way these crushers worked was simple, yet ingenious. Ore was fed down from the top into a chamber containing a rotating cone, or mantle, which smashed rock against the chamber's sides. The shattered material fell through onto a conveyor belt to be transported away. The job of those big electric motors was to rotate the cone, and our job was to adjust the gap between cone and chamber.

"How the hell do we adjust something of this size?" I thought to myself.

A man strode out of the control room and nodded all round; in comparison to our overalls he wore long pants, a collared shirt and was relatively clean. Having once been a well dressed office worker and now finding myself splattered from head to toe with grey mud, I took a mental note.

"G'day boys." He looked in my direction, "Ah-ha! Someone new. This should be fun." and winked at the Shift Boss Steve who grinned back at him in silent collusion.

I was introduced, "Curly, this is Steve."

I smiled knowing instantly that it was a nickname; it was obvious and so typically Australian. In a similar way that a redhead would have been called 'Ginger,' Curly's head was oiled, shiny and completely bald. The man in the clean collared shirt donned his helmet, nodded in my direction and smiled a bit like I imagined a wolf would just before it ate his prey, "Well Steve, let's get to it."

"Thanks for putting on the hat Curly, the glare was getting pretty severe." called out Merv, drawing a laugh; but two fingers raised in a familiar V was all the reply he got from Curly.

Harry, who knew the routine, had brought over several lead weights attached to wire and the operator bustled back into his control room releasing a short feed of ore into the crusher. The machine began to thump on its foundations and Harry dropped the lead into the chamber, then pulled it out again; it had been flattened to about 30 millimetres. The operator came out and had a look and this "leading" procedure was repeated several times at different locations around the cone. After the third time it was decided to adjust the crusher; the gap was too wide. Six kilogram sledge hammers were handed around; I got one of them and it was heavy.

Adjusting a cone crusher was a manual job and required timing, skill and some good luck. With the crusher running at idle, Steve instructed us to knock out all of the big steel wedges, which pinned the machine's body down and locked it in place. As it loosened, the sound changed—metal grating against metal—and slowly, very slowly the massive bowl began to vibrate and rotate. I relaxed, thinking that we'd just wait until it moved around far enough around; easy! I jumped a bit as the operator released a stream of ore and the big machine began to thump making a huge racket; the speed of its rotation picked up alarmingly. Steve, who had moved in behind me, allowed it to make a half turn and then yelled at the top of his voice, "Now! Now! Now!"

I lifted my hammer and swung it, but hit the post below the wedge. I tried again and struck the wedge on its bottom edge, which caused the damn thing to fall out onto the floor. I scrambled to pick it up and managed to get it back into the slot. With my heart pounding and legs beginning to shake, I swung and the hammer glanced off the post once again. I looked quickly around at the rest of the team all in action slamming wedges deep into their slots. The crusher was thumping and Steve was yelling at me. I swung once again, my arms felt like rubber and I missed. I looked up to see the boys all laughing at me and then Harry nudged me aside and set the wedge with three decisive blows. Smack! Smack! Smack! Rotation had stopped, the ore feed was turned off and the great machine returned to idle. I was sweating.

It was all over in a couple of minutes but seemed to have been much longer. With big grins on all of their faces the team applauded me and some slapped me on the back. I realised that I'd just been initiated, that they had all been through this and now I was one of the boys. I joined in laughing with them, mostly in relief. We retired to lean back on the handrails as Steve and the operator took another reading. I saw their heads nodding; it was good. Now all we had to do was repeat this for the remaining three crushers; it was an exciting start to my new job.

It turned out that only two of the four crushers required adjustment and when we were done we returned to shovelling mud under the conveyors until a siren wailed, signalling it was crib break. Crib was a word I'd not heard before; it referred to a meal break on any shift. In office work it would have been known as lunch at noon, but because Mount Isa Mines ran 24 hours a day, featuring three shifts, "lunch time" did not work at eight o'clock in the evening or at four in the morning so crib was used.

We all walked over to No. 2 Concentrator building where there was a crib room with tables, chairs, a refrigerator, sink and a big stainless steel urn. The others opened their crib boxes and retrieved sandwiches, fruit, snacks and the like; I sat down next to Harry.

"Where's your food?" he enquired.

"Didn't bring any." I replied. "Thought there might be a canteen or shop here so I could buy something."

"That's not good," Harry mused for a moment and handed over half of a cold meat and pickles on white bread sandwich. Merv had overheard and rolled me a green apple and someone else found me a Monte Carlo biscuit.

"Thanks guys." I said gratefully.

"Do you play?" Merv asked, shuffling a pack of cards.

"What's the game?

Merv looked up and said, "500." as if everyone in the world should have known that.

"No. I've not played it before."

"Well, you better learn then." said Harry, "We need you to make up the four."

Merv dealt out a hand each and they made me lay down my cards face up, while we played a round with Merv and Harry instructing and explaining how it could work, should work and might work; it seemed that there were many ideas, strategies and interpretations possible in the game of 500. I found it was similar to

Whist, though with its own peculiarities such as the Jacks being all powerful and known as left and right bowers. I'd played lots of cards with my family and picked it up quick enough. I got into some trouble with my partner when bidding for the kitty until I began to see that certain calls meant something, and a wrong call misinformed my partner, making him cranky.

"Crikey Steve. You called 8 diamonds without even having the ace or a king!"

"Give me a break will you. I just started with this game today!"

Cards, it seemed, were keenly contested; I would find out over the next few years that it was virtually Mount Isa Mines' national sport!

Crib was 40 minutes and the siren let us know it was time to get back to work. We went back to the crushers and spent the afternoon on the shovels. At four o'clock the siren sounded again and our shift was over; we made our way down to the security gate and headed home. My first day working for MIM was done; time for a cold beer.

Chapter 18

Just Let it Go

Our time at Pelican Street was done and Claudia and I moved into 102 East Street, next door to her parent's house. Our new flat was part of a block of four and we were up a flight of steps on the first floor, overlooking the street. We had upgraded to two bedrooms and it featured a combined lounge, dining and kitchen; there was a driveway along the south side and everyone parked their cars at the back. Shortly after our move I sold the HT station wagon and bought a green 1973 Leyland Marina. It seemed like my dreams of hot Australian sports cars had all but faded away as the Marina was a fairly conservative family sedan, but it had a four speed gearbox and a perky 90cc four cylinder motor, which was fun to drive. In addition and adding to the family theme, we'd bought a Siamese kitten and named her Kia.

My sister Karen had written that she was planning on coming up to Mount Isa for a visit and I replied that she could stay at our place as we now had the spare room. My life seemed to have settled into a comfortable routine of work, home and weekend barbecues and parties. The adventure of Darwin had begun to fade and Ray and I didn't talk about it anymore; it seemed that Mount Isa was fulfilling our current requirements. My job in the labor pool took me all around the mine but we were mainly located working at the crushers and No. 2 Concentrator plant; it seemed that there was always a mess to be cleaned up somewhere. The work connected me with many different areas of Mineside and whereas Union Minière had trained me in the treasure hunt of locating ore buried in the ground, I was now learning about extractive metallurgy, the practice of removing valuable metals from ore and then refining them into a purer form.

No. 2 Concentrator plant was designed to process ore delivered from the crushers, by feeding it first into rod mills and then on into ball mills. The rod mills were huge metal cylinders, about four metres in diameter that were about a quarter full of steel rods. The mills rotated slowly and the rods rolled around inside to grind down the ore and from there it passed through ball mills to become a fine grain. No. 2 handled zinc, lead and some silver, and the separation of metal from grain was done in a flotation system. Water, ore and reagents were mixed into a slurry and pumped into rows of holding tanks, bubbles were released from the bottom and as they rose the metal sulfides stuck creating a glossy, mineral-laden surface froth, which was sloughed off and dried, producing a fine concentrate. The resultant zinc was ready for market, but lead was further processed in smelters.

The concentrator was commissioned in 1966 and
featured an air conditioned control room, that was
clean, dust-free, soundproof and sported banks of
tall computer cabinets; again, I took note. One of our
not-so-favourite jobs was to empty the rod mills of
ore when they occasionally broke down. We, literally,
entered the mill and manually shovelled and hosed
them clean, removing as much ore as possible; then the
rods could be pulled out and any repairs done. It was
hot and humid in those cylinders and we all took turns.
While I enjoyed the team of men that I worked with,
and was certainly much fitter than when I'd started,
I knew that I did not want to make a career out of
labouring and started to browse local notice boards and
newsletters looking for alternative jobs within the mine.
I was pleased when the weekend rolled around and
while the crushers and concentrators would continue to
work 24/7, I got to have several days doing something
different.

On Saturday afternoon, I was refashioning the Marina's
rear seat shelf to accommodate a new set of stereo
speakers, when a brilliant yellow Holden Sandman
panel van pulled up behind me outside of our East
Street flat. It looked hot! And then, big surprise, my
sister Karen got out of the passenger's door; it had been
14 months since I had last seen her.

"Stephen, your hair is nearly as long as mine!" she
exclaimed and came running over for a hug.

I heard a chuckle and looked around; a tallish bloke
with moustache and tie-dyed tee shirt held out his
hand, "G'day Steve. I've heard a lot about you."

Karen made the introductions, "Stephen meet Kevin!"

And so I did, instantly liking him. "Great looking car Kev." I commented.

"308 V8 under the lid too," he replied.

"Yeh?"

"Yeh."

Soon the car's bonnet was up with its V8 engine burbling on idle. It was nice; really nice. A few revs to hear the exhaust note and then Kevin took us for a quick burn along East Street. That was it; mates forever.

We parked back outside the flat and I took them in to meet Claudia and put their gear in the spare room. The two girls were getting on really well, so Kevin and I went outside to finish off the Marina. Within 30 minutes we had it all back together and were ready to test the new speakers.

"Hang on." Kevin said and went off to his car. He came back, slipped *A Night at the Opera* by Queen in the tape deck and turned up the volume, "You'll like this Steve." We sat in the front seat listening to Bohemian Rhapsody; the Marina was rockin' and so were we!

The girls could hear the music from our flat and came out to investigate; everyone piled into the Marina and, accompanied by God Save the Queen, we did a royal tour up and down East Street; giving the royal wave to anyone we saw.

As Queen played the last few chords of their album we pulled into the kerb outside the flat and I asked,

"Anyone for a beer?" There was a big, "Yes!" all round. Kevin brought up his music collection and plugged *Wings At the Speed of Sound* into our tape deck, Claudia was up for cooking some dinner, Kia the cat got two new laps to sit on and I handed out chilled bottles of beer. We were all set!

Karen had met Kev at the Gold Coast Bulletin; she was working in administration and he in the sales department. They had become friends and when Karen mentioned she was taking a trip to Mount Isa to see her brother, Kev offered to go with her and they would drive up in his new Sandman.

The HJ Holden was distinct from its predecessor, the HQ, having a squared-off front and wrap around indicator lights. The panel van, intended as a commercial vehicle, was released with a special Sandman package in late 1975, with features adapted from the Monaro GTS models. It was distinctive, boasting bold colours, graphics and a host of sporty extras designed to appeal to a younger crowd. It had become very popular with Australia's thriving surf culture and to prove the point, Kevin had brought his surfboard with him in the back.

Sometime during the evening Claudia noted dryly, "Not much surf out here in Mount Isa Kevin."

But, the next day we took them out to Lake Moondara and Kevin was able to get his board wet and be a surfer in the middle of the desert. Actually, we all had a paddle and it was really great to get on a surfboard again. Ray, Margie and Debbie drove out in the Charger and joined us for a swim, beers and barbecue; it wasn't long before the Ford man, now a Valiant man, and the Holden man, now a LeyLand man, and the Sandman man were bantering about the superiority of their cars. I copped some flack about my "family sedan" and its "sewing machine motor," but there was strong rivalry between the other two. There was no doubt though that with his 5.0 litre (308cc) motor, Kevin held a powerful ace and Ray would come afoul of the big V8 soon enough.

I worked throughout the week while Karen and Kevin explored Mount Isa and surrounds. We all hung out together in the evenings, went out for dinner several times and had some beers at the Overlander Hotel, which was just up the road from the flat. Kevin told us he had gone there for a beer during the week to be greeted by a gang of local bikers having a brawl. I borrowed a phrase that was said to me when I first arrived in The Isa, "You should have been here a few years ago, when it was really rough!" Ray met up with us during the week and we made plans to take our visitors out to Mount Frosty on Saturday, but an event at work would prevent me from joining them.

On Friday the labour pool always adjusted the crushers so that they were ready to run all weekend. The work was going well until we got to No. 3. We all knew that the big machine was due for maintenance as its internal liners were worn and needed replacing, as a result it was more difficult to adjust. We had removed all of the wedges and the operator began to feed ore in, the crusher thumped and its cylindrical body began to rotate. Steve and the operator had decided to set the gap a bit tighter than normal to account for the excessive wear. Ore rattled down into the crusher and we stood, hammers ready, waiting for the call. It seemed like a long time before we heard Steve's, "Now! Now! Now!" the bowl was jumping aggressively and spinning fast. We leapt into action, but with the amount of vibration bouncing the machine it was difficult to hit the wedges accurately and the body kept on turning. We were getting those wedges set when there was a great shudder through the floor, dust went everywhere and the crusher groaned and jammed tight with ore pouring out of it, all over the crusher floor. We all leapt back and got out of the way fast. The powerful electric motor squealed loudly, and then tripped, the crusher operator cut the ore feed and it was suddenly silent.

The door to the operating room slammed open and the operator ran out, "Ah-h fuck it!"

I looked around; the crusher was partially buried in ore that spread out over the metal floor, and some had fallen down to the ground below us. Dust was still streaming up out of the machine, exposing rays of sunlight that played into the building. This was not a good look and particularly for the operator whose shift it had happened on. A machine being down affected production and all operator's bonuses and up through management were paid based upon through-tonnage; in addition, there was the time and cost to get this all fixed and working again.

"Not a good look at all." commented Harry as we talked quietly off to one side, awaiting instructions.

Steve, who had disappeared into the control room with the operator, emerged and came over to talk with us.

"Wait around here." he said, "They're sending an inspector over and then we'll have to clean up the floor. That'll take the rest of the day. Can you two work some overtime this weekend? They are going to bring in a crew to dismantle the crusher. They've moved its maintenance forward too and will replace all the plates while they have it apart." He shook his head slowly from side-to-side and lowered his voice conspiratorially, "They should've done that earlier instead of trying to squeeze every last drop out of it."

"Yeh, I can work this weekend." I said. Harry nodded too.

"Good. Okay. Merv will come in too and drive the loader. You'll be able to shovel some ore off the side down onto the floor; the rest will have to go into a wheelbarrow and down in the lift. "

Then he looked directly at me, "You better get to it. We will probably have some of the mine managers coming over for a look." He raised his eyebrows and the corners of his mouth turned down a little; a silent question.

"Got it Steve." I said for both of us. "Don't get caught slacking."

He nodded, winked and then turned to go back into the control room; Harry and I went off to find a couple of wheelbarrows. It was going to be a long day.

On Saturday we were joined by Ken, the overhead crane driver, engineers, a boiler maker, an apprentice, the control room operator and a shift boss; everyone gathered around the distressed crusher while the shift boss and engineer talked about the job. They sent the apprentice in first who set-to, blasting the machine with compressed air and sending clouds of fine dust high-up.

Ken yelled out, "Oy!" from his lofty perch and shook his fist as the dust rose up to meet him

Then the others got busy wire-brushing giant nuts and bolts and dousing them with oil. We had been able to clear away much of the ore spill on Friday, so Harry and I began tidying up around the periphery, taking the occasional wheelbarrow load down to Merv; we would be needed later when the machine was opened up.

The overhead ore chute was unbolted and lifted away by the crane, which then returned for the feed hopper; with the use of some large hammers this came clear and was deposited down on the ground floor. It was time for Harry and I; we stepped up onto the body and began shovelling ore out of the crusher into a wheelbarrow. While we toiled the others stood around, smoked and talked among themselves; occasionally entertaining themselves with loud comments about our apparent poor performance with a shovel, inability with women, extremely low tolerance to beer, small penises and other good-natured barbs and jibes. We, of course, defended ourselves and returned as good as we got.

"Half a shovel-full Steve? Come on. Is that all you've got. I'd take you out and buy you beer and steak if I thought it would help build you up, but you look beyond all hope!"

"So is that how you pick up your gay boy friends Jimmy; bribing them with drink and food to make up for you having such an ugly dial?"

"At least I've got some friends, ya looser."

"So you say, but it's not what I've heard!" Is that your photo on the wall at the Snake Pit? The one that says, 'Friends wanted. I'm desperate and will take anyone.' Is that you?"

"Get stuffed."

"Not by you buddy."

"You wish."

When we had cleared as much ore as possible, Harry and I stepped back out of the line of fire and new human targets took our place, working on removing the massive nuts locking the crusher's body section down.

"I'll bet that's the biggest thing you've had in your hands for a long time. Ha-ha!"

And so it went on ...

Bolts were loosened, a sequence of parts lifted away and at one point the crane and crusher were connected by a thick steel cable, which was used to unscrew the massive cylindrical adjusting ring and expose the crusher's heart, its mantle. Harry and I stepped in again to clean up. The rest of the crew busied themselves as one of the mine managers and our shift boss came to see how the job was going. They talked with the engineer, pointed a lot and looked over the naked crusher; then they left and Harry gave me a knowing wink.

"Time for a smoke Steve." he said, "They won't be back again today."

Stephe⊙ ti ram

And with that we walked down the steps to the ground
floor and found a quiet spot where we could finish
up our shift. After a while, I left Harry talking with
Merv and went back up to watch the crusher being
repaired and reassembled. It was quite extraordinary
to see its massive parts and pieces, no doubt weighing
many tonnes, flying through the air like a bizarre circus
trapeze act, controlled by master puppeteer Ken, way up
in the ether above us. At four o'clock the siren sounded,
signalling a change of shift. I bid farewell to the others
and went home with stories to tell of cranes and
crushers, but over a cold beer Kevin took the floor with
a tale of Ray Linwood and his beautiful orange Charger.

"Mate. You won't believe what happened today." Kev
began quietly.

"Yeh." confirmed Karen, shaking her head.

"Really?" I replied. "What happened?"

Kev took a long pull of his beer, as if pausing for effect
and then said, "Ray smashed up his Charger."

I was shocked. Cars were a big thing in our lives; they
gave us freedom to move, a private space that we could
customize, play music, kiss girlfriends or hang out with
our mates. And there was no doubt that it was fun to
cruise through town and watch heads turn, attracted
by a throaty exhaust or great paint job. Girls seemed to
like being in a nice car too, like Margie and Ray in the
orange Charger, it was a good look. So when Kevin gave
me the news I knew what it would be like for Ray, to
damage his ride, just as Kevin knew, just as every boy
knew.

Kev and I looked at each other for a moment and then I asked, "Is he okay?" and we both knew I wasn't asking just about his physical health.

"He wasn't too happy." Kev replied, "Broke an ankle."

"Yeh? Wow. So, what happened? I asked.

"Well, basically, he ran it off the Barkly Highway."

"Yeh?"

"Yeh."

Kev took a quick sip of his beer and leaned forward, "Ray and Margie took us out to Mount Frosty this afternoon for a swim."

Karen leaned back in her chair and nodded. Claudia, who had heard the story earlier, turned around and leaned back against the kitchen bench to listen.

"On the way back we drove out onto the highway and I put my foot down; I already knew we had a race on. I could see the Charger in my rearview mirror; it came drifting out of the dirt road in a cloud of dust and onto the bitumen; Ray gunned it and was after me. We raced towards Mount Isa; the V8 was a good 100 metres ahead when suddenly, the Charger went bush!"

"Far out!" I exclaimed.

"Yeh. Maybe it slipped on some gravel; I'm not sure, but I watched in the mirror as he ploughed into the bush, with dust and rocks going everywhere. We pulled up as fast as we could, did a u-turn and went back; it was about 150 metres in. Margie was okay but Ray had hurt his ankle; turned out later that it was broken. The car was pretty beat up."

Kev paused, revisiting the scene in his mind; he took a sip of his beer and finished up. "It had run over the top of rocks and scrub; buckled his front rims and messed the front-end up; there's some good-sized boulders out there you know."

"Chargers aren't really designed for bush-bashing. I replied. "How's Ray now."

"Yeh. True." Kev chuckled, "We put them both in the back of Sandman and went off to the hospital. Ray was pissed that he'd lost his wallet in the accident. He's okay. Got some crutches to get around on now."

"They were lucky." Karen said, "He managed to avoid some big boulders. If he hit any of them the car would have probably been totalled and they may not have gotten off so lightly."

"Yeh." Kev agreed.

"Well, it's a good thing I wasn't there in the mighty Marina; probably would have beaten both of you home!" I said.

"Yeh. Sure you would have." Claudia smiled at me and I grinned back.

My attempt at humour broke into the somber mood and we all lightened up a bit.

"Well, I'm glad to hear they're okay." I said. "I guess we'll catch up with them tomorrow. Let's get some dinner. Anyone for pizza?"

Everyone was excited about pizza but Karen said, "Maybe you should get cleaned up first, brother. You're a mess!" She pulled out her camera and took a photo of me sitting at the table. "I'm going to show this to Mum; she won't believe you've turned into such a grub."

I realised that I was still in my work gear; I got up and went into the bathroom. Looking into the mirror it seemed like there was a dirty coal miner looking back at me; his face black with soot and hair all streaked with dirt and sweat.

"I see what you mean." I called out, turning on the shower and picking up soap. "Goodbye mate." I said quietly, as the coal miner washed away down the drain.

The next day Kevin was up early, before me, and went back to the scene of Ray's accident. He was very excited when he came home.

"I found it!" he exclaimed; brandishing Ray's wallet. "I found his wallet."

"Wow. Ray is going to be pretty happy with you!"

Later in the morning we all went to visit Ray, and Kevin returned his wallet. Ray was stoked. He was sitting on the verandah at Margies parent's place with his bandaged foot propped up on a stool, a steaming coffee cup in hand.

"Look's like you're getting the royal treatment mate."

"Yeh." he winked at me and grinned, and I knew Ray was going to be just fine.

A tow truck had been organised to pick up the
distressed Charger and would take it to a holding yard.
Ray could get it assessed from there. He'd been smart
and had taken out insurance when he bought the car; so
there was a good chance it would be repaired and he'd
be back on the road again soon. No police had been
involved so his license would not be docked any points.
Apart from a sprained ankle Ray seemed in good shape
and was certainly enjoying being taken care of by the
beautiful Nurse Margie. We left them and went out to
Lake Moondarra for a swim.

Karen and Kevin stayed with us for about 10 days and
then headed off early one morning, beginning their
drive home to the Gold Coast. Kevin had taken two
weeks holiday for this trip and had to get back to start
work again. Shortly after they had gone Claudia and
I broke up. Our relationship had not been going so
well and while the visitors had galvanised us into being
good hosts, their leaving seemed to make it all the more
obvious. It was not a dramatic breakup but it was clear
that we were done living together. We would continue
to see each other as we socialised with our friends and
agreed that some space would be good for both of
us. Claudia took the cat and moved back in with her
parents, though she would be looking for her own place
soon, and I took up residence at Mount Isa Mines'
single men's quarters, know as The Barracks.

It was a big change and I was out of sorts for a while.
Having been *Stephen and Claudia* for the past year
or so, now, being single was quite different and it

seemed different from the last time that I had been single. Relationship was an insidious reality and it had cunningly got its hooks into me; the weird thing was that I had been aware of each sharp hook as it took hold but had also been love drugged enough not to care. Now that the girl was gone the effect of the drug dissipated quickly, but the hooks remained, especially the ones in my guts. I began mourning my loss, searching for what I'd done wrong, feeling guilty, feeling like I'd failed ... feeling. Friends became sympathetic, even people I didn't know well joined in, commiserating my loss. But beyond the emotional turmoil I was excited for something new and as I connected once again with that energy, of adventure, I started to come out of the fog.

Perhaps, in mourning the loss, I had blinded myself to what was actually possible as a result of it. And while breaking up with someone is not fun; not comfortable it is being uncomfortable that forces us to take action and create something different. While it seemed easier to mourn and be sad, and I certainly had a willing bunch of contributors, I knew it was not going to create the adventure of my life.

There are times when you simply have to get on with your life without really knowing what will happen next; there's no one else there to do it for you, no one cheering you on and it's all up to you. One day, after a period of being sad about our breakup, I just let it go. It was a choice for something different and with that choice, a lot of "different" began to show up.

Chapter 19

Getting Ahead

In the 1930s, United States company ASARCO owned
Mount Isa Mines and were experiencing a massive
turnover in workers,

> "In a given year, roughly half the employees left
> the site and were replaced with new employees
> who needed to be trained and integrated ..."—
> Ned White

The company had encouraged workers to construct their
own places and advanced them building materials at
very favourable terms, and even offered to partially fund
a home ownership scheme partnered with Cloncurry
Council. A shortage of suitable housing for married
employees had been an issue, because they couldn't
retain tradesmen and turnover was around 50%. As
a result of World War II and a massive increase in
American and Australian military in the area, a Base
Supply Depot was built near the railway tracks to
provide for the servicemen who were building tactical
roads in the Northern Territory.

Following the war, Mount Isa Mines converted those structures into dormitories, mess halls and an open air theatre for employees. Post-war employee turnover rose to a staggering 130% in 1947, and the company built 100 rental cottages. 1950 saw a doubling of its workforce and the Base Supply Depot's dormitories were converted into single men's quarters; in addition, new tent houses were commissioned.

Despite a developing town, worker turnover was still too high, averaging 65%. New mine management began a cooperative housing scheme in 1954, which started at Soldiers Hill; the 10 year community expansion program cost around £100,000 and included demolishing the many tent houses and temporary dwellings. 1960 and onwards heralded a private enterprize expansion of Townside and in 1968 Mount Isa was declared a city with its population surpassing 26,000 residents. The success of Mount Isa Mines' amenities and housing was reflected in worker turnover figures, now down to 17%, and married employees making up 70% of the workforce. The Base Supply Depot (BSD) buildings and similar new builds had become known locally as "The Barracks" and in later part of 1976, became my new home.

The Barracks were rows of long buildings each containing up to 40 single rooms; there was a central, shared bathroom and steps at either end leading onto a single access corridor. Each building was numbered as were all the rooms; I took up residence in one of the earlier builds. The rooms were simple with wooden floors and contained a bed, wardrobe, sink and small table; they featured a ceiling fan and louvred windows at each end.

I paid $26 per week, taken directly from my pay, which included full board; all meals were taken at the BSD Mess, a cafeteria style building capable of seating 600 men. It was great as I could go in the morning and have breakfast, then pick up up a crib pack to take to work; it seemed that my life had become much simpler. Another bonus was that the Irish Club was within walking distance across the railway track, and as there wasn't a lot to do at The Barracks except shower, eat and sleep, the Irish Club became my adopted lounge room.

New visitors had arrived, with friends Gary Hallard and Ian Mercer driving up in tandem from the Gold Coast. Gary arrived in his Toyota Corola and Ian sported a Holden Gemini, which we nicknamed Kermit in honour of the famous Sesame Street frog. The popular USA show featured on Mount Isa TV at eight o'clock each morning, presumably for children, but I loved it!

Ian and I had been friends since our early school days on the Gold Coast. At one point his parents had moved from the northern end of the Gold Coast, to live at Burliegh Heads in the south. Ian wanted to go to high school with his mates and convinced his Mum to allow him to attend Southport State High School with us, rather than the local school. Every day for two years he rode the 17 kilometres, one and a half hours, each way and completed his Junior Certificate at Southport. On Fridays after school, he would often come over to my place for the weekend, or I would ride to Burleigh Heads with him and we'd hang out at his parent's place.

We were like brothers and I was stoked when he and Gary turned up in Mount Isa.

They stayed for a week and we had fun in the hotels, playing pool, out at Moondarra and all the usual things that one did in the mining town. Ian was interested in work and spoke with a Mount Isa Mines employment officer; it seemed there was a job for him if he was willing to commit to 12 months or more and settle in the town. Given its long history of worker turnover, mine management was interested in people seeking long-term positions. Ian was excited by the conversation and went home with new things to think about. Gary still had an architectural position on the Gold Coast and while he enjoyed the cold beers, pool and catching up with Ray and I, it seemed clear that Mount Isa had not really connected with him.

I'd been having trouble with the Marina; it was doing this strange thing of occasionally purging engine oil and there were some overheating issues. I decided to sell it and bought myself a Yamaha V50 step through scooter to get around on; it was not particularly fast but a hoot to drive. Claudia and I were still seeing each other sporadically, and I got us a pair of matching matt black helmets; it was nice to feel her hugging me from behind as we zoomed around the place. And while I was a temporary scooter rider and not a big-time bikie, it was interested that the associate fallacy of simply riding a bike brought a different kind of attention from other drivers.

Ray's Charger was being fixed and he and I took the scooter to go out and see how it was going; we had arms and legs sticking out everywhere. The Valiant's chassis had been twisted during the accident and the repairers showed us the car loaded onto a substantial steel frame that was bolted to their workshop floor. They had attached chains to various points on the sub-frame and were, literally, bending it back into shape; tensioning the chains and putting the car under tremendous pressure. Once they had restored its structure they would get on with the bodywork and paint. We left them to their work, not really enjoying hearing the Charger groan and squeal as the big mechanical chiropractor made its calculated adjustments. Ray eventually got his car back on the road and while it looked good, he said that it didn't drive the same and I knew he'd be looking for something else in the near future.

Ray, who had been sharing a house with one of Margy's friends and the guy's mother, was offered an on-site caravan at Union Minière's yard. He hadn't been getting on well as son number two, and over at Ryan Road there had been some theft. So, the yard got a new security guard and he got his own place rent free and was pretty happy with the whole arrangement. The funny thing was that Mick Campbell had moved too and taken up residence in the yard next door to Ray; so the two were neighbours once again. Mick was driving trucks for the business that owned the yard. Ray told me that he'd been over to visit Campbell in his new place and the house was completely empty, not a stick of furniture, except for Mick's mattress on the floor.

"Well at least he's got heaps of space to store his used shorts and tank tops!" I joked.

Our lives rolled on and even though we were both earning three times our previous Gold Coast wages, much was spent on cars, booze, girls and having a good time. I was always broke before payday and either cashing in my small-change, selling some item off cheap or borrowing $20 from a mate so I could buy some beers at the hotel. It was not unusual to be paying for a pot by counting out five and ten cent coins at the bar when things got tight. Fortunately pay day came around regularly, loans were paid back and I was "flush" once again; instantly forgetting the pain of being broke until it, as regularly as pay day did, came around once again. I was blind to the cycle and it just seemed a normal way to live; didn't everyone do it like this? In my oblivion, I had not noticed that Ray was quite good with money and had savings, until one day he announced he had enough to buy a Ford GT-HO.

"I'm going to sell the Charger." Ray began. "It's never been the same since the accident."

"Yeh?" I replied.

"Yeh. I really wrecked it driving through the bush. It looks good though. They did a good job on the paint so I should get a good trade-in or sell it privately."

"What are you going to get next? I asked.

"With the Charger, I've got enough for a HO."

He watched my face closely, as my jaw dropped a little, "What? Really? Your going to get a HO?"

Ray laughed that big Ray laugh and I joined in. "Yeh." he said, "I'm going to start looking."

I was delighted for him and at the same time thought about my near empty bank account; the prospect of a

GTR-XU1 seemed a long way away. But is was fun to listen to him talk excitedly about the Ford and what he was looking for.

"Good on you mate!" I congratulated him and was seriously impressed with his news.

"Thanks" Ray replied, "You'll have to come for a burn Stevie, when I get it."

"I'll be there." I said.

We received another big announcement that week from Eden, who told us he was leaving Mount Isa. He'd completed his two year stint and was now returning to the Gold Coast. The carrot that Woolworths had dangled was, after he'd spent time working in a remote regional area he would be eligible for a management position back in the city. We all got together for some beers to see him off and several days later took our friend Eden out to the airport. I watched the aeroplane take off and thought about how he seemed, somehow, relieved to be leaving the mining town; it was curious. Images of home and family flitted across my mind and the fledgling idea of a holiday began to grow wings.

One morning at work Steve, our shift boss, pulled me off to one side.

"You seem to have a few brains Steve," he began, "Well, with a name like Steve, you'd have to be pretty clued up. Right?"

"Too right!" I said as we both laughed at the reference.

"One of the control room operators is leaving, so they are looking to train someone up before he goes; are you interested?"

"The crushers?" I asked.

"Yeh. You know the place well and you'd be a good fit for the job. You'll be working a continuous shift you know, but you get paid a bonus of the through tonnage. It's a cush' job. Think about it." He turned to go.

"Wait." I said, "I'm in! What do I do?"

"Ha-ha." he laughed out loud over his shoulder, "I thought you might be interested. Getting off the shovels. Right? I'll put your name forward and let you know."

"Who's leaving?" I asked.

"Curly."

Curly was the operator who'd freaked me out a little when I participated in my first crusher adjustment. I'd not felt at ease with him since then but 'Hey,' whatever it took.

"Thanks Steve." I called out to his departing back.

"No worries." he called out, "You're all right Steve. Great name too. Ha-ha."

And that's how it was done. A week later I came out of the labour pool and began training.

———

Claudia had moved into her own flat just north off Marian Street, sharing with a girlfriend. My relationship with her was deteriorating. I'd go to the hotel, get drunk and then show up at her place and stay the night; she never turned me away but it must have been a difficult time for her. A friend, Danny, who worked nearby the concentrator building pulled me aside one day.

"Steve. Mate." he counseled, "She still loves you but you're just using her. It's not nice and she's really unhappy. She doesn't know if she's going out with you or not. Let it go and get on with something or someone else."

I had no experience with ending a relationship and I wasn't even sure I wanted to but Danny was older than me and I listened; two things that he said stood out. The first was that my current behaviour was confusing to Claudia and she was stuck not knowing if she should hang in there and hope it got better, or leave and give up on the possibility of reconciliation. I still cared for her and contributing to this unhappy situation was not what I really wanted. The second thing was that I could, "get on," and in so doing release Claudia and explore something or someone new for me. There seemed to be a kindness in that, for both of us.

"You like her too?" I asked.

He looked down for a moment, dark framed glasses hiding his eyes, then he looked up again,"Yeh. She's a friend and I don't like seeing her upset this way."

"Okay. Thanks Danny." I replied. I had got the message, the whole message.

It all came to a head the following weekend; Claudia had walked across town to visit me at the barracks. Females were not allowed in the rooms but the rule was not widely enforced unless someone complained; we were all men living there and understood how this worked, so complaints were rare. She looked great dressed in short shorts, an orange boob-tube and wearing matching lipstick. Yum. We stayed in my room, had some fun for a while and then I got up and dressed.

"I'm going to the Irish Club." I announced.

"Can I come?" she asked.

"Nope. See you around." And I just walked out leaving her alone in the room. She called out my name twice but I put my head down and kept on going.

It seemed like a gutless act, not to stay and have a decent conversation about not seeing her anymore and I was not proud of myself. I wasn't even sure who I was, handling it in this way, being such an arrogant dick.

After some cold beers and a whisky boilermaker at the club I went and had dinner in the BSD and then walked home; the sun was just dropping behind Mount Isa's western hills and its shadows were long and deep. The door to my room was wide open but she had long gone. I leaned on the door frame, looked at the messed

273

up bed where we had been and took in a deep breath. After a while I stepped inside and closed the door behind me.

———————

The crusher control room was air conditioned and featured a full-length console along one wall, there were several TV screens mounted in the far wall and a functional metal desk sat in the corner near the door. Above the console was a wide expanse of double-glazed sheet glass that looked out to the crusher floor. It was Monday morning and I had reported for training with Curly. We both arrived at the same time and Curly was being debriefed by the night shift operator before hand-over.

"How's it going?" Curly greeted John who was sitting at the desk, a large log book open in front of him.

"Yeh. Good." he replied and yawned.

"Sorry if I'm keeping you awake!" joked Curly and we all laughed.

In the background, muffled by the room's two door airlock, I could hear the crushers working at a steady pace. In the time I'd been at Number 2 I'd come to know their sounds; today the heart beat was strong but measured, at other times it could be erratic and stressed. In this new job I would become intimately connected to that beat and even miss it when it stopped completely.

John was speaking, "Ore's very fine coming up; it's been like that most of the shift. I've been pushing it through. If it keeps on like this you'll get an easy day."

"That'll be good." replied Curly and then gestured towards me, "Steve's doing some training with us now."

John nodded my way, "I heard you were leaving." he said to Curly.

"Yeh. Heading to the coast. It's time to get out of this hot dusty hole."

"Well, good luck."

"Yeh. Thanks."

John yawned again, picked up his crib box and bid us good day; the noise of the crushers briefly invaded the room as he made his way out through the airlock.

Curly glanced around the room taking in the monitors and console's various gauges, and I knew that he was tuning into the beat; satisfied he turned to me, "There's a small crib room outside, around the corner, let's have a cuppa before the crew arrive to adjust the crushers. White with two please."

It was much louder outside; I found the room and made tea, each with two sugars, then took the steaming mugs back into the room.

"Just so you know," Curly spoke over his shoulder from the console, "there's no drinks allowed in here. You're supposed to shut down the crushers and take your crib in the room outside. But if we did that then we would lose tonnage. So, when the shift boss shows up make sure there's no cups or food left around the place. Okay?"

"Got it." I replied. "Tonnage is the name of the game."

275

He glanced back at me, raised an eyebrow and almost managed a half grin, "Right. Good. You might just do okay at this job Steve."

"Yes. I just might." I thought to myself as I took a sip of hot tea, and then sat down in a metal chair near the desk.

When we'd finished our tea I took the mugs back out to the crib room. When I got back Curly explained the big log book to me and we went back through several pages of entries. It was a similar idea to a ship's captain's log where events, or notes were entered and created a historical reference record. At the end of each shift the operator made a final entry about the through tonnage and verbally updated the new shift on handover, as John had done. Curly left me to browse the log until my old mates of the labor pool showed up to adjust the crushers. It was good to see them, and it was also different.

"Hi you guys." I called out when they appeared on the crusher floor, "How are you?"

"Good Steveo. Good. You?"

"Yeh. I'm good."

I wanted to pick up a sledge hammer and join in adjusting the crushers but I didn't. It seemed odd to watch them through the control room window, knocking the steel wedges out while Curly adjusted the ore feed. I realized that a part of me was still with the guys, it was like a call from the past, "Hey. Stephen. Come back." and another part of me was in the room. Curly began to talk, adjusting dials and telling me what he was doing, and I put my attention fully on him; the tug dissipated and then was gone. When we went out again to check the lead's measurement I was no longer a labourer.

Harry was leaning on the rail, "Looking good Steveo. Looking good."

Shift Boss Steve introduced Curly to my replacement in the labour pool, "Curly, this is Ed."

A tallish man in new, but mud splattered overalls looked up and nodded in greeting, "Hello."

"Ah-ha! A new boy. Should be fun." Curly said and winked at the Shift Boss Steve, who grinned back at him in silent collusion.

I knew exactly what was going to happen and stepped over next to Harry to watch it all unfold.

Chapter 20

When Illusion Fades

Whereas previously with the labour pool I'd been working day shift, continuous shift was a sequence of day, afternoon and night shifts that included weekends. A crusher control operator might start afternoon shift, 4:00PM to midnight, on a Wednesday, followed by a two day break, followed by day shift, a break and then night shift; it was a three week sequence that rolled forward by one day each cycle.

The best break was at the end of a full night shift, which was always followed by afternoon shift; in between the two I, effectively, had four days off in a row. Several times each year night shift ended at eight o'clock Friday morning, which meant a full weekend and that always seemed special.

Shift work forced a change of lifestyle. The Sunday Session at the Irish club took a hit as did some of the weekend parties and events. I discovered a different group of people who finished work at eight o'clock in the morning, visited the hotel for some beers and went to bed midafternoon, then got up at ten o'clock at night for breakfast ready to start work again. When their shifts aligned advantageously, some would head off on Friday morning to drive the 900 kilometres to Townsville, or 570 kilometres to Karumba for a fishing trip, returning on Monday afternoon to start afternoon shift. Curly told a funny story of such a trip; he had been driving back from Karumba when some cattle had run onto the road. His car clipped one beast's shoulder, spinning it around so that a big furry brown bum pointed directly at his open window. The cow's bowels had emptied leaving Curly in a big mess. He was in the middle of nowhere and there wasn't much to do except hold his nose and continue driving home. While there were long breaks to look forward to there were also the relatively short breaks where I might finish work at midnight Thursday and start work again on Saturday morning. Continuos shift had its advantages and disadvantages; one advantage was that my pay grade went up.

My training was finished and I was now a qualified Crusher Control Room Operator. My pay had gone up to $250 a week plus something new, loading. Loading was added to my base rate, as a percentage of the total through tonnage per period. I understood now why we didn't shut down the crushers for a crib break; it was to everyone's benefit when the crushers ran. There were three half hour crib breaks per 24 hour period and that totaled a potential 45 hours downtime over a month or the equivalent of 22 days each year, and tonnage was the name of the game!

Apart from day shift when, generally, there were more people around and the labour pool came visiting, the job was solitary; just me, the control room and my four crushers. I had a new shift boss now who checked in each shift, sometimes by telephone. There were times where the plant was running smoothly and I could read, or sometimes doze for short periods though coming instantly awake the moment there was a change of beat. And others when I was up at the console making fine adjustments to handle coarse, irregular or wet ore coming up from underground. The console featured four sets of identical controls and gauges designed to monitor and adjust each crusher and the ore feed it received. There were also buttons and instruments to control the various conveyor belts, as they could become overloaded and trip drive motors in certain conditions. The plant had cameras positioned in strategic positions that fed vision back to monitors in the room, so the operator could look into critical areas of the huge building. If I spotted a feed chute that had blocked and ore was beginning to back up then "bam!" Hit the red button! Stop the conveyor delivering the ore. Some nights at two or three o'clock in the morning I'd be on the shovel once again clearing out a blockage, or pulling out drill rods and wire that had become entangled somewhere in the system. I could have waited until the labour pool started work, but tonnage was the name of the game and my job was to keep those four hungry crushers working. At the end of some shifts my clothes were not so clean and when I got home I found the coal miner looking back at me from the bathroom mirror.

Ray had begun making noises about working for Mount Isa Mines. After nearly two years of prospecting and working out in the bush he was looking for a change. His relationship with Margy was going strong and demanded more attention, and even though he would have to give up his rent free caravan at Ryan Road, the lure of better income was tempting. It wasn't long before Ray began shaft and hoisting work at Mount Isa Mine's K57 shaft.

The K57 shaft was a relatively new construction, commissioned in 1966. It provided access to 21 mining, transport and crushing levels and penetrated over 1,100 metres deep into the earth. The shaft was just under eight metres in diameter, steel framed, concrete lined and contained eight compartments, which facilitated ore skips, men and material cages, air supply, piping and other services. In the process of sinking the shaft engineers had discovered a major, previously unknown copper ore body 900 metres below the surface; a nice bonus! Gone were the days of headframes being made up of an Eifel Tower like lattice of steel girders, struts and braces; K57's winding tower rose over 60 metres above ground level, was supported by four massive steel columns and capped with a simple sheet-metal clad box. This large structure dominated the area and was located just southwest of No. 2 Crushers; Ray and I were practically neighbours. During an afternoon shift, the control room's phone rang.

"Hey Outram. It's Ray."

His voice was lost for a moment in the roar of machinery working in the background.

"G'day mate. Where are you?" I asked.

"Working for the mines." he called out over the noise, "I'm over at K57."

"What's all the noise?" I asked.

"The winders. Monster electric motors. I'm right up the top of the winding tower. When I look out of the window I can see across to your crushers."

"Ha-ha! That's great. I can't see you from here. K57 is on the other side of the building."

"Yeh. Well, I better go. Just thought I'd give you a call mate. Ha-ha."

"Okay. I'll catch you later for a beer."

"Too right mate. Your shout! Ha-ha." and with that he was gone.

I put the phone down and listened to the crushers for a while; all was well. Earlier No. 3 had thumped hugely and it's ampere gauge's needle had shot up to maximum load; about 10 seconds of that would have tripped the big electric motor but it settled down before I could reach the feed's shut off button. Sometimes large pieces of metal—tools, broken drill rods or teeth from a loader's bucket—came through in the ore from underground and the crusher stressed as it attempted to process the alien material. It must have been similar to me chewing on some nice chicken stir fry and then biting down on that one shriveled, hardened corn kernel that shouldn't have been there. Ouch! But the crusher didn't get to stop, and had to keep on chewing until it jammed or the object finally got through.

Ray and I had been in Mount Isa for nearly two years now, we had good paying jobs, accommodation, friends and parties-a-plenty; our lives were good. With Ray now working for the mines, virtually just next door, I reflected on what we'd accomplished. It seemed to me that Ray's phone call had marked a key milestone, for several reasons.

Many people after they have lost a limb say that they can still sense the whole limb still being with them, even though they can't see it anymore. It seemed to me that something similar happened when a child was born and the umbilical chord was cut and tied; but even though there's a physical separation, energetically it still connects child to mother, to family. I had been away from my parents long enough to know I that could make it without them. With Ray's call that 20 year old umbilical connection had finally gone and now I had choices that had not been available before.

I knew that I could choose to *visit* my family, whereas up until now I would have been going back to them. It might have seemed that I was just shuffling semantics, but it was much more. Dad's earlier prediction of my upcoming failure, "You'll be back in three months." would not be fulfilled; and it wasn't even about proving my Dad wrong, it was about me being okay with me.

I would never go back to the way it had been and in those few moments, sitting quietly in the control room, I acknowledged that I had fully accomplished leaving home. It was now time to book a holiday and visit the family.

———————

Kevin Rogers and Ian Mercer arrived back in Mount Isa around about the same time. Kevin had sold the Sandman and was now driving an orange Holden Torana GTR. Its paint colour was officially Salamanca Red and the 1973 GTR featured contrasting black trim, a black interior and distinctive mags; not to mention the 173cc six cylinder motor fitted with a two barrel Stromberg carburettor. Ian, or Merce as he had become known, was still driving a Gemini. Mount Isa Mines fulfilled its promise and Merce was soon working at the mine's rail yard and had moved into The Barracks. Kevin, who had left his Gold Coast Bulletin job, found work with Woolworths in their men's wear store; he'd also applied to join the air force and was waiting to see what would come from that.

I was very interested in Kev's GTR; it was Holden's sports model and while it was no match for the XU1's 160 brake horsepower performance and handling, the body shape and general styling was similar. One evening while we were having some beers and talking, Kevin threw me the keys.

"Take it for a run Steve. See how you like it." he said.

"You sure?" I asked.

"Yeh. No worries mate. Take it." he replied with a big grin on his face. "It'll be better than that scooter you're getting around on. Might inspire you to buy some real transport!"

"Yeh. Right. It just might." I replied. "Thanks Kev."

The Torana was parked outside, it's orange paint demanding attention even in the street lamp's low-level sodium lighting; I unlocked the driver's door, got in and started her up. The motor roared into life and sounded good. Kev's stereo was up loud and Chicago's *If You Leave Me Now* flooded out of its speakers filling the cabin with their distinct, harmonised sound. I reached over and turned off the sound so I could be with the car; this was as close as I'd come to driving an XU1 and I didn't want any distractions. The GTR had an automatic transmission and I put it in drive and then pulled out onto the road. About 40 minutes later I returned the car to Kevin.

"How'd you go Steve? he asked.

"It was great Kev. Thanks mate. Really appreciate it."

"Yeh. No worries. It's a great car."

"She gets up and goes when you put your foot down!" I enthused.

"Yeh! I would have liked a four speed gearbox but the auto is okay." Kev replied. "But I loved the color and the Torana's got such a great body shape."

"It sure has."

"Yeh."

Later, in my room and lying in bed, I replayed my drive of Kevin's car several times, just to make sure.

I had learned something tonight; driving the GTR had certainly been fun but it was nothing like the expectation I had. My idea of what a hot Torana was, a GTR-XU1 no less, had been built over time, layer upon layer, based upon what I'd seen on television, read in magazines or what I had heard from other enthusiasts. It was a carefully constructed model with all the parts and pieces lovingly assembled and glued together. And it had allowed me to be a player in the competition between Aussy blokes. Ray was a Ford man, Gary drove a Toyota and with the support of a dream I could, in my mind at least, be a real rival to the others. And now that I'd driven the GTR, the illusion was beginning to crumble. It seemed that a GTR-XU1 was not what I wanted at all and considering that I was driving around on a tiny scooter these days, the illusion may have seemed a lot more real to me than anyone else. In any case, it was likely that Ray would buy his big GT-HO Phase III soon and trump us all; or would he?

Ray and I were on the move again having discovered Mount Isa Mines had its own fire brigade and periodically took on new recruits. There were some great advantages to being a member: extra pay, better accommodation, regular paid training and it was something we'd not done before. We both applied to join and shortly after moved into the fire brigade's own barracks.

The buildings were newer and had air conditioned rooms; in addition there was a community room with pool table, darts and a full kitchen, and out the back a series of sheds where we could work on our cars. We got paid for attending trainings and also for call-outs.

There was always a rush for call outs; when the alarm bells sounded firemen would run out of their rooms, often half naked and carrying clothes, socks and boots that had been snatched up along the way. The first five or six to arrive at the big red International fire truck got the job and quickly dressed in overalls, fire hats and other gear; disappointed latecomers were sent back to bed or whatever they were doing before the bells. Apart from the fun of being in the truck, racing towards an apparent emergency with lights flashing and sirens blaring, the supplementary pay was very attractive. And we got to see parts of the mine that would not have been available in our regular work.

Often the call outs were false alarms, or electrical systems simply tripping out that had to be investigated; occasionally we were sent underground and did get to put out our fair share of fires. There was also a level of respect and regard for the "fireries" and the mines allowed some flexibility with shifts so that larger scale trainings or events could be attended. And we found a good bunch of blokes, shared camaraderie and a high level of professionalism and pride in the work. All round, it was a good gig!

Greg Summers was in Mount Isa most weekends now. He said it kept him from going nuts, while living in Boulia's small town scene. He had been seeing a tall, attractive, blonde-haired teacher in Mount Isa and stayed at the education department's house that Jackie shared with two other teachers. Mick, Ray and I had a lot of fun with the teachers who always seemed to have a party or barbecue on the go. During one such event. Ray got talking to Greg, who drove a Ford, about buying a GT-HO Phase III.

"The HOs use a heap of petrol Ray; it will cost you a fortune to run it."

"Yeh?"

"Yeh. It hasn't got a 160 litre petrol tank because its economical! Ha-ha." Greg was on a roll.

"Ha. Yeh. True."

Greg continued his pitch. "You should have a look at the XW, like I have. Same body shape. My Falcon GT goes like the clappers mate. It's got the new Windsor V8 motor you know."

Ray looked thoughtful, "I like the look of the GT; good colours and it has got the 351cc V8. Gotta have the 351 Greg!"

"Too right mate!" They chinked their beer bottles together in agreement and both laughed out loud; entente had just been established. Ray was leaning forward, elbows resting on knees and his attention with the teacher.

"Have you driven one before? Greg asked casually while he glanced around; he caught Jackie's eye across the room, nodded and smiled.

"Na. Not yet." Ray replied.

"You can take the big GT for a run if you like." Greg patted his jean's pocket, virtually dangling car keys as if they were the proverbial juicy carrot.

"Yeh?" Ray responded; surprised and then pleased, "That would be really good Greg. Thanks."

"Yeh. No worries. See if you like the beast." Summers pulled the carrot from his pocket and paused for a moment, "I'm thinking of selling it, if you're interested." then dropped a set of silver keys into Ray's hand, turned and walked off towards Jackie; the deal was nearly done.

"Coming for a drive in a real car Outram." Ray invited; taunted.

"Na mate. This one is all yours." I replied.

Ray laughed. I could tell he was excited. He threw the keys into the air, caught them and walked off. A few moments later I heard the throaty sound of a big V8 motor coming to life, lights flashed and then a car drove off into the distance

Ray took the WX Grand Tourer for a long test drive. He came back later wearing a big smile; his eyes were bright and not just from alcohol. By the time the following weekend had rolled around Ray had bought the car; paid in full, all cash.

––––––––––

Christmas was fast approaching and 1976 was coming to a close; temperatures in Mount Isa had been steadily ramping up after some very pleasant winter months. It had been an interesting year for the city with Sherbert and the Ted Mulry Gang presenting their *Howzat* tour in June; we had gone to see them perform at the Barkly Hotel, featuring new guitarist Harvey James. July saw the opening of Frank Aston Museum by Mount Isa Mines' recently knighted chairman, Sir James Foots and greyhound racing began in Buchanan Park. September heralded a national ban on radio and TV cigarette advertising, which I must have somehow missed as I'd begun taking Drum tobacco and papers to work. On November 7, unlike the rest of the country, the mines continued working during Australia's premier horse race the Melbourne Cup; but as soon as Bob Skelton had roared Van de Hum across the line the word passed high and low like wildfire. More importantly though the ABC had cancelled its raunchy TV comedy show, Alvin Purple! The earlier films had been good fun with regular displays of tits, bums and the occasional penis, and we liked the idea of various women inexplicably lusting after poor Alvin, aka Aussy bloke Graeme Blundell.

I'd put in an application for two weeks annual leave, which had been approved for February, and booked a return flight to the Gold Coast. Mum and Dad had left their Narrow Neck apartment and bought a house over on the northern side of Main Beach; there was a spare room and I could stay with them. Karen was living at home and still working with the Gold Coast Bulletin and my Grandmother Rena, who I had not seen since leaving England 12 years ago, was visiting, so we could all have some time together.

Christmas 1976 came and went, the rainy season engulfed the region with major flooding and eventually dissipated. Once again I stood on the Leichhardt River's banks and looked across the river's raging torrent to the Bowls Club, isolated on its island, "Next year for sure." I promised myself. I'd bought a Kawasaki 400 motor bike as the scooter had not been running well and a local bike mechanic told me it was not worth fixing, and had started seeing a new girl named Penny.

Actually, I had been seeing several girls but Penny got my attention; she had fabulous hair hanging like a dark river all the way down to her waist and large soft breasts. The hair and boobs alone would have probably won me over, but she was easygoing, a lot of fun and I liked her luscious full figure and the alluring way she dressed it. Mount Isa's social scene was truly 'small world,' as Penny had just moved in to share a flat with Claudia.

The *small world phenomenon* had been discussed for years and was the subject of an interesting experiment by Stanly Milgram, in the late 60s. The United States psychologist sent information packs to randomly selected individuals, inviting them to be the starting point for a chain of correspondence. The participants were asked if they personally knew the person described in their pack and if they did, then they would forward a provided letter to that person; otherwise consider if someone else that they knew may know the target, and forward the package on to that person.

Amazingly, 64 letters did reach their intended target contacts. Some arrived within as few as two hops, but the average path length fell around five to six, and researchers concluded that people in the United States are separated by about six people. So, perhaps I should not have been surprised by the apparent coincidence of the two girls knowing each other.

It seemed a bit weird to be going out with Claudia's flat mate, and there were a few awkward moments. Claudia had taken up with a new boyfriend but we all managed to manoeuvre around each other; it seemed to work out okay. Anyway, my relationship with Penny was fun but short as just after my trip to the Gold Coast a new girl showed up and for the very first time I fell head over heels, completely in love.

Chapter 21

Family Revisited

Besides copious quantities of $H2O$, Mount Isa's rainy season also brought sweet pleasures; mangos. The huge shady trees grew wild in the region's semi-arid environment, and much to the delight of local Flying Fox colonies and residents, produced a fabulous fruit. We of Mount Isa Mines Fire Brigade had a considerable advantage over bats' wings and earth-bound people; we had a fire truck.

An important part of our training was to know how to use all of the equipment, and to that end we practiced extending the truck's long ladder up to the top of mango trees, where the very best mangos hung. Operators would skillfully manoeuver the ladder left, right, up and down to position it precisely where the point person high up on the ladder could carefully pick magnificent mangos. All agreed, from the Senior Fire Officer down to the lowest beginner fireman, that this was highly valuable training.

In the late afternoon we would return to the fire station and with large plastic bins full of glorious fruit and gorge ourselves. Even residents of nearby barracks would join in for the feast, and there was plenty to go around.

"I really don't know how we manage to put up with this job!" someone said as sweet sticky mango juice drizzled down and dripped off his chin.

"They're almost better than beer." suggested another sugar saturated mouth.

"Almost, but not!" was the consensus response.

As we ate and talked I glanced up to watch the first bats venturing out across the darkening sky, "Go get 'em boys. We've left you some." I called out.

In mid January news of Australia's worst train disaster penetrated the invisible shell of Mount Isa's regional remoteness. An eight carriage commuter train had left the rails while approaching Granville railway station on its way to Sydney. Many people were injured and 83 died; it was horrific and captured the nation's attention. Our local papers and news reported the disaster for days and it was the talk of the town; sobering news for the mining community who were familiar with rail. Even the upcoming event of Queen Elizabeth's royal visit in February was usurped by the far reaching drama of Granville. But news is fragile fare, to be consumed fresh, and the headlines soon changed to cover contemporary events. And my own news took center stage as the first day of annual leave finally arrived.

I caught an afternoon flight and later touched down in Brisbane's domestic airport around five o'clock. Dad was waiting in the arrivals area and waved when he saw me. It was a little strange at first, we shook hands, then laughed and hugged. He stood back for a minute and looked me over.

"Look at you." he smiled, "Long hair and what's that fluff on your face?"

Recently I'd grown and styled a Van Dyke beard, and my hair was quite long; shoulder length. I'd been fairly skinny as a teenager but physical work at the mines had changed my body ... a lot had changed.

He nodded; satisfied, "Come on son. I've got something special to show you and then we'll go home. Molly will have dinner ready for us."

As we walked to the carpark Dad explained that he'd been working in Brisbane and that's why the others had not come to meet me at the airport. We got into a Ford F100 pickup with a "Transpac" label on the door and drove off. Dad chatted about his work as a driver for the Gold Coast company, who made kitchens; he delivered their flat-packed products all over Brisbane and had come to know the city well. While we chatted I could see that he looked good; lines that had been engraved in his face from the Marlin Motel days had eased and he seemed happy and relaxed. He swung the long wheel base Ford into a carpark and we got out at the Breakfast Creek Hotel.

"Come on Stephen, I'd like to buy my son a beer; a special treat." He put his hand on my shoulder and guided me to through a door into the public bar.

We sat on stools at the bar where an old fashioned, five gallon cooper's cask was cradled in two wooden blocks designed to angle it down towards a brass tap.

"Two pots off the wood please." Dad placed his order with the barman and soon enough two cold glasses of clear amber beer sparked in front of us.

"Try that my son.' Dad said raising his glass, "This is the only place in Brisbane where you can get beer straight from a proper wooden barrel."

We both took a long satisfying pull and it was, indeed, delicious. The beer tasted clean and fresh; it went down a treat.

"That is a really good beer Dad." I complemented him.

"I thought you might like it."

He talked about driving in Brisbane and how he'd found this bar, "I pop in here for a quick beer on the way home sometimes, when I'm in the area."

I offered to buy another round but he declined saying we had better get home for dinner; the rest of the family was wanting to see me too. We got back into the pickup and made our way through Brisbane to join the southbound highway, after about an hour the lights of Helensvale passed by on our left, then the old Crab Farm and 15 minutes later I saw a familiar illuminated sign up ahead, it was our old place the Marlin Motel, we were in Labrador where I'd gone to school. Several kilometres on, Southport appeared to the right and Dad drove over Sundale Bridge, turned left into Main

Beach and eventually parked outside a house in Hughes Avenue.

"This is it." he said proudly, "The new house."

It was high-set and I could see the original front stairs had been built-in and framed with a wide set of windows that spilled light out over the footpath. It looked warm and friendly but unlike all of the other homes I'd lived in with my family this time it was different; different because I knew I was a visitor, a visitor who was very welcome but being welcome in someone else's home was different to being home. Dad locked the pickup, opened a white painted front door and directed me to put my suitcase in a bedroom just off the entry, then we climbed the staircase up to the lounge room.

"Is that my boy?" Mum called out from the kitchen and rushed over to give me a hug; Karen and Grandmother Rena were there too. It was great to see them all especially Rena; her eyes were soft with tears, she spoke with that lovely Yorkshire accent and there was a cute little gap between her two front teeth when she smiled. I didn't remember much of my Grandparents from England, but Rena and George had visited once when we lived in the Marlin Motel at Labrador; Grandad had since died and Rena moved from her home town of Bradford to live with Mum and Dad.

"I suppose you'll be wanting one of these!"

Dad put a glass of cold beer in my hand and then we all piled into the kitchen with Mum until she threw us all out so she could serve-up dinner. Molly was a great cook and we sat around the dining table tucking into

roast beef, crispy potatoes and vegetables all liberally
doused in her glorious, glossy gravy. We all ate, talked,
laughed and caught up on the last couple of years. It
was clear that Mum was delighted to have her own
house with a garden. As I looked at their faces and
listened to the conversations I could that see the choice
of leaving a full-time commitment and the relentless
work of a motel had allowed them to be more relaxed
and happier. Karen too was good, enjoying her work
with the newspaper and living once again in Main
Beach, where we had first stayed after arriving on the
Gold Coast in 1970. The family seemed in great shape
and it was fun to be with them.

I spent the next few days catching up with friends,
visiting my old architectural bosses Darrel and Ron at
Burling Brown and Partners, and enjoying the beach.
The weekend rolled around, as they do, and Dad had
invited a whole bunch of my friends over for a barbecue
on Saturday afternoon. Gary and Eden showed up,
Ray's brothers, some friends of Karen's and some
others dropped by over the afternoon. I started drinking
shortly after Dad came home from his morning game
of golf and didn't stop until later that evening when
we had a light meal. The next day Rena talked with
me over coffee; she had shaken her head and frowned
commenting that it wasn't how much she had seen me
drink that worried her, but that I was still standing,
chatting and making sense at the end.

I had learned to be a very good drinker in Mount Isa;
I could drink for 15 hours, sometimes more, get myself
home and do a full shift's work the next day. I didn't
think about drinking as being a bad thing, it was a way

of life in the mining town and beer was included in just about everything. I drank with some big men who could consume massive amounts of alcohol—I was a lightweight at just 65 kilos—but I knew how to hit that certain level of buzz and maintain it for hour after hour without losing control of my body or my mind. We drank full-strength beer at 5.5% alcohol; the brewing companies had introduced a light beer product rated at 2.5% but it was sneered at and there was little demand; many would have been insulted had the inferior drink been offered at a party or event. It was not uncommon in Mount Isa to go to a birthday party where the host had put on an 18 gallon keg of beer, and then after a night's drinking we'd return the next morning to finish it off. On some weekends a group of my mates might have arranged to meet at The Overlander Hotel at opening time; ten o'clock on a Saturday morning to begin a day's drinking, then migrate from hotel to hotel throughout the afternoon; this was regarded as good social fun and required stamina and skill. Sometimes I would let go of the control and the next day hear from mates about all of the silly things I did and had no memory of; but it was always a choice as I had taught myself how to drink and be a good Aussy bloke in Mount Isa.

While Rena's husband had been a drinker, and perhaps this was some basis for her concern about me, I doubted that she had experienced an Australian mining town where drinking was an integral part of its social fabric, a measure of one's worthiness to be there and amidst the intense heat, gritty dust and hordes of black flies, it was simply a glorious thing to consume a freshly poured chilled beer. People and places like to claim title to impressive drinking but it's unlikely they would remain standing after a bout at The Isa, going pot-for-pot with some of bottomless pits that I drank with. It was an interesting place and yes, we drank.

I looked across and smiled at my lovely English Grandmother, "Yeh. Sorry Nannna. I guess I got a little carried away seeing everyone yesterday." I looked down for a moment and then delivered the lie, "I don't normally drink like that."

She took my hand and said, "I'm glad to hear that Stephen." then, with a laugh, "And you don't seem any worse for it Dear."

We laughed together and I gave her a hug. I liked Rena and took a note not to cause further worry while I was there. I left her reaching for a book and went into the kitchen to make another coffee.

Before I left to return to Mount Isa Dad took us all for dinner at Twin Towns RSL Club; it was one of those places that the family had connected with and enjoyed since our early beginnings on the Gold Coast. It was located on the Queensland-New South Wales border and had a good restaurant on its top floor, which looked out over the Tweed River and surrounds. Dad and I had a standing joke; the first time we'd eaten there a large steaming seafood platter, designed to be eaten by two people, was delivered to a nearby table. We had already ordered but Dad located it on the menu and said that the next time we came to the club he and I would share one. But the next time we found that the price of the dish had gone up, so Dad said, "Next time Son." The next time, the same thing, the price had gone up and

Dad said, "Next time." This had been going on for five or six years now and was getting quite funny. We would sit down, look at the menu to check the price of the seafood platter and then look up at each other, "Next time Stephen, next time!" Karen and Molly who were familiar with the exchange just shook their heads and Rena, who was a relative newcomer to the game, didn't quite get it; Molly leaned over and explained. I knew that Dad or I could afford to buy the platter but that would spoil our game, so it was unlikely we would ever eat seafood together at Twin Towns.

My holiday at Main Beach had come to a close and early one morning I said goodbye to Mum, Karen and Rena, and went off with Dad on his work run to Brisbane in the F100. We made several deliveries around the city and he dropped me off at Brisbane's domestic terminal around mid-morning. It was a simple, no fuss men's goodbye and I stood for a few moments watching the pickup drive away; Dad's hand waved briefly out of the open window. I landed back in Mount Isa around midday and went over to the Irish Club for lunch. There were a few familiar faces in the bar and the manager took my suitcase to store it; I ordered a meal and a beer then sat at the bar and chatted for a while until my name was called out; taking a steaming plate of lasagne to a nearby table I ate quietly and reflected on the recent trip.

I found that I was in this strange space of not quite being fully in my body in Mount Isa, as if one part of me was still in the Hughes Avenue house. As I looked around the bar I had the odd sensation of lingering in the recent past.

"They are all okay Stephen." I said to myself, "You have seen that; you know they are fine."

And with those words I let go and was instantly home. I became aware of a warm, rich tomato taste in my mouth and contrasting cold sensation when I sipped the beer; across the room I heard the clack of pool balls knocking together and noticed the bar's general chatter and hubbub, someone I knew came over and asked how my holiday had been; a few moments later I finished up lunch and went to join him at the bar. Work would begin at eight o'clock the following morning; I sat on a bar stool, ordered another pot and allowed Mount Isa to claim me once again.

———————

Despite being located on the edge of the Simpson and Sturt Stony deserts, Mount Isa's arid surrounds contained hidden treasures. With our shifts coinciding, Ray and I took Margie and her best girlfriend Debbie out to "Painted Rock" for the afternoon. Its official name was Warrigal Waterhole, but these coveted places always seemed to have a local name that everyone used instead. We stashed an esky full of beer and food into the boot of Ray's GT and roared out of town along the Barkly Highway, heading towards Cloncurry. About six kilometres out Ray slowed and turned right onto an unmarked gravel track; he nursed the big Ford over the rough surface for another three and a half kilometres and then parked in what seemed to be the middle of nowhere. The V8's burble died away and suddenly it was eerily quiet out there in the bush. The girls lead the way with Ray and I carrying the esky. We made

302

our way through the scrub for about 100 metres and walked along the floor of a shallow depression, formed where two low hills folded together. Negotiating a tumble of rocks and boulders we joined the girls who, having gone on ahead, were waiting on a stone ledge for us to catch up. As we approached them the waterhole appeared below us; a cool semi-shaded oasis, set down in the earth and cupped in between weathered walls of ancient limestone. It was as if a great Aboriginal deity had smote his ancient stone axe down deep into the hillside to cleave out a catchment. Countless rainy seasons had softened all of the once sharp edges and worn an overflow through the far hill that ran away to the northeast, punctuated by verdant lines of eucalypts and acacias.

"Wow. How nice is this?" I said.

"Yeh. Very nice." replied Ray.

There's paintings too. Over there." Debbie pointed to the far left wall. "That's why we call it Painted Rock."

"Makes sense." I said, "Where's the paintings?"

"Just over there." Margie replied, "You can go closer to see them better."

"Is it deep?" Ray asked, looking out over the tea coloured water.

"It can get pretty full after the rains." Margie replied, "Probably about a metre deep now."

"Damn! No high diving off the walls then Ray." I joked.

"Definitely not today."

I took off my t-shirt, climbed down into the water, which was surprisingly cool, and carefully felt my way around checking for hidden rocks or logs. The bottom, which was rocky near the ledge, fell away into deeper water in the middle, but became soft and gave way under my feet as I moved towards the far end. I walked up onto a small pebble beach, picture framed with a copse of eucalypts, and turned to look back. The walls either side peaked at about 20 metres above me and fell sharply down, forming a V at the ledge where the girls still stood; Ray was already in the water.

The Kalkadoon had been here before, many times no doubt and going back centuries; they had left their amazing artwork now preserved upon the stone. As I paddled along the north wall I could clearly see the rendered shapes of people; one distinct ochre warrior outlined in amber stood high up, he featured an elaborate headdress and impressive manhood; there was a smaller figure alongside and to his right, a rock carving. Elsewhere I found the Kalkadoon's territorial emu foot symbol; Ray swam over and we stood together in the shallows, pointing, talking quietly and enjoying the open air gallery. Margie came over and Ray wrapped his arms around her; Debbie joined us too. For a few seconds it seemed that I expanded up high into the sky to look down upon the harsh, sparsely treed, hot and dry gibber landscape with its low spiky spinifex bushes and ant hills and there, tucked in the hillside, a tiny jewel flashed up at me as the sun's light kissed its liquid surface.

I heard Margie laugh as she and Ray fell backwards into the water with a gentle splash and soon we were all swimming, the sounds of our voices bouncing happily off the waterhole's hard surfaces. Later we drank some cool beers, ate and lounged on the rocks until shadows began slowly, stealthily to claim the space. We reluctantly packed up, walked back to Ray's car and made our way home. Painted Rock was a bit special and I knew I'd go back there again; maybe next time with my own special girlfriend to swim with and cuddle in the shallows.

In March Kevin announced that he had been accepted into the Royal Australian Air Force; he finished up his job and drove off to see his family on the Gold Coast, before heading to the RAAF's Laverton training centre near Melbourne. The next month Karen visited again for a week, staying with Claudia, Boulia celebrated its 100th birthday and Australians voted for a new National Song, 'Advance Australia Fair;' and there were several new things on the horizon for me, one in particular was going to change my life in ways I could never have imagined.

Chapter 22

Two Loves

I'd had the Kawasaki 400's fuel tank, side panels and tail piece repainted in a deep metal-flake burgundy and it was looking smick! My very first motor bike had been a pearl-white Kawasaki 250 with green trim. The series featured high revving, three cylinder two-stroke motors and went up through a very fast 500cc H1 Mach III model to an even faster 750, capable of a 12 second quarter mile time. The H2 750 had been tested against Ducati, Honda, Harley, Triumph and Norton bikes by Cycle Magazine and was found to be the fastest accelerating machine, and with a top speed of 180 kilometres per hour was quoted as being, "scarily fast." I wanted one!

In June, however, I walked past the Camooweal Street car dealer, and heard a sultry voice calling out to me, "Hey. Handsome. Over here."

I glanced through a wide polished glass window and stopped in my tracks. There, centre stage on the showroom floor was a gorgeous, gleaming Valiant Charger.

"Would you like to have me?" she teased.

I didn't need any more of an invitation and walked through the open entry doors up to the car.

The soft voice filled my head again, "Get in honey."

I reached for a sleek inline handle and swung open her generously proportioned door, then slipped onto the driver's seat placing both hands fully upon her black leather steering wheel.

"Yes." a murmur, "That's how we do it big boy."

Leaning back into a contoured high back seat that seemed to hug my body, I closed my eyes for a moment. It felt good, very good.

A salesman had come over, "Ah." he said, "I see you've already met the lovely CL."

A little surprised at the intrusion, I looked up, "CL?" I asked.

"Yes mate." he said, "She's a 1976 CL model. Been our showroom demo and so we're offering a great price. Only got a few thousand klicks on the clock; just run in. Really great car. I'll be sad to see her go."

"How much?"

"$6,495 and we have hire/purchase available. Do you work for the mines?"

"Yes. In the crushers. What's under the bonnet?" I asked.

"A big 245cc straight six and it goes some!" he leaned in and popped the bonnet catch, "Come and have a look."

The Charger's engine was amazingly clean. After driving around Mount Isa, a car's engine bay soon became covered in red dust. Seeds and insects got stuck on radiators or were deposited in nooks and crannies, and I had actually seen engine bays with their own unique flora and fauna. The engine's tappet cover proudly flaunted its new paint and immediately to the right a silvered exhaust manifold, with octopus-like tentacles, disappeared in under a large round air filter.

The salesman started her up and my hair was blown back a little as the radiator fan came to life and the motor was revved a few times; by the time he joined me it had settled down to a smooth, silky idle. We talked about motors and cars for a while and then came the question I was waiting to hear.

"Would you like to take her for a spin mate?"

My heart rate went up a little more, "Yeh. That would be good." I replied.

"Okay. I'll bring her out for you. Meet you out the front in a few minutes."

Ten minutes later I was cruising Camooweal Street in a sleek Amarante Red Charger, working through the gears and feeling its 140 horsepower engine push me back into the seat with each change. In front, a generous dashboard, array of gauges, centre console, light cream interior … I was in love.

The Valiant "V" series began in 1966 with the VC and included notable names such as the 16 second quarter mile, high-performance *Pacer*, and the *265 Hemi Six-Pack*. But by 1971 Valiant had lost its racy reputation and gained 'family sedan' status. Chrysler had wanted to enter into Australian motor racing and needed to change their conservative label; enter "The 29 Car" project. In early 1970 USA stylist Bob Hubbach arrived in Australia with some rough drawings to begin a secret project, and together with Australia's Brian Smyth crafted a new car. When Wheels Magazine broke the story mid-year, *Charger* was born. One night, in January 1971, Managing Director David Brown took the car out for a run and came back with a big smile on his face; he gave it thumbs up. The VH Charger was put into production and launched to great success with its popular marketing slogan, "Hey. Charger." It was soon followed by VJ and then VK models. The Valiant V series was changed in 1976 with the CL, which reflected Chrysler's corporate name. I didn't know it at the time, but despite Charger's popularity and being awarded Wheels Car of the Year 1972, the CL would be the last Charger.

I swung left off Camooweal, made my way onto Miles Street and after a while looped back around onto West so I could cruise back through town, eventually pulling up outside of the car dealers again. I turned the engine off and sat quietly, though I was pretty excited.

"How did you go?" the salesman had appeared at my door again.

"She's a beauty!" I replied, "You know. I wasn't planning on looking at any cars today."

He laughed, "Yeh. It can happen like that sometimes."

"Yeh. My name's Stephen."

"I'm Rob." he replied and we shook hands through the open car window. It seemed to open the door for his next question.

"Would you like to come in and go over some numbers?"

"Yeh. Sure." I replied.

"If you don't have a trade in," Rob the salesman mentioned. "I can talk with the boss and see if I can get you a better price."

I followed Rob into his office and we talked, and then I signed some papers. He said they would have to do a few routine checks: employer, credit rating, etc. and would be in touch very soon. Two days later I drove away from Rob's showroom in a gleaming Amarante Red Charger; I filled the tank with super and with both windows fully down and the wind snapping at my hair, cruised all the way to Cloncurry and back. I felt that I could have driven the Charger for days and didn't want to go home but my next shift at the crushers was due, and eventually pulled into the BSD carpark to go eat and pick up a crib pack.

The next day, after work, I went and visited Ray and then Mick and anyone I could find, I was so excited that I could hardly stand myself and didn't seem to be able to get the grin off my face. Sometimes I would

wake up in the night and look out of the window to
see her waiting for me and the soft voice would fill my
head, "Are you taking me for a drive now honey?" I
must have washed Mount Isa's red dust off her glossy
skin nearly every second day and soon had the standard
Chrysler radio unit replaced with a Pioneer cassette
player and speakers. It was awesome and I loved my
new car! It seemed impossible that my life could get any
better, but life has a great propensity for change and had
much more to show me.

Unbeknown to many, Mount Isa had a drag racing
track. Unofficially it was know as "The Drags," but
officially it had been named by Queensland's State
Government as the Barkly Highway. About 18
kilometres north of the town centre and west of Lake
Moondarra, someone had painted two white lines,
exactly one quarter mile apart, across the bitumen's
black surface. The strip was located midway along a four
kilometer long stretch of dead straight roadway, which
afforded generous views to the north and south.

The road's surface was in excellent condition, perfect
for racing; it had been upgraded by Mount Isa Mines
as part of their Hilton Mine development, located just
to the west. Often on Friday or Saturday nights, around
midnight and after the hotels had all closed, those in
the know would make their way out to The Drags for
a couple of hours racing. At that time of night the
highway was relatively quiet, but it was easy to see a
late-night driver or road train come around the most
northerly bend. As the twin beams of their head lamps

swung to point down the straight, it gave everyone time to clear the road and let them through. It must have been a strange experience, in the early morning, to drive through a cordon of 20 to 30 cars that had lined up on either side of the start line.

These clandestine events were organised on an ad hoc basis with someone, often a passenger, volunteering to be the starter and others positioned at the finish line. Sometimes there was a timer and a system of torched signals to indicate a race had started or finished. Drivers challenged each other and there was no shortage of contenders; racers might make bets amongst themselves, occasionally there would be an amateur bookie or onlookers would place bets on the outcome of a race, with their mates. Now that Ray and I had some decent cars we went to watch and to race.

It often began with something like, "You own the red Charger?"

"Yeh. Wanna race?"

"Yeh."

"Good enough. Ten bucks?"

"Yeh mate. You're on."

"Whattayou drive?"

"She's sittin' over there mate."

"Lookin' good. Whatta you got on it?"

"186 with dual Strombergs, a bit of head work and high lifter cam."

"Yeh?"

"Yeh."

"You?"

"Stock 245, three on the floor."

"Nice."

"See you down at the start line."

"Yeh. And bring your A-game. Ha-ha."

"Ha! Don't worry mate. I will."

"See ya later."

And with that the gauntlet had been flung down, ceremoniously taken up, wagers agreed and we were all set for, "Ready. Steady. Go!"

Occasionally the cops would drive out to break up the party, but somehow word got out and we'd already begun to disperse before they arrived, though not always and sometimes fines were handed out and drivers given a strong talking to. I suspected that the cops knew all about The Drags and turned a blind eye; perhaps as long as there were no accidents or deaths it wasn't such a bad thing to let the young folks have their fun? As someone who liked going out to The Drags I justified the event with that point of view, after all, there hadn't been any accidents …

I'd finished my week's afternoon shift on Friday night; it had been a rough week with the crushers hammering away at some large grade ore that was coming up from underground. Number 3 had become jammed with a lump of iron railway track that had gotten through, and there were several conveyor belt feed chutes that had been blocked with bent drill rods and steel mesh. With one I'd called in a boiler maker to cut away the jammed steel and then cleaned up the mess after he was done. And the big conveyor belt, the main feed up into No. 2 Concentrator, the bearings on its head drum had begun to seize, glowing so hot so that a cigarette could be lit off it. Engineers had shut the whole system down on day shift to replace the one metre diameter drum and while they were at it, another team checked and repaired the 260 metre long reinforced rubber belt. In addition to this I'd created my own night time drama and shut down the whole crushing operation!

Five hours into my last shift for the week, at around 10:00 p.m., I shut down the crushers to go and clear a partially blocked feed chute before it got too bad. It hadn't taken very long, about a half hour or so, and on the way back I made a cup of tea and then returned to the control room. The protocol for starting crushers was to allow 3 minutes for a machine to settle into a steady idle before starting the next one. The reason was logical; the big electric motors pulled a lot of juice, particularly at start and if several crushers were started at the same time it could overload and trip the system. If this happened an operator had to call in the shift's emergency electricians who would check everything out and then reset the switches. If he was lucky they might show up at the building within two to three hours; it was possible to be down half a shift, and tonnage was king.

The three minutes wait time could be manipulated and with precise timing an operator was able to start each crusher in a much tighter sequence and get everything up and running quicker; except when he was being sloppy and got the timing wrong. I started one, then two and managed to hit three and four about the same time. Number one's ampere gauge was settling down to idle but the other three were registering full load, their needles jammed hard up against the dial's little retaining pin. Then came the big bang, my control room's lights flickered and all four crushers began winding down, along with the plant's conveyor belts and everything else.

"Damn it!" I shouted and banged my hand down on the console in frustration.

My heart jumped, my stomach seemed to drop and suddenly it seemed very quiet at Number 2 Crushers. What to do now?

There had been a time when I was doing training with Curly and we'd had a trip-out for no apparent reason. He'd told me to stand by while he went over the concentrator, where the electrical distribution room was, and in 10 minutes we had power back on again. Before I called the job in, I was going to check that room out myself.

I put on my hard hat and walked across to the concentrator building; the sound of machinery getting louder as I got closer. It was always strange at night; the building's interior was brightly lit, its machines all running but not a human in sight. I looked around and just inside the main entry and to the left I saw a door labeled "Electrical" and pushed it open. Banks of pale green metal cabinets were lined up like soldiers at attention, singing loudly as they conducted massive flows of electricity. My body reacted viscerally and I felt the hairs on my arms move and lift. Each cabinet was labeled and as I walked along the rows, finally, I spotted "No. 2 Crusher." Unlike the other cabinets, its green light was not glowing brightly and the switch handle was positioned to the right; I took a deep breath, reached up and set it to vertical, matching all of the others. At first nothing seemed to happen and my stomach sank again; then, after a few seconds the green light winked once and came on solid. The cabinet started to hum and find tune with the main choir, and I knew it was going to be okay.

I pretty much ran all of the way back to the crushers, sprinted up the stairs and in my control room, even before the door had fully swung shut, pressed the red button for No. 1. Like music to my ears a warning siren sounded loudly and 30 seconds later the huge electric motor began to wind up. Its ampere gauge came to life, climbed quickly to maximum and then settled down as the big crusher rumbled at idle, ready for work. This time I waited for a full three minutes before starting the main conveyor belt and then the other three crushers. Everything came up, the plant was alive again and as I set the ore feeds a familiar and comforting vibration travelled up through my feet and into my lower body; Number 2 Crusher plant was talking to me once again. Woohoo! I pulled out a packet of Drum tobacco and without taking my eyes off those gauges, rolled a fat cigarette, lit it up and took a long pull. The smoke tugged my throat and then settled into my lungs, there was a warming sensation and a little nicotine buzz in my head. I felt my body begin to relax and went over to make a note in the log book, 'Plant down for 60 minutes - clearing a feed chute.' then returned to the console and sat down on a metal stool. It was 11:00 PM and in an hour I'd be on my way home.

On Saturday and after dinner at the BSD, I got ready to go to the Irish Club for the dance. I hadn't made arrangements to meet anyone there but thought I'd just turn up anyway. I left the car at home and walked over at six o'clock for a few beers in the Piano Bar. It was early, the place was quiet but there were a few faces I recognised and joined a couple of blokes at the bar. Around eight I got up and walked through the public bar and into the night club. A three piece band was playing but the dance floor was empty with most people gathered in groups at the bar. I made my way over, ordered a beer and looked around, noticing Penny with some girl friends. We'd not seen much of each other since my trip to the Gold Coast and she waved me over. As I negotiated the crowd another girl caught my eye, a really cute and shapely brunette. I'd not really connected with Sandra Wilson before but I'd watched her dance many times; she was hot. My heart beat went up a notch when she waved and smiled. I waved back just as Penny threw her arms around my neck and pressed her breasts provocatively into my chest.

"Hello stranger. Where have you been lately?"

She tilted her face up for a kiss and claimed my full attention as soft full lips and the sweet scent of Bacardi filled my senses. Penny looked great, hair falling long and loose down to her waist and meeting a full length

317

skirt under which I knew there would be fine lace and stiletto heels. My eyes lingered enjoying the tantalising view that her unbuttoned blouse yielded; she laughed and everything jiggled in a truly wonderful way.

She took my arm, "Come on and meet the girls." and chaperoned me off to join her group. How could I have refused?

I hung out with Penny and as the band and alcohol warmed us up we all danced to Pussyfoot's *The Way You Do It*, Dr Hook's *Walk Right In* and other popular covers; and everyone in the place must have joined in to sing the chorus of Wings' *Mull of Kintyre*.

While the band took a break I went over to order another beer. It was busy, mobbed with thirsty dancers, and I leaned back against the bar while I waited to be served.

"Hello Stephen."

I turned and Sandra Wilson was right there, "How are you?" she asked.

God she was cute! Five foot two, a soft curl to her shoulder length hair and a luscious body that somehow, she'd managed to squeeze into a skin-tight pants suit. All of a sudden my brain seemed to have turned itself off and I'd lost control of the tongue in my mouth. I fell back on the classic Australian auto-response, "I'm good. How are you?" Where was my witty repartee and engaging chat?

She laughed, "I'm good."

She chatted, smiled and laughed and I began to regain some faculties, and was able to communicate once again. Her pale green pants suit had a front zipper that was partially opened at the top; every time Sandra laughed the zipper pull flashed, catching the lights and I so wanted to reach out and slide that zipper further down. She knew, of course she knew, and seemed to enjoy me enjoying her. The band had started up again; after a while we went out onto the floor and she danced for me, something I would not forget easily.

I never went back to Penny and as the lights flickered off and on again, signalling closing time, I knew something had happened to me but didn't quite have words for it yet. Arm-in-arm we made our way outside with the crowd and then somehow were in a taxi being driven to my room at the barracks. As I unlocked the door, my arm wrapped around this gorgeous girl who was snuggling into my body, I truly thought I must have died and gone to heaven. Later, in the early morning, I slowly drove her home through Mount Isa's empty streets; it seemed like we were the only people on the planet. I eased the Charger up to stop outside of her parent's Fifteenth Avenue house, said I'd come and see her tomorrow afternoon and with a lingering, "Don't forget me" kiss she slipped away inside. That night my life had changed, I had changed and something big had just begun.

On Sunday I slept right through the morning, which suited as I was starting night shift at midnight and went to have a late lunch at the BSD. I sat quietly by myself totally enjoying the sensation in my body; the previous evening was a soft buttery impression that had not fully restored its original shape. I went back to my room and around half-two, not being able to wait any longer, jumped in the car and drove over to her house. She was there sitting in the front yard, enjoying winter's afternoon sun and reading. The tight pantsuit and high heels had been replaced with denim shorts and a blouse; vodka and orange transformed into a can of coke sporting its own red and white striped plastic straw. I wasn't sure what to expect or what to be: nervous, excited, amorous?

"Hello." she smiled. I walked over and sat down beside her. We kissed, she leaned into me, our shoulders touched, hands found hands, we laughed at each other's awkwardness.

"What are you reading?" I asked.

She told me about her book, then her parents and sister; we talked about her Dad working underground for the mines and she described her job with ANZ Bank in town. We chatted about anything that might extend the afternoon, which seemed to slip away much too fast. She took me inside where I met Mrs. Wilson and got a tour of their house; her bedroom, her books, her things. And as the sun slipped down behind Mount Isa's red western hills and their shadows darkened the streets, I made my way home with her kiss on my lips, my heart singing and a mid-week dinner date with a beautiful girl in my future. I had no idea how I was going to survive until then but knew that somehow, I must.

And so in the winter of 1977 and just a month before my 21st birthday, my relationship with Sandra Wilson had begun; one that would provide me the highest highs and the lowest lows I'd yet experienced. It would be different to any love I'd known before and be one that I'd never forget.

Chapter 23

Deep Underground

August found us all at Mount Isa's rodeo where Mick
went off to find, "... some black fellas to fight with."
This year's rodeo had been in some doubt as vandals had
run loose in the grounds, smashing electrical equipment
and some of the stalls, but the damage was repaired in
time for the big day. The rodeo was held at Kalkadoon
Park, which was located out along the Barkly Highway
at the northern tip of the airport's black tarmac
runway. Ever since 1959, when Mount Isa's fledgling
Rotary Club had galvanized local politicians, business
and residents into building the venue from mine site
salvaged materials, the rodeo had been staged each
year. Rotary originally created the event to foster civic
pride amongst the 15,000 strong population; they
maintained a herd of semi-wild horses, borrowed cattle
from local ranchers and ran the rodeo with teams of
volunteers drawn from all areas of the community. Most
of the audience would have been unaware that since its
beginning, the popular event had facilitated the club
distributing $270,000 into many avenues of service;

most of the audience, including us, were there to wash away the dust with cold beer and have a good time.

Sandra and I got seating up in the grandstand, and Ray, Margie and Debbie joined us, we didn't see Mick again until later in the day; he said he'd had a good time but didn't elaborate. During the afternoon we saw Greg, Jackie and some of the other teachers, and various people we knew; it was quite the social event! I was hoping to see Sid or Dick from Union Minière but Ray and I both agreed that it was unlikely our solitude seeking bush Dad Sid would be there; just too many people. By taking turns to go and buy beer or food, or just to have a look around, we managed to keep our seats and enjoy most of the events. Sandra spotted some of her work mates from ANZ Bank and we spent some time with them, and having lived in the city and gone to school there, she knew lots of people.

As we walked around I noticed the admiring looks and covert comments from the men. It was interesting to be with such an attractive woman, one that men looked at openly, their hungry eyes running over her body, glancing down her unbuttoned shirt, trying to catch her eye, and then checking me out, assessing their chances. She seemed to enjoy the attention, and why wouldn't she? But while there was desire for the pretty girl their behaviour changed with me, either to quickly looking away at having been caught staring or to glare at me in outright challenge. And I was well aware of their unvoiced taunt, "Well. What are you going to do about it mate!" As a man, being with Sandra, I was much more visible than I was used to and it was strangely uncomfortable. And with my attention on the men, I

missed the women that looked our way, that looked my
way, and missed their interest. We picked up a round of
drinks and made our way back to the grandstand to join
Ray and Margie for the finale, and it was good to be
amongst my mates again.

The annual rodeo was a big deal in The Isa and drew top
competitors from a national pool and internationally,
with prize monies totalling $35,000. We clapped
and cheered along with everyone else as Les Ball was
presented with the Mount Isa Mines saddle trophy
and Judy Crompton was named 1970's Rodeo Queen.
Afterwards, a bunch of us went off into town and had
dinner at a Chinese restaurant; all-in-all it was a top
day.

A few days before my 21st birthday a truck arrived
at the fire brigade and delivered a big cardboard box.
It contained a 21 inch colour television; a surprise
birthday present from Mum and Dad. I'd shouted
Karen a flight up for the weekend and she and Claudia
joined the party held at the fire brigade's recreation
room. The local boys were pretty happy with having a
new blonde, tanned, Gold Coast girl to flirt with. All
the firerees were invited as well as girlfriends and mates,
and I enjoyed introducing Sandra to the mob from the
fire brigade.

Merce had brought his new girlfriend too. Jan was older
than Ian, in fact she was quite a bit older than all of us,
but she was good fun and the two of them seemed to
be getting on really well. Jan was from Tennant Creek,
which was located about two-thirds of the way along
the Stuart Highway that ran nearly 3,000 kilometres
from Port Augusta at the bottom of Australia, up

through Alice Springs and on to Darwin right at the top. She'd told me that after living at "The Creek" most of her life she found the smaller town too confining and so had travelled 600 kilometers east to Mount Isa to have more people to play with.

"Well," I said, "now you have Merce to play with!"

"Yes I do." She laughed and playfully squeezed his denim clad bum."

She had some colour to her skin and was appealingly sassy reminding me of the singer Suzy Quatro, unshrinking and gritty, but I knew that below the surface she could be a real softie and I liked her instantly. It seemed that Merce was pretty well taken with her too as he had moved out of the Barracks, and they were sharing a place at Moondarra Caravan Park.

I had made sure there were enough beers to go around and everyone brought chips, snacks, sausage rolls and the like. We all pitched in at the kitchen, heating food up and dishing it out, though I noticed that after a while most of the girls had congregated there while the men were in the other room. It was interesting.

There was a cake, the obligatory candle blowing out and make a wish ceremony and then presents. It was all going well until I opened a long, crudely wrapped gift from the fire brigade; a yard glass. Actually, unwrapping the yard glass was not the problem, it was when they filled it up with beer and gave it to me to drink the damn thing that I became undone. With the crowd chanting, "Drink! Drink! Drink!" I gave it my best go and emptied its wide flared mouth, then carefully navigated the long narrow neck, but I was no Bob

Hawk. Thankfully someone else took it off my hands
and it was passed around the group until finished.
The next day I was told that I'd fallen asleep on a seat
and when everyone was leaving; Ken, one of the big
firees had put me over his shoulder, carted me off and
dumped me in bed. There had been a loud squeal as he
discovered that Sandra was already there and fast asleep,
having left me to my drunken slumber. My head had
pounded unpleasantly the next day but I rallied enough
to have several beers, "For medicinal purposes only." I'd
explained as we had lunch with Karen before putting
her back on an aeroplane to return home, ready for work
on Monday morning.

In late October, George Lucas' epic space film Star
Wars was screened at the Star Theatre and I flew with
Luke and Princess Leia three times, but Australia's
Prime Minister, Malcolm Frazer, was functioning in a
more down-to-earth galaxy and announced a federal
election to be held on December 10. Early November
saw Joh Bjelke-Petersen's Liberal Party gain its
fourth successive victory in Queensland; the country
seemed awash with politics but Ray and I were totally
ambivalent. The important news was that Ford, with
drivers Alan Moffat and Colin Bond, had managed
a one-two win at Bathurst and anyway, we had other
business to attend to, we were going underground.

There were two good advantages to working
underground that we could see: it paid better money
than surface work and it was shut down on the
weekends. This meant we could spend time with our
girlfriends who didn't work on the weekend, except
Sandra who sometimes was at the bank on Saturday

mornings. We both applied and after a few weeks Ray was reassigned to the crushers on Level 21 and I was to start work on Level 15 of K57 Shaft: I would begin later when a new control room operator had been trained to take my place at No. 2 Crushers.

There was a 55 metre layer of earth between each Level connected to K57's shaft and Ray began work over a kilometre down below the surface where he'd be trained on a massive crushing operation. It surprised me to learn that all of the ore mined, was transported down to the mine's lowest level, where it was fed through crushers and then hauled up to the surface. Level 21's crushers were a different type to the ones I'd been working with; they were jaw crushers designed to reduce large rocks down in size, ready to be processed on the surface by the rotary units at No. 2 Crushers. As the name suggested, ore was fed into a V-shaped jaw like structure where a hinged steel plate compressed material against a fixed one; the reduced ore fell through a gap at the bottom and was transported away on a conveyor belt. Ray told me that the machines were huge, driven by big electric motors and, "No." he didn't have to adjust the gap with a sledge hammer!

When my control room replacement was fully trained I left No. 2 Crushers to begin an induction course; my introduction to working underground. I would now be going to work via the northwest security gate, which was accessed by driving along Mine Road and around the old Black Rock open cut operation. Between 1957 and 1965 the pit had been mined to a depth of 165 metres, since then it was slowly being filled in with rubble from other operations; as I glanced out over 400 metres of open space to the other side, I noted that it was still a massive hole in the ground.

In 1930, Chairman Leslie Urquhart had commissioned a mining town to be built in this area with nearly 300 houses, single men's dormitories, clubs, stores, a post office, school, sport fields, hospital and banks. In fact, Mount Isa had two distinct and separate communities, Mineside and Townside; people identified as being from one or the other and there were regular inter-town football and cricket competitions. Twenty six years later a large silver-lead deposit was discovered below Black Star mine and another of copper on the Rio Grande; notice was given to occupants of houses and government agencies that the majority of buildings would be removed.

> " The company's old general office was carted away. The lofty staff dining hall was set afire. A long barracks that housed 132 single men, smaller rows of barracks, a guest house, 21 houses, five cottages, a post office, a branch of the Bank of New South Wales, were all removed in order to clear the ground for the open cut as it spread half way across the narrow valley."— Geoffrey Blainey, Mines in the Spinifex

In 1955 the centrepiece of the older settlement, the band rotunda, was relocated to Townside and houses were demolished to clear the way for a new road system. By early 1956 the Isa Mines State School had been relocated and the community store closed; this worked to focus the township to the east of the Leichhardt River, and mining operations to the west. As I drove to work and looked out over the open cut's cavernous crater, there was nothing left of the Isa Mines settlement, not even the ground that it had rested upon, save ghosts, dust and perhaps memories now long and forgotten.

Underground had a very different environment to my previous surface work and required different equipment, procedures and safety awareness. The more obvious things were the use of a headlamp and battery, respiratory filters were critical in heavy dust areas and loud equipment operating in confined areas required ear protection. The amount of gear a worker had to carry on-person, was significant.

Everyone had a brass identity tag; it's main purpose was safety and not wearing it to work was grounds for dismissal. The safety officer, an old miner himself, explained that the business of mining was, "bloody mining!" Mining involved explosives and he stressed that explosives were, "bloody dangerous things!" He held up his hand and I saw that the thumb and top joint of its index finger were missing; the old wound's pale scar tissue obvious and in the silence that followed his point had been well made.

"What are they?" he asked suddenly looking around the room for someone who dared not to have the correct answer.

Fortunately we all knew the required answer, "Bloody dangerous things!"

"Very good." he acknowledged, nodding his head in agreement. "Very good." and lowered his damaged hand.

The mining levels fired at crib and end-of-shift and unless all of the tags were hanging from a board in the crib room, the synchronised firing of all explosives on the level would not be triggered.

"Anyone who comes in late and caused a firing to be aborted will be deep in the shit!" he told us.

"Where will they be?"

We knew the drill well by now and responded in choir like unison, "Deep in the shit!"

"Very good." came the expected reply, "Very good."

Miners worked to have their mine face ready for blasting. A delay meant the explosives, primed and ready to detonate, would be cordoned off for half a shift, no ore was released and the miners may not be able to continue their job. This impacted the level's production and bonuses were paid based on mine production. Deep underground, as on the surface, tonnage was king. Of course, if someone had not returned and there was an empty hook on the board then the shift boss would lead a search party through the level to find them, as they may have been hurt or trapped somewhere. During the training I quickly realised that working underground was risky, and there was a reason that the money was much better than on the surface. I would experience that risk first-hand, in the months to come.

Training finished on Friday and as I had now officially been transferred to underground, the weekend was mine; no more continuous shift. I took Sandra for singing lessons with Victor at the Piano Bar on Friday night and the teachers were having a Saturday night birthday party barbecue. We couldn't seem to get enough of each other and used venues or social events to be together though not in the social way of interacting with other people, but employing our own two person inclusive bubble to exclude. Friends shook their heads knowingly and made jokes about, "the honeymoon period" or "the young lovers" but we were oblivious to their jibes and I was most certainly head-over-heels in love. It was a totally new experience and having taken love's potent elixir everything seemed to be good and right with the world, as if we were shielded from all the harsh realities of life. Illusion, though, does not make life less real, but it can filter out that which does not support a less-than-delicious fantasy.

Shortly after Karen had flown home Sandra commented, "It was really strange at your 21st where you hugged Karen. More like she was your girlfriend than your sister."

My sister and I had always been close but I made a mental note to alter that behavior so that Sandra would not be disturbed by it anymore. It was one of many things I would give up to be deeply in love.

On Sunday morning we met up with two mates at the fire brigade who had just returned from holidays. David and Patrick had done something different to the majority of residents, whose holiday plan was to head north or east to the coast and get as far out of the area as possible. The two men had gone bush to camp at Mount Surprise, a small town located in Far North Queensland's Gulf Savannah.

They'd both originated from Melbourne and had
been working at the mines for about a year. David was
smaller and quite intense at times, while Patrick was a
big strong Irish lad who liked acrobatics and flexing his
muscles. They were a little bit of an odd couple but good
fun and we got on well. They'd taken camping gear,
food, shovels and picks and pitched tent near O'Brien
Creek. For a week they'd dug through the creek
bed, under boulders and in among tree roots to have
recovered 12 bags full, mainly of topaz but some other
types of gemstones as well. It was an extraordinary haul
and my jaw had dropped when they'd opened the back
of Patrick's Toyota.

"Amazing!" I exclaimed as I handled some of the
stones. Even in their uncut, unpolished natural state I
could see the sunlight working its magic with the gems.

"What are you going to do with all of these?" I asked.

"We've got a contact who is a gem cutter." David
explained. "He's going to cut some of the really good
ones and sell them and we'll split the money."

"Wow. Great deal." I replied.

"I'd like one, or three." Sandra said.

"Or ten!" David laughed.

"We'll show you when we get some back from the gem
cutter." Patrick nodded enthusiastically.

And so they did as later in the week David revealed a
magnificent pale blue topaz that was nearly the size of a
10 cent coin.

"The first one." he said reverently.

The stone was fabulous, the cutter had skillfully captured its subtle blue colour zone and the 69 faceted oval cut played happily in the sunlight every time David moved it.

Early Monday morning, I checked in through mine security and walked on into the building at the base of K57. I was conspicuous in my shiny new orange hard hat but at least my clothes, boots and crib box were already work worn. In the change rooms I found an unused locker and noting its number attached a padlock claiming it as mine, then walked on through into a large hall. There were rows of benches and right at the far end the shaft gate. Starting at around seven thirty a powerful rush of air would be pushed into the room as a huge steel box known as "The Cage" containing 180 men on two decks would speed up the shaft at 50 kilometres per hour coming to rest at the gate. The cage would be emptied of those finishing their shift, refilled with those starting and then released to hurtle back down into the mine delivering workers to their level; air would be sucked back down the shaft until the cage's pulling power dissipated.

There were a few men standing around and several flatbeds loaded with drill rods and other mining gear waiting outside the shaft gate for their turn. I walked across to the battery room and an elderly man looked up.

"New hat. New boy?" he asked.

"Yeh." I replied.

Stephe❾ ꞁ ram

"Well, you'll need one of these then." he said and placed a black battery about the size of a paperback novel on his counter in front of me. Handing me its headlight, he flicked a switch and the small bulb lit up strongly.

"Not much sunlight down there son." he smiled at his own joke, probably told a thousand times, and glanced around the hall as I connected the light to my hat and slid the battery onto my belt.

"What level?" battery man asked.

"I'm down on fifteen."

"Ah. One of Dick English's boys."

"Dick?" I queried.

"Yes. Your shift boss. He's down on fifteen."

"Is he good to work with."

"Yeh. He seems okay from what I've heard. You could do a lot worse." he chuckled; another classic.

"Great. Thanks." I said and nodded in thanks.

"No worries. See you tomorrow son."

I visited another window, picked up a respirator and then found a seat near the shaft gate and waited. The hall began to fill with men and battery man was doing great business; soon all hats were adorned with their own mini suns. The air pressure in the hall began to increase as the cage rose up towards us; I heard a big winch motor brake and wind down, the shaft's safety gate was pulled open, then the cage's internal doors and some 90 men burst out, eager to be above Earth's crust and on their way home.

When they were clear the gateman yelled out, "Twenty one! Twenty one!" and Level 21's shift made their way inside. Gates were slammed shut, the cage lowered about two metres and then its upper deck emptied and refilled. Finally, when everyone was locked inside and the shaft's safety gate closed and latched, the cage was dropped into the depths heading for the lower levels.

This was repeated over and over, and the hall had begun to empty. Finally I heard, "Fifteen! Fifteen!" and followed a group of men into the maw. We were packed in tight, shoulders almost touching with most observing that strange silence that overcomes people in lifts. Steel gates clanged, a few seconds wait and then the drop, a sense of weightlessness, darkness and the roaring wind. The cage's guide wheels rattled as they ran on vertical railway lines, flashes of light indicated passing levels and then gravity's earthy reminder as we braked hard approaching Level 15. The cage bounced several times as its long steel cables, elastic under load, stretched and then came to rest. The gates were opened, we all walked out. I was over 800 metres underground.

"It's like being in a cave Steve. Hot as hell!"

Ray's voice was in my head as I followed the men along a short drive, then turned left into the crib room and control centre. The room was hewn out of the rock; not one wall was straight and not a square corner in sight. Rows of benches and tables were soon covered with crib boxes and I noticed the ceiling was covered in steel mesh that had been bolted in place. To the left was a

makeshift counter and some desks, which were used
by the shift boss and his assistants; a tall stocky man
put his crib box down on one of the desks; I heard his
English accent and figured this was probably Dick.

"G'day. Dick?" I asked.

"Yes. I'm the dick." He replied with a chuckle, "Who
are you?"

"Stephen Outram. Just starting today."

He looked down at a clip board and pointed, "Yep. Got
you here. Hang around a bit and then you can come
with me. I'll show you the level as I do my rounds."

I sat on one of the benches while Dick issued orders
and fielded queries; gradually the crib room began to
empty as workers went off to find their jobs.

"Right. Stephen. Come with me." Dick put on his hard
hat. We switched on our lights and I followed him back
out near the shaft gate where he pointed out the Mule's
battery charging room, an Armory, which contained
all the explosives and then we turned right into a long,
large drive. Dick explained that while there was some
mining done on fifteen, it was mainly a transport level.
Vertical shafts connected to various mining levels above
us were continuously filled with ore, the ore was loaded
into 20 ton rail cars and then dumped down another
shaft that fell all the way to Level 21. As we walked, a
diesel locomotive rumbled by followed by a dozen steel
rail cars that were about two metres tall.

The driver nodded and slowed the train, his light bobbing up and down, "New boy?" he called out above the big diesel motor's idle.

"Yeh." replied Dick. "Stephen, this is Jimmy. Don't listen to him. He's a bloody Scot!"

Jimmy's face broke out in a big grin, "Aye! And proud of it you pommy bastard."

Dick looked at me, rolled his eyes, and then turned back to the Scotsman, "Hey, apparently one of the chutes is blocked in six so pull out of nine for a while until we get it cleared. All right?"

"Okey dokey boss." Still chuckling Jimmy tugged an imaginary forelock, applied pressure to the locomotive's throttle and slowly pulled away.

"He's a cheeky bugger." Dick said over his shoulder, shaking his head in mock resignation. "But a good worker."

The main haulage drive that we walked along was about six metres wide and five metres high, hewn out of the living earth; its floor was reasonably level though our boots occasionally crunched on ore that had fallen from passing rail cars. Streaking off into the blackened distance were lines of pipes, electrical cable trays and other services ran overhead supported on galvanized steel hangers bolted directly into the rock ceiling. A single railway track ran the drive's entire length branching off into side drives, one of which Jimmy's train had disappeared into. A strong breeze pushed into my face and played with tiny beads of sweat that had begun to pop in the warm, humid environment.

Up ahead and far off in the inky darkness a lone yellow light moved slowly towards us, accompanied by a much smaller light floating above it.

"Ah. There he is." said Dick and picked up his pace a little.

Gradually, the light increased in size and after a several minutes the steel rail tracks at our feet began to hum, then came the whine of an electric motor and gradually it became obvious that this all belonged to a small locomotive and its driver.

While 3,000 year old donkey dung had been discovered in what was thought to be King Solomon's mines and mules were popular in many counties for their ability to carry considerable weight, these two animals never really caught on in Australia; they were passed over in favour of horses, bullocks and camels. Donkeys and mules may have been employed in Queensland and Western Australian mining from around 1890 - 1920, but the industrial revolution had been well underway long before the first convicts had arrived in Botany Bay and steam engine power had been working in Australian mines since 1825. It turned out, though, that some traditions die hard and the humble mule, albeit in name only, had survived to work underground at Mount Isa Mines; in fact, one had pulled up in front of us!

Its driver was busy winding a wheeled handle; brakes rasped, steel on steel and a yellow three and a half ton electric mule came to rest next to us.

"G'day Dick." the small light bobbed.

"G'day mate." the tall shift boss replied. "Damian, this is Steve. He's just started and will be working with you. Will you show him the ropes?"

The small light nodded and a hand reached out, "G'day Steve. Glad to meet you."

The handshake was firm in contrast to his soft pleasant drawl and loose grin.

"Where are you working?" asked Dick.

"Just delivered some gear to the miners and I'm heading back to the shaft to see what's there."

"Okay. Good. I'll catch you two later." and with a salute Dick walked off.

Now, turned away from us, he was less visible though I could track him by following the spray of light from his headlamp that moved and bounced over floor and walls, and for a while heard a breathy whistled rendition of, *When the Saints Go Marching In.*

"Hop on mate."

The mule was largely a big battery on wheels with a small driver's station containing a metal seat, brass wheel for applying brakes and an accelerator handle; there was just enough room for one person sitting and the other standing. I stepped up onto the machine and we moved off, an empty flatbed rattling along behind us.

"The battery's getting a bit low so we'll go and change it over, and see if anything has come down the shaft." Damian explained.

"Okay." I replied, "How long have you been working here?"

"Three weeks. Dick will arrange some training so you can get your mule ticket. It's not hard."

We approached the drive that led to the shaft; it was obvious as fluorescent light blazed out into the main drive. Damian spun the brake wheel and the mule came to a stop.

"Throw the points will you." he asked, pointing to the ground. "And then reset them when I'm through."

I got off and found a weighted lever and threw it over; he was referring to a switch that allowed the mule's wheels to move onto a different line. As the weight hit the ground a light above changed from green to red; a signal for locomotives using the drive. When the trailing flatbed was clear I returned the lever back to its original position and reset the points so that trains using the main line didn't get any nasty surprises; the green light came back on. Damian continued along and then waited again for me to change another set of points leading into a battery charging station. We used an overhead winch to lift the spent battery over to a charging bay, and then loaded a new one back onto the mule. When the battery was locked down in place Damian took out a packet of Winfield reds.

"… anyhow, have a Winfield 25s." he said.

It was the slogan that Paul Hogan had successfully used in a popular series of commercial adverts for Winfield cigarettes. Similar to, "Hey Charger" it had really caught on with the Australian public. Eight hundred metres below the surface in an unlikely white-painted cave humming with electrical charge, two men burst into laughter and instantly became friends; that moment would never be touched by sunshine or its sound carried on a breeze but was nonetheless real for having been kindled deep in the ground.

After we had caught our breath again and Damian could actually hold the packet steady, I took one of the offered cigarettes, we lit up and chatted for a while. The crib room was empty with all the men out working though I could sense the rumble of a laden train making its way up the main drive.

As the locomotive passed Jimmy spotted our mule and called out, "Dick's on his way."

Fortunately the cage had arrived and a flatbed full of gear rolled out. We hooked it up to our refreshed mule and set out to deliver items to various parts of the level. The job quickly became clear to me, we were like postmen, delivering the new and retrieving the old, and anything that was worn, broken or no longer required was returned to the surface for repair or to be recycled. It was a great job as I got to explore every part of Level 15 and met everyone who worked there. Many a time a hot and sweaty miner had gratefully swigged down a cool drink from the freshly filled water canteens we delivered, replaced their worn drill rods with resharpened ones or was able to finish charging a face because we'd shown up with a new supply of explosives from the armory. We were a key supply link that kept the level fueled and working and as in days of old, in mines all over the world, the mule worked faithfully with us.

By the end of week one working underground I had
my mule ticket, was integrated into a regular game
of cards— of course it was 500, which seemed to be
Mount Isa Mines national sport, and had discovered
that Sandra's Dad worked at Level 15 too though on a
different shift to me. While rail dominated transport on
Level 15, it had been fun to find out that Land Rovers
and Toyota four wheel drives were used underground
too. Damian and I had been at the shaft one afternoon
when the cage arrived and a vehicle simply drove out;
two geologists added their ID tags to the crib room
board and then headed off down the main drive. The
cage was a lifeline that supplied everything from huge
ST-5 scooptram machines, 60 ton locomotives, two
metre diameter tyres and powerful Deutz V12 diesel
motors to explosives, pumps and foam insulated water
bottles. Machinery that was too big to fit was delivered
in parts and then assembled in huge underground
workshops, some would spend their entire working life
underground; it was an extraordinary operation.

On Friday afternoon around four o'clock I stepped
out of the cage and took a deep breath of cool, fresh
surface air. I was now one of those men I'd watched five
days ago as they burst out of the cage eager to be above
Earth's crust and on their way home. Afternoon shift
was waiting for its turn to go down in the cage and in
eight hours time they would return having finished the
working week. Then the mine would be quiet except
for the movement of air along its deserted drives or the
occasional echo of a pump. Those of us who worked
underground would never know the empty mine or hear
the quiet mine, it was a realm that could only exist in
our absence.

342

Chapter 24

Big Stack

The red and white striped wizard's wand was the vision of Mount Isa Mines Chairman, 1953 - 1970, Sir George Fisher. Begun in 1958, "The Stack" was constructed of over 1,900 cubic metres of concrete, more than 200,000 fire bricks and rose up from its concrete base a full 153 metres in the air; it symbolised Mount Isa's upward growth and had become, as Fisher predicted it would, "… a landmark of considerable significance in North West Queensland …" The mighty chimney served the copper smelter at a time when the mine produced half of Australia's copper and nearly one fifth of its lead.

Fisher also predicted great growth for the mining town, "… as operations expand, our national contribution will grow until the name of Mount Isa is a household word to every Australian." Just as The Stack had surpassed the 73 metre high, lead smelter's steel chimney over a decade ago, history was repeated in December 1977 with the beginnings of a new construction that would be known locally as "The Big Stack." It would dominate the skyline at 274 metres in height and be the tallest chimney and free standing structure in Australia; perhaps exceeding even Fisher's vast vision of the future.

In the process of smelting lead, at a stage called sintering, gaseous sulphur-dioxide is produced; it was the beautiful plume of white smoke that elegantly wafted down onto Union Minière's Ryan Road yard and set Ray and I coughing, our eyes streaming and noses running with its toxic fumes. Even with bag filtering and discharging at 153 metres above the town, air quality was becoming unacceptable. Mount Isa Mines commissioned a study to see if they could reduce emissions and commercialise the gas.

All proposals for turning the gas into revenue did not stack up and during 1972 and 1973 the mine instituted a program of closely monitoring air quality and shutting down smelter production when target levels were exceeded. While there was some success with this method it was realised that the stack's plume was influenced by adjacent tall buildings, at times causing considerable downdraft and unacceptable local pollution. A decision was taken to build a taller stack for the lead smelter and to refine and continue with the air monitoring program.

Word filtered down from the fire brigade's officers that we'd be involved in the new stack's build. The brigade was being asked to provide firemen on site during construction and initial briefings were being held with the mine and contractors. There was a general buzz around the station as this was an unusual and prestigious assignment, after all, it wasn't every day that a big new stack was built. The newspapers and media were already reporting on the upcoming event and Sandra was impressed when I told her about the job.

"Can you take my camera up there and get some good shots?" she asked, "You will probably be able to see my house."

"I'll probably be able to see Brisbane, by the time it's finished." I laughed.

I thought of Sid and our conversations around the campfire at Mount Elliot; the old brick chimney in the dark behind us, still standing tall after 70 long years. I wondered if in 200 or 300 years, when we and Mount Isa were long gone, would Big Stack remain, a silent sentinel keeping watch?

"Where are you?" she asked.

I came back to the present, my reverie broken and laughed, "Somewhere?"

"Yeh? Well let me see if I can distract you! she laughed, reached up and kissed me full on the lips, pressing her body into mine; that certainly got my attention.

Nearly 2,000 kilometers away in Melbourne, studies were conducted resulting in designs for a 265 metre tall, reinforced concrete chimney, providing support for an internal steel liner or flue that would extend up above the structure and eject gasses high into the atmosphere. The chimney, nearly 22 metres in diameter at its base, was supported on a three and a half metre thick concrete footing; it would taper to just over 12 metres diameter at full height. It was the system's great height that would allow gasses from the lead smelter to be dispersed over a much wider area and meet the air quality standards that had been adopted.

During the week the fire brigade was training over at Mineside and we drove the fire truck along Miles Road to have a look at the site. There wasn't a lot to see yet but we noticed the existing free-standing lead smelter stack was located very close by.

"They reckon there's only 28 metres separating the two." Colin the truck driver explained. "They're worried that the wind kicking off the new stack will knock that one about; and then there's the blasting required for the new footing that might shake it up a bit too. It's going to be fitted with steel guys, like tent ropes, to make sure the old bugger stays up."

It turned out that old steel tower wasn't so happy about having a new kid on the block and would pour its toxic outflow over the builders; it might also recruit the copper smelter's stack, which was 660 metres to the southwest and together they could, literally, fumigate anyone who worked in the area.

"Good thing we've got air tanks and masks." I noted.

"Yeh. But what about the rest of the workers?"

I knew it was a rhetorical question but took a crack at it anyway, "It might make a new Guinness Book record."

"What? How's that?"

"Australia's tallest chimney, built by scuba divers in the desert!" There was dead silence for a while they digested that one and then the penny dropped, and I was howled down as we drove off back to the station.

To avoid a possible six month shut down of the lead smelter the idea of a "cocoon" was born; a protective environment with its own air supply could be built around the top of the stack, supported on its formwork. Incorporating a lightweight steel frame that would be clad in aluminium sheeting, the cocoon would be pressurised and thus prevent fumes entering and affecting workers. As the chimney's concrete skin would be formed during a series of six continuous pours, known as slides, the 15 metre high cocoon would move upwards with the slipform, effectively leading the way.

Slipform construction was a method where, as concrete was being continuously poured, it's formwork was slowly moved upwards by manipulating 120 hydraulic jacks, effectively self climbing. The rate of climb could average around 220 millimetres per hour, with six and a half metres possible in one day. Along with other fireman I was rostered to work as the slipform was assembled. Having come from an architectural background I was particularly interested in its design and function, and enjoyed chatting with the engineers from Tileman Australasia, when they did their inspections.

The first slip began in early December up to a height of 24 metres and the second in January 1978. There was a four week stop to assemble and test the cocoon; once again the fire brigade provided men while the work was being carried out. Once the cocoon was ready the slide would continue in four steps; the target was to have the pour completed by the end of March.

While Big Stack was making progress there were two other notables: I had accomplished a personal target and Boyds Hotel had been making national headlines. With the heavy December rains I managed to get myself stranded in the middle of a flooded Leichhardt River; instead of standing on the river bank and looking out across at Mount Isa Bowls Club's lights, this time I was in the club looking out.

News was out that there'd been heavy rain in the Selwyn Range's catchment where the Leichhardt rose under Rifle Creek, and I'd arranged to meet up with Harry from the labour pool for a few beers one evening. We were chatting when the club bar manager came over with a warning; or was it an invitation?

"Looks like the river's coming up gentlemen; unless you're planning to stay for the night or a few days, it might be a good time to, 'Break on through to the other side.'" he did a reasonable impression of a line from *Break on Through,* by The Doors.

I looked at Harry, he grinned back at me and I replied for both of us, "Thanks mate. It's probably just a rumour. It hardly ever floods in Mount Isa this time of year."

The manger touched his nose with a finger and gave us a wink and a nod. "Have fun." and walked off to talk with other patrons.

Harry and I picked up our beers and moved to a table near a window overlooking number one green; it was dark and raining but we hoped we'd see the river coming up. We talked, drank, ordered and ate dinner and around nine o'clock someone called out, "Here she comes."

Mount Isa Bowls Club could only be accessed off Fourth Avenue; visitors drove down across a shallow concrete causeway and then up onto an island. The club was located off to the right and there were a couple of houses to the left. On the far side, to the island's eastern shore was the Leichhardt's main channel. The island was about 600 metres long and 120 metres wide with the building pretty much dead centre at its highest point. It was only raining lightly and we took our beers and walked outside, alongside the green and onto the sand. Across the far eastern bank the lights of Lorraine Street twinkled and behind there was Camooweal Street and the hospital. It took a while for our eyes to adjust but as we looked down I began to see movement, froth and foam swirling around in the bed, filling up all of the low-lying pockets and depressions and raising anything that could float; the mighty Leichhardt was alive! I knew from my experiences out at Kajabbi that creeks and rivers could come up very quickly; Harry and I went back to the warm, dry bar but ventured out again and again to follow the river's progress as it swelled and grew in volume and sheer intensity.

Sometime later in the night it was announced that the causeway had gone under and we were now officially living on a island. Harry and I went out to inspect the river once more and it was massive; the beach where we had stood a few hours ago, now, completely under a dark, vast expanse of churning raging river, speeding along its way towards the Gulf of Carpentaria. I thought of Ray who had scratched his name into a can of Coke at Lake Moondarra's dam wall several years ago, predicting he might find it in the Gulf one day; looking out over the racing water, I was convinced he had been right. A huge tree trunk swept past, being tossed and tumbled as if it were a matchstick; there was little that would withstand such extraordinary power and force, except maybe a 600 metre long spit of sand and rock that had probably been here for thousands of years. Shaking our heads in amazement and awe, Harry and I tossed the rain out of our hair, turned and walked back to the bar.

Sometime during the night I must have dozed off in my chair; I awoke around six o'clock and saw Harry was still sleeping, his head resting upon folded arms on the table. The club was quiet except for several blokes at the bar, still drinking and talking. One of them saw me stir and saluted and then raised his glass in my direction. I waved back, then got up to stretch away the kinks in my neck and back.

I walked past the boozy group, "Morning. "Still at it?"

They were amazingly coherent; probably had drunk themselves sober, "Not much else to do mate. It's not the greatest weather for bowls!"

We all laughed at the joke, and the response, "Or swimming!"

Still chuckling I pointed at the bathroom and walked on.

"Going to siphon the python mate? If you shake it more than twice, you're playing with yourself son!"

It was old toilet humour; an off-colour joke that had probably been told a thousand times, but they all cracked up in like a bunch of 12 year olds hearing someone fart.

With my hand on the bathroom door and my bladder requiring urgent attention, I delivered the best early morning response I could muster, "Only men with small dicks would only shake twice." and disappeared into the bathroom accompanied by a salvo of badly aimed verbal abuse.

The bar was beginning to stir and staff, having slept on makeshift cots in the storeroom, were putting on coffee; later on we were able to order breakfast and enjoyed bacon, eggs and toast with lashings of tomato sauce. Harry and I rang work to let them know that due to an unforeseen Act of God, we wouldn't be able to make it in for our shift. I also rang Sandra and managed to catch her before she went off to work at the bank.

"Well, I guess I'll see you in a few days when you surface." she said. "Gotta go to work. Catch you later."

The rain had eased considerably and after some food we went outside to inspect the river; it had dropped, but was still flowing strongly in the main channel. We walked around to the causeway and it had dropped too; it seemed likely that it would clear during the morning and allow cars to pass.

"Well Harry." I began, "Having waited for over two years I wasn't sure if I was going to be able to chalk this one up, but finally we got it done."

"Yeh." he reflected, gazing out over Fourth Avenue towards Mineside, "Stranded at the bowls club. Apart from he scintillating conversation, of course, it wasn't really that exciting."

"Something to tell the grand kids though Harry!"

"Yeh. Maybe. One day Steve. Ha-ha!"

We turned, walked back up the road and went back into the bar to, once more, order a cold beer and wait it out. I mean, what else could we do in such difficult circumstances?

"Right Harry?"

"Right Steve."

"Cheers!"

The other event that made a big splash in Mount Isa, and with the National media, was staged in our local "Boydies."

There were a lot of stories about Hotel Boyd and what had gone on behind its walls over the years.

> " In the mid 70's Boyd's was the roughest, toughest, shootin', tootin'est pub in town. [In the Snake Pit,] beer came in cans only and the spirits came in old Vegemite jars"—Dead Flies and Oose

From the day Jim Boyd opened its doors in 1951 the hotel pushed boundaries, flaunting liquor licensing laws by reopening at midnight to serve free beer to miners after their shift; it's told that drinkers were backed up from the bar along Marion and West Streets. There was an unwritten rule, Aboriginals could not drink in the public or private bars … there was another bar for them, which was called the Pluto Bar but everyone knew it as the Snake Pit.

Its name came about because drunks, both black and white tried to borrow money from just about anyone who walked into the bar. The practice was known as "bite" and their opening line was something like, "Can I bite you for a quid mate?" Apparently there was so much biting going that the name Snake Pit was coined and stuck. It could be a rough place to drink; a barmaid told us that the bar was over a metre wide so that patrons couldn't lunge over and grab the girls who worked there, and drinks were never served in glasses as they would be broken and used as weapons during the many drunken brawls that broke out.

Neville Bonner, well known for being Australia's first Aboriginal Senator, was visiting Mount Isa and dropped into Boyd's public bar for a cold beer and to read the paper. The barmaid refused to serve him saying, "We don't serve darkies here." This didn't go down very well with the good Senator who quoted the Race Discrimination Act and mentioned $5,000 fines; he eventually got his beer. Despite Boyd's rules being aired and discussed right across the country, following the incident, I never saw an Aboriginal drinking in the bars and my sister who later worked at Boyds for a time said that the rule still held.

Harry was Aboriginal and I asked him if he ever went to the Snake Pit; he told me that he didn't, "It's a shit fight in there Steveo, full of drunks and idiots looking for a fight. I'd give it a miss if I were you"

One night Harry and I had been out for a beer and at closing time he invited me to go with him to another place, "You'll probably be the only whitey there!" he laughed.

We walked across the river bed to some buildings there and went inside; it was full of "darkies" talking, drinking and some were dancing. The bar was a small hatch in the wall and Harry got a rum and coke and a can of beer for me. He was right, I was the only whitey there. We hung out and talked with some people that he knew, one giggling girl came up and invited me to meet her sister who, apparently, was interested; but I told her, "Thanks and I already have a girlfriend." At one point Harry went off to the toilets and I was standing by myself in the middle of the room; I sipped my beer and looked around, a few people glanced over but I knew there was no real trouble here. I thought about the black kids I'd played with while growing up in Port Hedland—my family had just emigrated from England and I was whiter-than-white back then, spoke with a pronounced Pommy accent and was most obviously the newcomer—but they'd been good and I had black mates almost from day one. I wondered about how they were doing, the boys who taught me how to fish off the old wooden jetty and whom I'd played marbles with at school. Harry came back and after a while I said goodbye and left; it had been an interesting night.

The rainy season was in full swing and so Sandra and I entertained ourselves at the movies, drank and danced at the Irish Club or hung out in my room at the fire brigade. The seasonal big wet always seemed orchestrally dramatic with huge grey clouds, powerful wind, massive rain falls all accompanied by the Leichhardt River's roar as it raged along its bed. Lake Moondarra was full and we drove out to marvel at its enormous expanse of grey water surging furiously over the spillway, the river driving east across Gorge Creek Fault then, beyond our view, sweeping north to be obstructed once again by Julius Dam before breaking free to hurtle under the slender railway bridge at Kajabbi and sprint onwards towards Burketown; finally plunging into the Gulf of Carpentaria, pushing out a massive fan shaped stain that could probably be seen from space if the thick cloud layer were to part for a moment and reveal the river's spectacular crescendo.

Later, dry and back in my room and listening to Meat Loaf's *Bat Out of Hell*, we got talking about having our own place; getting a flat together. While Sandra had been away from home on holidays, she had always lived at her parent's house.

"I'm not sure how Mum and Dad will take it." she replied when I broached the subject.

"I can get a flat and you come and stay on weekends, at first; we can see how it goes."

She thought about that for awhile, "Na. If we are going to move in together then it's better to be up front with them. I'll talk with Mum first. I can't stay living at home for ever you know."

"And it's not like we are leaving Mount Isa. They can still see you anytime." I offered pragmatically.

"Yeh." And then her eyes brightened and she smiled that smile that I adored, revealing the cute little gap between her two front teeth, "Where will we live? I wonder what our place will be like? This is exciting!"

"Guess we'd better get looking!" I laughed. "I don't want you moving out of home before we get a place!"

"Yeh. That would not be good. Homeless before I even got into my first place!"

While we were on a roll I introduced another topic I'd been considering for a while.

"I haven't seen my family for a while." I said quietly. I was thinking of going for a visit soon."

"Yeh? I always forget that they're a fair way away. I live with mine so I get to see them every day."

"Yeh. Right." I laughed.

"When are you thinking of going?" she asked.

"Soon." I replied vaguely. "Maybe next month. I have to put in for the time off work." Then I asked, "Have you been to the Gold Coast?"

"Yeh. Once. My parents took us for a holiday when we were children. It was great. We went to Marine Land and saw the dolphins." Then she looked at me again, head half cocked, eyebrows raised, the corners of her lips turned upwards with the suggestion of a smile if my reply was the right one, "Why?" she asked, purposefully drawing the word out.

"Well, would you like to come for a holiday to the Gold Coast with me? There's all the beautiful beaches and surf; you'll get a great suntan, and we can probably stay at my parent's place; you can meet them, and Karen too; they're really gonna like you … ."

My voice trailed off and she laughed, "Yes! I'd love to go. It sounds great."

"Okay. Great!" I let my breath out in relief; I hadn't realised I'd been holding it in or just how much I'd wanted her to say, "Yes!"

But wanting her to come was really an overlay, my own, personal subterfuge. Now the real want; the real need could begin to surface. The one I wasn't really willing to be aware of, the one that had been created a long time ago and buried deep, the one that might be more difficult to accomplish, the one I didn't know much about and may never do, the one where my parents would like her, the one where they'd be totally okay with my choice, the one where Mum and Dad got to judge, where Mum got to judge Sandra, the one where she'd approve of her … but I didn't quite have words for all of that. It was more like a fluttering, hanging around near my stomach, not yet defined, not yet clear, waiting for its moment to be satisfied.

Chapter 25

Holding Strong

Australia had an abundance of the highly controversial mineral, uranium. In the 1950s, we'd supplied the British with the uranium, and then allowed them to test their nuclear weapons on Western Australia's Monte Bello Island, and at Emu Field and Maralinga in South Australia. The government signed a Non-Proliferation of Nuclear Weapons treaty in 1972 and hotly debated France's atmospheric testing of nuclear devices at Moruroa atoll in the Pacific, taking them to the International Court of Justice in 1973; this resulted in France moving their testing underground.

Primarily due to a rising uranium price, Mary Kathleen mine was reopened in 1975 and in the same year the government undertook an inquiry of the Northern Territory's Ranger deposit. In May 1977, anti-nuclear protesters in Melbourne managed to prevent the loading of yellow-cake at Swanson Dock and the ship was forced to leave without its valuable cargo. In August, the Fraser government approved full scale mining and exportation of uranium, and seven of Australia's biggest unions declared their opposition. Left wing unions alongside Friends of the Earth and others, staged huge rallies in Melbourne and Sydney, and banned its members from working in uranium mines, effectively shutting down Mary Kathleen. But the Australian Workers Union came out in favour of uranium and lobbied government heavily. To add to the melee, Bob Hawke, president of the Australian Council of Trade Unions demanded a referendum, threatening bans on mining and transport if this was not done within one month. In October, the government who had contracts to supply uranium to Europe and Japan drew up plans to use the defence forces, supplemented by heavy legal firepower, to break the union's blockade of Mary Kathleen mine.

> "MKU [Mary Kathleen] must be maintained as an operating mine. If it fails as a result of union pressure, the effect on the domestic industrial relations scene and on the international front would be irreparable from the Government's standpoint."— Australian Government, 1977

The unions backed off and work at Mary Kathleen was allowed to proceed.

While I was a union member, I was not particularly interested in their involvement in Australia's nuclear debate. It seemed to me that the different unions were using the topic in an attempt to increase membership and gain power. But with Mary Kathleen being, literally, down the road, it was difficult not to be caught up in what was going on; the national and local media were full of it, as were the hotels and their bars.

"The ACTU say they'll actually allow existing mining contracts to be worked now."

"Yeh?"

"Yeh."

"My mate Tom will be happy with that. He works down at Mary Kathleen."

"Good. What's he do?"

"On the tools."

"They're not going to allow work on any *new* uranium mines though."

"No?"

"Na. Not until the mines make it safer for workers."

"Ah. Probably not a bad idea."

"But the AWU's not interested. They reckon there's heaps of new members joining them, in support of opening Roxby and Nabarlek in the Territory."

"Seems like a shit fight. No one really knows what's going on."

"Yeh. True."

The conversation fell away for a moment and then, "Have you heard Meat Loaf's new album, *Bat Out of Hell?*"

"Na. Any good?"

"Bloody ripper mate. You should get it. They say he has to have oxygen during performances"

"Yeh?"

"Yeh. It's a beauty."

"Allrighty then. I'll look it up. You having another beer?"

"Yeh. That would be good."

"I'll have one too thanks, now that you've offered."

"What? Ha-ha! Good one. You got me that time ya bastard. No worries. Two more over here Johnno; when you're ready. Thanks mate."

The next day at work, during crib some of the old-timers spoke of the 1964 dispute where the mine's owners, ASARCO, had refused to consider an Australian Workers Union demand for a £4 rise in the bonus. They spoke proudly and described a different kind of event to the normal union controlled show of strength. The miners, their wives and many of Mount Isa's residents took on ASARCO, one of the world's biggest mining corporations, despite open hostility from the company, the unions, Queensland's Government and the mass media. The miners voted to come off contract, which was linked to production, and work for wages. As a result mine production slumped dramatically, pressuring the big company.

Patrick, an Irishman who worked on the trains with Jimmy spoke up, "It wasn't a strike. We didn't stop work." he explained, "The mongrels locked their gates. We didn't work for eight long months. There's no

money when you don't work. I used all my savings
to survive. We used to line up for groceries and veg'
provided by the unions."

"Sounds like it was a tough time Pat." I said.

"Yeh. There were about two thousand workers involved."
he continued, "A popular fellow named Pat Mackie
lead the fight for better pay and conditions but the
AWU didn't like him much and tried to get the mines
to sack him. But we all backed him and told the mines
and the bloody unions to go to hell; there would be no
negotiation without Mackie.

The AWU called a meeting and a thousand or more
workers showed up. Now that was really something, I
tell you. We all voted to stay working on wages."

Pat nodded, lips set in a thin line. He looked around the
room but his eyes were far away.

As the '64 action continued, Mount Isa Mines had been
hurting. Mine production was down and the effect was
being felt as far away as the Townsville copper refinery,
the docks and Bowen's coke works. Railway freights fell
and Australia changed from being a copper exporter
to an importer, with the price rising over 65% in three
months.

ASARCO hit back viciously and announced that
it would close down its copper mine, causing the
government to react and declare a State of Emergency
and order the miners to accept contract work under
penalty of a fine or six months jail. On December 13
the AWU called a meeting and 1,500 men voted to
ignore the government and hold strong on wages. Just

10 days before Christmas 1964, the mine, authorised by hastily amended Government legislation, dismissed all of the workers, closed down operations and shut its gates.

The fight went on and in January 1965 the Nicklin Government legislated police greater power, and bolstered their numbers in the troubled city. Within 48 hours, working class Australia reacted strongly with strikes and protests throughout the country. The government eventually backed down and withdrew.

In February, ASARCO offered work to those who had previously been on their books. Of the 2,000 workers, around 140 reported for work on the day, though later, picket lines were formed in an attempt to stem the daily trickle of desperate and broken men. In late March, delegates from 38 unions met to discuss a full statewide work stoppage to support the miners but now, with enough men back at work, Mount Isa Mines was able to resume operations after more than 100 days of zero production.

"We lasted out until the end of March." Patrick continued, his soft brogue dancing lightly on our ears, "Even though we didn't have a firm work agreement with the mines, Mackie told us to get back on the job. After such a long hard slog it was a bombshell. Some felt that we'd lost the fight, but we all voted on it. In April we went back to work."

"It might have seemed bad then Pat, but we've got some good benefits now." Dick called out.

"Yeh. It's good now. A lot of good folks left town you know; there were quite a few suicides too. Not good that. I lost some mates that way."

He fell silent for a while and then Dick called out, "Crib's over boys; let's get back at it."

Patrick stood up, gave me a wink and called out loudly, "Well, there was one really good thing that came from the sixty-four dispute Dick!"

"Yeh? What's that Pat?"

Pat's eyes lit up and his cheeks turned rosy, "I did get a new daughter. I mean. Well, there's not much else to do when you have no job and no money. Ha-ha!"

We all joined in, laughing with the red-faced Irishman and then packed up our gear and headed back out into the mine. I walked alongside Patrick who was still chuckling to himself.

"Thanks Patrick." I said.

"What for?" he asked, puzzled.

"For holding strong during all those months, in sixty-four. My life's better now because you did that back then."

He paused for a moment and then looked across at me, nodding, "Yeh. That's good. That is good. Yeh."

He reached out and shook my hand. It was just one firm shake, and with that we went off to take up our jobs again, far away from the surface and disputes and unions and governments and 1964. And "Yes," it was good.

———————

I got talking with Ray about getting a place with Sandra and he mentioned that he wanted to move in with Margie, but she wasn't willing to leave her parent's house yet.

"What if you and I and Sandra moved into a flat together?" I suggested, "And then Margie could have some of her gear there with you, but officially, she would still be living at home. She might go for that mate."

"Yeh? That might work Steveo." he nodded thoughtfully. "Thanks."

"Have a talk with her," I suggested, "and I'll ask Sandra too."

It turned out that Sandra was willing to give it a go and Ray said Margie thought it was a great idea; she could maintain her status at home and also play house with Ray. We searched around and found a great two bedroom flat in West Street. The funny thing was, it was number 1/102, the adjoining flat to the one that Claudia and I had lived in, right next door to her parent's house!

"Too funny." I laughed, glancing around the building to see the bulldog wagging its short tail in their front garden.

"At least we're on the other side of the building this time Steve." Ray joked with me, "You can sneak in without being spotted!"

"Yeh. Ha. Maybe one day I'll find out that there are other places to live, in Mount Isa, besides the Barracks and next door to Claudia's parents in West Street."

And so we all moved in, Ray and I exiting the fire brigade barracks, Sandra moving out of home for the first time and Margie with a foot in both camps.

The happy house lasted just three months; Ray and Margie wanted their turn in the main bedroom having, initially, taken the small second bedroom, Sandra and I were having alcohol fueled lover's quarrels,it seemed that one minute we were fighting furiously and the next we were in bed. It got very intense one night and Sandra moved out, then we all moved out. Ray and I went back to the barracks, Sandra had returned to her parent's place and Margie, who was probably the smartest one of us all, simply packed an overnight bag and moved her clothes right back home.

I didn't see Sandra for about a week. At first I was fortified by my own righteousness and that I would just get on with my life and forget about her, but that point of view rapidly dissolved after about four days. It was horrible; once the drama had subsided I found that I missed her terribly. My biggest fear was that she would find someone else and I'd never be with her again; that constant thought filled my head and gnawed away at my guts.

Eventually, desperate to see her, I plucked up enough courage to go and knock on her parent's front door.

Her Mum answered, it was clear that she wasn't thrilled about seeing me but I'd rather it was her than Sandra's Dad. Rather than call out and alert the whole house I noticed that she went quietly and got Sandra, who came out. We went outside into the garden and talked. It was as awkward as hell and she seemed distant; it was like I didn't know her anymore. I grovelled and said I was sorry, that I missed her and that my life was not the same without her. Finally she confessed that she had missed me too, and a glimmer of hope entered my world. With that it seemed that something had changed and I invited her out for a drink at the Irish Club.

After a while we held hands, then we kissed and my stomach began to settle with the alcohol helping to quiet nerves that had been jangling together loudly in my body. The drinks seemed to help in pushing down the barriers we'd erected to insulate ourselves, and the recent past passed by, moving further and further away. I began to flirt, she responded and our smiles returned; we could look fully into each other's eyes again and something else began to happen, our bodies began to talk to each other. We ended up back at my room in the barracks and afterwards, laying in a tangle of sheets and sweat, talked about getting our own place; just the two of us.

"It was fun, at first, with Margie and Ray." she said, "But maybe we should have just gotten our own place to start with."

"Yeh. It was pretty cramped with the four of us." I added. "How is it at home now?"

Stephen Bram

"It's the same as it was. Dad drinks a bit you know; he and Mum have some fights. My sister had moved into my room and I had to get her out; she wasn't very happy about that."

"So, would you like to get our own place?" I asked. "I really miss you."

"Yeh. Me too. But if I moved out straight away I think they'd disown me. Let's leave it for a while and when Mum is in a good mood I'll talk with her."

"Okay. Well, in the meantime," I offered, "I'll see if I can find something for us."

A few weeks later I found a nice one bedroom place on Marion Street and while it was not right next door to Claudia's parents this time, it was near the West Street intersection. It was a ground floor flat, simply arranged with four rooms forming a rectangle, and the laundry located out the back under a small, open lean-to. The bedroom and lounge looked onto a busy street, which also doubled as the Barkly Highway and was the entry and exit point for every road train, truck and car travelling through the city. Despite the road noise, we liked it being newer than the other flat with tiles throughout and good sized rooms.

Sandra had picked her moment and talked with her Mum, and while not totally happy with the news of another move, she supported her eldest daughter. Once again I moved out of the barracks and Sandra left home for the second time. Her parents were not thrilled with the new arrangement but knew that it was impossible to stop their daughter doing what she wanted once she'd made up her mind. Our flat came furnished and we had a lot of fun at Kmart buying sheets, towels, kitchen gear and filling up the refrigerator with food and drink. The five million dollar Kmart Plaza had been opened by Queensland's Premier, Bjelke-Petersen and Mayor Frank Born in late 1975 and was Mount Isa's first shopping centre; Ray and I had visited there frequently with our various moves in and out of the barracks. Fortunately for Sandra and I it was just down the road, as was Mount Isa's best pizza shop, and nearby to our flat in the other direction, the Overlander Hotel became our local.

Ian and Jan had also moved out of the caravan park and into a house at Winston. Jan had two young daughters who had really taken to Ian, and he adored them. We ribbed him about finding a ready made family but he seemed very happy with the situation. It was fun to hang out with them sipping scotch and coke at their kitchen table. The fine grit facade that Jan usually wore when she was out disappeared in her own home and she was funny and warm. It seemed that life was working for both of them and I was delighted to watch and enjoy their good time together.

"You'll be married soon, you two." I jibed the happy couple.

"Naa. No way!" Jan responded with a laugh, "I'm not doing that one again!" and all the while Ian's eyes just sparkled.

"And what about you two?" Ian asked with a big grin, waggling his finger at Sandra and I, "When are your wedding bells going to ring?"

"Take it easy mate." I replied, "I hardly know the girl. We only just met yesterday. Ha-ha."

"Hmm." said Sandra, "So I wonder who it is that I've been waking up with then? Hmm. Do you have a twin brother? Another Stephen? Who could it be that was in my bed?"

"What? There's another man?" I play acted dramatically, placing a hand across my brow in a classic pose, "I can't believe it. My heart is a broken, cast in pieces upon the floor!"

"Something else will be broken if you don't get me another drink."

"Coming up right away Ma'am." and I kissed her gorgeous face.

In June, Sandra and I flew down to the Gold Coast to visit Mum and Dad at their new house. There was no one to pick us up this time and we caught a bus from Brisbane down to Southport, where Karen was waiting in her green Holden Torana; it was her first car.

"Sis. You got your license!" I called out when she got out to greet us.

"Yes. And I intend to keep it a lot longer that you did!" she joked with me.

"Good luck with that." I replied.

Even though they had met at my 21st birthday party, I introduced Sandra, we put our suitcases in the boot and Karen drove us five kilometres inland to Koolewong

Parade, Ashmore and pulled up outside a large white brick, high-set house.

"Impressive." I commented, "But no beach Sis."

"Yeh. I know." she replied, "I do miss Main Beach but this is nice. Dad will tell you the story. Come on you two!"

It was late afternoon and Dad was not yet home from work; Mum welcomed us at the door and then took us on a tour of their new home. She directed Sandra into the spare room and had set me up in the study.

"But Mum, Sandra and I live together in Mount Isa; can we have a room together here?"

Mum was very clear, "No. I'm not having you two sleeping in the same room in my house."

Sandra and I looked at each other for a moment, bemused, and then she went and put her suitcase in on the bed.

"Thank you." said Mum, "Trevor will be home soon so you can entertain yourselves for a bit while I get dinner ready." and with that she went off leaving us to unpack.

We found Karen in the lounge room watching television and joined her; full program TV was a novelty for us and it held our attention until Dad came home. We had a couple of drinks and then dinner while Dad told us about their move to Ashmore. He explained that he'd gone into partnership with a builder to build the house but it hadn't sold. The builder was used to developing larger houses and though Dad had preferred a smaller project, he agreed with his partner and they had gone for a four bedroom, two bathroom design. Dad had been right; the market was ripe for smaller properties and the big house didn't sell. Eventually, hemorrhaging money paying out interest on the loan, they had bought out their partner and moved in themselves, planning to sit tight until things changed and then sell.

Later that night after the others had all gone to bed, Sandra and I were talking quietly in the lounge, "Your mother doesn't like me." she commented.

"Of course she does." I replied, attempting to comfort her. "They all like you."

She was not convinced, "Not really. Your Dad seems okay with me but not your Mum. I knew it when we first met."

"Give it a little more time. She just needs to get to know you better. It will be okay."

In my eyes everything was going wonderfully. I had so wanted my Mum to like Sandra and approve my choice that I was virtually blinded to any other possibility; I had already created their loving relationship in my head and that's all I was willing to see. Later, I would discover that Sandra was correct and it hadn't been such a fun experience for her, living with my parents in their house. Especially when I had gotten drunk one day and then gone off drinking with my mates, leaving her behind at home.

I made sure that I paid Sandra more attention and we got out and about. We hitched rides in and out of Ashmore when they were available and caught busses or taxis when they were not. We hung out with Gary and Eden and caught up with Skin and Kevin, who were renting a house in Southport and growing their own marijuana in the backyard. Sandra and I visited the beach, spent a fun day at Marine Land and did our best to be good tourists on holiday at the Gold Coast. The time passed quickly and soon enough we were back in Brisbane Airport and on our way home; it was Sunday afternoon when we opened the front door at Marion Street, and I was due to start work at midnight.

The movie *Grease* was sweeping the world and Mount Isa was not immune to its romantic, boy-meets-girl charms. It was especially cool that Australian singer, Olivia Newton-John was cast in the lead with John Travolta. My sister and I had enjoyed Travolta, as the young rebel student in the TV series, *Welcome Back Kotter* and we knew Olivia for her hit songs, *If Not For You, Banks of the Ohio* and others that were played frequently at our local roller skating rink in the early seventies; the owner Trevor just loved Olivia. Sandra and I saw Grease several times at The Star and later, it was fun to watch people trying to impersonate the dance moves or singing along with the songs.

The subject of uranium hit the headlines again in July as the French Government continued their nuclear activity in the Pacific. During one underground test at Mururoa atoll, codenamed "Tydee," a 120 kiloton device got stuck halfway down at 400 metres, where it was detonated. The blast caused a submarine landslide and a significant chunk of the atoll broke away generating a three metre high tsunami, and a two kilometre long by 40 centimeter wide crack, effectively breaking the

373

Stephe⊙ ꞇ ram

atoll. There was great public concern around radioactive material being released into the ocean and Australian protesters voiced their concerns again.

Just over 8,000 kilometres away from Mururoa, dead west and just down the road from us, work continued at Mary Kathleen. Further north the federal government was in talks with the Northern Land Council over rights to mine the Ranger uranium project, which the Mirarr Gundjeihmi and other groups fiercely opposed. The tantalising carrot of land rights was being dangled in exchange for mining rights and their long, drawn out negotiations continued.

Sandra and I were having our own detonations and negotiations, and after a particularly vicious fight one night, she moved out of our flat into an ANZ Bank staff house. Our relationship seemed to swing from intense rum-and-raisin dark chocolate passion, to skipping playfully through spring's daisy studded meadows, and then on to summer's blood-orange sunsets of intense fighting and destruction; then we would loop back to start all over again. We seemed to spend more time at the extreme edges of the pendulum's range than in the middle; the middle was more like a quick holiday, passing through on our way to the fringe. Just before she left the flat we had been fighting one night and I did something I hadn't known I was capable of.

We'd been out socialising and drinking, were on the verge of summer's sunsets and fueled with drink had begun fighting on the way home. The fight escalated when we got into our flat. I couldn't even recall why it had begun or why we were so angry, but at one point I opened my hand and slapped her. It changed everything. Time froze for a long moment. We were both shocked and she ran off into the bedroom screaming and crying. I was devastated. A million thoughts ran through my head. How could I have done it? I felt like a monster. Fuck! This was not me; was it? I quickly followed her, apologising over and over and over. Held her while she wept. Cried, my face pressed into her soft hair, desperate for this to be different. Finally, her tears began to subside. I felt so totally guilty and at fault. We calmed down and got under the covers. I held her all night, hardly sleeping; I was afraid of the morning and what it would bring.

The next day revealed the telltale blue blush of a bruise; she wore sunglasses to work and made up a story that she'd slipped and fallen. It was awkward. We were awkward together. Something had broken. Our shared trust was gone and I had lost trust in me. There were some things that couldn't be undone nor taken back; words can be powerful but actions much more so. A few days later I came home from work and she was gone. Somehow, I was not surprised. I'd half expected it. From then on, every time I went to work or came home I drove past the ANZ house hoping to see her or even to gain a glimpse of her, but its windows revealed nothing and the front door was always closed. It seemed she was no longer in my world and that I'd lost her forever.

I recall a female psychologist being interviewed about women's support systems who was asked what men could do when faced with a broken relationship or heart; she said derisively, "Men always have the pub." and that's where I went. I drank beer and talked with mates at the hotel.

The consensus view was, "Women; who can ever understand them mate? Not me that's for sure."

The alcohol worked to push away the thoughts in my head and numb the churn of my guts, my job underground kept me occupied for a third of each day, and despite some moments when I couldn't block her out it seemed I had a strategy to survive. As it turned out, a tragic incident at work would assist me in ways I could not assist myself.

———————

Despite Mount Isa Mines being one of the safest in the world, mining was a risky business. Even with all of the training, we still took some risks in our jobs, pushing boundaries to get something done a bit quicker or with less effort. Accidents in varying degrees happened regularly and there was good medical support, but there is no bandage or stitching that works for death; it's a done deal and one of the more permanent features of life.

On September 12, 1978 a young geologist was on a sampling assignment down on Level 15; he'd recently come to live in Mount Isa with his wife and baby and had taken up a job working for the mine. He came down around ten o'clock in the morning after the main cage runs were finished, put his tag on the crib room board and walked out into the drive; Dick was out on inspection so there was no shift boss to report to.

Later, at crib, Dick noticed a lone brass tag hanging on the board and led a team out to investigate; after 30 minutes he sent back for reinforcements to join in the search. Word came back later that a pair of boots had been spotted poking out from under a 60 tonne rock on the sublevel; it looked like there had been a fall from the brow of a draw-point. The guy was doing some rock sampling and had ventured into an area where the ceiling had not yet been rock-bolted and safety mesh installed. There were danger signs and somehow he had missed, or ignored them.

It wasn't until after a doctor had been sent down and the man pronounced dead that the huge rock could be lifted off, and his crushed and battered body retrieved. Later in the afternoon Dick instructed me to go and pick him up and bring his body back to the cage. Damien had reported in sick that day and I drove the mule along to a workshop where machines from the sublevel were serviced and maintained; there was a small siding adjacent to the main hall where we normally left supplies for the mechanics, and I backed the mule in.

A single flatbed was parked there and I could see the body had been wrapped in grey tarpaulin and laid on top, a pair of fairly new work books stuck out from beneath its frayed edge, dried mud still clinging to the soles. One of the miners was waiting with the body and helped me with the coupling, and then I set off again to deliver my cargo to the cage. I had not seen a dead body before, let alone been in charge of one, but there we were, just me and him travelling along the deserted drive. Actually, I was okay with taking care of him on this part of his journey, on his way back to the surface. I didn't know the guy from Adam, but was honoured to be his driver. I drove slowly, checking back on him from time-to-time to make sure his body hadn't rolled or moved, but it hadn't and eventually I saw the crib room's familiar lights blazing out brightly up ahead. I set the main drive's points and backed the mule up to the cage gate; Dick was already there, waiting for us, and made a telephone call to the surface. A short time later the cage announced its arrival, jostling the folds of the young man's tarpaulin; some of the mine's mud had dropped off his boots. The safety gate was opened, we pushed the flatbed inside and they took him away.

It was the second fatality at Mount Isa Mines for 1978 and fortunately, the last one. In Queensland, four men had been killed in mining type operations in 1977 and five the year before that; mining was a risky business and I had now seen that firsthand.

Dick put his hand on my shoulder, "Best thing is to get back to work now Steve, and make sure that you're not as stupid as him. I don't want to have to go out looking for you. Okay?"

"Okay Dick. Thanks. You won't have to."

"Good." he replied, "See you later mate." and walked off.

I stood there for a moment, quiet, still, thinking about life, death and the young geologist but there was no more to be done here. The body was now in the hands of others who would pass it to his family and they would do what was required to eventually place it gently in the ground, and then they too would move on with their lives. The ebbing, flowing, constant and sometimes dramatic evolution of life would pull them along, away from the past and into their future, whatever they chose it to be. I put the mule into forward and pulled away listening to the familiar whine of its electric motor, the low rumble of its steel wheels, and feeling the breeze pressing upon the skin of my face that seemed to propel me into the future, whatever I would chose it to be.

I thought about Sandra and about how life could be unexpectedly short. The young man under the tarpaulin would never be able to look into the eyes of his wife again, but I still had that chance with Sandra. I realised that my numbness and avoidance was not going to create what I really wanted. I knew I had to find a way to talk with her, to truly know if there was anything left that we could work with. Either way, I needed to know.

Something changed while I travelled slowly along the drive, 800 metres below the surface, and the cold, damp, fog of my despair and misery began to lift and dissipate. I knew what I had to do now and somehow, I was going to do it!

Chapter 26

Year of Endings

Sometimes it seems that Fate, God or the Universe steps right in and gives you a hand, perhaps, when you least expect it, when you're stuck or when you really need some help. I was working night shifts and on this particular night drove in earlier than usual. There wasn't much traffic around and passing by the bank's staff house I slowed right down. Given the number of times I'd done this, hoping she would appear, it was a bit of a shock when she actually did! The house's front door opened and Sandra stepped out onto the footpath. She looked up, saw my car and I pulled over on the side of the road; she came over and leaned in the open window.

I couldn't help myself and started to sob uncontrollably, "What are we going to do?" I asked miserably.

She opened the door, perched on the side of the passenger seat and put her hand on mine, "I don't know." she said softly, "But I've put in for a transfer with the bank. I need to do something different, get a fresh view on us, on living in Mount Isa, on everything

... " her voice trailed off for a moment then, "I still love you."

"Where are you going?" I asked. I hadn't totally missed that last thing she said but I was processing the "transfer" part.

"There's an opening in the Southport branch, on the Gold Coast. I'll be leaving in a month."

"Oh wow. That's a big decision. Can I see you before you go? I love you too. I wasn't expecting you to be leaving the area." The reality of what she'd said was beginning to sink in.

"Yeh. I know. It's a big move." she replied, "I'd like to see you. I'm staying here until I go. I didn't want to move home again with Mum and Dad. Do you want to have a drink after work tomorrow? I get off at four?"

"Yes please. That will be great. Shall I pick you up here? Five o'clock?" ... thank God I had managed to stop blubbering and was beginning to function again.

"Yeh. See you then." she leaned over and kissed me gently and then got out and closed the door.

I pulled the Charger out onto the road and watched her in the rearview mirror, waving. I was calmer now; she was leaving but we had a month and it was a lot more than I had 10 minutes ago!

I saw Ray in K57's waiting hall; he was coming off afternoon shift, "How you goin' Steve?"

"Good mate. I just saw Sandra."

"Yeh?"

"Yeh. Looks like it's back on. Well, we talked." I'm sure I looked a little sheepish right then.

Ray rolled his eyes, laughed out loud and shaking his head said,"I don't know. You two. Well, good luck mate."

"Yeh. Thanks mate. She's leaving The Isa in a month; going to the Gold Coast." I said.

"The Gold Coast?" Ray frowned. "Why there?"

"She says she needs a break. I'm going to miss her when she goes."

"I'll bet! How long?" he asked.

"I don't know yet."

He nodded, "Hang in there mate. It'll work out somehow."

"Yeh"

"Who knows," he laughed out loud, "You might even get back to the Gold Coast Stevie. It'd be better than this dump! Ha-ha!"

I laughed with him and it felt good; Ray could always get a laugh out of me."See you later mate." he said and still chuckling walked off to have a shower.

During the first half of our shift Damien and I got our work done quickly and slipped down a side drive for a cigarette and a chat. He lived out of town on a holding with his partner Sheryl where they raised horses; they'd brought their horses with them all the way from Victoria, when they moved up to Mount Isa. I had visited Damien at his place, apart from horses, they also had dogs, cats, goats, chickens and, of course, lots of flies. The first time I went there we went inside his house for a cup of tea. Later, we'd gone outside again and found a goat standing on the roof of my new Charger! We'd coaxed the damn thing down with food so it wouldn't startle and scratch the paint. Fortunately it had come down stepping like a trained ballerina specialising in adagio and no damage done. I knew that Damien had been with his partner for about 12 years and while we smoked, I talked with him about Sandra.

"Women are a lot like horses Steve." he explained, "You have to talk softly, move slow, brush them gently, stroke them and when they get nervous and run away, then give them some time to come back. Horses can spook really easily, it's in their nature, but they are curious creatures and can be coaxed back. It's like a game, when they move away then you move away and give them some space; you watch and wait, when they are ready they'll let you know, but if you go chasing after them too soon, then they'll run even further away."

"What happens if they don't come back Damien? I asked, "What if she leaves Mount Isa and I never see her again?"

"Never is a very long time Steve, and sometimes you have to be patient. It depends how long you are willing to wait for what you want. And waiting doesn't mean you become a monk, hide in a cave and do nothing. Sometimes you being unavailable, can be more interesting to a woman than if you're all over her with your tongue hanging out. You can still have a lot of fun while you're waiting, and at the same time keep your eye on the big picture."

"What do you really want Steve?" he asked.

"I want her and me together." my reply came quickly.

"Then for you mate, that's the big picture. Make sure you keep it in sight."

Damien Shine gave me a totally new perspective that night at work; it was one of those great conversations where a whole new world of possibility had become available. I'd not considered that relationship was like a game, and that some people were good players and some were not. I thought that relationship was about two people who were in love, and love was all that was required. I was beginning to see that there was much more required and I needed to improve my skills or I was going to lose. The more I explored the "game" idea, the more I realised that it was not about winning or losing but about playing; as long as the game and its players continued so could the relationship. My current game with Sandra kept ending, and then it took a huge amount of work to bring the players back together and start it all up again.

What if the game, like a dance, went on and on, evolving and changing to be different, as we changed and were different. What if there didn't have to be an end. What if the boom and bust cycle of our relationship could simply be evened out a bit, into rises and falls, like waves rolling onto the beach, like sunrises and sunsets, like riding a horse, like sex, like just about everything! I had one month before she left and that was a lot of game time.

I began to play and relationship became less serious, and more fun. Even though I wanted to see her as often as I could within the month we had left, sometimes I was not available; and if we were becoming a little irritated with each other, then I gave her some space. When we were together I talked softly and stroked her gently; it was different, it was weird but it started to work.

On the Monday before she was due to leave Mount Isa we both took a "sickie" and drove out to Paroo Waterhole located to the northeast of the city; there was no one else around and we had it to ourselves. It was a lovely spot nestled alongside ancient limestone outcrops and we saw red winged parrots, goannas and a variety of flying insects dancing lightly across the water. We stripped off and swam; the trick with Paroo was to find areas where the local cattle had not been, but we had lots of choice that day. Later we ate a picnic lunch in the shade of pale ghost gums, sipped chilled wine out of water tumblers and relaxed in the beautiful bushland setting. It was a really great day, one to be remembered fondly, and for a very long time.

We had dinner during the week and then on Friday, met up with her friends and work colleagues for a farewell drink at Boyds. On Saturday morning at eleven o'clock, along with her family and some friends, I waved as one of Ansett's aeroplanes lifted Sandra up off the tarmac and took her away. Damien's wise words filtered into my head, "… sometimes you have to be patient …"; patience was not my greatest capacity but I was determined to improve that, starting now. I took-in a deep breath, drove home to my Marion Street flat and marked six months on a calendar. I could do six months and as Damien had said, I didn't have to become a monk and hide in a cave.

I rang up Gary Hallard that afternoon on the Gold Coast and asked if he would keep and eye out and make sure that she was okay; he said that he would. There didn't seem to be much else I could do right now, so I walked to the Overlander Hotel for beer and game of pool, and ran across a mate, John MacDonald. Everyone knew him as Macca and, for a Kiwi, he could be a funny bugger. He liked impersonating a fictional British rodent puppet called Basil Brush; the puppet would tell jokes always accentuating their punch line with, "Boom! Boom!" Macca would apply it vigorously and the number of "Boom! Booms!" he uttered, and the volume with which he uttered them, increased in direct proportion to the number of beers he'd consumed. An evening with Macca was invariably accompanied by a number of, "Give it a rest will you Macca. Jeez!" But these requests rarely worked. We posited a theory that people who came from New Zealand, apart from their many other failings, which were way too numerous to mention, simply went deaf when drinking good Australian beer, and that sometimes it was best to go where said afflicted Kiwis were not.

Macca had recently bought a new F-Series pickup and he also had a gorgeous Kawasaki 750cc bike; I wanted that bike and had asked several times if he would sell it to me but each time I'd got a, "No." I was about to bring up the subject again when, unexpectedly, a single word leapt into my head, "Patience" and I stopped myself. Hmm, maybe this game idea could work for different things. Boom! Boom!

At work Damien and I trained and received our ST2 and ST4 tickets; these were load-haul-dump machines with two and four square metre capacity buckets designed to work underground in the narrow drives. The Wagner machines were articulated in the middle and could bend at 45° allowing them movement around corners and to operate in tight areas. The driver sat amidships, able to look out over the rear, where a Duetz diesel motor roared, or to the front where the bucket and hydraulic rams were located. The ST4's wheels were taller than me; around two metres in diameter and I could stand up or lie down fully, in its bucket. The larger unit was eight and a half metres total length and sported a big, grey, meaty, German V6 motor. The ST4 was often used up on the sub-level for cleanup and some mucking and so we mainly had the ST2; we used it to clean the haulage drives of fallen ore or spillage, sometimes we had to dig out a buried ore carriage, or rerail one that had jumped off the tracks and it was great to lift heavy items on or off the flatbeds we worked with. While driving a mule was good fun, these machines were a whole new level of brute power and huge capacity, and Damien and I would race each other to be the first to get in and drive them!

Dick mentioned that he'd probably get us trained on the locomotives too, so we could fill in when the regular drivers went on holidays. It all sounded great to me.

During a shift Damien and I were larking around, while waiting for the cage to arrive and pick up some gear we had ready. One item was a small steel trolly designed to carry drilling rods. We had been out to the miners and picked up all of their blunt rods and had them ready to go to the surface for sharpening. Damien jumped atop the trolly and was riding it like a surfer as it trundled down the gentle slope towards the cage, it hit some rubble in the tracks and his feet slipped on the smooth steel frame. I watched as his long, lanky cowboy body tumbled over the rods in slow motion. His leg got caught in the trolley as he rolled and jammed; it didn't break but it wasn't good and he spun awkwardly hitting the concrete apron with a thump.

I ran over, "Mate." I called out, "What are you doing to yourself?"

He sat up hanging onto his damaged leg, "Ah, man. That hurts a bit."

He tried a laugh but I could see the pain creasing across his face. I gently eased up his pants leg and saw the skin was lacerated and there was already swelling under his knee; the bruising would run deep.

"Wait here mate." I said and ran off to the empty crib room.

"I don't think I'll be going anywhere fast Steve." he called after me.

I was back in a few minutes, "I called the cage. They are on their way down. We better get you up to the medical room where someone can have a good look at you Dameo. I'll stay here so I can tell Dick what happened. Here's your tag. I'll go get your crib box."

"Wait a minute." he said.

"Yeh?"

"What will you tell Dick?" he asked.

"That you fell over your own two big feet stupid, and hit the bloody trolley. That it looks like you may have twisted a knee!"

"Yeh. That's it." he said, "Thanks mate."

"It'll be fine. Just look after yourself. Okay?"

"Yeh. I will." he winced, "Thanks."

By the time I got back we could feel the air pressure beginning to push at us and hear the whir of massive steel cables flying up the shaft. It wasn't too long before Damien, his damaged knee and crib box were on a small flatbed being whisked up, up and away to the surface. I saw Dick later and reported the incident.

"He could fall up stairs that bloke." said Dick, shaking his head. Thanks Steve, I'll put it in the book. Man down."

It was that easy, a bit of fun, a small lapse in concentration, maybe not enough sleep the night before and, "Ouch! Man down." Damien was off work for the rest of the week and when he did show up again, sporting a handy limp, guess who got to do all the driving while I did all the work? Jeez!

———————

About 10 days after she had left I got a letter from Sandra. She had moved into some temporary accommodation provided by the bank and was now working at the Southport branch. A picture of the building flashed into my head, located in the centre of Southport on Scarborough Street, opposite the old Cecil Hotel; I knew exactly where she was. She wrote that her work mates had taken her out for drinks one night and that had been fun, that the job was going good but she missed home, missed me and wasn't too happy with where she was living; actually, she didn't like her roomies that much.

The Gold Coast and its people were very different to Mount Isa, where there were a lot of social connections and interaction; there was always someone to visit, have a drink with or a party to look forward to. The Gold Coast was a 20 mile long tourist strip that attracted a transient population—there was an incessant flow of people moving in and moving out—and the idea of locals and vibrant, personal social infrastructure, though it did exist, was much harder to find and connect with than in the mining city. For Sandra, essentially a country girl, all of the social systems that she'd been brought up with and as an attractive, clever girl was valued and sought after within, stood for little where she was now. As a new-kid-on-the-block, especially a sexy, young, single woman, she would be seen by existing couples as a threat, other single women would probably not welcome the competition and men of all ages would take aim at a juicy new target; mix that up with ephemeral relationships, part-time jobs, ebbs and flows of the tourist dollar, huge population swings over the year and you had a unique playground that some people thrived in and others didn't. I had no doubt that Sandra could make it there but she was going to have to change, adapt and learn some new skills. She had included the phone number of her new place and I called her on the weekend.

"Hi. Is Sandra there?" I asked into the phone. It was my second call and the same bloke had picked up.

"I'll check. Hang on." he said and I heard the receiver clunk on a hard surface.

A few minutes later, "Hello." and it was her.

"Hi Sandra. It's Stephen." My heartbeat was up and suddenly nervous, I reverted to my fallback Aussy standard, "How are you?"

"Hi! I'm good. How are you?" and then, "Oh, it's good to hear your voice." and my nerves faded away.

We talked for nearly an hour and she told me that she was living out near Molendinar in a shared house; it was out in the suburbs so she had to catch busses everywhere and there wasn't much to do. One of her house mates smoked pot and watched television a lot and the other was often at her boyfriend's. Sandra said it was just temporary accommodation and she'd have to find another place soon, but it was difficult getting around without a car. Her work was fun; she was enjoying the larger branch but she felt socially isolated and missed Mount Isa, her family and friends and me. She told me that she'd talked with her Mum a few days ago and they'd cried together on the phone.

"I've got a long weekend coming up; I could fly down and help you get a place. I know the Gold Coast. I'm sure Gary would drive us ..." I offered tentatively.

Stephe⋂ ᴛ ram

"Really? You'd come down and help me?" she seemed incredulous.

"Yes. Of course. You know I would. I don't want to see you homeless, you know. Ha. It's not a good look."

"Oh Stephen, that would be wonderful. I'm not really sure what to do right now."

I had phoned her from a public telephone and inserted my last 20 cent coin into the well scratched slot; bare metal was beginning to show through and I rubbed at it with my finger, "Hey, I'm almost out of coins. I'll book the flight and let you know. Okay?"

"Yes. And hurry. I wanna see you soon!" she laughed happily and then there was a hollow, electronic sound, just as I heard the coin drop through with its now familiar and distinct, "Clink." and she was gone. Hanging up the receiver I stood in the telephone booth for a while gazing out across Marion Street, replaying our conversation, the sound of her voice in the speaker, her last words, until someone knocked on the glass, impatient for their turn.

Lost in my reverie I jumped a little, "Sorry mate." I opened the door, stepped out and made my way home. I was excited.

I was able to get a flight booked during the week leaving Friday and getting back in time for afternoon shift on Monday. Gary would be available to drive us around on Saturday to look at some flats. The week seemed to drag by but eventually my last night shift was done; I had a quick breakfast, packed and was on the late morning flight to Brisbane. Even though I was keen to see Sandra I spent the evening with Mum, Dad and Karen at the Ashmore house, and made arrangements to see my girl the next morning. Gary picked me up early, we got Sandra and established head office at a local burger bar in Labrador. Gary had brought a copy of the Gold Coast Bulletin and we poured through the classified adverts and real estate section over coffee and breakfast. We found three places that might work and pumping coins into a pay phone I contacted the various agents; by nine thirty we had secured three appointments for two properties in Southport and one in Labrador. Sandra was excited, I was excited and Gary, while not particularly interested in flats, was excited to drive.

The Southport flats were a bit expensive, one being old and quite run down. By the time we got to the last flat, our spirits had slumped. The nature of Gold Coast real estate was that we only had Saturday morning to get a place; all the agents shut shop for the weekend at midday. We crossed over Loders Creek bridge and entered Labrador, turned right into Robert Street and parked. Number eight was a long narrow building with two flats on the ground floor and another two on top; we walked along its tight driveway towards the back, up a set of timber stairs and had a good look through the offering. While the outside was old, 1960s beach shack construction, the inside looked good with fresh paint and furniture. There was a good sized bedroom and bathroom at one end, kitchen and entry in the middle and a lounge at the other end; the whole floor was connected with a walkway come veranda.

"What do you think Sandra?" I asked, "Will this do?"

"Well, it's the last one so I guess it will have to," she laughed, "Yes. This one will do. It's close to Frank Street so I can get a bus to work and just five minutes walk to the Broadwater."

"And the shops are just over there." I said pointing back across the creek.

She looked around the room, back to me and then turned to the waiting real estate agent, "Okay. I'll take it."

"Good." replied the agent handing over a business card, "Meet me at my office and we'll complete the paperwork. You'll need rent in advance as a deposit; cash will do. Some ID; all the normal things." She looked at her watch, "We should be able to get you the keys today if you hurry."

Suddenly we were all excited again and Gary sped us off to the bank to get the cash and then on to the agent's office where Sandra signed a six month lease and got a set of jangly brass keys. We went back into Southport for a counter lunch and beer at the Pacific Hotel to celebrate and then shopped for bedding, kitchen stuff, vodka and other flatting essentials. By five o'clock in the afternoon Sandra had officially moved into her new place; I gave Gary fifty dollars to buy petrol and a six-pack and he headed home. Finally, it was just her and me and we got some drinks, takeaway fish and chips and made the most of our one night together.

We caught a bus home to Ashmore the next day and had lunch with the family and later, I borrowed Karen's car and we went back to Sandra's flat. I stayed until after dark and then said goodbye. It was horrible and she cried; we both cried. As I walked down the stairs I could hear her screams and went back to comfort her but she was beyond that, beat me away and locked the door. I left. I was confused. It seemed that we'd really connected again and accomplished something together. I'd flown all this way to help, Gary and I had got her a nice flat and now she'd have her own place while on the Gold Coast ... what else could I do? Nothing. We all make our choices and have to ride the wave of what gets created. The next day I caught a bus to Brisbane Airport and arrived back in Mount Isa in time to begin afternoon shift at four o'clock. I was still confused but satisfied that I'd been able to get her set up. It seemed that patience included more than I'd first realised.

Damien was back at work, limping a little but in good spirits.

"Watch out you don't fall over your big feet again cowboy." Dick called out, chiding him in a good natured way.

I talked with Damien about my Gold Coast weekend and he shrugged his shoulders, "Probably not much more you can do there right now Steve; get on with your life."

When I got home from work that night I looked over the calendar that I'd marked up; it was now less than six months and I could still do it, and I knew it was time to come out of the cave.

Gerry Rafferty's brilliant song *Baker Street* was hitting the charts big time and it seemed to match the energy of moving on. The chorus, "When you wake up it's a new morning. The sun is shining, it's a new morning

… " followed by Raphael Ravenscroft's soaring alto saxophone solo helped lift my spirits and I began going out more, met some new girls and played; it was good.

Sandra and I wrote regularly and I knew that she was also getting out and about; it wasn't easy to swallow but we were getting on with our lives. And anyway, I put and end to our communication by sending her the "crazy" letter.

The crazy letter was my attempt at copying Peter Cook and Dudley Moore's popular *Derek and Clive* conversational sketches that, it seemed, were playing in everyone's tape machines in Mount Isa. The comedy sketches were freeform, often bizarre, where both comedians tried to break the other's deadpan and austere performance, by introducing outrageous or unexpected twists to their dialogue. The letter I wrote seemed funny to me but Sandra didn't find it humorous at all. It seemed that she took great offence at my comedic attempts and accused me of being a nut job, replying that I must have gone crazy and not to write to her anymore.

My 22nd birthday had passed, as did the 1978 annual rodeo and the lease on my Marion Street flat came to an end; I didn't renew, moving back into the fire brigade's barracks. It was timely as I got to be a part of Big Stack's completion and see some things that few people would. Perhaps 1978 was a year of endings or perhaps a year of beginnings; who really knew?

Chapter 27

Silence is an Ocean

In early October 1978, Australian rocker Johnny O'Keefe died from a drug overdose at the age of 43 years, and the world of Rock 'n' Roll mourned the loss of their Real Wild Child. Related to O'Keefe, only by the month of their death, three bodies were discovered east of Mount Isa Airport in late October and the Spear Creek Murders claimed local and national media attention.

Spear Creek flanked the northern tip of the airport's runway and wound in tightly behind the rodeo grounds before crossing under the Barkly Highway and making its way in a northeasterly direction, to join the Leichhardt River before it entered Lake Moondarra. One of their decomposing bodies were found in the dry creek bed by a couple out walking their greyhound dogs, while the other two were located the following day, 100 metres away in the spinifex. All of the victims had been killed by a single shot to the head and their ID stripped away; it was a grotesque event that baffled police and sent shock waves throughout the city.

"Do you think he's a local? The killer? Maybe he's still around?" I asked.

"Dunno." Danny replied, "The police seem to have no clue at all!"

"They were visitors from down south." Paul, a mate from the fire brigade joined in, "The three of them were travelling together. Makes no sense that they'd all go out in the bush to Spear Creek and get themselves killed."

"Yeh. They say each one was shot in the head by a twenty two rifle. He would've been close when he pulled the trigger you know; a twenty two is not that powerful."

"I dunno, you can do a fair bit of damage with a twenty two." I replied.

"They found a watch in the grass. It was the woman's. You know, the bloke that found the bodies used to be her neighbour." Danny was on a roll.

"What? Really? That's an amazing coincidence."

"Yeh. Must have been a shock, finding her like that."

"The other two blokes were Kiwis. School teachers. They'd been working down at The Alice."

"The police are looking for a brown and cream Landcruiser. A '77 model."

"What colour is yours Paul?"

"Well, it's supposed to be white; when I clean it. But it's looking brown at the moment."

"You better get busy then. Ha!"

"Yeh. Guess I better. You having another beer?"

"Yeh. Thanks."

It was a grisly and intriguing mystery that fueled gossip and speculation in bars and crib rooms across the city. Despite receiving thousands of pieces of information from the public, police were unable to solve the murders or identify a killer and like all news that is not fed regularly, the story gradually disappeared from the media as the public's attention was directed elsewhere.

My attention was on my car! I'd read that the CL model had suffered a drop in power due to stricter emission laws, and I was itching to do some work on the motor to see what else it could do. Chrysler used a single barrel Carter carburetter and their motors were well known for taking a long time to start; you could always recognise a Chrysler starting because they cranked over-and-over-and-over before actually firing up. I wanted to replace the Carter and ordered a 48 DCOE, side-draft, dual-throat Weber unit and manifold from Sydney. And I had saved a magazine article all about porting and polishing engine heads. Now that I was back at the fire brigade and had access to the work sheds, it wasn't long before my Charger was taken off the road and the work began.

I took the head off the Charger's motor one afternoon and set it up on one of the heavy duty work benches. The job involved using various grinding stones to

smooth out and polish out any casting irregularities
in the combustion chambers, inlet and exhaust ports.
I'd also bought some glass burettes to help measure
the volume of each chamber, and make sure they all
ended up the same size. It was fiddly, tedious and time
consuming work but after a couple of weeks I could see
the beginnings of a glossy, reflective surface, almost like
chrome; it looked great and my head became a talking
point in the station. It was not unusual for people to
drop by to check on progress, or for a bunch of us to
hang out at the sheds with a few beers and talk about
our various projects. It was a big day when the Weber
finally arrived and we pulled a good crowd when I laid
it out on display.

It took about a month of work to polish the head; then
I used the burette to make final adjustments. With the
head setup dead-level and it's chambers facing up, I put
a known amount of water in a buret and then dripped
the liquid down into one of the chambers and filled it
up; a simple calculation gave me the liquid volume of
the chamber and I repeated this six times. Now I knew
which chambers to take a little more metal out of, so
that in the end they would all be exactly the same size.
These adjustments took another week and finally, it
was done. I sent the head off to Townsville to have it
milled and so increase the motor's compression, and its
horsepower.

It took over two weeks before the Charger's head
was returned to Mount Isa; that's a lot of patience! I
picked it up at the railway depot, tied the 35 kilogram
deadweight of iron onto the back seat of my Kawasaki
and drove home very carefully. There were a couple of

blokes at the sheds and we unwrapped the package to reveal what was, from my point of view, a dead-set work of art. The head gleamed back at us; it was gorgeous, and I actually delayed refitting it to the motor so I could look at it longer. I knew that once it was bolted back on, my work would never been seen again; and I also knew that if I didn't I would never know what improvements it would make to the car's performance. On a sunny Saturday afternoon, a couple of blokes and I refitted the head, new manifold and Weber; it looked awesome! We spent some time adjusting the throttle linkages and fuel line and finally, it was ready. It took a few turns of the starter motor to pump fuel into the big new carburetter and then she simply started up.

"Hi handsome." purred CL. "I'm back!"

There was a cheer, some clapping and then lots of enthusiastic motor revving. The first thing I noticed was how smooth the motor ran at idle. I knew it required professional tuning but even with that, it was very nice. I cleaned up and then took the Charger for a run; she was strong with impressive acceleration and pull through the gears, and the typical Chrysler starting issue was completely gone. I was stoked and was already planning a midnight visit out to the Drags!

———————

Paul Dawson was one of the blokes who played cards in our group at crib; he worked on the trains with Jimmy and Patrick but was also being used, more and more, to drive the big ST5 mucking machines up on the sub-level. Dick booked me in for training on the locomotives so there was always someone available to

make up the haulage team. It was important for the
trains to run all shift, every shift, as they were a key
component in mined ore getting down to the crushers.
There were two tickets required, one for the electric
and another for the diesel locomotive; both machines
weighed 12 tonne each and pulled 12 ore cars; when
full of ore, each car weighed 20 tonne. The locomotives
were not fast but had massive torque; low-down, grunty,
pulling power that could move a 250 tonne mass of
metal and rock from a cold, standing start to top speeds
equivalent to a running man and, most importantly,
stop it.

Empty trains were run backwards, with a signalman
standing up in the front car. His job was to pull on
overhead cables, which operated the railway track's
points and direct the train into the drive it was
hauling from; every crossing was controlled by a set of
overhead traffic lights, synchronised with the points.
The switchman also operated a buzzer that rang in the
driver's cockpit; one buzz for stop, two for forward and
three for backup. As the train swept into a drive at full
speed backwards, the driver was watching for white
reflective markings on the wall, these indicated where
he should stop so that the first empty car would be
located directly under the overhead ore chute; he had to
stop in such a way that all of the 12 cars rolled out and
fully extended their couplings, and this was done with
skillful application of the brake. The signalman would
then climb down off the car, and then up a ladder to the
ore chute, where he would operate a control to pour ore
into the ore car until it was full. When the first one was
done he signaled the driver who moved the rig forward
by one car; this operation was repeated 12 times.

The full train was driven to the top end of the main
haulage drive to a special chamber where the cars were
pulled over a tipping ramp; each car was tipped in such
a way that it's full side door swung open allowing ore
to tumble down into a vertical shaft that was over 300
metres deep, and fall all the way down to Level 21
where the crushers were. That was the job and it was
repeated over and over again during the shift, delivering
ore from above to below. The haulage team were on
a different bonus to miners, shift bosses, mule drivers
and the rest, but we all benefitted from Level 15's
production, which was measured as the amount of ore
the trains delivered. As such, the train crews were given
priority and enjoyed a certain status on the level; they
could also be very unpopular when they screwed up!

On my first day as trainee with Patrick, I was working
the ore chute, dropping ore down into a car; Jimmy
was the driver. The task involved manipulating a lever
that controlled a huge metal gate located in the ceiling;
opening and closing its jaw to control the flow of ore.
I timed it badly and overfilled the car; ore poured over
the sides and buried the damn thing. Jimmy came
storming back and hurled a tirade of verbal abuse at me;
he was pissed with what I'd done. We had to split the
train, haul the free cars out of the drive and then get the
ST2 in to dig the stuck one out. It took over an hour
before we had the rig back together again and were able
to resume loading. Patrick put me right back on the
chute and with shaking hands and my heart seeming
to be beating in my throat, I managed to get the whole
train loaded. During crib Jimmy made sure everyone
knew about my incompetences and inadequacies, but
Dick backed me and the irate Scotsman eventually let

it go. Paul and I managed to beat the nasty little Celtic prick hands-down at cards; it was something at least and I smiled directly into his face when we took the winning trick.

"You won't get away with that again son. You two will be buying the lottery ticket this week; don't doubt it." he said.

"I don't think so Jimmy." I replied happily, "Bring your wallet because you're going to need it. And make sure it actually has some money in it."

"This will be a bit of an event Steve." Paul joined in, "We better get the newspapers alerted. You don't see a Scot opening his wallet very often, you know."

Even Jimmy managed a chuckle at that one!

———————

As I'd begun working with the fire brigade again I got to spend some time with Big Stack. At various stages of its construction the mine's firemen had stood watch on the growing chimney, usually when there was welding work being done or other potential fire hazards. We were raised up to the cocoon in a site lift that, like a bullet in a rifle barrel, sped upwards inside of the tapering concrete tube, the journey's distance and time increasing with every metre the pour team added to Big Stack. Occasionally I spent some time with the hydraulic jack operator who skillfully steered the climb from a central console. He explained that while maintaining a steady speed was important, to work with the concrete's setting time, he also had to control the rig's tendency to twist. Laser equipment and plumb bobs were used to provide feedback to the driver who could then adjust and compensate, to keep the whole thing on track.

"It would not be a good look if the stack had a bend at the top." the driver chuckled.

"A veritable, Leaning Tower of Mount Isa!" I joked back.

At four thirty in the morning, on March 30, 1978 the pour topped out and the concrete chimney was finally done.

When it was time to dismantle the cocoon the fire brigade was required to work in continuous shifts of four hours each. I watched as bolts were ground away and steel welds carefully cut through, and piece by piece it came apart and was lowered safely down to the ground. There is a scene in Tolkien's book, *The Lord of the Rings* where Saruman throws Gandalf the Grey up to the very roof top of the Tower of Isengard and imprisons him there. With the wind howling and threatening to topple him over the edge, Gandalf looks down the tower's dark stone walls to the ground and it's a very, very long way ... as Big Stack's cocoon slowly disappeared so did the safe, spatial sensation it provided, and Gandalf's plight at Isengard took on a whole new meaning!

One very special day in April I was rostered to do a morning shift at Big Stack. I walked up to the chimney passing by now familiar six metre diameter steel tubes that were being assembled to form the internal flue, and took the lift up a full 265 metres to the top. I was

405

there to start my shift at eight o'clock and stepped out
onto the platform, the cocoon was completely gone and
morning sunlight filled the once enclosed space. Below
me and to the east the city was dwarfed by a huge
expanse of landscape stretching out as far as I could
see. The mighty Leichhardt looked like an adolescent
snake winding off towards the north and east, houses
seemed the size of squares of Cadbury Fruit & Nut
chocolate, cars had become almonds and people looked
like tiny raisins; I watched a road train slowly drive
north and head out past the airport. Behind me, to the
west, Mineside stretched out; in contrast to the east it
featured the deep pitted scars of long-term mining work
dotted like pock marks found on adolescent skin. Six
hundred metres to the southwest I located Black Rock's
open cut maw and some three kilometres away the head
of Mount Isa Mines tailings dam, which flushed dark
grey a further five kilometres southwest to form a series
of lakes nestled in amongst the ochre hued volcanics
and sediments of the Western Fold Belt's ranges.

I located No. 2 Crushers and then K57 nearly half a
kilometre to the west, projecting a paltry 60 metres
above the dust and rocks and clearly no match for Big
Stack; or was it? What if I picked up Big Stack, inverted
it and then lowered it into K57's shaft? Big Stack would
only reach down about one third of the distance that
I worked underground and one quarter of where Ray
was on Level 21. Though hidden from view without a
skyline to dominate, at over a kilometre tall the shaft
dwarfed Big Stack massively. Similar to an iceberg with
the majority of its mass hidden below the surface, K57
was a giant in hiding. The thought reminded me of a
cartoon, where an architect was leaning out of over a

huge rectangular hole in the ground, frantically waving drawings of a high-rise building and yelling down to the contractor, "Stop work! Stop work! The plans are upside down!"

Recalling the cartoon I chuckled quietly to myself and wondered how my architectural mate Gary Hallard was doing on the Gold Coast. A boilermaker had begun work and I glanced around the platform locating its fire extinguishers and giving the flurry of red hot sparks he was producing some attention; a breeze was teasing them over the edge away from timber work and danger.

While I looked out again into the seemingly infinite space of sky, I realised that I had now worked at Mount Isa Mines' highest highs and its deepest depths and was one of only a small group of people who would ever stand atop Big Stack and see the unique and magnificent 360 degree view it afforded. Despite the mine's historical precedence of big, bigger and even bigger, it was unlikely another "Bigger Stack" would be built and so named, but I was sure that for a very long time, earth bound people would gaze up and wonder what it was like to be where I was standing right now.

I raised up an imaginary glass of cold beer to all of them, "Cheers!" and took an imaginary sip, in toast.

The boilermaker, who had paused in his work had glanced over; he laughed out loud, "It's a bit early for a beer isn't it mate?"

"It's never too early. Never too early." I replied knowingly and raised my glass in his direction.

He came over and leaned on the rail with me, wiping sweat from his brow, "Amazing view." he said.

"Yeh. Something to tell the kids about, if I had any to tell." I replied.

"Well, I've got a couple, so I'll tell them for you."

We were quiet for a few moments he and I, looking out over the world; words sometimes fail and silence can say everything that's required, which was nothing. He touched my shoulder and smiled; I nodded and the tradesman returned to his work. It was enough and as the Persian poet Rumi had written over 700 years ago, "Silence is an ocean. Speech is a river. Silence is the language of God, all else is poor translation."

Chapter 28

Return of the Prodigal

As we approached December, the clouds and humidity building up around Mount Isa heralding the big wet, two other water related events made it into the newspapers.

Following the Frost inquiry earlier in the year, Australia's only whaling station, which operated out of Frenchman Bay near Albany in Western Australia, harpooned its last sperm whale and closed operations. In April 1979, The Fraser Government was scheduled to endorse Sir Frost's report, *Whales and Whaling: Report of the Independent Inquiry*, which recommended a total ban on whaling. Cheynes Beach Whaling Company had worked the whaling station since 1954, catching nearly 16,000 humpback and sperm wales. The TV showed gruesome footage of whales being harpooned, then their huge carcasses were hauled tail first up a stained concrete ramp and butchered for oil. I was glad it was over and welcomed the distraction of Ken Warby, who made a blistering run of 510 kilometres per

hour on Blowering Dam in New South Wales. It was a
world record and he instantly became the fastest man
on water. Warby built *The Spirit of Australia* in his back
yard, around a military surplus Westinghouse jet engine
that he bought at auction for $69. The Spirit's body
was constructed of wood and fibreglass and the whole
project was simply covered with a tarpaulin whenever
it rained. It was a compelling homegrown story and
everyone seemed interested.

Perhaps inspired by Warby's new speed record or just
keen to show off the Charger's enhanced performance,
I took CL out to The Drags late on Saturday night. Ray
and Margy went too as we'd heard there would be an
American muscle car racing, a Ford Mustang no less.
It was a great event and I had lots of races; the car had
performed well. Around three o'clock in the morning
the crowds were beginning to thin out and a friend of
the Mustang crew asked if I'd like to have a fun run
with the big V8. No one, including me, expected the
Charger to win but it was a novel idea and I agreed.

We lined up revving our engines and then the starter
dropped his arm and I floored it, smoking rubber off the
line. Even over the noise of my engine I could hear the
V8 bellowing like an enraged bull and coming up fast
behind me. I had been little quicker off the start and
quickly dropped into second gear, my foot pressing the
accelerator flat to the floor when, bang, suddenly I was
spinning round in a circle.

My foot was still hard down with the rear wheels
spinning and smoking, my right shoulder pressed hard
into the driver's door; lights flashed into the cabin and
I had a sense of something hurtling off the road behind

me. Eventually CL's tail end slowed it's wild slide and I got my foot to the brake and brought the car under control. We'd spun a full 360 degrees; smoke and the acrid stench of burning rubber invaded my nose and lungs. I eased the Charger over to park her on the highway's gravel verge, and turned off her engine. The silence was startling.

People came running over to see if I was okay. I got out, looked around and saw another group running down the embankment towards a huge cloud of dust, which had begun to slowly drift off, revealing the Mustang with its rear end poking out from the rocks, spinifex and hardy low-level scrub that lined the Barkly Highway.

Ray put his hand on my shoulder, "You okay Stevie?"

"Yeh." I replied, "What happened? How's my car?"

"He fishtailed the Mustang and lost it mate." Ray explained, "Then drove into the back of you and spun you around." Ray pointed over to the other distressed car. "Huh. He ended up taking it bush bashing. Ha. We know what that does to a car. Hey Stevie?"

"Yeh. We sure do."

We walked around to the Charger's rear passenger side and it was clear where the big bull had struck; she was scraped and dented from just behind the door to the rear panel, but no broken windows and the rear bumper was untouched.

"You were lucky mate." Ray said, running his hand over the torn paint work, "It looks just like panel damage; nothing structural like when I smashed my Charger."

He was right. Fortunately for me with the Charger being lightweight in its rear end, the Mustang had virtually swatted us aside on its feral charge towards the bush. If he'd hit me dead centre then the impact would have probably rolled CL and me over, and down the embankment. We would have been the ones lodged in the bush with the Charger a total write-off.

Ray and I watched as the Mustang's owner and his mates climbed out through the passenger door's open window; gnarly wattles and kapoks were preventing the doors opening. Ray, Margy and I walked over.

"How are you mate?" I asked the driver; I didn't know his name.

"Damn it." he said miserably. "My wife's going to kill me."

We looked over his car and in reality, it wasn't too bad. The passenger's side-guard was dented and scratched from charging into me, with steam rising up from under the bonnet there was, clearly, some radiator damage and various other body work would be required to heal the effect of sticking the beast into the local bush.

"How's your car?" he asked.

"Damage to the rear end where you hit me, but not too bad." I replied. "What happened to you?"

"Yeh. Sorry about that mate." he said, "I was fishtailing off the start when the rear tyres got into the gravel and spun me out; when they bit into the bitumen again the car was pointed right at you. It was happening so fast I didn't have time to correct."

"Probably a good thing you did hit me. Slowed you down a bit." I replied, "You might have launched yourself further into the bush and be in a real bad way."

"Yeh. Could be."

"Yeh."

I thought about our situation for a moment or two; it was his poor driving that had caused the accident but I knew that we were both contributors, "So, what if you fix your car and I'll fix mine," I proposed, "and we'll call it quits?"

"Yeh?"

"Yeh." I reached over, offered my hand and we shook on it.

Looking around I saw that a lot of people had left and gone home. I was suddenly very tired.

"What are you going to do?" I asked Mustang man.

"I dunno at the moment." he looked around. "I hope the cops don't come out here for a look. Someone's bound to have told them."

"Yeh. I've got a tow rope in the boot." I said, "Let's see if we can get you out and onto the road."

413

Ray asked if I'd be okay; he wanted to take Margy home. I said I was good and they headed off back to the city.

I backed my car down the embankment, up to his, and we connected the rope; it was tricky for the rear tyres to get much purchase on the gravel verge, but with some people bouncing and pushing the Mustang and several others sitting on the Charger's rear end, we managed to pull it clear. His radiator was gone but tyres and steering seemed okay. I drove around to his front, we hooked up the tow rope again and I was able to pull the car up onto the road's verge. We were the last two cars at The Drags, everyone else had gone.

"I may as well tow you home mate." I offered.

"Yeh? That would be great. Thanks." he replied. Mustang man and his two mates got into their injured bull and we set off for the city; one smashed up Charger towing one smashed up Mustang. If anyone had been around it might have looked like a peculiar procession; something similar to the blind leading the blind. I drove slowly and skirted the city centre hoping to avoid any attention, official or otherwise; I needn't have bothered, the streets were deserted. As I pulled into the kerb outside his house the eastern horizon was beginning to lighten, tinted with pale oranges and yellows. It was around four thirty when we untied the tow rope and shook hands once again.

"Thanks mate." said Mustang man.

"Hope you get her fixed up."

"Yeh. You too."

414

"See you later mate."

I didn't know Mustang man's name and he didn't know mine, and it was unlikely we'd meet up again. Strangely though, perhaps via the event's drama, or that we'd worked as a team to get him home or maybe because we simply enjoyed cars, there seemed to have been a bond created. Maybe we would meet up, hopefully with both our cars in great shape once again; who knew? I drove home and parked outside my barracks' room. It was five o'clock and the sun was already shimmering over the eastern hills. I went inside, locked the door, pulled all my curtains and got into bed.

"Damn it!" I thought to myself and then fell asleep, exhausted.

————————

Christmas 1978 was uneventful, saved by the fact that Ian bought himself a Panama Green HX Sandman Panelvan, and that I was invited to have Christmas lunch with Paul from work and his fiance Christine. I spent New Year's Eve with Ray, Margy and what seemed to be most of Mount Isa packed tight like sardines into the Irish Club. Shortly after the holidays I decided to have a go at repairing the Charger.

Searching through the wrecking yard I'd discovered an earlier model Charger body and fortunately, the rear panels matched CL's. The panel I was interested in was largely spot welded in place and I spent an afternoon drilling out all the welds and freeing up the panel; there were a couple of cuts required but it all came out in reasonably good shape. I was stoked. Wrapped up in an old bedspread to stop it scratching, I managed to get part of it into CL's boot, tied it down and drove us to the work sheds. Once again my car came off the road while the damaged panel was drilled out and removed, and then the replacement fitted. The new panel was Harvest Yellow, which shouted out in shocking contrast to CL's Amarante Red!

"Jeez Steveo. She's looking a bit like Saturday night's pizza. Maybe you should swap a few more panels over and then we can call her Gelato Jenny!" said Ken, a fellow fireman who was giving me some lessons in welding.

"It all depends on your perspective of life Ken." I replied, "If you come over here to the driver's side then she looks fantastic. I'm not really sure what your problem is."

"The problem is, Steveo, that I'm on this side and I suggest you get some paint on this car or you'll have a bunch of starving Italians chasing you down the road thinking that you're dinner. Ha-ha!"

"It is pretty bright." I agreed.

"Bright ain't the word my friend; it's more like pukey."

"Puke?" I replied, feigning hurt feelings, "That's a little harsh Ken. You'll hurt her feelings."

"Get some paint. Soon." were his final words on the subject and we got back to welding the offending pukey pizza panel in place.

Over the next few days I sanded back the yellow paint and applied body filler, or "bog" as it was known. The process was to apply a thin coat of bog, let it harden, sand back and then repeat; building up layer after layer.

"It's just like making lasagne." Ken told me, running with his Italian food theme. "You'll soon be in the restaurant business with this car!"

I didn't have tools or gear for this job and did it all by hand when I had spare time after work. It took a while but I began to see the shape of my car returning. On close inspection it was clear that while my basic shaping was good, the surface was not yet ready for paint. The high gloss finish would reveal every imperfection and when I wet it, I could see fine scratches and marks across the surface. My mentor Ken had gone off on a trip and not being very sure what the next steps were, I bought several spray cans of primer, masked the area off and painted over the repair work to protect it. I was done for now.

It took a while for me to notice but I began to lose interest in the Charger. It seemed that now she was damaged I stopped taking such good care of her; the regular Saturday morning washes and vacuuming became less regular, and polishing was a thing of the past. I'm not sure why I didn't book her into a paint shop and get the repair job finished, but I didn't. One day I was talking to one of the other firees about the car and Paul hinted that he was interested.

"When are you going to get her painted Steve?" he asked.

"I'm not sure. I haven't gotten around to it yet." I answered vaguely.

"If she was mine, I would get her down to the panel shop. She's a great looking car!"

"Yeh. She is." I agreed, "And the engine goes really well with the head done and Weber."

I talked with him about the porting, polishing and carburetter, "Do you want to take her out for a run?" I offered.

"Really? You wouldn't mind?"

"Na. Go for it." and I handed over the keys.

About 20 minutes later he parked the Charger back outside my room, "How'd you go?" I asked.

"Really nice. Really nice to drive and she's got some pull too. Thanks a lot Steve!" his eyes were bright and I recalled how I had been when I first met CL. Was she talking with him now?

"Yeh. No worries." I replied.

And as the last word left my mouth the fire brigade bells went-off and we all ran for the truck, grabbing gear as we went; both Paul and I managed to get on for the call out and soon the truck was roaring off towards the mine with its sirens a-wailing. It was always a good moment being in the truck with our adrenalin pumping, the officer shouting out his instructions and everyone excited with the prospect of whatever was to come. Paul and I had forgotten all about CL but she had not forgotten us.

———————

Even though Sandra and I had not communicated for a while now, Mount Isa's grape vine was alive and well. I heard that she was finishing up on the Gold Coast and would be coming back to the city. I acted indifferent but deep down a small spark reignited, perhaps one that had never gone out, one that I'd hidden, even from myself, and one that the northwest's big wet wouldn't extinguish either.

January in north Queensland produced Australia's highest daily rainfall, with a record 1140 millimetres being recorded at Bellenden Ker. The cyclone season reached across from the east coast to fill creeks and rivers and February saw flooding over the Carpentaria. While the papers reported that our old friend Senator Neville Bonner was awarded Australian of the Year, and that cyclones Peter and Greta were invading Cairns, they missed our own local cyclone story, as Maurine swept into Jan and Merce's lives.

Maurine showed up one Saturday night at the Barkly Hotel. I don't recall how she joined our group, perhaps introduced by a friend. She was attractive with dark hair and wearing a short blue-black dress with matching heels that showed her legs off nicely. She didn't seem to be with anyone and I noticed that my instinctive "single girl" alert jangled; Maurine took a seat down the table from me near Jan and Merce. Around nine thirty Jan had to go home to relieve a baby sitter who'd been taking care of their two girls. We said good night to the couple but half an hour later Merce returned, alone, and joined us once again. I didn't think much about it and as the evening progressed we all got up for several dances and enjoyed the band, our drinks and rowdy chat. When the house lights flashed, indicating closing time, we all hung around outside for a while, not willing to let go of the night just yet. It turned out that Maurine and her girlfriend didn't have transport and were going to order a taxi, but Ian got in before me and gallantly offered to drive them both home, and we gradually dispersed and headed off to our various homes and beds or whatever was next.

I didn't hear from Merce for quite a while after that night out at the Barkly, which was a little unusual, so I bought some beers, scotch and coke and went around to his house. It was a Thursday evening and with my box of goodies tucked under one arm I knocked on their back door.

"Who is it?" Jan called out.

"It's Steve. Let me in I've got some cold drinks." I replied through the locked door.

I heard a latch being released, the door swung open and Jan seemed confused, "Steveo? What are you doing here?"

"Nice welcome." I joked, "I haven't seen you guys for a while so I've come-a-visiting!" and proffered my box, it's bottles clinking merrily together.

She didn't smile or say anything but stood to one side so I could enter, "Where's Ian?" I asked.

Jan hesitated and then said, "He's not home right now."

"Oh well, then he's going to miss out on a free drink." I joked again and poured Jan a scotch and coke and opened a beer for myself.

We sat at the kitchen table, just as we'd done many times before and chatted, but it was odd. Eventually I asked, "What's up Jan? You seem distracted. Are you okay?"

She thought about that question for a while and then looked me straight in the eyes and replied, "Ian said that he was going out with you tonight Steveo, so I'm puzzled as to why you're here."

"Out with me?" I frowned, "I've not seen him for a while now, which is why I came around."

We were both quiet for a moment, lost in our thoughts, and then she burst out crying. I wasn't sure what to do as I'd never seen her cry before. I reached out and placed my hand gently on her shoulder, "Jan, what's going on?"

She sat there sobbing for a while and then looked up at me once again; her voice firmed up, "I think you'd better go mate."

I still wasn't sure what was going on but I nodded, "Okay. I'll see you later."

Jan packed up my box and without another word handed it over to me; I left. It was the strangest night.

I made a point of catching up with Ian a few days later, "Not real smart mate, using me as a cover and not telling me about it!"

"Yeh. Sorry Steveo. I wasn't expecting you to come on over." Ian was a little sheepish.

"How'd it go when you got home?" I asked.

"She wasn't too happy with me." he explained, "We had a big fight."

"She wasn't too happy with me either, when I knocked on your back door." I laughed.

"Yeh. I can imagine."

Ian looked up, "I'm going to move back into the barracks."

"Yeh?"

"Yeh."

"Not so good at home?" I probed gently.

He looked away for a moment, "Well, I'm seeing Maurine now so it's best that I make a clean break of it."

"Aha!" I teased, "So, that's why you were out with me when you weren't." We chuckled together.

"Yeh. That's why."

"Okay." I replied, "Well, let me know if you need a hand with anything."

"Thanks mate. I will."

And that was that. A few days later Ian got himself a room in the barracks and was going out with Maurine. I wasn't so foolish to think that we'd seen the last of Jan, Mount Isa was a small place socially, but the circumstances would turn out to be somewhat uncomfortable, for me.

———————

A week or so later I went out to the Overlander Hotel on Friday night. Harry, his cousin and some mates would be there, and a live band. Mick Campbell, who I'd not seen much of for a while was going too. I arrived just before eight o'clock and the place was packed. Squeezing in between the mob at the bar I got a bar maid's attention and then found Harry; he'd saved me a seat at their table.

We all bantered and talked about stuff for a while and then Harry put his hand on my shoulder and inclined his head, one eyebrow raised, directing my attention across the room.

"Who are we looking at mate?" I asked, not quite getting it.

He remained silent, repeated his gesture and I looked once again. At first I didn't quite recognise her; the hairstyle was different, now permed and frizzy, she'd lost some weight and was smoking a pipe of all things. I watched her take a puff, raise up her cute little chin and then release a plume of smoke into the air above her table. My heart jumped and I took a quick pull on my beer.

"She's back then." I said to no one in particular.

"Apparently so." Harry commented, a half smile on his face. "Are you going over?"

"Na. We haven't talked for a long while now." I said, glancing over in her direction again, "I heard that she was coming back to town, but not from her."

"Fair enough mate." Harry replied.

I tried not to pay Sandra any more attention but it was a little unsettling that we were both in the same room. Mick got my mind off her when I visited the men's toilets. He was splashing water over his face and everywhere, and looked up when I walked in.

"Outram!" he called out loudly.

"G'day Mick. How are you mate?"

"Punch me!"

I was a bit taken back by his demand and played it down, "Mate. I like you too much to be doing that. What are you up to?"

"I've got a fight. Get me ready. Punch me."

The silly bugger stuck his chin out so I swung and landed one, my fist slipped on his wet skin and the ring I was wearing scraped leaving a thin red cut.

"Blood! Excellent!" he grinned a little too manically to be totally sane right then, "Thanks Steveo!"

"Go get 'em mate!" I cheered and with that he boomed out of the room and stormed outside. "God help the one who is outside waiting for him." I thought to myself.

Several blokes who had retreated—well, as far away as one can in a crowded men's toilet—during Mick's pre-fight preparations breathed a sign of relief and we all got on with our business. I didn't see Mick again that night but the man was a bull, a good boxer and I knew that he'd be all right.

Later on I went up to the bar to order a round of drinks and noticed that she was also queued, just a couple of metres away. She wore a white, short sleeved cotton top and cutoff denim shorts, and was still smoking the pipe. When I got through to the front of the line and ordered, I glanced at her reflection in the mirrors and it was clear that she had seen me too. It was a very strange sensation to be so close and yet so far. I placed all the drinks on a carry tray and returned to my table; about half an hour later I left the Overlander and went over to visit Paul and Christine. We had a couple of drinks and a chat and then I drove home to the barracks. Laying in bed I found myself thinking about pipes, permed hair and her before falling asleep.

During the next week Merce moved back into the barracks. He came and found me one afternoon to let me know where he was. We sat on the steps, had a cold beer, chatted for a while, and later walked over to the mess for dinner. He told me that Jan had not handled the breakup well and her two daughters cried and had begged him not to leave.

"It was one of the toughest things I've had to do Steve." he said, shaking his head.

425

I'd known Ian for a long time; we'd been mates since school and his home life then had not been the best, "Well, you made a real nice family life with Jan and the girls mate. You seemed pretty happy with it."

"Yeh. It was good." he admitted, "Anyway mate. New things to look forward to." and we raised our bottles of beer and chinked them together.

Over the next few days I thought about Jan and that she might not be having a real great time now, with Ian gone; I decided to pay her a visit and see how she was going. I'd really enjoyed her and Ian as a couple and we'd all had some good times together. Once again I bought some beers, scotch and coke and one evening drove on over to her house.

When I knocked on the back door Jan called out, "Who is it?"

I had a flash of déjà vu, "It's Steve Jan." I called out, "How are you?"

"Ahh. Well, you can't come in here Steveo." she giggled back at me through the locked door.

"No. No. No. You can't get in here. Ha-ha." It was a mail voice and I thought I recognised it as Chris's, one of the gay guys we drank with sometimes.

"I came to see how you are doing Jan." I said.

And then there was another voice; a female that I recognised but couldn't quite place, "Get lost dick head! We don't want you around here."

There was a raucous burst of laughter from behind the door and it was clear that I wasn't going in. I turned away, got back into the Charger and drove back home. By the time I unlocked the door to my room I was fully angry. "Fuck them all right back! Jan, Chris and the other idiot." I was done with the stupid bitch. Good riddance. I hoped never to see Jan again but Mount Isa is a small place and I wasn't to get my wish.

A few days later, I cleaned up after day shift, picked up the local paper and then went over to the Irish Club for a few beers before dinner. I didn't notice them at first but there, over at one of the tables in the public bar sat Jan, another girl I didn't know and Sandra.

Jan waved me over, "Hey, sorry about the other night Steve." Sandra seemed to snigger and then quickly picked up her drink and looked away, "I'd had a few drinks ..." Jan continued, "Anyway, why don't you join us?"

I found that I was really annoyed with the whole idea of these bitches being in my drinking hole; and having treated me like shit, now acting if everything was all just fine. And my stomach had dropped the moment I saw Sandra, so I wasn't sure what to do with that either.

"Na." I dismissed her offer, "I don't think so Jan. I've got better things to do with my time!"

And with that said I turned and walked over to a far table near the pool tables, settled down and read the paper. I'm not sure I really understood any of the words that my eyes ran over but I put on a damn good act. Later, I noticed them get up and leave and took in

a long, deep breath before refreshing my drink and
hoping for the distraction of a game of pool.

I didn't understand it. After all of these months. How
this girl could still have such an unsettling effect on me.
She just sat there; we hadn't even said a word to each
other. I knew, deep down, that I wasn't really angry with
Jan or Sandra, but with me. I was angry that I didn't
get it, that I didn't seem to be in control, that the whole
thing was confusing, that I still wanted her so badly,
that I was aware of the trap but knew I was going to
step in it again, that I didn't seem to have a choice and
that I knew it was, at some point, going to hurt.

Chapter 29

The Very Last Time

It seemed inevitable, like a record on repeat, playing the same song over and over, that I would find myself once again with Sandra. And there she was, the morning after, tucked up asleep in my bed. I watched an inquisitive finger of light creeping across the pillow, moving silently onto her hair, then her cheek and lips. It attempted to assail my pale blue wall but slowed and then retreated.

The mystery of the mystery voice behind Jan's door had been solved last night. Sandra told me that she'd been hanging out with Jan and Chris recently, and they'd been having a private party at the house when I knocked. She'd apologised and said Jan felt bad about it too; they'd come to the Irish Club hoping I'd be there but it hadn't worked out very well. She moved and began to stretch but in the confines of a single bed, soon pressed against my body and opened her eyes.

"Hello." she said sleepily.

I smiled, reached over and kissed her, then snuggled in against her warm body.

After a while she sighed and then sat up, "Gotta go to work. Can you give me a lift home?"

"Yes. Of course." I replied.

We dressed and went out to the car. It was early and the barracks were quiet. There were still a few hours to go until change of shift at the mines and we left the car park unnoticed. I dropped Sandra off outside her parent's house and then went back home to shower and have breakfast. I saw Ian's panel van in the barrack's mess carpark and found him inside enjoying a plate of scrambled eggs.

"G'day mate. You on day shift?" I asked.

"Yeh." he replied, "You?"

"Starting afternoons. How's Maurine?"

We chatted while we ate, mainly about girls and relationships, and then he left for work. Paul from the fire brigade was sitting a few tables away and waved me over. I got myself another cup of coffee and joined him.

"I've been thinking about your car." he said after a while.

"Yeh?"

"Yeh."

"Would you be interested in selling it? Maybe we can do a good deal."

"I'm always open for a good deal mate!" I laughed.

"Well, I was thinking of my car, along with some cash." he began, "I need to keep some money aside so I can get the Charger's body work finished and painted; how about $1600?"

It didn't seem like much cash but I knew that I'd lost interest in the Charger and would probably never finish the repair I'd started, "I'm interested." I replied, "Let's go and have a look at your car."

I knew Paul had a Valiant station wagon but hadn't really taken much notice of it before; it turned out to be in immaculate condition.

"It's been in my family since new." he explained, "Mum and Dad gave it to me for a 21st birthday present. She's been really well looked after and the VE was Wheels' *Car of the Year* in 1967 you know."

I looked the car over and we took it for a drive. It had an automatic gearbox, was soft, sedate and comfortable and a car that I probably wouldn't be taking out to The Drags on Saturday night, but it would do and I liked the simple fact that it was something different. I'd finished paying off the Charger's hire-purchase loan a few months ago so I had no debt left in CL ... it only took a few minutes before we shook hands on $1800 plus the grey Valiant VE Safari wagon, with its slant six motor and white walled tires. I knew that Ray was going to have a field day with me over the conservative new wagon, and I was right.

"Far out Outram!" the expected roasting began, "What? Are you planning on starting a family now mate? Dog and kids in the back. The missus in the front. Off to Moondarra for a nice picnic after church on Sunday? Ha-ha! You're all set mate."

I thought he was done but ... ,"You'll have a bunch of ankle biters running around after you in no time mate. Better get a trailer hooked on the back to cart them all around. Ha-ha!"

There was no doubt that Linwood was on a roll and thoroughly enjoying himself, but in the great tradition of cars and blokes we sniffed around under the bonnet together and then took the VE for a drive. Ray mentioned the "family" word again, several more times, commented on how sluggish it was compared to the Charger and then feigning boredom, laid back his seat and pretended to sleep. On the way back he nicknamed her the Grey Ghost, which I actually liked. Finally, he roared off in his big Ford gunning its V8 engine and laying down rubber. The smoke and dust cleared and it seemed that I'd survived for now, but no doubt there would be a Mick roasting to come and probably a few others, and I would survive those as well.

At work during the week Paul quietly announced that he and Christine had finalised their wedding plans and invited several of us around for drinks at their house to celebrate. They would be married at Airlie Beach, on the coast, and Paul handed me an invitation.

"I hope you can make it Steveo." he said, "Be great to have your there."

"Thanks mate." I replied, "That's really nice. I'll see what I can organise at work with Dick to get some time off."

While Christine and Paul were formalising a life-long partnership, my relationship with Sandra took a deep dive once again. She had discovered who I'd slept with while she was away on the Gold Coast and one girl in particular had really annoyed her.

"I can't believe you slept with her! Out of all the girls in town you had to pick her. Don't you know she's a bikie mole? She'll shag anyone. Who knows what diseases she has. It's disgusting!"

We'd already had a couple of drinks and the argument was escalating; I also had my sources of information and hit right back.

"Well, what about you with Kevin on the Gold Coast?" I threw at her, "He's one of my mates and you jumped right into bed with him soon after I was gone. I dropped everything, came down there to help you out and you just turned around and bedded him. Thanks very much!"

"At least he's a decent bloke. Not like the dirty slag you went with. I can't believe you'd do that to me."

And so, we officially broke up again.

Macka and Ian Drake, known as "Drakey," had a three bedroom house in Seventeenth Avenue, advantageously located just down the road from the Irish Club. While I was nursing my emotional bruises one evening at the Piano Bar, Macka mentioned that his brother Ollie had moved out and they had a vacancy, if I was interested.

"I'm not really sure Macka." I said.

"What do you mean?" he replied, "It's a great place and much better than the barracks."

"It's not about the house mate. Considering that you're both Kiwis, I'm not sure I can put up with all the sheep you'll have around the place. Bah-ha!"

He shook his head and laughed, "Boom! Boom! Outram. You're a riot mate."

It turned out that I was interested and once again moved out of the barracks, made the obligatory visit to Kmart for sheets, towels and the rest, and moved in. It was a good choice, and I had a lot of fun with the two New Zealanders, even though they did speak funny!

While it was good to be in a new place with a couple of great flat mates I was still struggling with my broken relationship. It seemed that in no time at all Sandra had procured another boyfriend; a black belt in Karate I was told. I wrote to her a couple of times and included some nice photos that I'd taken, but word got back to me on the grape vine that she'd threatened to publish my letters if I sent anymore. Given that she'd got herself a new man, who could probably beat my brains out, it was clear to me that the door had been slammed shut and I stopped all attempts to contact her. It didn't make it any easier that I saw them in the various places we all socialised at, but life goes on and I tried to be cool and calm, and make it work. It wasn't too long though, before my "cool" was really put to the test.

A bunch of us had met up at the Barkly Hotel on Saturday night. It was the current popular place for our group and often had a live band playing on the weekend. Gary Hallard had driven up for a visit and

434

even Danny, who I knew from No. 2 Concentrator, was there. We pulled some tables together, managed to get everyone seated and ordered drinks. The band was good and several couples got up to dance but I stayed and chatted with Gary and Danny. During the night someone pointed out that Sandra and her new boyfriend were here too, seated over on the other side of the room. I watched her up dancing several times but kept my distance. Later, Sandra slid into an empty chair just two seats away and began to hurl abuse at me; it was clear that she was drunk. It wasn't fun to be treated this way in public, at my table, surrounded by my friends, but I stayed calm, sensing that any retaliation from me would just make things worse. The tirade continued and then she threw her drink at me, glass and all. It smashed against a concrete column near my head, and shattered glass, ice cubes and vodka sprayed all around. Some people moved to hold her back but Karate Kid, who'd been standing in the background, stepped in and took her, still screaming at me, away. I looked up into his face and he wasn't very happy with the whole scene, but concentrated on getting Sandra away, back to their table before the bouncers came to investigate.

"Well done mate." Danny said, helping to pick shards of glass from my shirt, "You handled that well. I knew that if you reacted there would be a big fight. I saw the boyfriend watching you; he was looking for any excuse to step in."

"Thanks Danny." I replied, "It was pretty full-on!"

Merce was at my side; concerned, "Are you okay Steveo?"

"Yeh. I seem to have more vodka on the outside than I do on the inside." I tried a joke.

"Ha. Yeh. Maybe you can try and suck it in through your skin."

"I'll do my best." I replied.

"She was out of control." he noted.

"Yeh. She's pretty drunk right now. I hope she's got it all out of her system."

I went off to the bathroom to clean up and when I returned the table had been cleared of debris. I ordered a beer and sat down again but really wanted to get out of there, even for a while.

"Gazza?"

"Yeh?"

"There's a pretty good car shop across the road," I said, "Wanna go take a look?"

"It's night time." he puzzled, "Won't they be shut?"

"Yeh but they've got a big display window and there's heaps to see."

"Okay. I'm game." he replied and we got up and walked outside.

It was good to be in the fresh air and away from all the noise and bustle of the bar. I led Gary across to the other side of the highway. We had just started to talk when several blokes came up behind us; Karate Kid was one of them.

"You. Outram." he raised a hand and pointed at me.

There was no doubt about it, the guy was buff. He wasn't big framed, maybe a bit heavier and taller than me, but he looked to be in good shape. The words "black belt" filtered through into my mind and I knew if this went beyond words it would be a fight that I'd lose, and badly.

"G'day mate." I replied, "What's up?"

He looked across at Gary, "Who are you mate?"

"I'm just up here visiting from the Gold Coast." Gary replied, "I don't know anything about this."

Apparently satisfied, Karate Kid's attention came back on me. He was angry, about the scene at the Barkly, about photographs I had of Sandra, he was probably angry about me even being on the planet, but I stayed calm. On the inside every molecule of my body seemed to be shaking violently, but outside I was icy cool.

"Mate. I don't have any fight with you." I replied, "I have history with Sandra but I'm happy that she has someone to take care of her now. I'll send her all the photos if that helps. And if you two are going out together now, then it's all good. I didn't know, at the time that she was seeing you. I'm not interfering mate. Are you okay with that?"

His face and posture relaxed a little bit, but then he glanced around at his mates and looked back at me with a snarl, "You get those photos to her mate. No more letters and stay the hell away. All right?"

"Yeh. Can do." I replied quietly.

437

I knew that we were at some kind of inflection point and didn't speak again. He looked at me for a while, nodded once then turned away and strode off towards the Barkly Hotel; his mates all followed and we were done.

I took a long deep breath, "Phew. Sorry Gary. I wasn't expecting that."

"Yeh. That wasn't great Steve."

"Yeh. You're right."

And with that I turned back to the big glass display window and took up our conversation again. While we were talking my flight-fight response shut down, the adrenalin pounding around my body began to dissipate and later we walked back and went into to the hotel again. I had one beer, said good night to everyone and left. On the way home I noticed the Piano Bar's lights were still on, and dropped in to find Macka and Drakey there. Even Macka's regular "Boom. Boom." was comforting and I laughed at all his jokes even though I'd heard them many times before. At eleven o'clock we all went home and soon enough the house was full of shadows, snores and sleeping.

Before I dozed off I thought about Sandra, Karate Kid, and Damien with his horse stories. It was all well and good being patient but something wasn't working very well here. If they broke up next week and then she and I got back together again, I felt that I could confidently predict the outcome. I hoped that somehow I would find a few useful answers as I couldn't keep going like this; I'd only just survived this last debacle. I knew I was trapped, but at least now I was consciously looking for the way out.

I decided to take a break from the city and all of its dramas, and combine Paul's wedding with a visit to the Gold Coast and family. I hoped that I would be able to get my head straight and figure out what to do with myself. Perhaps some time-out at Mum and Dad's place would provide me with a fresh perspective on life; I sure could use one, or two or ten.

I spoke with Shift Boss Dick during crib and he wasn't too pleased with the idea of two train drivers being away from work at the same time, but agreed to approve my holidays when he knew it was for Paul's wedding.

"Taffy doesn't have many friends Steve." he called out loud enough for Paul to hear, "It'd probably be a good idea if you go and support him."

An amused chuckle rippled across the crib room; Paul rose from his bench and tipped an imaginary cap in our direction, "Thank you Mr. Dick!" he replied in his mildly Australianised Welsh accent, "And may the good Lord bless you too."

I kept my promise to Karate Kid and posted all of the recent photographs I had of Sandra to her parent's address. I was a little annoyed at having to do this, after all they were my photos, and had ripped them into pieces. I didn't include a letter deciding that this would be the last time I'd send her anything. If I'd thought that it would pacify Karate Kid and keep him off my back, I was wrong. One night we were both in the Irish Club and at closing time he was very drunk. As we all filed out of the club he was waiting outside, yelling and threatening to tear me into little pieces. While the bouncers moved him off, Sean the bar manager ushered me back through the building and I made my escape out of a side door unnoticed.

"Thanks Sean." I said gratefully.

"Glad to help lad." he replied in his lyrical Irish accent, "We'd been having trouble with him lately so we're keeping a good eye out. God bless."

Once again I had managed to avoid a difficult situation, but it was getting a bit stressful constantly being on alert every time I went out. My trip away couldn't have come soon enough and I was quietly relieved to be packing my gear into the station wagon early one morning. I drove across town and when Big Stack magically disappeared from my rear view mirror I was able to take a deep breath and leave my recent troubles behind.

It was really good to be out on the open road once again and see familiar towns passing by. Cloncurry was first, then Julia Creek, Hughenden, Charters Towers flew by and then I headed southeast at the coast. About 13 hours after leaving Mount Isa I turned east, off the Bruce Highway, and entered Cannon Valley. The road was flanked by verdant sugar cane reminding me of the drive that Ray and I did some three years ago along Murder Highway and into Sarina. The VE ambled along Proserpine Shute Harbour Road and through Cannonvale, where I had my first glimpse of the ocean, then we drove into Airlie Beach a few minutes later. The car had handled the 1,100 kilometer drive faultlessly, but I was very glad to be pulling into the Airlie Beach

Hotel's carpark to join Christine, Paul and their other wedding guests for sunset drinks overlooking the wide, blue-green expanse of Pioneer Bay.

"Apparently you do have friends 'Taffy.'" I joked with Paul.

"Yes. Apparently I do." he replied with a wink and we clinked glasses, toasting absent shift bosses.

Later, after finding my room and settling in, I joined them for dinner. Paul made a surprise announcement, followed by a request.

"Steve, the Best Man had to cancel on short notice and Christine and I would like you to be our Best Man tomorrow; will you do that for us please?"

I thought about it for a moment and asked, "What would I have to do? I've never done that before."

"Well, you get to hang out with the Bride's Maids." Paul began with a knowing wink. "Christine's nieces. Very nice mate."

Christine jumped in, "They are hot looking girls, you know. Oh yes!"

"You sit with us up on the top table wearing a fancy suit and we get served first." Paul continued enthusiastically, "Oh yes, there's the ring; you have to come to church and hand me the ring. It'll be great mate, you're involved the whole way through."

"The *whole* way through?" I joked with them.

They both laughed, "No Steve. Not everything. You don't get to come to bed with us. We already did that part several years ago. Ha-ha!"

"We'll take you over to the tailor tomorrow morning and get you measured up for the suit, and then you're good to go." Christine added.

"Okay." I replied, "Sounds great. I'm in."

Paul reached over and shook my hand, "Thanks mate. I really appreciate it."

"It'll be my pleasure."

"Oh!" said Paul with a big grin, "I forgot to mention one more thing."

"Yeh. What's that?" I was suspicious now.

"The speech."

"The speech?"

"Yeh." he chuckled, clearly enjoying his sophistry, "The Best Man has to give a speech."

My heart jumped a bit, I was not good standing up in front of people. It had been a big problem for me at school and I'd avoided any kind of public speaking ever since. Even at my 21st birthday party I'd managed not to give a speech.

"I'm not real good at that, you guys." I was already nervous.

"You'll be fine mate." Paul spoke reassuringly, "Tomorrow we'll have a few early beers while the girls are getting ready and write something up. You'll be great."

I wasn't totally convinced but I was tired after a long drive and feeling fairly mellow, what with the drinks and a nice meal, "Okay." I resigned, "I'll give it a go. But no promises. Best Man doesn't automatically mean best speech."

"Don't worry Steve." said Christine, "You'll be great. And thanks. You're a lifesaver."

So, it was done and I was now, officially, Best Man. We had dessert and then I bid my friends good night. It had been a big day and I was weary. Back in the room I took a quick shower, got into bed and despite the 'speech thing' fell fast asleep. I had the room to myself tonight and would meet my room mate, Christine's brother, when he arrived in the morning.

I met them again for breakfast and then we drove to Proserpine for a suit fitting and returned to welcome mothers, fathers, brothers, cousins and other family members and friends who were arriving for the big day. Many were from Christine's side of the family who lived in the area but Paul was represented as well. As promised, the Bride's Maids were hot and Paul's sister, who I knew from Mount Isa, was there and had brought a girlfriend. While the women went off to get ready Paul and I were allocated a room where we had a couple of beers and talked about the day. I got some notes down for my speech and he gave me a few telegrams and cards from people who were unable to attend the wedding. They were pretty tame so I made a few up for fun. Like the one from his other wife asking him where he was and what she was supposed to do now with all of his kids, and another from the South Wales Police reminding him that he was out on parole and wasn't supposed to have left the country; would he return to Wales as soon as the wedding was finished please!

Christine's Dad and brother joined us for a quick beer then left and we put on our suits and were ready. There wasn't a lot to do except wait so we went to the hotel's bar until someone came to get us saying the wedding cars were ready and it was time to go.

There's a well known formula to weddings; a process that allows everything to run smoothly and so people know what to do and when. Paul and Christine's wedding was a lot of fun and though I had not participated in one before, I kind-of knew how they worked. I managed to have consumed enough drinks to get myself through my speech and it seemed to go down well; I even got a laugh with my bogus telegrams and was proud to finally offer up the Best Man's toast, "To the Bride and Groom." One of my duties was to join the wedded couple out onto the floor and dance with a Bride's Maid. I had no idea how to waltz and was self consciousness about being in front of so many people, with so little skill, but we managed to get through it without stumbling or standing on toes.

When all was said and all was done the wedding party got back into the cars and were driven to Airlie Beach and the hotel bar. It seemed that Christine and Paul had already practiced and completed the, 'consummate their wedding' part and would not be disappearing upstairs to fool around. I hung out with Paul's sister and girlfriend and as things were winding down we went back to their place for a nightcap. It was pretty much the last thing I remember until I woke up the next morning in bed with both of them. We were all fully dressed and apparently, replete with good booze, good food and good times had all tumbled into bed and crashed. I had the worst hangover ever; I hadn't realised that the Best Man also got to have the best hangover and staggered back to my room, got into bed and slept through until eleven o'clock. The only reason I got up was because we had to vacate the room before midday.

A shower and change of clothes did not ease my thumping head much and not feeling well enough to be even slightly sociable, I simply put my gear into the station wagon and set off for the Gold Coast, nearly 1,200 kilometres south. Somewhere between Marlborough and Rockhampton I found myself nodding off at the wheel. It's a very strange sensation, where you know that you have to sleep but just can't seem to make the choice to pull over. At one point the VE veered off the road and I woke hearing the wheels kicking up gravel. I managed to steer the car back onto the road and with my heart thumping like crazy I was now alert enough to stop. A few kilometres on I found a side road and pulled over into a clearing; it was fairly exposed but I crawled onto the back seat, locked all of the doors and fell into a desperate sleep.

After a couple of hours I woke again feeling fresher and more alert. Gladstone was about 200 kilometres away, a bit over two hours drive, and I decided that would be my target for today. It was just on dark when I arrived and was very happy to see a motel's red vacancy sign

beckoning. I booked a room, cleaned up and then went
to the closest hotel for a hair of the dog that bit me. The
first half glass of beer just about needed a stick to poke
it down with, but after that I got the hang of it again
and ordered a second and then a third. Feeling mellow
with a slight beer buzz occupying the space between
my ears I was able to find a local eatery and enjoyed my
first decent meal of the day. As the food and alcohol
worked through my system it wasn't long before I was
back at the motel. I made a quick phone call to Airlie
Beach and let Paul know where I was. He said they'd
wondered where I'd gotten to and were glad to hear
all was well. Then I gave Mum a call so she'd know I
was arriving tomorrow. The TV was on but it wasn't
long before I was fast asleep in bed, with the room's
air conditioner purring quietly in the corner; the world
outside seemed a long, long way away.

The following day with the car full of petrol, I
continued to retrace the route that Ray and I had
driven several years earlier down through Maryborough,
Gympie, passing by the Sunshine Coast and on through
Brisbane; about 600 kilometres and eight hours later I
pulled up outside the Ashmore house.

"Hello love!" Mum called out from the front door and
came down for a hug, and then helped with my gear.

Dad and Karen came home after a while and we had
a beer and then dinner. They asked about the wedding,
my trip and then told me all their news. It was a really
nice night and I was very glad to be home. Mum and
Dad went to bed early and I sat with Karen watching
TV for a while. Apart from the TV's audio it was
quiet and peaceful and I felt my body relax. Until this

moment I had not realised how 'on alert' I must have been these last few months. My mind drifted to Sandra and Karate Kid but they were vague as if part of another world; it did an association hop to the legendry Island of Avalon that was known to reappear out of the mists and then mysteriously disappear again ... I shook my head clear before Morgan le Fay had opportunity to enchant me further. It was time for bed.

"Nite Sis."

"Nite Bros. See you tomorrow."

"Yeh."

I had a really pleasant week with the family, including catching up with friends, but it was not a wild week, not a boozing week, but a week where I gave myself the space to rest and with a clear head consider what I was doing in Mount Isa. I spent some time exploring my on-off relationship with Sandra and patterns of behaviour began to reveal themselves, and I also discovered that I had a relationship with Isa. It was clear that the city had charmed me and unless I made a conscious choice to leave and do something else, I could be there for a very long time. I had a good look at why I'd first gone on this adventure with Ray, what was different some three years on and asked myself, 'What would I like now? Six days later, on a sunny Saturday afternoon, when I got into my car to begin the 2,000 kilometre trip back to Copper City, I knew what I was going to do.

This time I decided to take a different route to Mount Isa and turned west just after Beenleigh, skirting the city of Ipswitch and headed inland towards

Toowoomba, Southern Queensland's biggest country town. The Warrago Highway continued northwest and passed through Dalby, Miles. I made it to Roma at nine thirty, with just enough time to have a cold beer at The Commonwealth Hotel before it closed for the night. Somewhere after Roma the bitumen surface changed to unsealed gravel and my tyres hummed a different tune. Mitchell was next up and then at Morven I left the Warrago, and swung almost dead north joining the Landsborough Highway, which would eventually take me most of the way to Cloncurry. The VE and I motored on, passing through Blackall just after midnight and later, turned left onto the Capricorn Highway at Barcaldine. Longreach was fast asleep and missed our passing but as the sun began to paint the eastern sky I pulled up into Winton's awakening.

The landscape that Winton sits in amongst is Mitchell Grass country; rolling plains, mostly treeless and featuring huge open spaces. The Landsborough Highway turned sharp left to skirt around the town's fringes but I continued straight ahead, turning left at the hospital and making my way across town onto Elderslie Street where I parked. It was Sunday morning and the town was quiet, shops and offices closed. I walked around, stretching my legs and poked my nose into the Australian and then North Gregory Hotel, finding a door open and some noise coming from the kitchen; the Gregory had accommodation and was preparing breakfast for its guests and I was in luck.

Winton was the place where much loved Australian poet Banjo Paterson had first performed the country's unofficial national anthem, *Waltzing Matilda*, and it was also the birthplace of Qantas Airlines. Originally named Pelican Waterhole, the story goes that in 1875 Postmaster Robert Allen became tired of writing its long name on letters and renamed the town Winton. He must have had some influence in the area as the new name was formalised in 1879, just four years later.

Filled with hot sweet tea, toast, bacon and eggs, I strolled down to the Tattersalls Hotel and then back to the car to resume my journey. It was a simple matter of following Elderslie Street out of town where it joined with the highway. On the way, I pulled into a small petrol station on the outskirts and filled up and was soon motoring again.

As I turned onto the highway I noticed two hitchhikers and stopped, "Where are you headed mate?" I asked when they came over.

"North. I'm going up to Darwin." one replied.

"Yeh. Me too." the other joined in.

"So, you're not travelling together?" I asked.

"Well, we weren't." the first guy laughed, "But we've both landed here so if you're happy to give us a lift then we are now!"

We all laughed, "Okay then. I'm going to Mount Isa so can get you that far." I offered.

"Yeh, that will be great. Thanks."

We piled all of their gear into the back and then drove off into millions of square kilometres of open country occasionally relieved by distant hills, dry creek beds and a few triumphant eucalypts.

As we got closer to Kynuna the graded road's surface deteriorated badly; it was gouged deeply with ruts that threatened to bottom-out the wagon. I stopped to the assess the situation and could see that during the wet season, trucks, road trains and other big vehicles had ploughed through and torn up the softened surface; now in summer's heat it had baked rock hard. I'd heard stories of trucks that had become stuck out here and waited several weeks for a bulldozer to arrive from Winton and tow them free. I decided to drive on and position the car's wheels on a center ridge, putting the rut directly beneath us. It was easier said than done and there were some anxious moments when we dropped alarmingly and I floored the accelerator, scraping the VE's undersides while we bumped and jumped and attempted to power our way out before getting stuck.

The rough treatment was too much for one of the rear tyres, which blew out with a bang and a whimper. I was able to manoeuver the car to a halt, straddling a deep rut, and get some purchase for the jack on the higher ground. There were several tense moments and burned fingers, though, while we got the red-hot rim off the car and a spare tyre back on, all the while wondering if the earth ridge that the jack sat on would hold strong. The flat tyre left us with only one good spare and I hoped to get that repaired soon; I knew from my bush work with Union Minière that one spare was never enough out here.

We got going again and further on passed a semitrailer about 20 metres off the main road that was buried up to its axles. It looked like it must have tried to negotiate a different way through and gotten bogged; who knows how long it had been there. It was hot, hard, dusty work in a car not designed for these conditions and we were all very grateful to arrive in the tiny town of Kynuna, looking forward to a couple of cold beers in the famous Blue Heeler Hotel.

A license plate nailed above the hotel's front door read JP Patrick and I took a chance when we walked in and the barman looked up, "G'day Mr. Patrick."

He nodded in greeting, "G'day mate. Barry will be fine. What can I get you boys?"

"Four XXX for me." I turned to the other two.

"Yeh. Same"

"Me too."

"Too easy. We only do stubbies and tinnies." he said and turned to get our drinks as we sat at the bar.

"You come in from Winton?" Barry asked as he put the beers down in front of us? How's the track?"

"Rough mate." I replied, "We bottomed heaps of times and blew a tyre. Glad to be here."

"Yeh. It's chewed up." he agreed, "Where you all headed?"

"I'm heading home to The Isa; these blokes have a bit further to go."

"Darwin." Josh confirmed.

While we chatted with the publican and each other,
I glanced around the room and spotted a well known
name, "Banjo?" I nodded at the print on the wall.

"Yeh." said Barry, "He used to be around these parts."

And then, right out of the blue, my hitchhiker piped
up, who had never been out here before, who was from
Melbourne, who, it turns out, had a literary degree and
who knew the whole story; he even gave us a writing
lesson no less!

"There's a theory about another story that Banjo hid
within Waltzing Matilda." Josh from Melbourne began,
"But first you have to know some local 1894 history and
then you have to understand allegory."

Barry nodded in agreement, "This should be good."

"In the early 1890s," Josh began, "the powerful
Australian Shearer's Union laid down a new rule that its
members could not work alongside non-union workers.
Some Queensland station owners continued to hire
low cost Chinese labour and in retaliation, the shearers
went on strike. The strike quickly spread and got nasty
with shearers taking up arms. When it seemed that
central Queensland was on the brink of civil war, the
Queensland Government brought the military in."

Josh paused, clearly enjoying the moment, not only did
he have our attention but it seemed as if the ears of the
hotel were listening too.

He took a pull on his beer and continued, "At Dagwood
Station though ..."

"Just out from Winton." Barry interjected.

"Yes." confirmed Josh,"At Dagwood in 1894, striking shearers set fire to the woolshed killing about 100 sheep. The police chased one of the men, pursuing him out to Four Mile Billabong and there, it is told, Samual 'Frenchy' Hoffmeister shot himself in the head rather than being taken in.

"What's this to do with the song Josh?" I asked.

"Well, in January 1895, Banjo was visiting Dagwood Station with his fiancee, and undoubtably heard the story as the station manager Bob Macpherson had been with the police who chased Frenchy! And it's likely that Banjo was shown the billabong. He wrote the words there at Dagwood Station and the score is attributed to Bob's sister, Christina."

"So, Banjo used the tale of the shearer's strike and Frenchy's death … " Bob added.

"Right." replied Josh, "And now to the way Banjo wrote the lyrics. Allegory is a literary device where the writer uses 'veiled language;' interpretation is required to reveal the true meaning skillfully concealed within a story or a poem. With Waltzing Matilda, Banjo Patterson wrote a political allegory and lament!"

Josh was done and sat back in his stool. We all nodded; it was a great story.

"It was first performed down in Winton at the North Gregory Hotel in April 1895; there was a banquet for the Queensland Premier." Barry said. "And of course it gets sung a lot around here at the Blue Heeler! Especially when everyone's had a few. Ha-ha!"

It was good and we all laughed with him.

"Where can I get a tyre fixed around here? I asked.

"You can try over there. It will be the only place around here that might do it." he replied, pointing across the road. Wanna take one for the road?"

"Yeh. Thanks mate. I'll come back for it after I find out about my tyre."

I drove the wagon across to the petrol station and found its owner but he was unable to do the repair, so I had no choice but to carry on and hope that my one good spare would not be required. I topped up with petrol, picked up my passengers and a round of beers, and we headed off towards Cloncurry, which was about 200 kilometres northwest.

Just after the town of McKinlay, having crossed its nine kilometre wide dry river bed, another tyre blew and I used my last spare. I was really tired and Josh took over driving. I tried to sleep but I was not fully confident about my passengers; I must have dozed and missed Cloncurry but woke as Josh braked suddenly and pulled over on a gravel verge.

"What's up?" I asked.

"Front tyre just went." he replied and we all got out.

After about 24 hours of driving I just wanted to get home, and made a decision to fit the flat tyre on the rear and bring the good one up front. Being sleep deprived I probably wasn't thinking very clearly and took over the driving. I experienced some weird hallucinations, trees morphing into monsters, but after some 30 kilometres of slow driving, hammering along on a steel rim, we parked in the Overlander Hotel's carpark. We got our gear out of the back and I shook hands with the two hitchhikers, wishing them a good trip on to Darwin. I watched them walk off towards the city centre and then called a taxi. Half an hour later I got home and fell into bed, fully clothed and exhausted. As I drifted off to sleep, I knew that I had made that trip for the very last time.

Chapter 30

Everything Changes

A shocking thing happened to Mount Isa and her citizens in April 1979, the city's beer supply was threatened. Over 2,000 kilometres away five semitrailer drivers parked their rigs across the Hume Highway at Razorback Mountain in New South Wales, and demanded the abolition of road taxes. Word was quickly spread via CB radio and over the next few days, they were joined by over 4,000 trucks maintaining blockades at 40 points around the country, and tough talking truckie Ted 'Greendog' Stevens became the face of a nine day long action.

Being remote and relying heavily on road transport for the delivery of food and other goods, Mount Isa felt the impact almost immediately; local rumours quickly spread about an imminent beer shortage and people began to stock up.

"I've heard that 4XXX won't be coming up from Brisbane." Macka commented, "The roads are blocked with trucks."

"Yeh. It's bad news mate." Drakey replied, "I saw some cartons of Cascade in the bottle shop today. First time I've seen that. They must be running it up the centre, through South Australia."

"Cascade? Bloody hell. That Tasmanian stuff is terrible."

"Yeh. But if the blockade continues, it's better than nothing mate."

"I'm not so sure about that Drakey," Macka scowled, "Cascade's a rough drop."

"I know, but after the first dozen you won't even notice! Ha-ha."

"Yeh. You're right mate. It's getting the first dozen down that worries me, and then keeping it down."

"Practice makes perfect Macka." I said.

"Yeh. Ha. It's a hard job, you know, but someone has to do it."

"Exactly!"

"We'd better get a few more of these 4XXX down our throats before they all bloody disappear." Macka said.

"Nice one mate." Drakey replied, draining his glass, "I didn't realise you were feeling so generous today. I'll have a pot please!"

After four days, national support for the Razorback Blockade campaign began to unravel, except at Razorback where they refused to budge. The state's premier, Neville Wran, met with Greendog and the truckies several times and instructed his minister to present their case to the Trade Practices Commission. Eventually, transport ministers agreed to scrap the tax, the Hume Highway cleared and the blockade was written into Australian history.

It turned out that we did have to sample some of Australia's oldest brewery's Pale Ale, resplendent in its shiny green cans with gold trim. And Macka was right, it was bloody terrible. But, remarkably, as predicted by the amazing Mr. Drake, immediately upon finishing the 12th can, everything seemed to be all right with the world.

"Where does that bloke get it from?" Macka said nodding towards Drakey.

"I have no idea mate." I replied, "But I think he might be God in disguise."

"Bloody good disguise mate. Boom! Boom!

My wages from work, as with many other employees, were deposited directly into an account with Isa Mine Employees' Credit Union; the bank had loaned me money to buy the Charger and various other things. I had mainly used them to withdraw money to spend and consequently had few savings, which was something I wanted to change.

While I was away I'd realised that even though my income was the highest it had ever been, I was spending everything I earned. I went in to meet with an account manager and we arranged to have a percentage of my pay placed into a savings account before I even saw it. While I had come to Mount Isa in 1975 on the back of $500, I wanted to leave with a decent stake. Every two weeks the balance increased and so did the interest being paid. I was enjoying that a lot, and there were changes at work too.

Working at the mines became very interesting when Dick asked me to do the training and get my Explosives Ticket; also one for the big ST5 machines. I was becoming a valuable all-rounder on Level 15 and enjoyed the variety of work, and while I liked all the jobs, working with explosives was the most fun.

Level 15 had its own armory; a special secured, strong room where various explosives were stored. Dick had the key and those of us working with the material could have access. As a mule driver Damian and I had delivered gelignite and fuses to the miners, and I already knew that staying in the armory too long could result in headaches and drowsiness; it was good practice to load up quickly and get out. The training had covered the health aspects of using explosives with a large focus on safety. Emphasizing the increased risk, my wages increased noticeably.

There were three main areas on Level 15 that required a shotfirer and I got to work with them all regularly. The most familiar were the overhead chutes used to fill ore cars; from time to time the chutes blocked and needed freeing up. The technique involved bundling sticks of gelignite together, tieing them to the end of a long pine pole and then carefully placing the bomb up in the chute near its blockage. The bomb's fuse was then wired into the level's firing line to be fired during crib or at end of shift. While firing had been a background activity, a powerful rumble and air blast that we experienced twice each shift but took little notice of, now I was fully invested. I could hardly wait for crib to end so I could go and see the results of my work. And I really enjoyed those stubborn blockages where my craft required the strategic placement of bombs using the least amount of explosive to do the job. Some blockages took days to clear, working over several shifts, and it was a great thrill to be the one to bring them down.

Up on the sublevel the muckers placed rocks that were too large to go down a chute, off to one side to be broken up. These required another type of treatment and every rock was different. I had to identify the rock's weakest point and place one or two sticks of gelignite, then pack the bomb tightly with damp mud; it was the mud that made this all work. If gelignite was simply set on the rock and ignited, all of its explosive force would blow up into the air, the path of least resistance. By applying mud and creating an air-tight pocket around the charge, the blast was concentrated and directed down, fracturing the rock. Using a small amount of explosive and directing the blast accurately, was the skill.

While highly interesting and fun, both of these tasks paled in comparison to the clearing of the massive vertical chutes that the ST5 muckers worked with. These chutes could be hundreds of metres tall and were huge columns containing thousands of tons of ore sourced from mining levels above us. They were part of a complex network of levels, drives and chutes by which ore was moved down through the mine and to the crushers on twenty-one. When they blocked it was big!

At start of shift Dick directed me to investigate a blocked chute up on the sublevel. I got supplies from the armory, loaded up an ST2 and drove across the level.

460

A short trip up an access ramp took me up and onto the sublevel and I parked. It was quiet in the area as the big machines had been directed to muck elsewhere. I could hear the distant, muted noise of mining activity and feel the light touch of moving air. Except for the soft glow of illuminated exit signs, my single headlamp provided the only light. In some areas, if I turned off the lamp, literally, I couldn't see my hand in front of my eyes. It could be a little spooky underground sometimes.

Normally the ore at the base of a chute tumbled out until there was enough piled up to stop the flow As a mucker removed bucket after bucket, the ore dropped from above replenishing the pile. I had walked into the area and found there was no pile. As my light climbed up high into the chute, there, some 20 metres above me, a roughly formed, arched stone ceiling looked down. It was crude, yet majestic and looked as if a poorly skilled mason had cobbled together stones of all sizes and shapes to form a rough cathedral ceiling. It seemed that I was the congregation of one. Wow! At first glance it was breathtaking.

I wasn't standing directly under the ceiling as that was way too dangerous. It was impossible to tell if or when the construction would just let go and fall, instantly releasing hundreds of tons of ore. If it let go and I was near, there would be no escape; my mind flicked to the young geologist and I squatted down on my haunches to review the job.

The mucker had cleared the floor and I could see there had been no recent falls. I walked over to a store area and picked three extra long pine poles and then placed them near the chute. I lugged three bags of

461

Stephe⊙ ⊓ ram

ANFO from the ST2's bucket along with several rolls
of Cordite and began to assemble the bombs on the
ground. ANFO being mixture of prilled ammonia
nitrate, a type of fertiliser, and diesel fuel, which when
detonated can produce a powerful explosion. When I
had placed a knot of Cordite in every bag and then tied
each to the end of a pole, I was ready.

The poles were long, about 10 metres, and an ANFO
bag weighed about 20 kilograms though it seemed a
lot heavier waving around in the air. The idea was to
hoist the bag high up and lean the pole into the chute,
without actually entering the chute and risking a big
rock dropping on my head. The reality was that the
bag needed to be in the chute to be effective and so
sometimes I seemed to be a lot closer than my safety
training had recommended. When all the bags were
in place, I bound all of their fuses together and then
connected them to a firing line.

I was sweating profusely and my arms ached, whether
it was the exertion, the excitement or a combination of
both I couldn't really tell. The job was done and I went
back to my machine, took a long drink of water and
then went off to take care of some large rocks located
in a side bay. It was still several hours until crib; I would
have to be patient and wait for the firing. Oh well, at
least I got to come back afterwards and see the results!

"Yeh!"

After crib I was one of the first out and went straight
back up to the sublevel to inspect my work. The
ventilation system was clearing blast dust, and I could
see that some rocks had fallen but the ceiling still held.

The once tightly packed jigsaw of stonework had pieces missing now; it seemed more vulnerable and with that, more dangerous than before.

I returned to the armory and this time picked up four bags of ANFO and fuses, then returned to my site. Once the bombs were ready I swung them carefully into position and wired the fuses. There wasn't much more to do here and I inspected the side bay to find good fracturing through the rocks I'd charged before crib. These would probably break apart once an ST5 picked them up. I heard the deep rumble of ore moving and walked over to see a high pile of rubble begin to fall in on itself. Down below on the transport level, Patrick operated the chute loading his first ore car; they would work this chute until empty and then move on to richer pickings. If my blast was successful then the mucker would return during the next shift and this area would be productive once again.

When my shift was finally over and we were all gathered in the crib room waiting for the cage, Dick fired the level. I listened to the crackle of explosives being detonated in various parts of the mine and then there was a deep, distinct rumble, a pulse of air and I knew the cathedral had come down. I couldn't help but smile.

Dick knew it too, caught my eye and nodded, "Good work mate."

It was Friday night and I'd arranged to meet up with Ian, Maurine and a few friends at The Tavern that evening. His green panelvan was already in the carpark when I arrived and I found them inside. We had a few drinks and then ordered dinner. It was a nice, relaxed evening and I told them about Paul's wedding, the Gold Coast trip and then later, talked quietly with Ian.

"I'm thinking about leaving The Isa mate." I began.

"Yeh?"

"Yeh."

"How come Steveo?" he asked.

"Well, it's been a bit rough lately, what with Sandra now going out with Karate Kid. He seems to want to punch my lights out every time he gets drunk." I explained, "And I still miss her. So, I thought I'd get some money together and head back to the Gold Coast."

"How long have you been here now?" he asked.

"Nearly four years mate. It seems much longer though. What about you; how long are you staying?"

"Dunno. "Ian mused, "I hadn't really thought about it much. Job's good. Company is good." he glanced at Maurine who was chatting across the table; she caught his eye and smiled back."

"Yeh." I said, "It helps when the company is good."

"Yeh."

"Well, you've been here a while mate and maybe a change is what you need." Merce was philosophical for a moment and glanced over at Maurine again, "Or a bloody good woman! Ha!"

"Ha-ha! Yeh. Maybe that would work." I laughed at his joke but I knew that it wouldn't.

It was nice hanging out with my friends, a pleasant distraction, but I wasn't right and my mind kept drifting to Sandra. Just before ten o'clock I said good night and left.

"It's a bit early Stevo." they called out, "It's not even closing time yet."

"Yeh. I know." I said, "Gotta go guys. I'll catch you all later."

I knew Drakey was at The Piano bar but opted for an early night, drove past the Irish Club and went home to bed. The alcohol and food did its job and I was soon fast asleep; I didn't even hear Drakey come in or know that he wasn't alone, until later.

Sometime during the night I drifted up out of a deep sleep. I only came up a few levels as my bed covers moved and then the mattress depressed. My sluggish mind vaguely suggested that it was probably Macka's brother Ollie, who sometimes stayed and slept on the couch in the lounge room. The fuzzy logic offered was that this used to be his room, he was probably drunk and had forgotten that he didn't live here anymore. I went with that and a few moments later was back in theta wave heaven and oblivious to worldly goings on.

I woke up about eight o'clock and glanced over to see a mop of curly hair on the other pillow and where the sheet had slipped down, I was somewhat hypnotised by a very nice full breast that gently rose and fell in time with its owner's shallow breathing. Clearly this was not Ollie, but who was this mystery woman?

I slipped out of bed, quietly put on a robe and visited the bathroom; when I returned mystery woman's eyes blinked, then opened, brown and a little glazed from sleeping.

"Good morning." I said and I'm sure my brown eyes were dancing merrily, "How are you?"

She stretched and the sheet slipped a little further, "Mmm ... I'm good."

Then she sat up and my most wonderful sheet gave up all pretence of cover. My morning was just getting better and better!

"I have to go to the bathroom." mystery woman looked around, "Oh. Where are my clothes?"

"I'm not sure." I replied, "Here. You can use my robe."

"Okay." she nodded, "Thanks."

I took off my robe and put on a pair of jeans. She got out of bed and a now very naked mystery woman leaned in, kissed me, slipped on my robe and walked out into the hallway. I had no idea what was happening but this sure was a helluva lot of fun.

After a while she came back in and propped herself up in bed. She'd washed her face and tidied her hair, and I noticed she filled my robe out very nicely.

"Would you like a cup of tea, coffee, or something?" I offered.

"Yes. Tea, white with two would be nice. Thanks."

"Okay." I smiled, "Back soon."

Macka's door was closed and Drakey's room empty, his bed a tumble of sheets and pillows. I went into the kitchen, made tea and then returned with two steaming mugs and sat on the bed. Finally, my curiosity got the better of me.

"So, who are you?" I asked and I'm sure my eyebrow was raised just like James Bond did when he met a mysterious female spy.

Her brow furrowed a little and she looked at me with a quizzical expression, "I'm Julie."

"Well, I'm Stephen" I smiled, "Nice to meet you Julie. It may seem an odd question, but I'm sure we didn't come home together last night. I would certainly remember that."

"Really?" she exclaimed, "Oh my goodness!" Then she laughed, "I was wondering why you didn't cuddle me when we woke up. I mean, we'd just spent the night together. Though now I get it because, actually, we didn't."

"Well, we did spend part of the night together, the sleeping part. " I corrected her with a smile, "Did you come home with Ian? Drakey? Tall, slim bloke with dark hair?" I asked.

"I guess I must have. I had a lot to drink." she replied, "I got up in the night to pee and must have come into your room by mistake. Sorry. Oh my goodness. How embarrassing!"

"It's okay." I said, "It was a nice surprise when I woke up."

"Um." Julie glanced around my bedroom, "Can you see my clothes anywhere; a black bag?"

"Not in here but I'll have a look around."

I went out and checked through Drakey's room, being careful not to stand on anything slippery, and then looked around the house, finding nothing that resembled women's clothing or a bag.

"Nothing." I said.

"Oh. Really?" Then she thought for moment, "Oh! We were in his car fooling around. I must have left them in the car."

"Well, Drakey is not here and nor is his car." I replied, "He's probably gone to work."

"Oh wow!" she said, "This is really embarrassing. No clothes, no money, no cigarettes and no keys to my car. They are in my bag."

"And no Drakey's car."

"Yeh." she agreed. "That doesn't help the situation at all. Ha."

I had to give this Julie due credit, considering she was naked, penniless and virtually homeless, she was handling this all rather well.

"Don't worry. You can keep my robe, or borrow a shirt or something. I can give you a lift home."

"That will be great. Thanks. Well, that will teach me to have that one last vodka."

"Yeh." I laughed, "It's always that last one."

"Yeh."

I went and found one of Drakey's T-shirts. I figured that he'd had all the fun and could pay. He was tall and the shirt was long enough to work as a dress. Later, we got into the station wagon and she directed me over to the other side of the Irish Club where I dropped her off outside a house. I took a note of the address.

"I'll tell Drakey to drop your stuff around when I see him." I said.

"Thank you Stephen." she replied, "I owe you a drink or two. See you around."

"Yeh. Bye."

And off she went. I drove away with a big smile on my face, and I was really looking forward to hearing Drakey's side of the story when he got home.

A few weeks after mystery woman's visit I was in the kitchen making dinner when Macka walked in, got a beer out of the refrigerator and leaned up against a bench.

"You still interested in the bike Steveo?" he asked.

"Are you selling it mate?" I replied.

"Well, Drakey and I were talking about taking a holiday and doing a drive up to Darwin. And I think, after that, its time for her to go to a new owner."

469

Ian Drake had a magnificent orange Ducati 900 Super
Sport that sat alongside the Kawasaki and my 400 in
our carport; it always sounded wicked when he started
it up. I could just imagine the two big bikes on the
road up to Darwin, they were both head turners. I was
interested, of course I was interested, I'd been interested
for a long time, but this was out of the blue and I
needed a little time … I led the conversation on to his
trip.

"Darwin mate. That's a good drive. What is it, about a
3,000 kilometre round trip?" I asked.

"Yeh. That's about right. We'll just follow the
Barkly Highway out through Camooweal and on to
Warumungu, and then turn north onto the Stuart
Highway all the way to the top end. It should be good."

"Sounds like it. When are you thinking of heading off?"
I asked.

"Probably in a couple of weeks." he said, "There's
another bloke who might come along. We're waiting for
our leave to be approved."

"Good on you mate. That's going to be a great trip."

Macka drew me back to his question but I was ready
for it now, "I know that you like the bike and wanted to
give you first dibs."

"What are you asking for it Macka?"

"I was thinking of $1,200. It's a beautiful bike."

"I've not even ridden it yet mate; can I take it for a
run?"

"Yeh. No worries. You want to go now?"

I wasn't going to pass up a chance to ride the big Kawasaki and pulled my dinner off the cooker, "Yeh. That'll be great." We went out the back door into the carport and he pulled its covers off.

The Kawasaki Z1 was the company's first big four stroke motor. It had been originally designed with a 750cc engine but with Honda releasing their CB750 model, Kawasaki's engineers changed their plans and went for a big 900cc power-plant. It was quick and in tests had clocked over 220 kilometres per hour! The Z1, known as a Super-4, first came out in 1972, but the one Macka was selling was the 1975 Z1B; it was to be the last of its line.

"I bought the bike after it had been fully rebuilt." Macka explained, "That's why it has the wrap-around racing fairing, drop handlebars and custom paint job. The bloke hit a cow on the way back from Cloncurry and launched himself over the front and into the bush."

"He hit a cow?" I exclaimed, "Jeez, that would have hurt."

"Yeh. He was pretty knocked around. But they got a new frame, wheels, and all the parts and rebuilt the bike with sports fairings. You won't see another one like this."

It's beautiful Macka." I nodded in agreement, "I've always liked it."

He handed over the keys and a helmet, "Here. Take it for a run Steveo." And so I did.

It was, without a doubt, the biggest and most powerful bike I'd ridden, and I treated it with respect. It was much heavier than my 400 and I backed it carefully out of the carport. It started the instance I pressed the ignition button and the sound of four exhaust pipes burbling behind me was sweet. I dropped it in first, pulled out of the driveway and all sensation of weight disappeared; I hadn't even gotten out of second when the end of our street appeared. I turned onto Buckley Avenue and made my way onto Railway Avenue where there was a bit more room. I twisted on the accelerator and opened her up a bit through several of the gears; the acceleration was extraordinary and it wasn't very long before we ran out of room again. It was enough and I turned around and cruised on home. I was very excited.

After I came back Macka and I talked some more and then shook hands on $1,000 cash with one proviso, that he brought the bike back from Darwin in one piece!

"Thanks Damien." I said quietly to myself. Patience, it seems, can work.

Several weeks went by quickly and one sunny Saturday morning Macka and Drakey pulled out of the driveway to begin their 3,000 kilometer drive. While they were gone I managed to get several bites on the Valiant station wagon and sold it for $650, which meant I only had to add another $350 for the Z1B. My Kawasaki 400 had been sitting idle for a while so I had it serviced and used that for transport; it seemed small compared to its big brother.

While I enjoyed my two flat mates it was quite nice having the house to myself for 10 days, but one evening the distinctive sound of a powerful Ducati echoed down our driveway and I knew the boys were home. Before I'd even got the back door open there was a crash and a shout. Drakey, stiff from the long ride, had not been able to get his leg out in time and he and the bike had gone down in the carport. Macka already had his helmet off and was laughing out loud at the distressed Drake who, weighed down with helmet, full leather jacket, pants and boots was trying to get out from under his bike. I went down and helped lift the orange beast up off him and he crawled out, gaining his feet a little unsteadily. He was fine and we all had a laugh while they stretched and complained about their aching backs and bums. Apparently they'd done a big run to get home, and it wasn't long before we were in the kitchen with cold beers and I was being regaled with stories of their trip.

After a while Macka looked at me, "Hey!"

"Yes mate." I replied.

He reached into his pocket, pulled out a set of keys and placed them in my hand, "She's yours mate. Take good care of her."

"Thanks Macka." and we shook hands, "I will. I've got some money for you."

He raised his hand to stop me, "It's fine Steveo. Later. I trust you and anyway, I know where you live mate. Boom! Boom!"

And so I became the owner of a beautiful sunburst yellow Kawasaki 900 Z1B and, for my money, it was the world's first super bike! Later, when the others had gone to bed, I walked out into the carport and said hello to my new bike. She was grubby from the recent trip, but it was more like an athlete who'd been training, had worked up a light sweat and was now ready for the big game.

"You and I are going to have a lot of fun." I said, turned off the light and went back inside.

It seemed like the recent dramas of my life had receded, maybe gone. While I thought about Sandra from time to time, heard about her on the grapevine and occasionally saw her out and about, it was not so upsetting anymore. I knew that I still loved her but I also realised that I was in love with what had been, and since she'd returned to Mount Isa from the Gold Coast she was not the same person; nor was I. I had been trying to connect with or recreate those first heady months when we had been so deeply into each other and it was simply another time, another place and not the now that I lived in. If we were to get back together again, then I had to take off my rose coloured glasses and see her for who she was now and ask, "Can I love who she is now?"

And while I pondered contemporary Sandra, I had to acknowledge that I was not the same either. I was not the same person who had left home nearly four years ago and I was not the same person who had broken up with Sandra nearly four months ago. Life changes, circumstances change, people change.

Would I like to see her again? Yes. Would I like to go out with her again? It was a different question, one that I wasn't so clear on, and also, one I wasn't so blind about. Six months ago, the answer was unquestionably, "Yes!" but now …

My recent idea of returning to the Gold Coast had provided a new target; something different to aim at and with it, my life seemed larger. I was not focussed on Sandra and Mount Isa as my only future, now there was something else and in that I had to consider that the Gold Coast and the people I knew there would be different too. So whether I stayed here or went, and provided I was willing to see what was actually in front of me, the change in everyone and everything would create the adventurous life I so enjoyed exploring.

It seemed that I had become so engrossed, so totally captivated and so stuck in my relationship with Sandra and Mount Isa that I'd been unable to see the constantly changing, full colour, spectrum of life that was available. It's not that I was wary of relationship, but that I was becoming aware that relationship has to be allowed to change too. If I was to go out with Sandra again then I had to let go of my grip on the past, and if I didn't go out with her again then I still had to let go. It was really simple, if I was living in the past then I had no future.

The purchase of the Z1B, the excitement and enthusiasm I had with that choice was future, but when I thought about going back with Sandra it didn't generate any enthusiasm at all. As I drifted off to sleep that night I tried to look further ahead, and wondered what a future with Sandra would be like. I was a

475

little surprised to find that I had no response to that
question.

Chapter 31

I Guess This it It

Ray came around with news that Ian had taken a bad
fall at work, on the trains and had been taken into
emergency. He wasn't sure what had happened so we
drove across town and parked in Camooweal Street,
opposite the Base Hospital. Ian had already received
surgery and a nurse at reception directed us to his room.
We found him propped up in bed with his leg in a
full plaster cast; our poor mate looked pretty knocked
around with bruising, cuts and scrapes clearly evident.

"Merce. What have you been up to? Did you slip-up on
the dance floor after too many scotch and cokes?" Ray's
jest was rewarded with a weak smile, but Ian's eyes were
dull and I knew that he was not good.

He told us that he'd been standing on a flatcar when a
line of freight cars had been shunted into position. The
impact of coupling had thrown him off the car and his
leg, which got trapped in a handrail, snapped like a twig.
He'd hit the ground pretty hard and was knocked out;
considering his injuries, it was probably a good thing.

"… but you should see the other bloke!" he finished up, attempting a joke.

Merce was on strong pain killers, which dulled him down a fair bit and worked to insulate him from reality; but I knew his accident was a big deal and that he'd be out of action for months while his injuries healed, and then what?

We chatted for a while. Well, actually, Ray and I chatted around Ian who slipped in and out of consciousness; eventually he drifted off to sleep. We found a pen and, as good mates do, embellished his cast with appropriate profanity and then left.

"Not good Steveo. Not good." Ray commented soberly on the way out.

"No mate." I agreed, "Not good at all."

We went into Boyd Hotel for a quick couple and then he dropped me home. Having seen Ian so battered and beaten we didn't seem to have much appetite for a big session.

Merce wasn't the only object to be reacquainted with gravity in July, as NASA's Skylab also fell heavily to earth. The United States first space station had been launched in 1973, abandoned one year later and had recently started to breakup. Unlike Ian's fall, though, where it was obvious that he'd land in Mount Isa Mines' railway yard, no one seemed to know where Skylab would come down.

NASA and the world's media were on the job feeding us with reports, predictions and commentary until

finally, in the early hours of July 12, Skylab crashed
into Western Australia, scattering itself across the
Nullarbor Plain and eastern goldfields. It was an instant
worldwide sensation.

NASA were quick to arrive in Esperance and got busy
collecting their debris, but not before the local Council,
equally quick with a joke, sent them a $400 fine for
littering the town with space junk. While we followed
the extraordinary story in local media, it was the
littering fine that caught on.

"Better not drop that empty tinny on the ground mate!
Esperance Council will be here in a flash with your very
own, special space-littering fine."

"I hear they start at four hundred bucks you know!"

"Ah. No worries mate. I'll just send it on to NASA.
Apparently they have lots of money. I mean, they just
donated a $2.2 billion dollar space station to Western
Australia. Nice chaps those Americans!"

It was Friday night and I'd gone to the Piano Bar,
arriving early. The place was quiet; it was that in-
between time where afternoon patrons were finishing
up and heading home, and evening revellers had not
yet arrived. I gave Sean the manager a wave, said hello
to the bouncer, whom I knew, then ordered a beer and
sat down on one of the couches. My back was to the
door and I didn't see him come in, but I did notice the
bouncer come to attention. karate kid walked by and up
to the bar. I watched him order a rum and coke, then he
turned around and came over to where I was sitting.

I'd heard gossip that he and Sandra had broken up and I wasn't sure what was about to happen, but he sat down next to me like we were old mates.

"G'day Steve. How are you?"

I glanced around and the bouncer was watching, but karate kid was looking down at the floor and didn't seem to notice.

"You heard that we broke up?" he asked.

"Yeh mate." I replied, "How are you doing?"

"A bit rough mate. A bit rough."

He spoke quietly so that his voice only carried far enough to reach my ears. I realised that he was trying to be inclusive. We two blokes had gone out with the same woman and both arrived at a similar destination. Through that common and sometimes difficult experience there was the thread of a connection. It was weird but right now, we were mates.

Even though he seemed calm I was being very aware of what I said, not really sure where this was going, wondering if, at any moment, there would be an explosion; but there wasn't and we chatted about Sandra, and relationships and things men don't seem to understand about women.

"You know, she put a big kitchen knife through the door trying to get at me. I had to get out. It got crazy."

"Jeez mate." I said, "Yeh. She can get wild sometimes, especially with some drinks in her."

"Yeh. We can all get a bit silly with the drink."

"True." I agreed.

After about 20 minutes karate kid finished his drink, placed the empty glass on a side table and stood up. I stood too and we shook hands. He apologised for having been aggressive towards me, I wished him the very best and then he left the bar. The bouncer caught my eye and nodded; all was well.

Later, as I leaned at the bar waiting for a fresh beer, I thought about that handshake; it had been firm and genuine. We had been two blokes who had never really met before, except by association where we'd become unwitting adversaries, ready to fight the other; tonight we could put our weapons down, end a war that never really was and move on. Relationship had to be one of the strangest things I had ever come across!

As Australian band Mental as Anything stormed up the charts with their song *The Nips Are Getting Bigger*, Sony changed the way we listened to music by introducing the Walkman, and Japan changed the way we talked to each other by launching the world's first mobile phone network in Tokyo. A few years earlier Microsoft had been founded, the digital camera and laser printer invented, the first personal computers introduced and in Melbourne, Australian scientists developed the first bionic ear. Technology and the change it brought with it was sweeping the world. But change and firsts were not limited to technology as conservative Britain elected its first female Prime Minister, Margaret Thatcher. Locally, in Mount Isa, I began organising my own changes; my departure would not be the first time I'd left the city, but it would be the first time I wasn't coming back.

August had slipped by quickly featuring the annual rodeo and my 23rd birthday. Merce had come out of hospital and was convalescing; he was faced with a decision that would create some change for him too. He could either stay on wages while he healed and then go back to work at the rail yard, or sue Mount Isa Mines for compensation and never work for them again.

Since her break with karate kid I'd seen Sandra several times. She had some new girl friends and I'd sat chatting with them at the Overlander Hotel, and we'd hung out together at several parties. She looked good and I'd felt that familiar tug, and while I still wanted her, often strongly, the possibility of reunion was getting further away as the past began to claim it, and the future increasingly pulled us in different directions.

One day in September, as Mount Isa was slipping away from winter's cool touch and reaching for the promise of spring, I stepped off Level 15 and took the cage up a final time. Dick had let me off early and I was the only passenger. Not buffered by the hot, sweaty, male bodies that normally packed it at end-of-shift, a chill wind freely invaded the empty space. After several minutes our rate of accent slowed, then stopped and the cage's steel doors were slid open. I stepped out into the waiting hall; it was fairly empty with only a few early birds sitting on the benches. At the battery room window the attendant took my lamp. It was the same old man who had been there on my first day underground; I guess some things don't change much.

He didn't recognise me but I shook his hand anyway and said goodbye.

"You leaving us son?" he asked.

Suddenly I was choked up, close to tears, I just nodded.

"Where are you headed to?"

"Gold Coast." I replied.

He looked up and his rheumy eyes seemed to clear for a moment, meeting mine, "Don't worry son, if it doesn't work out you can always come back."

"Yeh." I smiled with him.

"Well, the best of luck mate." he said, then picked up my lamp and turned away.

I walked towards the shower room, surprised by how much attachment I had for this place; my head seemed to be full of doubt and I wondered if I'd made the right choice to leave. It seemed a long walk, a lonely walk and I wanted to stop, sit on one of the benches and wait for all of the miners to come pouring out of K57's shaft, then join them and be part of their chatter and excitement as we headed home; but I didn't stop, I kept on going.

I found my locker, took off muddied boots, sweaty socks, dirty overalls and underwear, dropping it all into a rubbish bin. I placed my coveted hard-hat with its attached ear muffs on top of the locker; perhaps someone might like to have it. The showers were empty and water pressure would be high. I turned the taps on full, stuck my head deep into the powerful stream and

cried a bit. I told myself there were new adventures
to be had, that Mount Isa wasn't the only city in the
world, that I had more to do with my life … but I knew
I was going to miss this place a great deal. I'd arrived
here young and green, with not much of a clue about
life, and she'd provided-for, sheltered and nurtured me.
This wasn't an ordinary goodbye, there was much to be
grateful for and much that I would remember for a very
long time.

Later, washed and dressed in clean clothes, I cruised
the Kawasaki slowly around Black Rock's pit trying
to take in every dry, dusty detail. The copper smelter
and Big Stack swung into view on my far left, then I
passed administration buildings and the mine gate. I
stopped at Mineside's eastern boundary and waited for
traffic to clear then turned right on to Railway Avenue.
Straightening up I dropped the bike into second gear
and hit the throttle; the motor roared and we leapt
forward like a Scud missile on steroids. It was done. I
was officially unemployed!

The next day was Thursday and I spent the morning
delivering my gear and the two bikes to Mount Isa's
rail depot. It would take several weeks but they would
eventually get to Beenleigh, just north of the Gold
Coast, where I could pick them up. I visited the bank,
withdrew the balance of my account and closed it. It
was terrific to have a great wad of cash and I was really
pleased that I'd made the savings. There wasn't much
else to be done and anyway, it was time to go to the
Irish Club!

It was a local tradition, when someone leaves The Isa
that they put on some beers. I'd purchased an 18 gallon

keg of beer in the public bar and put out an open invitation to come and have a some free drinks, on me. I got there about eleven o'clock, poured myself one of my free beers, and was joined by a few blokes I knew. Later I had lunch and then throughout the afternoon people drifted in and out to share a drink and chat for a while.

There weren't that many people who showed up; perhaps because it was a work afternoon, or maybe they hadn't heard, but I was fine with that. I went home, feeling quite merry, about six o'clock, had dinner and a few more beers with Macka and Drakey and went early to bed. Another part of leaving, it seemed, was done. I lay in bed for a while and mused on how no one really meant goodbye; it was more of a, "See you later mate." The preference being that we would meet again sometime in the future. I knew that for many of the blokes and women, we would not see each other again. Some friendships or relationships become locked in time and by location, and it's unlikely that I'd be back. And even if I did return, that they'd be here.

The next morning I got up with the boys, we had coffee together and said, "See you later mate." and they went off to work. I would put my keys in the letter box when I left. I had some hours to kill as my flight was not until the afternoon so I caught a taxi into town and entertained myself for a while and then went over to the Irish Club for lunch, a last game of pool and some beers. Finally it was time and I walked home, showered and changed, and then packed my suitcase.

I heard the Ford's twin exhausts burble as Ray pulled up in the driveway. He came in and we chatted for a while and then it was time to go. I gave my old mate a manly hug, I was going to miss him heaps.

I looked around the house for the last time and then locked the door. I threw keys into the letter box, loaded my suitcase into the car and we got in. Ray backed out into the street, slipped into first gear and then floored it, laying down a burn of smoking rubber up Seventeenth Avenue. I waved goodbye to my old mate the Irish Club as we went past.

"We've had some good times in there; hey Stevie?" Ray said as he swung the Ford, turning right.

"Yeh mate. We sure did." I replied as the Irish Club was captured in the rearview mirror to become past, and the subject of stories yet to be told. I didn't look back.

Ray pulled us out onto Railway Avenue and I watched the barracks and then Mineside slip past, Big Stack came and went, as did the copper smelter, the Bowls Club and many other memories.

"Did you get to see Sandra?" he asked.

"No." I answered, looking out of the window, "I thought she might have come to the Irish Club for a drink yesterday, but she didn't."

"Ah well."

The Grace Street bridge passed by, I knew the mighty Leichhardt's river bed would be dry and wide, and then we drove onto the Barkly Highway passing by its namesake hotel, Miles End and Soldiers Hill.

The houses and buildings began to disappear, replaced by low-lying Spinifex, tussock grasses and Snappy Gum. As Ray picked up speed, the turnoff to Lake Moondarra beckoned but quickly dropped behind us and a few minutes later Ray braked, turned left and we were greeted by Mount Isa Airport's welcome sign.

He slowed the Ford right down and looked over at me, "I guess this is it mate."

"Yeh." I replied, "It is."

The End

Some young men leave home seeking adventure,
Others are forced to escape.
And some young men never leave home,
Until it is all very too late.

Afterword

Becoming a Man

I'm sure that becoming a man is not something that any boy sets out to do. I know that at nineteen years old I didn't say to myself,

"Okay. Now I'm going to go out into the big wide world and become a man!"

The idea never even crossed my mind; it seems like something a parent would think, or older people; all nodding their heads wisely and saying,

"Yes, he's leaving the nest now and going off to become a man."

Perhaps, in their conclusion, forgetting what it was really like for them many years ago.

What excited me was the adventure; creating the adventure of my life. Up until now my life had been a subset of my parent's.

When I did return to my family; to those who had known the boy, I was certainly different. A man though? Maybe, but what is that? What does it mean? Probably many different things to many different people, and different in every culture.

I'd learned to drink convincingly and be an Aussy bloke, smoked cigarettes for a year, including big fat Cuban cigars; I knew I could work and make money, live in my own place, and I'd experimented with girls, relationships and sex. Is that being a man? Perhaps but more likely that was me, being the me I was then; and though it may have looked similar to my peer's experiences it would be different for each one of us, for example, I know that if Ray had written this book he would tell a very different story.

It seems that being a man or woman is something other people define based on some made up criteria, or disguised as a right-of-passage to be judged, approved and made real. But it wasn't real for me and none of my mates brought it up or discussed it, ever. Doesn't it seem bizarre that Ray, I and the others, the *then* 'becoming a man' generation, knew absolutely nothing about it and were not even remotely interested in becoming a man anyway? So, who is making all of this up?

Even now at nearly 60 years old, I still think I'm a boy, around 18 or so … that I'm me and life is an adventure at every turn waiting to be created. Sometimes I look out of my eyes onto a mirror and think to myself,

"Who is that old person looking back at me?"

When we accept, without question, that we are this or that, as prescribed by someone else, do we become that?

491

And does that definition and the many, many others we are offered begin changing us in ways that create what we are not: an employee, husband, father, mortgagee, divorcee, single Mum, hopeless with money, depressed, stupid, retired … dead?

I wonder what a life could be like if we never accepted other people's definitions of who and what we should be, and remained true to who we knew we were? What would my life be like if I never ever became a man, and was simply me?

Epilogue

Where Are They Now?

This book is based upon a true story, and most of its characters were real people. What follows is a brief update on their ongoing stories.

Stephen Outram became partner in an architectural business on the Gold Coast, then moved to the United Kingdom for nearly 10 years. He returned to the Gold Coast in 1997 starting an IT business, later moving to the Sunshine Coast. He is now Global IT Development Coordinator working for a worldwide group of companies, Access Consciousness, and lives just northeast of Brisbane with partner Simone.

Ray Linwood left Mount Isa for a short while and then returned, staying a total of 10 years. He made his way across to Western Australia and, in his early forties, married Linda. They have a daughter, Phoebe, and live south of Perth.

Ian "Merce" Mercer sued Mount Isa Mines, received settlement and returned to the Gold Coast. After a variety of jobs he joined Queensland's police force. He and Maurine married and had a son, Nicholas. Later, Ian married again. Ian is now a retired Snr. Detective and lives with his wife in Bargara, near Bundaberg.

Karen Outram was married to Ken Gay in early 1990 and they had two sons, Daniel and Joshua. She later divorced and still lives on the Gold Coast, working in accounting.

Kevin Rogers became an officer with the Royal Australian Air Force, stationed in Butterworth, Malaysia. He married Jeannette and they have two children, Colby and Josh. On returning to Australia they spent many years in Harvey Bay, then explored Australia extensively to settle for some years in Daly Waters in the Northern Territory. They now live just west of Harvey Bay, in Queensland.

Sandra Wilson was married in Mount Isa, in the early eighties.

Eden Devon worked with Woolworths on the Gold Coast and then left for a management position with Florsheim. He later married and opened a restaurant at Gallery Walk, North Tamborine.

Ian "Drakey" Drake worked for the mines for many years and is now retired, living near Queensland's Sunshine Coast.

Bibliography

Research

This book is based upon a true story and contains many factual historical references, mining and geological information and other inclusions.

BICC. "Coal Mining in Blackwater." - *Blackwater International Coal Centre*. N.p., n.d. Web. 29 Jan. 2015. <http://www.bicc.com.au/coal-mining-in-blackwater/>.

Keyser, F. De. *Geology and Mineral Deposits in the Paradise Creek Area, North-West Queensland*. Rep. N.p.: Department of Natural Development, 1958. Print.

Mackay Historical Society and Museum. "Mackay History." *Mackayhistory.org Your Web Portal for Mackay History*. Glen Hall, n.d. Web. 30 Jan. 2015.

Qld Dept Natural Resources And Mines. "Geological Framework." *Queensland Minerals - Geological Framework (n.d.): n. pag. Queensland Mining and Safety. Queensland Government*. Web. 6 Feb. 2015. The geological framework provides a basic overview of the geology of Queensland and draws particularly on work completed by the Australian Geological Survey Organisation and the Queensland Geological Survey Office.

Queensland Government. "Creation of a State." *Queensland Government | History of Queensland.* N.p., n.d. Web. 29 Jan. 2015.

Queensland Government. "Exploration Permits, Minerals, Queensland." *Mines Online Maps.* N.p., n.d. Web. 4 Mar. 2015. EPM 17527 Kajabbi area, Queensland.

Department of Mining & Surveying. "Town of Kajabbi." Department of Mining & Surveying, 1976

Queensland Government Department of Mines and Energy. *Mineral Development Licences (MDL).* Rep. Queensland Government, Aug. 2008. Web. 04 Mar. 2015.

"Carl Friedrich Gauss." *Wikipedia.* Wikimedia Foundation, 26 Feb. 2015. Web. 07 Mar. 2015.

Raymond, O. L. *Mt Isa Inlier and Environs Mineral Deposit Database.* Rep. no. Version 1.0. N.p.: BMR Publications, 1992. Print. Record 1992/66.

"Herb Was the Man behind TV in Isa." *The North West Star.* N.p., 01 May 2013. Web. 23 Feb. 2015.

Queensland Airports Ltd. "About Mount Isa Airport." *Mount Isa Airport.* Queensland Airports Ltd, 2015. Web. 14 Aug. 2015.

True, Everett. "Prehistoric: The Punk and Politics of Brisbane's Darkest Days Rebooted." *The Gardian*. N.p., 24 Sept. 2015. Web. 7 Sept. 2015.

Barrett, Chris. "I Was Not the Tony Soprano of Brisbane." *Brisbane Times*. N.p., 22 July 2009. Web. 7 Sept. 2015.

The McWhirters Project. "The McWhirters' Building 1898 - 1931...A Pictorial History." *The McWhirters Project*. N.p., 30 Dec. 2010. Web. 07 Sept. 2015.

CQ University Australia. "Stepping Back into the Badlands." *Be* 12 (Dec. 2011): 24-25. Print.

Bradley, Keith. "The Weckert Murders." *Australian Police Journal* March (2015): n. pag. Print.

"Two Shot by Sniper at Caravan." *The Sydney Morning Herald* 18 Sept. 1967, Late Edition ed.: 1. Google News. Web. 18 Sept. 2015.

Leichhardt, Ludwig. "Chapter II." *Journal of an Overland Expedition in Australia [1844 - 1845]* (2004): n. pag. *Project Gutenberg*. 25 Sept. 2004. Web. 15 Sept. 2015.

Charters Towers Regional Council. "History." *Charters Towers Regional Council*. Queensland Government, n.d. Web. 22 Sept. 2015.

Eckford, Shirley, and Julia Creek Historical Society. "Mount Isa Centre for Rural and Remote Health." *Towns - Julia Creek*. Faculty of Medicine, Health & Molecular Sciences, n.d. Web. 26 Sept. 2015.

Stephens, Kate. "North-west Queensland Pub from A Town Like Alice Destroyed by Fire." *ABC News*. N.p., 26 Mar. 2015. Web. 25 Sept. 2015.

Behnke, Stephen G. *The Savage Kalkadoons*. Australia: Stephen G. Behnke, 15 Sept. 2015. PDF.

Sutton, Chernee. "Kalkadoon History and Culture." *Chernee Sutton Contemporary Aboriginal Artist*. N.p., n.d. Web. 12 Oct. 2015.

Tibbett, Kevin. *Community Specialisation, Standardisation and Exchange in Hunter-gatherer Society: A Case Study from Kalkadoon Country, Northwest Queensland, Australia*. Thesis. James Cook University, 2005. Townsville: JCU EPrints, 2005. Print.

McLeish, Kathy. "Boulia Rodeo Brings Isolated Families and Farmers Together." *ABC News*. Australian Broadcasting Corporation, 09 Sept. 2011. Web. 22 Jan. 2017. <http://www.abc.net.au/news/2011-09-09/boulia-rodeo-brings-isolated-families-and-farmers/2879150>.

Boulia Shire Council, Office of Economic and Statistical Research, Queensland Treasury and Trade. *Population and Dwelling Profile, Boulia Shire Council*. Brisbane: n.p., Apr. 2012. PDF.

0001 R826236 7548173. Perf. Kathy McLeish. *YouTube/ Boulia Rodeo 2011*. Land Line, 06 Nov. 2012. Web. 31 Jan. 2017. <https://youtu.be/MuuwAFZT10E>. Segment of the full Land Line television show, uploaded by jillOroo

Pettigrew, John D., BSc(Med) MSc MBBS FRS. *The Min Min Light and the Fata Morgana. An optical account of a mysterious Australian phenomenon.* Thesis. University of Queensland, 2003. Brisbane: U of Queensland, 2002. Print.

Chalker, Bill. "The Min Min Light Revealed Nature Unbound?....Part 1." *Bill Chalker Archive.* N.p., 1983. Web. 31 Jan. 2017. <http://www.auforn.com/Bill_Chalker_8.htm>.

Beatty, Bill. "The Mystery of the Min Min Light." *The Sydney Morning Herald* [Sydney] 25 Jan. 1947: 13. *Trove.* The Sydney Morning Herald. Web. 02 Feb. 2017. <http://trove.nla.gov.au/newspaper/article/18012995>.

Derrick, G. M., I. H. Wilson, A. Y. Glikson, and J. E. Michell. *Geology of the Mary Kathleen 1:100 000 Sheet Area, Northwest Queensland.* Rep. no. Bulletin 193. Canberra: Australian Government Publishing Service, 1977. Print.

Hewit, Karissa, ed. "Zinc Lead Concentrator and R62 Shaft Celebrate 50 Years." *Mine to Market* 149 (2016): 1-3. Web. 10 Mar. 2017. Historical reference to 1966 commissioning event

White, Neil. *Company Towns: Corporate Order and Community.* Toronto: U of Toronto, 2012. Print.

Kirkman, Noreen Suzanne. *Mount Isa Mines' Social Infrastructure Programs 1924-1963.* Thesis PHD. James Cook University, 2011. Townsville: James Cook University, 2011. Print.

"Media - Chrysler Articles/Road Tests." *Wheels Car of the Year - Charger (Wheels Magazine January 1972): Chrysler Articles/Road Tests: Media: Charger Club of WA*. Charger Club Of WA, n.d. Web. 29 May 2017.

"History of Chrysler in Australia." *The Valiant Made a Place for Itself in Australian Motoring History*. Ozmopars, n.d. Web. 29 May 2017.

Pratt, Charles W. "Starts Here." *The Rotarian - Apr 1975* (1975): 17-19. Print.

Young, Suzy. "Community rodeo endures 45 years in the outback." *The Rotarian - Jan 2004* (2004): 12-13. Print.

Donahue, Michelle Z. "Found: Fresh Clues to Mystery of King Solomon's Mines." *National Geographic*. National Geographic, 02 Apr. 2017. Web. 20 June 2017. <http://www.nationalgeographic.com.au/history/found-fresh-clues-to-mystery-of-king-solomons-mines.aspx>.

Birrell, Ralf Winter. *The Development of Mining Technology in Australia 1801 - 1945*. Thesis. The University of Melbourne, 2005. Melbourne: Minerva Access, 2005. Print.

"Fisher Era." *Mimag, July 1970* 20.2 (1970): 5-9. Print.

"Sir George Fisher 1903-2007." *Mine to Market* 76 (2007): 3-5. Print.

Blake, D. H. *Geology of the Mount Isa Inlier and Environs, Queensland and Northern Territory*. Rep. no. 225. Canberra: Department of Resources and Energy Bureau of Mineral Resources, Geology and Geophysics, 1987. Print. BRM Bulletin.

Clements, Raymond D. "Chapter 1 - Recreation Mt. Isa Style." *Aussie Rogues and Rebels.* Place of Publication Not Identified: mango, 2014. 3-18. Print.

Bramble, Tom. "Campaigning on the Political Front." *Trade Unionism in Australia a History from Flood to Ebb Tide.* Cambridge: Cambridge UP, 2008. N. pag. Print.

Cameron, R J. *Year Book Australia 1981.* Vol. 65, Aust. Bureau of Statistics, 1981

Gregory, Denis. "Watering Holes." *It's All about Australia, Mate,* ReadHowYouWant, 2012, pp. 120–121.

"Waltzing Matilda an Old Cold Case." ABC - *Australian Broadcasting Corporation,* ABC News, 12 Feb. 2010, www.abc.net.au/news/2010-02-12/waltzing-matilda-an-old-cold-case/329506.

Clarke, Roger. "The Writing of 'Waltzing Matilda'." *Roger Clarke's Website,* Xamax Consultancy, 2010, www.rogerclarke.com/WM/Banjo.html.

"Truck Blockade of NSW Highways Continues despite Talks." *The Canberra Times,* 5 Apr. 1979, pp. 1–1.

"Troops Available If Requested, PM Says." *The Canberra Times,* 9 Apr. 1979, pp. 1–1.

About The Author

Biography

Stephen Outram has authored 10 books on a variety of topics. and published titles for several other authors. He haa background of some 18 years in architecture, and since 1997 has worked as a graphic artist, website developer and IT consultant. More recently presenting seminars and working globally as an IT development coordinator.

His family emigrated to Australia, from England in 1965, landing in Fremantle and spending five years in the northerly town of Port Hedland. In 1970 the family drove across the country from west to east and settled in Queensland's Gold Coast, where his parents and sister still reside.

Educated in Queensland, Australia, Stephen studied at Brisbane's University of Technology in the early 1970s; he returned to study in 1995 at Dundee University, Scotland, achieving a Master of Science degree in Computing.

Stephen enjoys a diverse and wide range of projects including work, writing, music and song writing, boats and some sport. He was active with Surfrider Foundation Australia and is interested in sustainable and flourishing coastlines and waterways, free of plastics and pollution.

Visit the website for more information visit www.stephenoutram.com

The First Five Years: Port Hedland 1965-1970

Imagine leaving everything you know—your job, family, friends; your country—and setting off on a journey that will take you 20,000 km across the planet to a remote, isolated town where you are not known, have no job and must begin creating your life; would you do it?

"This is brilliant scene setting; what was then, what had been and when you guys arrived, it was just awakening. Awesome story telling! I am still intrigued and want to read more."

"Every time I read this I am amazed by the 'Yes!' attitude and zest for life."

Stephen Outram's new book, The First Five Years, tells the true story of a small English family that left home to go and forge a new life in Australia. Their first five years in the small, isolated town of Port Hedland, which regularly experienced searing heat, cyclones and offered very basic facilities, required courage, guts and the willingness to do whatever it took and not give up on their dreams.

Wedding Speeches

For many, being asked to give a Wedding Speech is the first time they will speak to a larger group, and these speeches may be done only once in a lifetime. Copying and pasting someone else's lines off the Internet is just not good enough. This book will assist you in creating your speech, with ease!

Professional speaker and coach Stephen Outram connects you with everything you need, to accomplish what may be one of the most important speeches of your life!

- Discover a simple idea with 3 parts and begin organizing and preparing your Wedding Speech.

- How to convert what's in your head, into a vital resource.

- Detail descriptions of the 5 key wedding speeches, including the Bride's Speech—a woman's role in transforming long-standing traditions

- The real job of a wedding speech and your role in accomplishing it

- 9 things that you may have to handle that no one tells you about!

Over 80 pages of information, ideas and techniques, designed to assist anyone who has been asked to give a Wedding Speech.

Dealers: Buying, Selling & Making Money

Dealers are people who can make things move! They are market creators and facilitate the flow of ideas, objects and objectives, connecting sellers and buyers. Dealers make money as a consequence of their ability to move energy and create results.

The ideas, concepts and tools that this book contains will connect you with the dealer that you have always wanted to be, but have not yet been introduced to; until now!

- What deals you will not walk away from that are costing you more than you know?

- The 5 key characters that you need, to be a dealer and make money.

- Are you speculating about making money rather than making money speculating?

- What is BIRGing and are you using it to disadvantage?

- Do your investments resemble losing football clubs that you loyally support with your money?

Treasure Hunter, Collector, Bargainer, Speculator and Investor—which are you using to your disadvantage and how do you turn that around?

Find more books and information on the website at
www.stephenoutram.com